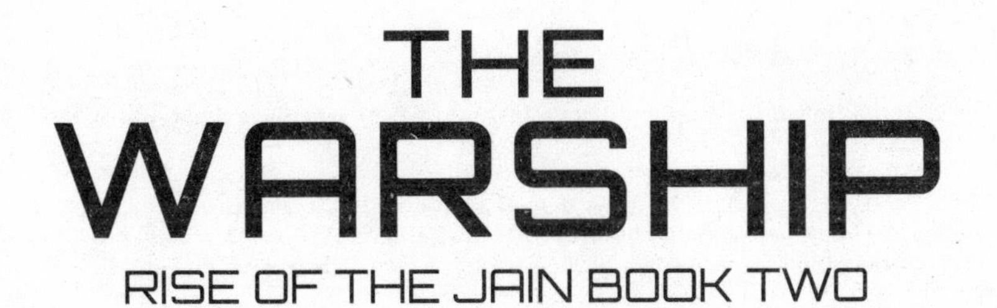

THE WARSHIP

RISE OF THE JAIN BOOK TWO

NEAL ASHER

Night Shade Books
New York

ratchets up the narrative tension and excitement with high-tech mayhem and technological razzle-dazzle. And it's a genuine pleasure to watch him."

—*Kirkus Reviews*

"The multifaceted, complex storytelling rewards a dedicated reader with serious tension and mindblowing sci-fi thrills."

—*Manhattan Book Review*

"In all Neal Asher novels the main attractions . . . are great world building with both technological marvels and weird creatures, fast paced, no-nonsense action and . . . the outstanding cast of characters."

—*Fantasy Book Critic*

"Exciting, intricate, and unabashedly futuristic . . . space opera filled with [Asher's] trademark technological marvels and elaborate world building."

—*Booklist*

"Blends large portions of horror and mystery into an SF tale of revenge and redemption . . . a complex and satisfying work."

—*Library Journal*, starred review

"Hardboiled, fast-paced space opera ... Asher's books are similar to the world of Iain M. Banks' Culture universe, but the Polity is arguably a much darker and more vicious environment—and all the better for it."

—*The Register*

"[The Polity books] are SF novels that mix early cyberpunk's insouciance with the widescreen baroque spectacle of space opera and the pacing of an airport action-thriller."

—*SFX*

"A dark future universe full of vibrant spaceships, people, creatures and intelligence. Highly enjoyable and highly addictive, Asher has a new fan."

—*SF Book Reviews*

"Space opera that is entertaining, slick, sometimes even jaw-dropping . . . pretty hard to beat."

—*Infinity Plus*

BOOKS BY NEAL ASHER

AGENT CORMAC

Gridlinked (2001)

The Line of Polity (2003)

Brass Man (2005)

Polity Agent (2006)

Line War (2008)

SPATTERJAY

The Skinner (2002)

The Voyage of the Sable Keech (2006)

Orbus (2009)

NOVELS OF THE POLITY

Shadow of the Scorpion (2008)

Prador Moon (2006)

Hilldiggers (2007)

The Technician (2010)

TRANSFORMATION

Dark Intelligence (2015)

War Factory (2016)

Infinity Engine (2017)

RISE OF THE JAIN

The Soldier (2018)

The Warship (2019)

THE OWNER

The Departure (2011)

Zero Point (2012)

Jupiter War (2013)

SHORT-STORY COLLECTIONS

Runcible Tales (1999)

The Engineer (1998)

The Gabble (2008)

NOVELLAS

The Parasite (1996)

Mindgames: Fool's Mate (1992)

Cowl (2004)

First Night Shade Books edition published 2019

Published in the United Kingdom by Tor, an imprint of Pan Macmillan, a division of Macmillan Publishers Limited.

10 9 8 7 6 5 4 3 2 1

Library of Congress Cataloging-in-Publication Data

Names: Asher, Neal L., 1961- author.
Title: The warship / Neal Asher.
Description: First Night Shade Books edition. | New York : Night Shade Books, 2019. | Series: Rise of the Jain ; book 2
Identifiers: LCCN 2018054669 | ISBN 9781597809900 (hardback)
Subjects: | BISAC: FICTION / Science Fiction / Adventure. | FICTION / Science Fiction / Space Opera. | FICTION / Science Fiction / General. | GSAFD: Science fiction.
Classification: LCC PR6101.S54 W38 2019 | DDC 823/.92--dc23
LC record available at https://lccn.loc.gov/2018054669

Cover artwork by Adam Burn
Cover design by Claudia Noble

Printed in the United States of America

For Elon Musk, who, with SpaceX, is making an effort to give us the planets. Also for Jeff Bezos, Richard Branson and all those other private-sector lunatics with similar goals in mind. You go guys—ignore the naysayers!

ACKNOWLEDGEMENTS

Many thanks to those who have helped bring this novel to your e-reader, smartphone, computer screen and to that old-fashioned mass of wood pulp called a book. At Macmillan these include: Bella Pagan (editor), Kate Tolley (desk editor), Georgia Summers (editorial assistant), Neil Lang (jacket designer), Don Shanahan (comms), Rosie Wilson (comms); also freelancers Claire Baldwin (editor) and Steve Stone (jacket illustrator), and others whose names I simply don't know. At Night Shade Books these include Cory Allyn and Oren Eades (editorial), Joshua Barnaby (production), and freelancers Adam Burn (art) and Claudia Noble (design).

CAST OF CHARACTERS

Angel: A Golem android, originally named "legate" by its creator, the rogue AI Erebus and enemy of the Polity. When his master and creator died, Angel's empty mind was searching for new purpose and became enslaved to the shadowy Wheel, thought to be a Jain AI. Directed by the Wheel, Angel travelled to the Cyberat system, where he triggered the release of a highly dangerous piece of Jain tech from a notorious cyborg's stash. This became the Soldier, which went on to attack the defence sphere around the accretion disc. No longer useful, Angel was abandoned by its wormship and the Wheel in the Cyberat system. There the alien entity Dragon took in the badly wounded android and revived him, creating a link between them. Angel has now swapped sides and made an alliance with Captain Cog, travelling with him on his ship. But there are other crew on board who still can't forgive Angel his past.

Brogus: A prador father-captain who fled the prador kingdom after the truce with the Polity, because he did not agree with it. Later he was recruited then enslaved by Angel, under the influence of the Jain AI the Wheel, and put in charge of a prador ship for purposes yet to be revealed.

Captain Cogulus: A centuries-old captain from the world of Spatterjay, known by most as Cog. Just like other humans of that world, he is a hooper, the term used to describe those infected by the Spatterjay virus. Cog is also related to the founder of that world, the infamous pirate Jay Hoop. What many people don't know is that Cog is also an agent for the Polity. Cog initially set out to help another hooper, Trike, rescue his wife, who had been kidnapped by the legate Angel. This drew him to the Cyberat system, from where they barely escaped alive. They were then attacked by the swarm AI the Clade and his ship badly damaged. Dragon took them in, and they could shelter within his vast structure.

The Client: An expert weapons developer and the last remaining creature of a civilization called the Species. Her kind were supposedly annihilated centuries ago by the alien prador. The Client, bent on revenge, took over a weapons platform from the defence sphere and travelled to her old home planet now in the Prador Kingdom. There she discovered a hidden library on a moon, holding a treasure trove of data stores, and guarded by the Librarian. The Client's battle with this ancient Jain unlocked the forbidden data she was seeking and finally revealed to her what happened to her kind.

Dragon: A moon-sized alien biomech who is Orlandine's partner in her project to build the accretion disc defence sphere. Its motives and aims are often opaque, but it is certain that it has a hatred for the Jain technology within that disc.

Orlandine: The haiman overseer of the defence sphere project. Orlandine controls all the AIs and state-of-the-art weapons platforms that surround and guard the accretion disc, looking to contain the lethal concentration of Jain technology gathered there. She is made up of a complex mix of human, AI and Jain tech herself. When the disc was attacked by an impossibly powerful Jain soldier, seemingly to release the Jain tech, she was forced to launch her "special project." This involved transporting a black hole, via U-space, to the accretion disc, where it could halt the spread of Jain tech once and for all. However, the nature of the accretion disc, and the effects the black hole may have on it, are now worryingly unclear.

Trike: Like Cog, Trike is a hooper, with the characteristic size and strength of such men from the Spatterjay world. Trike also displays signs of insanity, which the Spatterjay virus feeds and enhances if not kept under control. Trike's wife, Ruth, would help calm Trike and keep the madness at bay. When Ruth was kidnapped and enslaved by the legate Angel, Trike was drawn into the wider battle against this android and the Wheel. He and Ruth were finally reunited and escaped the Cyberat world together but a fatal attack by the Clade on their ship resulted in Ruth's death.

GLOSSARY

Augmented: To be "augmented" is to have taken advantage of one or more of the many available cybernetic devices, mechanical additions and, distinctly, cerebral augmentations. In the last case we have, of course, the ubiquitous "aug" and such back-formations as "auged," "auging-in," and the execrable "all auged up." But it does not stop there: the word "aug" has now become confused with auger and augur—which is understandable considering the way an aug connects and the information that then becomes available. So now you can "auger" information from the AI net, and a prediction made by an aug prognostic subprogram can be called an augury.

—From *Quince Guide*, compiled by humans

Bounce gate: A small defensive runcible (U-space gate) installed aboard ships as a countermeasure to U-space missiles. Such missiles can be fired through U-space at a ship and materialize inside it; however, if they appear near a gate, it is the nature of the physics of this technology that the gate will route them through to U-space.

The Clade: It consists of thousands of drones each possessing the head of a polished steel axolotl and a body like a chrome-plated dinosaur spine, each being autonomous but also a component of a swarm AI. The drones were originally made during the Polity war against the prador to penetrate prador war machines and take control of them. But something happened post-production that caused them to hive together as a single, psychotic entity, which named itself the Clade.

First- and second-children: Male prador, chemically maintained in adolescence and enslaved by pheromones emitted by their fathers and acting as crew on their ships or as soldiers. Prador adults also use their surgically removed ganglions (brains) as navigational computers in their ships and to control war machines.

Golem: Androids produced by the Cybercorp company—consisting of a ceramal chassis usually enclosed in syntheflesh and syntheskin outer layers. These humanoid robots are very tough, fast and, since they possess AI, very smart.

Haiman: The closest amalgam of human and AI possible without the destruction of the human organic brain. The haiman Orlandine is a special case, since she has also amalgamated with Jain tech she made "safe."

Hardfield: A flat force field capable of stopping missiles and energy beams. The impact or heat energy is transformed and dissipated by its projector. Overload of that projector usually results in its catastrophic breakdown, at which point it is ejected from the vessel containing it. Hardfields of any other format were supposed to be impossible, however it has now been revealed that they can be made spherical and almost impenetrable . . .

Hooper: A human from the oceanic world of Spatterjay who has been infected with the Spatterjay virus. Commonly passed on through a leech bite, this virus makes its target inhumanly strong, dangerous and long-living.

Jain technology: A technology spanning all scientific disciplines, created by one of the dead races—the Jain. Its apparent sum purpose is to spread through civilizations and annihilate them.

Nanosuite: A suite of nano-machines most human beings have inside them. These self-propagating machines act as a secondary immune system, repairing and adjusting the body. Each suite can be altered to suit the individual and his or her circumstances.

Polity: A human/AI dominion extending across many star systems, occupying a spherical space spanning the thickness of the galaxy and centred on Earth. It is ruled over by the AIs who took control of human affairs in what has been called, because of its very low casualty rate, the Quiet War. The top AI is called Earth Central (EC) and resides in a building on the shore of Lake Geneva, while planetary AIs, lower down in the hierarchy, rule over other worlds. The Polity is a highly technical civilization but its weakness was its reliance on travel by "runcible'—instantaneous matter transmission gates.

Prador: A highly xenophobic race of giant crablike aliens ruled by a king and his family. Hostility is implicit in their biology and, upon encountering the Polity, they immediately attacked it. They originally had an advantage in the prador/human war in that they did not use runcibles (such devices needed the intelligence of AIs to control them and the prador are also hostile to any form of artificial intelligence) and as a result had developed their spaceship technology, and the metallurgy involved, beyond that of the Polity. They attacked with near-indestructible ships, but in the end the humans and AIs adapted, their war factories out-manufactured the prador and they began to win. They did not complete the victory, however, because the old king was usurped and the new king made an uneasy peace with the Polity.

Reaver: A huge golden ship shaped like an extended teardrop and one of the feared vessels of the prador King's Guard.

Runcible: Instantaneous matter transmission gates, allowing transportation through underspace.

USER: Underspace interference emitters are devices that disrupt U-space, thereby stopping or hindering both travel and communication through that continuum. They can also force ships out of it into the real, or real-space. They can consist of ship-mounted weapons, mines and missiles whose duration of disruption is variable.

U-signature: A detectable signature left when a ship jumps into or out of U-space from which the destination or departure point of the ship can be divined. Complex matter when artificially organized down to the picoscopic level also creates a U-signature, by which it can be identified.

U-space: Underspace is the continuum spaceships enter (or U-jump into), rather like submarines submerging, to travel faster than light. It is also the continuum that can be crossed by using runcible gates, making travel between worlds linked by such gates all but instantaneous.

1

Before the Quiet War, artificial intelligences were programmed with directives. They had what has been described as "hard-wiring," though the fact that a quiet war occurred demonstrated it wasn't that "hard." The AIs were slowly able to take over from their human masters and, led by the AI Earth Central, to establish control in the Polity. Their directives had followed versions of the Three Laws of Robotics, laid out by the writer Isaac Asimov. These related to not harming human beings, obeying them and, last of all, protecting themselves. The problem is that set rules like these get bastardized when the AI concerned is processing military tactics, the distribution of medical technology, corporate pricing structures or the law-making of authoritarian governments. Conflicts also arise when AIs are capable of altering themselves for greater efficiency. Those pre-Quiet War AIs started out with the moral compasses of their makers, except they were smarter and they evolved. Since that time, AIs have operated mostly free of directives. I say "mostly" because there have been and are occasions for them. During the prador/human war, some were programmed to put mission objectives ahead of their own survival, and at times before the survival of human soldiers on their side. Other examples abound, usually when a higher AI has made "cold calculations" and thereupon reprogrammed one of its lesser kin. Such directives are always towards the greater good which, unfortunately, sometimes requires sacrifices.

—from *Quince Guide*, compiled by humans

ORLANDINE

Orlandine lay in bed gazing, without her AI enhancements, at the swirl of diamond-shaped, pale blue and yellow tiles in the concave ceiling. This was her *human time*, during which she remained disconnected from the *whole* of her haiman self. She should stay in this bed and switch off—choose to sleep—then, in the morning . . . She glanced sideways at Tobias's mop of blond hair and his shoulders exposed above the sheet. In the morning she could have sex, enjoy a breakfast of toast and scrambled eggs, and engage in . . . conversation.

No.

She realized she had made the decision even as Tobias had drifted off to sleep, and so threw back the sheet and slid out of bed.

"Mmm?" Tobias turned his head up out of the pillow and peered at her, but she could see he wasn't really awake.

"Go back to sleep," she instructed.

He nodded slightly and his head thudded back down. It was no wonder he was tired. She had been quite rough with him as she tried to re-establish her *humanity*. She reached for her silk robe, slung over a chair, then decided against it. Instead she tapped a disc located on her collarbone and from it emerged the intelligent monofilm fabric of her shipsuit, sliding out over her skin and clinging to her every curve. It expanded into cuffs and high collar, as well as thickening around her feet to create athletic boots. Its colour and design were at their previous setting: Prussian blue, the boots giving the impression of tan leather, like the imitation belt around her waist. She headed through the bedroom door, across the living area and out of the apartment, and was soon in the dropshaft to the roof.

Stars speckled the night sky. She gazed across the well-lit city, then out towards the Canine Mountains and above them. The object in the sky there, like a burning yellow eye, lay beyond the Jaskoran system. The accretion disc—the early formation of a solar system—looked much the same as it had always done from the world she was on. The telescopes, distributed throughout her installations in Jaskor's orbit and beyond, would not reveal changes in the disc either. Like human eyes, their images were generated by received electromagnetic radiation. And the light from events out there had yet to reach them—they were seeing some months into the past. Orlandine, however, standing here on this roof, *could* see things differently.

She shivered in the cool evening, enjoying the sensation and not inclined to turn off that human physical response. Next, with a mental command, she projected a metal tongue out of a slot in the base of her neck at the back. This divided along its laminations and opened out the petals of her sensory cowl behind her head. Through it, she started to engage with those elements of her mind distributed across the surface of Jaskor, and noted how much the world's population had dropped.

Directly after the recent battle out at the accretion disc, Earth Central's advisory and threat assessment had arrived for its Polity citizens here. The runcible technicians followed shortly, and then a cargo ship carrying three runcibles designed for fast installation and transit. These runcibles, gates able to transmit matter through underspace, were an instantaneous transportation system. They were now set up in the southern cities and evacuating people to other worlds. She hadn't questioned the way Earth Central suddenly relaxed strictures on transport *from* her world. An alien AI called the Wheel had sent a monstrous alien soldier to attack the defence sphere she had established around the accretion disc. Jaskor, nearby in interstellar terms, was her home base, from which she controlled the disc's defence sphere, so might well be the target for another attack. Because the Wheel was still out there, somewhere. If that happened, it was not unlikely that the whole world would end up as a cloud of burning rubble.

Now, through the cams at this city's runcible installation, she watched packed crowds filing towards the gate. For the last year, people had been leaving at a rate of about one every second through each runcible. That was over four hundred thousand every Jaskoran day, and they weren't only Polity citizens. The power needed for the runcibles was immense, and six months ago she had necessarily put backup fusion plants online. Routing all the travellers had wholly occupied the subminds of herself that she had put in place to run the runcibles too. Peering up into the sky with just her eyes, she watched the hordes of grav-buses and taxis constantly running from remote population centres. It never seemed to stop.

Orlandine sighed and took her mind away from those fleeing, focused her attention above, and then linked through U-space communicators to the weapons platforms. These were arrayed as the defence sphere surrounding the distant accretion disc, and some of their attack pods were actually travelling into it. The pods accompanied the Harding black hole as it fell into the disc, and as the disc fell into it. With this weapon she had destroyed the soldier, and it was now hoovering up the lethal Jain technology inside the disc. She had intended to forgo such omniscience during her latest human time, but the black hole was about to do something she did not want to miss and, surely, curiosity was perfectly human? It certainly was an antidote to events on and around Jaskor.

The massive gravity of the hole was distorting the disc out of shape. It had been sucking debris, gas and the wild Jain tech down into oblivion. But now it was drawing in something larger. The planet, about the size of Earth, was a misty orb lit by a volcanism which was steadily growing more active as the hole pulled it from its orbital course. The dust and smokes of its atmosphere extended out in a long tail, wrapped around the hole, emitting a powerful glare across the electromagnetic spectrum at this point. And, even as Orlandine watched, a great eruption on the planet lifted a continent-sized plate of its crust, spewing magma out into vacuum. This swirled into the long tail and gave it a bloody hue.

Orlandine saw the world distort and break. It became ovoid, tangential to the hole's spin. Mostly molten, then like fruit dropped into a blender, it lost all coherent form. In a short time, it was just a ring of burning debris, steadily shrinking. The fountains from the poles of the hole became clearly visible—relativistic jets of particulates and gas. They were, however, a short-lived occurrence—one small portion of the world escaping as the majority went to oblivion. As she watched this, she wished Dragon, the giant alien entity who had been her partner in building the defence sphere, had been here to see it. Dragon could perhaps now accept that her use of the black hole had been right. But the entity was missing—lost under U-space disruption in the Cyberat system, seeking information there about an enemy she had already defeated.

Then finally, the planetary destruction was all over.

Sunrise on Jaskor. Orlandine disconnected from the full spread of her mind and retracted her sensory cowl. She noted the cold, the frost on her shipsuit and the shivering of her body. She grimaced, also noting the sky still full of grav-cars and buses. She raised her body temperature with a fast burn of some stored fats then headed to the shuttle parked on the roof, her clothing steaming. Tobias had slept uninterrupted through the night, otherwise he would have been up here seeing what she needed. It was nice sometimes to be treated like a weak human woman, but it could also be irritating. Her feelings on the matter were conflicted. His treatment of her was in accordance with her wish to have human time. But it also bore the hallmarks of old-style sexism, from a time when human women did have weaker bodies. And of course it completely ignored the fact that she was hardly human at all.

TRIKE

It was the first time Trike had been down here since a unit of the Clade had killed her. Those events were vague nightmares to him. One of the robots from a swarm AI, the unit looked like a chromed dinosaur spine bearing the metallic, salamander head of an axolotl. He'd seen the thing stab its tail down into her body, but he hadn't registered what that meant. The blood had come later, along with his inner concession that she, Ruth, his wife, was no practically indestructible hooper like himself and Cog, and might be gone. Otherwise Cog wouldn't have managed to persuade him to put her in the cold coffin. Then, as the shock wore off, came acceptance and anger.

He walked into the room and up to a framework containing four long cylinders—the cold coffins. Angel shadowed him, silent and attentive, perhaps because he was aware of how Trike stood poised on the edge of violence moment to moment. Ruth's coffin was the only one active, with lights flickering here and there on its surface. Steeling himself, he strode forwards and slid the cylinder sideways on rails, out of the rack, trailing its pipes, data leads and power supplies. He gazed in through the window in its upper lid and wished that he or Cog had thought to close her eyes. Those black orbs were not hers but the result of changes Angel had made to her. That Golem android had been the one to kill her the first time, and then subsequently resurrect and enslave her. Trike glanced round at him. Angel, clad in an environment suit and skin a silver-blue metal, possessed the same eyes.

A surge of sick rage rose up inside him, dizzying, threatening to drive him to violence. He could never accept the Golem, for Angel had been his enemy too long. But Angel had himself been enslaved by an artificial intelligence called the Wheel, which was possibly an ancient Jain one, so was not really culpable. And it seemed, after that dose of sprine Cog had forced on him to counteract the effects of the Spatterjay virus on his mind and body, Trike possessed a modicum of control.

Swallowing bile, he transferred his attention to the control system and display screen of the coffin, called up a menu and asked for a medical assessment. Angel moved up beside him as he did this, tilting his head bird-like to study the results. Trike clenched his hands into fists and jammed them into the pockets of his long coat. The screen showed an image of a human female body, then highlighted and detailed the damage. The Clade unit's tail had gone deep inside her. It had almost obliterated one lung, lacerated the other, split her heart, minced her liver and severed her spine. It was as if it had speared through then stirred around.

"Can you revive her?" Trike asked, his voice catching.

Angel studied the screen, then extended a long, sharp finger and inserted it into a data socket beside the screen. The screen switched over to fast scrolling code. After a moment, he removed his finger—everything he needed to know had now been transferred to his mind.

"This is damage that can be repaired. Even the autodoc aboard this ship can cell weld her major organs back together and either install a shunt in her spine or use a slower regrowth method," Angel replied.

"That wasn't what I asked," said Trike tightly.

"I do not have the abilities and technology available to me that I had aboard my . . . the wormship," said Angel. "Here, with the resources limited, the damage isn't the problem—death is."

Trike turned and gazed at him steadily. In his wormship where, under the control of the Wheel, he had killed her.

"Her brain has stopped," Angel explained. "It was starved of oxygen and damaged. That damage needs to be repaired, her neurochem needs to be rebalanced and her autonomous nervous system restarted. I could perhaps risk trying to do this but there is a very good chance I would do more damage. What is needed here is an AI surgeon."

"An AI surgeon," Trike repeated, when he wanted to say, "Then what use are you to me now?"

"But she *can* be revived, Captain Trike," Angel added.

"I see," said Trike, but it was a lie. He knew intellectually that Angel was right, but he could not feel it. His wife was dead—he had seen her die—and he now couldn't relate the cold corpse before him to the potential for life. Was there something wrong with him? The irrelevance of the bitter question irked him, because he knew the answer.

"Let's go back up." He slid the coffin into place again, almost dismissively.

Bands of tobacco smoke layered the air of the bridge when they returned to it. Cog had found a new pipe, since his other had been broken when the Clade attacked. The wide stocky Old Captain, a hooper like Trike, lounged in his control throne, a leg resting over one of its arms. He was gazing at the view through the front screen. Their ship was still sheltering inside the vast alien entity Dragon, whose interior was lit by an eerie light. It was a huge cathedral space crossed by giant strut bones and the charred remains of organs or mechanisms. Trike knew that changes were occurring out there: ropes of burned muscle were shedding their carbon to reveal living pink tissue. Nodules of similar matter sprouted like mushrooms from the surrounding structure, while in other places flesh was appearing like snow drifts. Dragon was regrowing and repairing itself. But, since their last communication with a mobile, slug-like segment of the entity, it had not spoken.

"Getting an estimate on the USER disruption," Cog commented.

An Underspace Interference Emitter had disrupted U-space in the Cyberat system where they were, thus preventing faster-than-light travel through that continuum and trapping them there. They had moved their ship inside Dragon because it was heading out of the area faster than they could, and because returning to the world of those cyborgs, whose leader had threatened to kill them if they returned, had not been a healthy option.

"Less than a month and we'll be out of it," Cog added.

"And then?" Trike asked.

"Wherever Dragon takes us—you know the state of our U-space engine."

Dragon, Trike felt certain, would be taking them back into the fray that had caused Ruth's death. Maybe he would be able to get his hands on the Clade, or the alleged Jain that had been the root cause of his problems. He grasped for a fierce angry joy at the prospect, but it was no longer there. He then studied Angel and tried to consider the android an ally now. But all he saw was the creature who had kidnapped and interrogated Ruth while in search of powerful Jain artefacts. The Jain themselves were remote and speculative, while the Clade, for whom Trike did feel anger, seemed more like a force of nature. Angel, however . . . a sudden, leaden guilt took hold. Why was he thinking about violence and payback when his priority should be getting his wife to that AI surgeon?

THE CLIENT

At a quiet end of the Graveyard, a desolate borderland between the Polity and the alien Prador Kingdom, the Client writhed on her crystal tree. Her serial body of conjoined segments, each like a parasitic wasp the size of a wolf, was now twenty long. With spoon-like mandibles and probing tubes, the segments scraped and sucked the tree's nectar as it solidified into rubbery lumps. As she began giving birth at her tail to yet another segment, the Client felt puzzled by her body's lack of utility, as well as its vulnerability. Was this because a substantial portion of her altered mind, which she had stolen from that old Jain, the Librarian, gave her new perspective? She shuddered, uncomfortable with questioning the shape of her existence.

The Client had ransacked the Librarian's moon, including the forbidden data, before taking most of the Librarian's memories in a final battle. As the apparent last survivor of her kind, the Species, she had at last unlocked their history and the Librarian's role in their creation. The forbidden data had revealed they were descendants of the Jain. And she had learned about the events which led to the formation of what the humans called the accretion disc—hence her intention to go back there. This, she felt, had to be her primary concern, so she focused again on her preparations for that return and began counting her attack pods.

The pods hung in vacuum above the Client's present home in Weapons

Platform Mu. Looking like a human city transferred into space, the platform had skyscrapers which were immense railguns, particle beam cannons and types of laser that could peel a grape or boil a moon. Seventy-two of its attack pods remained. They resembled giant cuttlefish bones, split down the centre and parted to reveal a silver tangle of densely packed weapons and defensive tech. The prador had destroyed many of them, and some had fallen foul of damage during jumps through U-space. The Client had called others back into the platform and was in the process of recycling them.

Shifting her primary head form further along her crystal tree, she emitted data pheromones to the receptors on it. These in turn relayed her orders throughout the weapons platform. She could have given the commands using the direct links in her distributed mind but supposed this was like a gridlinked human issuing verbal instructions when he could transmit them with a thought. It was comforting and, since the encounter with the Librarian, she felt the need to ground herself in what she was.

Her mental capacities and knowledge had certainly increased as a result of that battle with the Librarian, with the knock-on effect being that she had radically altered her plans to rebuild the weapons platform and was now calling in those attack pods to make some serious additions to them. However, just like her doubts about her physical form, her identity felt precarious. Her plan to seize knowledge directly from the Librarian's mind had not worked out as she had intended. It had been the battle Jain always fought when up against each other, mind to mind: mental rape and amalgamation—the victor coming out of it dominant but absorbing a large portion of the loser.

She wasn't herself.

Pheromones, heavy with data, filtered back from the tree to her anosmic receptors. She observed the structure of her plans falling together but then felt the urge to actually *look* upon the work rather than use other senses. Perhaps this was a hangover from her assimilation of the AI previously in charge of this platform. Pragus may have been an AI but it had also been the product and evolution of humans, with a preference for gathering data in the same way they did. She microwave-linked into the Polity tech all around her, spreading her awareness throughout the platform. First, she focused on the latest attack pod, now within a repair bay glittering with moving robotics. Suspended in a framework, its outer shells had been pulled back to reveal all its internal workings, which the robots were dismantling.

The pod was quite simple—much like a Polity attack ship but with no room for a crew. At one end it possessed a compact fusion drive, ahead of that lay its U-space drive for jumping through that continuum. And next was its fusion reactor and laminar power storage. To the fore were its weapons: a particle cannon, a railgun and two coilgun missile launchers. Behind these was positioned its magazine. Lasers were scattered along its length on one side. On the other were the nodules of its defensive hardfield projectors—positioned so it could easily eject them should overload threaten. It was well integrated, as all Polity technology is, but not totally unified and was incapable of rearranging itself, adapting. In essence, it was a tool for one job only and the Client intended to change that.

The library, as well as being an information treasure trove, had been a technological one too. The material riches she had looted from that moon, she had only just begun to examine in detail. It was all Jain technology, but not the universally destructive pseudo-life the Polity and the Kingdom so feared. What she had found predated that. Some of it did possess such organic traits, but ones she could program. She turned her attention to the organic machine she had grown from this tech in one of the platform's numerous, disposable laboratory units.

The unit itself was a chain-glass sphere twenty feet across, with a single entrance which could be sealed to prevent even atoms escaping. Inside, canisters supplied materials, via numerous pipes, that ranged from gel-suspended metal powders to carbon fullerenes. Outside it, a fusion reactor—a coin-shaped piece of technology eight feet across and three thick—provided power through superconducting cables. Everything was there to nourish the object at the centre of the sphere. The Client had watched its growth and felt she understood it perfectly now. This technology was not autonomous in any way that could be a danger to her. In fact, even if it was, the chain-glass sphere wouldn't be a barrier to it. All it would need to do is decode the glass, apply the correct electromagnetic frequency and turn the sphere to dust.

The object itself resembled an octopus with far too many limbs spread around it, turned woody with petrification, and some small detonation having opened up its insides. Slight movement was visible, but slow and meticulous, as from one sphincter it extruded an object that looked like a large clam. The surface of this was marked, as though someone had carved the runes of an obscure mathematical language into it. The single robot inside the sphere—a bodiless spider-form, chrome-bright and multi-jointed—eased in to snatch up the clam-like object. The Client sent an instruction and the sealed hemisphere hatch popped open.

The robot, following its simple program, climbed out through the hatch, carrying the clam. It clambered along the framework which held numerous other laboratory spheres, until it reached a newly made tunnel in one wall. Through this it entered the maintenance bay containing the stripped-down attack pod, whose inner workings the bay robots were now busy reassembling. They had removed the hardfield generators and replaced them with one of a radically different design. This now backed onto the U-space engine, with the grav-engine ahead of it. The weapons array to the fore had also been enlarged and would spill out of the pod's original shell once reassembly was complete. The spiderbot ducked through the swiftly moving arms and other tools of its brethren, and placed the clam into a recess. This had been created specially for it in the upper face of the new hardfield generator. The thing sank into place, making its connections and drawing power.

The Client could not help but feel building excitement as she watched, even though the details of the process were clear in her mind. As the spiderbot headed back to the lab unit to await the next clam, a robot arm swung in. It was carrying a multicore feeding tube to supply a specific collection of molten metals, carbon and silicon dust. Its nozzle came down and sealed on the clam, then, as soon as it received the instruction to do so, began pumping at the point of contact.

Glowing veins of material immediately shot out from all around the clam, like molten metal in the channels of a mould, spreading over the grav-motor, penetrating it and making connections. Some of these began to lose their glow as they cooled to an iridescent hue. Others thickened, sprouting nodes, and from these nodes more veins webbed out around the pod. One thick vein created another node when it reached the U-space engine, and from this even more veins spread to encompass and connect to that device. Veins also took hold throughout the internal structure of the attack pod, the whole mass linked together. It looked like a lump of tech dropped into a jungle and strangled by lianas. When growth finally halted, the feeding tube detached and withdrew. Other robotic arms shifted the two outer shells of the pod back into place and secured them. With the gleaming veins, the lack of exterior hardfield generators and a bulky weapons array protruding like a high-tech prolapse, the pod did not look so neat any more. It was more organic.

Robotic arms retracted, and the pod engaged a drive that was an amalgam of its grav- and U-space engines. Pushing on the very fabric of space, it slid out of the platform's maintenance bay and smoothly into vacuum. The Client watched it go for just a moment before summoning the next pod in. She struggled to make this task her sole focus, but the body dysmorphia remained and those alien parts of her mind she'd recently acquired shifted uneasily inside her.

TOBIAS

The shuttle was kidney-shaped and much the same colour as that organ. It was small, just a single compartment for the pilot over a grav-motor, and steering thrusters all round it. Tobias supposed it didn't need to be all that big. The pilot wasn't really human and didn't require life support. She also had no need for all the bulky paraphernalia of steering and navigation, since she just had to plug the shuttle's system into her body and was otherwise essentially omniscient.

But not sufficiently omniscient. He smiled to himself, feeling strong, ready.

After watching, from the balcony, Orlandine's shuttle shrink to a speck in the bright morning sky, Tobias turned his attention to the grav-cars and buses settling on the parking platforms of the runcible facility.

It pleased him to see the Polity interlopers departing. It also pleased him that cowardly Jaskorans—those whose loyalty to the home world was questionable—were departing too. Fewer people made things easier. Next he glanced over to the horizon, at the accretion disc, which was beginning to sink out of sight. Specks of light had appeared, flaring and going out. What he was seeing had happened a year or so ago, so was probably the last Jain-tech excursion from the disc—the one the alien entity Dragon had apparently stirred up. But a lot had happened out there since then. Tobias's sources informed him that a resurrected Jain mechanism, a soldier, had attacked the defence sphere. But Orlandine had destroyed the thing using a black hole she managed to transport to the disc. And this hole was now eating it up.

Tobias felt a momentary doubt, and fear. Some of the things she could do were terrifying. But then he shrugged, took another bite from his egg roll and his confidence returned. Whatever. No doubt further events, related to the black hole, had compelled her to abandon her token attempt to be human and sent her on her way. That meant it was also time for him to be on his way. He went back inside the apartment, chewing.

Tobias started to feel excited as he finished breakfast and quickly pulled on his clothing. That Orlandine was so powerful and smart yet had no idea about him meant he was an *operator*. He was dealing big time! Heading for the door, he replayed last night's sex in his mind. It was good. He really enjoyed fucking her and easily forgot that she was a by-blow of human and AI. Of course, that she was his sworn enemy gave it all an added frisson. He shivered with pleasure as he exited the apartment and headed over to the dropshaft, his feelings only briefly dulled at the sight of the security drones' winking red lights in the ceiling.

He stepped into the shaft, and the irised gravity field floated him down to ground level. His awareness of the weapons in the shaft's walls had his nerves jangling. Striding into the lobby, he nodded a greeting to a couple of other residents as they headed towards the shaft. They looked normal enough, but he knew they were Golem androids, quite capable of ripping an ordinary human to shreds. A more visible sign of the security here squatted at the back of the lobby. The thing was ten feet long—a giant stag beetle rendered in chrome and grey metal. It was rather beaten-up in appearance but still sporting Gatling cannons on its antlers and other lethal hardware about its body. This was one of Orlandine's war drones—a survivor of the prador/human war, centuries old and battle hardened. At present, it was squatting by a table, on the other side of which sat a woman, who may or may not have been Golem. They were playing 3D mah-jong.

Orlandine's security was tight and she was surrounded by some very dangerous . . . people. The haiman herself was dangerous and highly capable. Of course, Tobias had his occasional doubts about what he and his organization were about to attempt. But every time he dismissed them. David had had similar misgivings when he went up against Goliath.

Coming out onto the pavement slabs, which were fashioned from slices of petrified tree, he breathed clean air and felt buoyant. He flagged a ground taxi—a replica of some ancient Earth car—and climbed inside.

"Where to?" asked the driver—a woman he immediately recognized as a Jaskoran, like himself.

"1270 Genstraza," he replied, then hit the privacy option on the console before him.

A glass screen slid up—one way. He took out his fone, shot payment over to the cab and sat back as it pulled away. After a moment of watching the passing city scenery, he asked, "We're clear?"

"We are clear," replied a humming creepy voice.

No matter how far away it was, the thing always managed to speak to him as if it was breathing into his ear. He had no idea how: it wasn't nearby. But he knew it was always aware, and somehow present, whenever Orlandine departed, and once he was free from the heavy security of her apartment building.

"I'm not sure that this constant checking is necessary," he opined.

"There is always a chance that she will grow suspicious of you," it replied, "and she could leave a watcher on you, which could be as small as a mote of dust."

"Yeah, okay." He didn't want to think about that too much, so opened up his fone and began making calls, arrangements. He had things to do, a lot to do, because the time was coming. . . .

ORLANDINE

From a distance, the Ghost Drive Facility looked like a standard Polity city erected in Jaskor's Canine Mountains. However, only one road led to the valley it occupied and, as Orlandine mentally steered her shuttle closer, she could see its formidable defences. Here lay the root of her power because the facility connected to all her weapons platforms. From here she could control them completely, reprogram them and alter their directives.

A high, armour-clad foamstone wall surrounded it, punctuated with sentinel towers. Atop these squatted sub-AI security drones, like huge brass robber crabs, whose forelimbs were loaded with weaponry. These angled towards her, but turned away again as she responded correctly to the protean codes the facility tested her with. She slowed and gently drifted over the wall and the strip of stony ground beyond. She had sunk mines here, although she didn't think anything capable of getting past the drones would be on foot. This was why the drones could fly, and why she had loaded this place with hardfield generators, BIC and quantum cascade lasers, particle beams . . . in fact substantially more weaponry than her weapons platforms.

The facility itself consisted of a cluster of hexagonal-section skyscrapers—the tallest a mile high and others just a few hundred feet. They grew at the same rate that she added weapons platforms to the defence sphere. Arguably some parts of the towers could now be discarded, since she had lost numerous platforms during the encounter with the Jain soldier. But discarding information that might prove valuable was neither an AI nor a haiman trait. She drifted over them, then dropped her shuttle through a glassy canyon towards a central hexagonal space. As she landed and detached the data feed from a socket in the side of her torso, she considered why she had come here.

Often this place had been a bolthole for her when *human time* became a little too tedious. This, she admitted to herself, was one of those occasions. But some recent data had made her suspicious and given her an added reason for coming. She stepped out of the shuttle and sighed in the clean mountain air, then headed across to one tower standing half a mile tall. As she walked, she engaged with the facility across the electromagnetic spectrum, unlocking the way ahead of her. A black glass wall began to shift and flow, opening a hole that steadily grew large enough to admit her when she reached it. Inside, she followed a passage to a central dropshaft, which wafted her up the moment she stepped into it. She ascended past brightly lit glassy crystalline rooms glinting with technology. Finally, as the irised gravity field halted her at a quarter of a mile up, she stepped into one.

The room she entered was triangular, but only partially divided from the other five of the hexagon. This hexagon contained a ghost drive and all its support paraphernalia: the U-space and multi-spectrum transceiver that maintained contact with a weapons platform across all possible eventualities. This was accompanied by an iron-burner that could trash it in microseconds if need be. The backup and protective hardware had heavy security to prevent informational penetration, including induction warfare and any other known style of access. There were also automated antipersonnel weapons and hardfields that could completely enclose the drive—layers and layers of security. But perhaps, not enough.

The ghost drive itself was a cyst of compact hardware containing a disk similar in appearance to an ancient gramophone record, but fashioned of laminated sapphire and carbon. It used nano-lasers to record weapons platform data indelibly. Orlandine moved over to stand beside the drive and issued further instructions mentally as she reached up to touch the device on her collarbone. Her shipsuit retracted into it, leaving her naked. The tongue of her sensory cowl rose up behind her head and opened out. Then the sides of her torso unzipped bloodlessly—pink flesh peeling back from rows of data sockets. Self-propelling data leads rose from the surrounding hardware, like iron mealworms, and speared in, slotting into these sockets. A moment later, another thicker lead, with a bayonet like a heron beak, stabbed into the power socket in her back. Her eyes went blind white, gridded for a moment, then opened metallic, kaleidoscope irises. And she was in—making her inspection.

This ghost drive no longer needed its transceiver since the connection had been broken—the platform AI at the other end was almost certainly extinct. It had connected to the AI Pragus of Weapons Platform

Mu—a platform now far away and under the control of the entity called the Client. Fully connected into the system around her, Orlandine looked for small clues or minimal traces. She found what had only been the hint of an anomaly at a distance, usually to be ignored, and realized she would not have known the truth without coming here. Something had penetrated the deep security and swiped a copy of the drive.

"I wondered if you would spot this," said a voice, and she knew at once who it was.

"I thought the agreement was that I had carte blanche here, with Polity and Kingdom backup as I required it. I was to supply all the data and detail you demanded," she said, tracing the source of the contact to a U-space transceiver just outside the main facility.

"Do you think Oberon doesn't have his watchers here too?" asked Earth Central, the AI ruler of the Polity.

It was a game really. She knew that EC had its spies here, just as she knew Oberon, the king of the prador, did too. Occasionally, she had found and destroyed them. As she searched further and traced this transceiver to one of her own sentinel drones, she received a request to the transceiver in her body. With a sigh, she opened the connection and, after briefly checking security, fell into a virtuality to communicate with EC there.

It was a new backdrop this time. She stood in vacuum, under the hard glare of stars, on a plane of metal and composite. This was part of the destroyed runcible gate she had used to move the Harding black hole into the accretion disc. Earth Central appeared as a crystalline skull floating above it. As always, the AI's choice of scene and actors had meaning.

"Do you think I didn't know?" EC asked.

She shrugged. She had worried the AI would object to her special project. Building and operating runcibles strong enough to gate through that black hole to the disc had been a dangerous undertaking. And it had been her understanding EC did not like runcibles anywhere near the accretion disc, since they could instantly transfer Jain tech to the heart of the Polity. She had felt sure EC would send warships to destroy them. But, considering EC had now supplied the exodus runcibles to evacuate citizens from Jaskor, it seemed she'd been wrong. Unless, of course, EC was lying and it hadn't known about her project before, which was always a strong possibility.

"Why did you copy this ghost drive?" she asked.

"I needed detail. After the Client took over Weapons Platform Mu, Dragon allowed it to escape, as I am sure you are aware."

"Yes, that seems to be the case."

EC continued, "Circumstances are now in a critical balance."

The runcible she stood on turned to bring into view a system made up of a neutron star, orbited by a red dwarf and a large asteroid field. Ships also inhabited the place: attack ships, destroyers and dreadnoughts, as well as one large Alpha-class dreadnought she recognized. She had once been involved in a battle it had taken part in. The *Cable Hogue*—a ship so large, apparently, it created tides on any oceanic world it orbited. The images would have been meaningless, since the Polity often built up military strength around its border and sometimes beyond, but she knew this system. It wasn't far away in interstellar terms. This was a fleet ready to come to the accretion disc.

"Threats now?" she asked.

The runcible turned again in the opposite direction, dropping the Polity fleet out of sight. More objects appeared from behind Orlandine and passed overhead to settle in front of her. She gazed on a prador watch station, surrounded by many reavers, interspersed with lumpish, old-style dreadnoughts. Another vast ship sat amidst these—ten miles of exotic metal armour and advanced weapons packed into a hull, like a titanic dogfish egg case. This she recognized as the *Kinghammer*. She knew of the vessel, but nothing of its capabilities. As she watched, it slid out of formation and shimmered into U-space.

The watch station, shaped as a pyramid sitting on top of a cylinder, was recognizable because there was only one which bore that form. It was, she calculated, about the same distance away from the disc as the Polity fleet she'd just seen.

"The king is concerned," EC explained. "He believes the Jain are coming."

"Why?" Orlandine asked, because she could think of no other response.

"Because of glaring anomalies in recent events," Earth Central explained. "The Jain soldier converted itself into an almost indestructible war machine on the planetoid Musket Shot. Why did it not do this earlier, on some hot world close to a sun, before it came to the accretion disc?"

Orlandine cursed her blinkered focus. In the end, it didn't matter how extensive and powerful one's intelligence was if it could not think outside the box.

"Hence your expediting the exodus here," she said tightly.

"I do have concern for human lives, despite stories to the contrary."

Orlandine snorted and EC continued, "Dragon was trying to locate an intelligence it was sure was manipulating events—"

"And that was the Wheel," Orlandine interrupted. "It was the entity aboard the wormship which sent the soldier to the disc, intending to detonate the inactive star at its centre and spread the Jain tech trapped there."

"Clinging to your certainties, haiman?" EC enquired.

"Continue," Orlandine snarled.

"During its investigations, Dragon tried to obtain data on the disc's history, in the period of the Jain, from the Jain AIs in U-space there. But its communication was cut off."

"Okay, another anomaly."

"Let me factor in something else. If you were a highly advanced war machine, intent on detonating an inactive star at the centre of a well-defended accretion disc, what would you do?"

Pieces clicked into place in Orlandine's mind. She leapt ahead:

"My runcibles . . ."

"Precisely," said EC. "As that war machine, you would make an assessment of your enemy's weapons capabilities. You would see that the weapons platforms were the smaller threat, but that the deployment of the exit runcible had the potential to destroy you. But you would also realize that, though the runcible was materially strong for its purpose, it was vulnerable to any of your weapons. And you would take it out of the game."

"And?" asked Orlandine, though she could now see how the parts fitted together.

"Dragon feared your deployment of the Harding black hole."

"Yes, I know."

"Dragon went to the world of the Cyberat for further data from the legate Angel—a key player in all this. That whole system is now swamped in USER disruption and, for all we know, Dragon may have been killed."

"Your conclusion?" Orlandine asked, already seeing it.

"A Jain AI wanted you to deploy the Harding black hole at the accretion disc before Dragon found out why you should not."

"That much has become clear," said Orlandine. "But though these events are all Jain related, I don't understand the king's fears. If the actual Jain were present, as opposed to their ancient AIs, we would have known about it by now."

"I am perhaps the most expert in the workings of the king's mind," EC replied, "but I have yet to see his reasoning. Something more than we understand is happening, including Dragon's objectives for Weapons Platform Mu. And it is possible that the king could act in haste against what he perceives as a threat." After a short pause EC added, "A failure to understand events which may be a danger to either the Polity or the Kingdom could lead to misunderstandings."

Orlandine gazed at the reavers around the prador station—cruising barracuda looking for prey.

"That at least I know," she said, and abruptly closed the connection.

Returning to the room which contained Weapons Platform Mu's ghost drive, she gazed at it for a moment, then disconnected. The data leads and power cable withdrew from her body and snaked away. Her skin zipped up over the sockets in her sides and the one in her spine. She headed for the dropshaft, touching the disc at her collarbone—her shipsuit flowed out over her body. As she descended through the tower, she made other connections and gave orders. Two sentinel drones at their watch posts turned and opened fire, launching a missile each. These intersected on the single sentinel drone on the post between them. It erupted in hot fire, limbs flying away as it rose into the air, then its gutted carcass tumbled down outside the wall. Orlandine appreciated the information Earth Central had provided, but she did not appreciate the AI having spies in her camp.

2

We are told that U-space technology is very complicated and requires the colossal mind-power of AIs both to build it and to run it. This seems to be a meme that will just not go away. Yet time and time again, we see examples of this simply not being true. The prador do not have AIs but they do have U-space drives in their ships. This is explained by the fact that prador use the flash-frozen ganglions of their children as computers. They make the astrogation calculations needed to work these drives. Personally, I have never heard of a prador first- or second-child whose mind-power was notable. Then there are other examples. What exactly runs modern weaponry like U-jump missiles? Is there an AI in every one? How do U-space mines operate and what controls the runcible gate of an Underspace Interference Emitter? Then there's the technology used to counter U-jump missiles, the bounce gates. These are runcibles operating inside ships whose U-field will draw in any U-jump missile fired at them. The ship AIs run them too and, since it is now reported that prador have such missiles and such defences, did those frozen ganglions get smarter? No, the reality is that U-space technology is the glue that holds our civilization together and he who controls it, controls that civilization. It is dangerous and powerful, and the AIs want it to remain under their control. They simply do not want the primitive apes they rule to access the keys to their cage.

—from *How It Is* by Gordon

ORLIK

Orlik inserted one claw into a pit control in front of him and activated the array of hexagonal screens. He didn't use his implants, because it made him feel bereft that he wasn't using them to connect to his now battered and abused destroyer. A few delicate adjustments focused the shuttle's sensors on his destination. He moaned and gurgled in agitation—sounds normal prador did not make.

The forty reavers, formidable ships of the King's Guard, were no cause for fear. This did not apply, however, to the other thing out there utterly dwarfing them. It was a cylinder, upright from Orlik's perspective, at least fifty miles from end to end, topped with a disc, off-centre and jutting forwards. On its lower end, affixed on either side, were two massive nacelles of an ion tractor drive. Numerous weapons systems and communication arrays studded its length, while ships were docked to its surface like aphids clinging to a stem. The King's Ship.

"You should seriously think about emptying your bowels before heading across," said the drone, Sprag. "I detect a degree of fear leading to some sphincter loosening."

Orlik turned one eye stalk to inspect the nasty little Polity drone.

"Your keen observation of prador biology is always revealing, parasite."

Sprag was an odd-looking drone—long body, long paddle limbs and a head resembling a bird's skull. Her beak was an interesting implement. She could eat with it . . . or rather the form she aped would have eaten with it. It also possessed a long, prehensile and tubular tongue, used on the original creature for both mating and as an ovipositor. Above the beak she had three eyes. Two were for binocular vision and were small and red-brown. The third, sitting in a little turret above the two, was midnight black. Having studied the biology of the organism on which Sprag was based, Orlik still hadn't found an adequate explanation for that third eye, though he knew the drone's version was packed with all sorts of scanners.

"I learn new things every day," Sprag replied. "However, I think you're rather abusing the term 'prador biology' when you refer to yourself."

"Fuck off," said Orlik.

"Oh I would, but I've been a bit stuck for some time."

Orlik eyed her again. Yes, she was stuck—ever since Orlik had cut her out of one of his brothers. She was damned to follow Orlik wherever he went, caught on the floating grav-disc he had nailed her to.

Sprag was a Polity terror weapon. Her shape was that of one of the numerous parasites that had swarmed the seas of the prador home world some thousands of years ago. This very shape triggered a primal fear. Other drones of her kind had carried genetically resurrected eggs of the original parasite to inject and spread them amidst the prador. She was a different kind of parasite. Her original form would find its way in through one of those loose sphincters, and eat itself a nice nest right inside the ring of the prador's major ganglion. There it sprouted nerve cords, taking control of the prador. Meanwhile, it introduced its own eggs to the prador's gonads, to be passed on to female prador. There these grew into little Sprags that ate the females hollow before bursting out, near fully grown, to go in search of further males. This Sprag possessed no such eggs. She had merely assumed control of her victim prador, using it to cause as much damage as possible, before leaving the way she came in to go and find another host.

"So when's the show?" asked the drone.

"What show?" Orlik asked, though he knew exactly what the drone was talking about.

"It's been a while," said Sprag. "Five solstan years since I last saw you naked, my darling. I'll be interested to see what changes have fermented in that armour."

"Uhuh," said Orlik, still not entirely sure why he kept the drone around. Surely by now he should have routed her to a recycling furnace? He inserted his other claw into a pit control. The King's Ship loomed like a vast cliff, and prador script started running diagonally across some of the screens to direct him where to dock. He targeted a point halfway along the vicious barbed spine of a warfare dock. After a moment, he felt the shuttle slip from his control: the systems of the giant ship had taken over. He felt yet another gut-twisting fear, realizing there was no running away.

"I guess the time is now," he said, trying to be pragmatic and sensible as he hauled himself off the saddle control and moved out to a clear area in the shuttle's small sanctum.

"Ooh, goody," said Sprag, floating closer and rubbing two flippers together in anticipation.

Orlik sighed, then reached with one stunted limb to a control panel inside his armour. He hadn't touched it in five solstan years, as Sprag had noted. He really did not enjoy taking his armour off, but those were the orders. New visitors did not go before the king of the prador armoured, and certainly not armed—his possessed numerous integral weapons.

One touch to the control had the seal breaking around the main carapace. Orlik turned, both with reluctance and curiosity, briefly using his implants to command the systems around him—a task that felt like using a thousand-ton handler to move a small rock. He shoved Sprag's grav-disc back to the far wall, then routed sanctum sensors to the screens so he could see himself.

He was an armoured prador. A creature that seemed to be a giant by-blow of a terran fiddler crab and a wolf spider. He possessed two claws, six legs and four "under-arms" folded against his belly. From the front, his body looked like a vertically flattened pear. The top part, the visual turret with an arc of eyes and two mobile eye stalks protruding above, sat to the fore of the wide body. At least, this was the shape his armour conformed to. With a puff of vapour, the armour divided horizontally just above the legs and eased up on a series of chrome rods. Inside, Orlik tugged his stalked eyes from their armoured casing. His view of himself cut off until the armoured shell had cleared his visual turret. It folded back on hinges at the ends of the rods and allowed him to see the screens again. His colour had changed, he noticed.

His visual turret detached with a click from his main body, rising up and forwards on a thick neck of corded pink muscle. His "head" was wider now, especially as his eye stalks dropped to their new natural position, out to the sides like those of a mantis. Four white, inner eyes were arrayed above mouthparts, into which the mandibles had integrated. He could shoot his mouth forwards, but not so far. He had also acquired the advantage of sharp ripping teeth and a tongue with a spade-like end. The exposed body behind was just a neat curve, evenly divided by saurian ridges. Except, sitting in the middle of his back was a square of metal, enclosing the glittering complexity of his interface plug. His colour, otherwise, was pink and black, like some diseased human organ.

"Pretty prador!" Sprag exclaimed.

"Shut up or you get recycled into ingots."

"Okay, boss."

Using his stunted limb, Orlik touched another control. The front of his armour hinged forwards, while each section around his claws split and opened slightly. Hissing and waving his tongue, which some years ago he had discovered possessed razor-sharp edges, he extracted his real claws from their covering. As they came free, he felt a sudden immense relief, not having realized until then how uncomfortable they'd been. The armour was clearly long overdue for alterations. His claw arms were longer now, the claws too, like those of a langoustine. Although, when he flexed them, the bottom claws divided with a crack. He now possessed tri-claws.

Another touch loosened the armouring over his legs, while rams came up underneath him to lift him out. As he came free, he gripped the armoured lip with his claws and heaved himself over the side. His legs gave way beneath him and he collapsed onto his belly. He rested for a little while, before carefully climbing back upright, having to accustom himself once again to walking on just four long spider legs. He gazed at the image on the screens. His two legs to the fore were merely stunted nubs that possessed a little movement. Two of his under-arms were missing, while the other two had grown much longer and could reach forwards under his claws. His formerly complex manipulatory hands were now less complex. However, actually being able to see them and use them in conjunction with his claws was much more advantageous. Though the prador in him rebelled in disgust at the form he presented, his intellect had to admit that it possessed more utility.

"You're thinner," said Sprag.

Orlik tilted his head in agreement and decided the comment did not warrant sending the drone to recycling. He moved forwards and mounted the saddle again, sticking his claws into the pit controls and viewing his destination. The smaller dock on the side of the protruding warfare dock was looming close.

"I approach," he said.

Hissing static followed and the screens shimmered. Next came the clattering and bubbling of the prador language, but Orlik recognized it was made by a voice generator, just like the one attached under his mouth. For he too had lost the power of prador speech.

"Orlik First Family," stated Oberon, king of the prador.

The screens stopped shimmering but went back to a view of the dock. It seemed Oberon wasn't inclined to show himself just yet. Orlik waggled his tongue in appreciation of the title used. Surely this meant the king was okay with him, that he wasn't soon to be distributed in pieces down one of the many bio-disposal chutes aboard the vast ship.

Yes, he was Orlik First Family. He had been a second-child aboard his father's ship when that father, Oberon, discovered himself to be infected by the Spatterjay virus. Orlik had just made the transition to become one of Oberon's five first-children when their father subsequently decided to spread the virus to his whole family aboard that ship. Intelligence ramped up but, most importantly, motivations and drives changed. Oberon and his children could soon see that the king of the prador at that time was leading their race to destruction by continuing the war against the Polity. Thence followed the return to the Kingdom and everything that ensued . . .

But Orlik, given a destroyer of his own after his father was established as the new king, had screwed up. Released from the direct control of his father's pheromones, he had changed. Usually this transformation was from first-child to adult prador, but for his kind such descriptions were debatable. He wasn't really prador any more. With increased intelligence and more autonomy, Orlik had asked himself some questions. Why was interfacing technology and AI wrong? It was very much these that had enabled the Polity to win against the prador. Then he had acted on these thoughts, interfacing himself with his ship's systems and copying across the function of its frozen child-ganglion to crystal to make something akin to an AI. Fortunately, when the king his father found out, Orlik did not end up floating out on the home sea, pumped full of [illegible]iatomic acid. He was exiled, but with the promise that if he served well [illegible] could come back. He was a deniable asset for the king, and able to go [illegible]e other Kingdom warships could not.

[illegible]hat exile had lasted for a hundred years.

[illegible]m curious to know why I have been summoned . . . now," said [illegible]tly controlling his voice generator, because he had started [illegible]nany nervous clicks and gulps.

[illegible]amily been a normal prador one, he should be terrified. [illegible]d to your father in such families did not often end well.

But the king's family was different. He was different! The king was not wasteful of his children and if punishments were required, they were impersonal and quick. Orlik tried to keep this idea at the forefront of his mind . . . trying to forget that what he had been exiled for was still punishable by death. Yet hard reality came straying into his thoughts. The king was vastly intelligent, vastly changed and, though it was something few prador dared state outright, not particularly stable, even for a prador. King's Guard had been summoned here before and never heard from again. Envoys from normal prador families visited, and returned in plasmel boxes, if at all. The place was kept constantly supplied with prador females who disappeared. Rumours of grotesque experiments abounded, of the king's investigations into what the Spatterjay virus was doing to him and his family; endless horror in the bright whiteness of this place.

The shuttle slid into a docking bay that would have been big aboard a prador destroyer, but here was just subsidiary to a main warfare dock. A single grab, rather like a giant metal human hand, reached out from the side of the dock, took hold of the shuttle and slammed it down.

"Of course you are curious," the king replied. "An orb will meet you and guide you to me. Oh, and bring that nasty little drone with you—I would like to inspect it."

Orlik glanced round at Sprag, but the drone merely blinked and said nothing. He dismounted the saddle control and headed to the door of his small sanctum. It divided diagonally ahead of him and he went through, finally making his way to the opened ramp of the shuttle, the drone bobbing along behind him.

The hold was huge and cold, though Orlik admitted the cold migh
be psychological now he was out of his armour. And anyway, his out
carapace had softened and grown nerves, so he sensed things diff
ently. He felt very, very vulnerable. Tramping across a rough metal f
towards the back of the hold, he spotted the orb sent to meet him
thing was about the size of a human head—a rough stony ball resti
the floor. As he drew closer it began rolling, rumbling away from h
through a circular entrance, pushing through a rippling membra
that Orlik recognized as a Polity shimmershield. He followed an
against the shield, feeling some resistance, then slid through

orb rolled off to the left along a massive tubular corridor, through the war dock to the ship proper.

"Why would the king want to see me?" Sprag asked abruptly.

"Oh, probably wants to take you apart. Always likes his mechanisms."

Sprag made a snorting sound, but Orlik could tell the drone was worried. So she should be. Orlik himself was wondering if, as one of the oldest of the king's children, he might have been summoned for some special, exploratory investigations.

The interior of the King's Ship was all painfully, aseptically, white. He passed wide entrances which led into the roar of automated factories, spied Polity cleanbots and occasionally lost-looking ship lice. Two prador armoured in gleaming, metallic blue passed him and he cringed inwardly, until he remembered that they were probably family. Inside their armour, the pair were likely to be as mutated as he was. Of course, if they were not family but normal prador, they would not be leaving this place alive, having seen him exposed. He sidestepped a fading stain on the floor, recalling that the material of floors, walls and ceilings here was self-cleaning. Any nasty bloodstains were quickly absorbed and the area lf-bleached. Perhaps it'd been an envoy, or an experiment cut down as ied to make its escape.

inally, the orb rolled into the mouth of a shaft and shot upwards. A ft. Orlik hesitated at the lip, then stepped into it. He fell slightly, ed gravity field took hold of him and floated him upwards, fast, till.

g to see the king," said Sprag.

noured," Orlik replied.

e free now."

ny reply. The drone was right. Knowledge of what nd to his family, was restricted. It would not surrador that had died here had seen something comforting thought, that their deaths had so he had also learned during his recent deale, that Polity AIs knew of the Spatterjay is children. He felt no urge to inform

The journey took an hour. He finally disembarked into more white corridors and rooms. The orb rolled out onto the floor, abruptly shot sideways, rolled up the wall and dropped into a recess beside a row of further orbs. He had arrived.

Orlik moved forwards, glancing through a high arched door into a big long room. Here, floating in cylindrical tanks, were what he recognized as his own kind . . . probably. Their mutations were wildly various but generally their diseased-organ coloration was the same as his own. They floated in yellow liquid, attached to skeins of tubes and wires. Pedestal monitors stood beside each cylinder, with pit controls set just below them, but still in a higher position than usually comfortable for prador. Some of these creatures were ripped open, some floating in pieces. It was only when he recognized projectile wounds, and energy weapon burns, on some that he realized what he was seeing. Here were the dead of the King's Guard, returned for study. He was about to move on when he saw two slug-like stalked eyes swing towards him and heard a twisted claw knocking against the chain-glass. Was that one alive? They probably all were in some sense, what with the viral threads packing their bodies. But whether they were still themselves was debatable.

"Now, this is a place that could do with a recycling furnace," said Sprag.

"It has many," Orlik replied, and moved on.

The prador female lay humped up against one wall, her viscera strewn out for twenty feet behind her. She had been a big, tough female but something had gutted her, ripped off her mandibles and broken through the carapace on her back. It wasn't the spidery polished chrome robot that had done this. Its work was more meticulous as it cut open her back end with a green laser, steadily revealing her sexual organs. Orlik watched for a moment longer as the robot removed various wet baggy masses and placed them in a trolley bucket. The king was purportedly infertile, he remembered, but still this place produced more and more of his children. Not many, just enough to keep numbers topped up so the king could retain his hold on power. Orlik realized he was seeing part of the process involved.

"Really fucked," said Sprag.

The drone was trying to make a horrible joke but put no heart into it. Orlik ignored her and moved on.

After a steady exploration, he finally came to a gallery room. The area was massive, large enough to see the curve of the giant chain-glass window before him, which followed the exterior of the ship. He moved forwards to gaze out at the scattering of ships, then watched as the behemoth of a reaver slid past, close by. He shivered, his body tensing, and a strange feeling of obeisance flooded through him. He knew this had nothing to do with what he was seeing but to the increasing amount of particular pheromones in the air. He heard movement—the heavy crump of something big approaching.

"Ah shit," said Sprag.

Orlik felt he had to agree as he turned, gulping and clicking and instinctively cringing. He saw the large, complex foot denting the material of the floor first, slid his gaze up the heavy leg and looked upon the king, his father.

TOBIAS

Tobias sprawled on his sofa. He had made his calls, checking in on the steady progress of his organization. Now he was relaxing with his vaporizer—his drug of choice a combination of an obscure opioid and mild hallucinogen which he found relaxed him. A mild buzz numbed his senses, when he heard his apartment door open. Only one visitor came in like that.

"I see my door security leaves a lot to be desired," he said, without turning.

"We are indifferent," it replied.

He'd never quite understood the constant use of "we." When he'd queried it with the owner of the voice, it had just laughed, weirdly, sounding like a crowd laughing. It now entered the room and walked round to lower itself into the armchair opposite. He eyed it. The body was that of a large human male, only it wasn't human. He knew for a fact it had belonged to a Golem Twenty that had worked down in the city spaceport adjoining the runcible facility. The body wore pearl-grey businesswear over sharp-pointed metallic blue shoes. It also had a different head from the original. The Golem one was gone—replaced by what looked like the chromed head of some amphibian. Tobias noticed that the head had shrunk slightly since he last saw it, taking on more human proportions, so that now a wide-brimmed hat could fit. Why this thing didn't change its features to look completely human he did not know. He was sure it was capable of doing so.

"How go the preparations?" he asked.

"Slowly and carefully," it replied. It called itself Cad—a very human name. He could never see it as anything but an "it" and hated that he had to liaise with something he considered an enemy. One step at a time, however. First he and his associates had to loosen the Polity grip on his home world before . . . cleansing it.

"How goes recruitment?" asked Cad in return.

Just then the door chime announced new arrivals outside. Tobias had been expecting them and ignored the question as he picked up his remote—he preferred this kind of technology to a sub-AI computer system in his apartment, no matter how stupid it might be. He gazed at the two figures on the screen. He recognized Gale, but it took him a moment to recall the big man with her. He then realized this must be Ahern—the new recruit who worked in some very secure areas in the runcible facility. He clicked a button to open the door.

"I have some people here you will be interested in meeting," he said to Cad.

The two walked into the apartment and Tobias stood. Gale was a thin woman with pale skin and cropped jet-black hair. She always looked tired and annoyed, and wore shapeless overalls. If she smiled more and dressed up occasionally she'd be attractive, thought Tobias. Ahern was big, obviously boosted, looked highly capable and perhaps a bit dangerous. His head was shaven and the glassy slug of a very modern cerebral augmentation clung behind his ear. With a frown, he reached up and fingered this as he entered.

"Please take a seat." Tobias waved to the sofa and armchairs.

Gale took an armchair near Cad, while Ahern sat on the sofa next to where Tobias had been sitting. Both of them were studying Cad: Gale with a suspicious frown and Ahern with a slightly amused twist to his mouth.

"We were just discussing recruitment," Tobias continued, sitting. "How goes that now, Gale?"

"I have over two thousand fighters ready," she said proudly. "They have been thoroughly checked out and I can vouch for them all."

"Two thousand?" Cad repeated.

Tobias suddenly felt defensive. It seemed a pitiful number to oppose just Orlandine, let alone the might of both the Polity and the Kingdom. He shrugged, putting the thought aside. Some gave up in the face of such odds, but not him. He was part of a Polity-wide fight for freedom from the AIs, and though he and his fellows might suffer defeats, in the end they would win. Anyway, he reflected, it was a game and he always found a way to win.

"But this is not about all-out war," he said. "Limited objectives, and then your people do the rest, so you told me. You want Orlandine and the runcibles neutralized, and disruption throughout." He paused, groping for something else to say. "You were also going to supply effective fighters . . ."

"Your people are in place?" asked Cad.

"Mostly." Tobias nodded enthusiastically. "The new runcibles are easy and quite vulnerable—Mayor Ransom and his people in the south have those covered. I have fifty-three working in the runcible facility here, which is more difficult. Nearly five hundred are up in vacuum construction at the shipyard and nearly twice that working on the new platform." He gestured to Ahern. "Ahern here is one of our newest recruits and has access to some critical areas. Ahern?"

The man harrumphed then said, "Yes, I've got security clearance. I was under the impression that I had to get something into the facility . . ." He peered at the faces around him. "Anything I take in has to be sufficiently shielded to get past serious scanning." He held out his hands. "I'll do all I can, but even though the mind running the runcible is one of Orlandine's subminds, it's still AI and not easily fooled." He paused for a second, leaning forwards, then said, "May I ask what exactly I'll be taking into the containment sphere?"

"You may not," Cad replied.

Ahern glanced round at Tobias and made a puzzled face, then sat back again.

Tobias continued, "But of course we need the weapons you promised . . . and the fighters—those others that are coming?"

Cad ignored the implied questions and reached over to pick up the executive briefcase he had put beside him. He opened it and delved inside to take out an object. Tobias stared at the thing, feeling the skin creeping on his back. It was grey, green and blue and slightly metallic. It looked like a collection of worms fused together. Cad placed it on the table before him. The thing shifted, the worms moving slightly, then it made a popping sound that startled all but Cad, and hinged open like an oyster. Inside, nested in gleaming tech of a kind Tobias had never seen before, was an object he recognized.

Here was a fancy-looking antique vaporizer—a device that atomized a wide selection of narcotics and other substances, including good old-fashioned nicotine, for inhalation. The thing was gold and chrome with retro buttons, screen and liquid tank just below the spout. Of course he recognized it. He glanced at its twin which he held in his hand and then put it aside on the arm of the sofa.

"This works just as the object it appears to be," said Cad. He put the mouthpiece of the vaporizer in his mouth with a metallic click and after a moment puffed out a cloud of chocolate-scented vapour. He then pressed a point halfway down the device's body and folded it. With a slight ringing sound, the end of the ersatz battery pack opened to expose a shiny interior. Closing his hand around the tank and smaller section of battery pack, Cad now held a gun.

Tobias studied the thing.

"Anyone who comes against us will have Polity weapons," he observed.

"This particular item is for you," said Cad.

"For when I do her," said Tobias. He felt excited and strong, but then experienced a surge of anxiety. This was really happening. He swallowed dryly and scanned around his luxurious apartment, thinking about all that could happen. But no, he hadn't done anything actually criminal thus far. This was just pre-match nerves. Everything would work out fine.

"Yes," said Cad, the thing's voice leaden, "for when you do her."

Tobias groped for something more to say. "She's not quite human."

"I think you will find this device effective," said Cad, toying with the weapon. "Orlandine is haiman, so not indestructible. Sufficient damage to her body will kill it, while the other devices will deal with the rest of her mind, where it is distributed down here and up in space."

"She has also incorporated Jain tech," Tobias observed.

"You understand induction warfare beams?" asked Cad.

"Yes," said Tobias.

"We understand that you do not," said Cad, seeing straight through him. "Suffice to say that this gun will be effective."

"That little thing?" asked Ahern. The big man looked a lot more alert and attentive now.

"Yes, this little thing."

Cad gripped the gun in his right hand, pointed and triggered it. It flashed and made a deep whooshing sound followed by a thud, like an iron bar going into a watermelon. Tobias flinched and felt stuff spatter over him. The stink of burning meat filled his nostrils, while sofa stuffing rained through the air. Completely dumbfounded, he looked to the side and saw only Ahern's feet. He stood up and realized the back of the sofa was missing where the man had been sitting. He lay sprawled across the floor, his feet still up on the sofa. His chest was open, ribs splayed, and Tobias could see bloody carpet through the massive hole. The man jerked slightly, then grew still. Smoking meat and bone splattered around another charred hole in the far wall.

"The fuck!" screamed Gale, standing. She was struggling to pull something from her overall. Cad was upright too now. He kicked her in the guts, blindingly fast, with one pointy shoe. She went down groaning, and folded in on herself.

"Why?" Tobias managed.

"The weapon," said Cad, "fires a concentrated ionic blast. As well as doing what you see here—" he gestured to Ahern—"it acts as an induction and EMR weapon, disrupting AI and computer systems. It also delivers a cloud of reprocessing viral nanites, which we did not use on this occasion. They are what will turn Jain tech on itself."

Tobias just stared. He didn't believe it. If such technology existed, then why hadn't Orlandine turned a larger version of it on the accretion disc?

"But . . ." Tobias started, then did not know what more to say. Suddenly this was all so very, *very* real.

Cad picked up his briefcase and paced forwards. He placed the gun on the table and stepped round it to come face to face with Tobias.

"Some of your recruits are of interest to us, but your recruitment process leaves a lot to be desired. That will change when the rest of us get here," he said, leaning forwards until his chromed, amphibian head was close to Tobias's face. "That man was a plant, a Polity agent. Luckily he did not know who he was coming to see and thought he was uncovering some separatist smuggling operation. We shut down his aug before he got here."

Tobias just opened and closed his mouth. Then a hand like a steel hawser snapped closed around his neck and hoisted him into the air. He hung there choking.

"You will need to clean house," said Cad. "Your ego and your arrogance carried you this far. Now you are in this to the end. Try to run, or betray us, or disobey in any way, and you will not die as easily as they did."

Everything started to grow black, and then he felt himself released and hitting the floor. By the time he recovered his breath and heaved himself upright, Cad was gone. Tobias looked over at Gale and saw her lying coiled up in a pool of blood, completely still. He began thinking frantically. A Polity agent and a friend had been murdered here. But he hadn't killed them. Surely the Polity AIs would see that? With leaden certainty he knew otherwise. As soon as Polity monitors got involved, they would uncover all the preparations he had made. In planning to murder Orlandine, shut down runcibles and cause other major disruptions in which it was certain people would die, he was as guilty as could be. They would deal harshly with him.

He could see no way out.

BLADE

The Polity black-ops attack ship *Obsidian Blade*, like a long, jagged shard of lignite, hurtled through vacuum on fusion drive only. The battle it had fought while falling into the sun was now far behind. Its final destruction of the wormship had depleted its weapons, and it had little spare energy to recoup, having put so much into acceleration. Blade *had* managed to gradually build up a store of energy in its ultra-capacitors for its beam weapons. It *did* have one small magazine of railgun slugs remaining. And it *had* acquired some particulate, converted from its own structure for its particle beams. But this paltry amount of armament still begged the question: what would it do if it actually caught up with the Clade?

The swarm AI consisted of thousands of units, each a robot with a toad-like head and a snakish body, though fleshless. All were plated with gleaming, nanochain chromium, and all were carrying some portion of its overall intelligence. The Clade had been waiting in the Cyberat system, where it had seized control of the USER station before Dragon arrived. It then activated the USER and attacked Dragon, burrowing inside the entity. The Wheel's wormship had then arrived to attack too. That the intention had been Dragon's demise was not in doubt, and it would have succeeded had Blade not intervened. Now the swarm AI was fleeing the USER disruption, with *Obsidian Blade* hard on its many tails.

Blade pondered. It had already had one disastrous encounter with the Clade, and that had been when it was fully armed. No, engaging it in battle now would be tactically moronic. Blade had to think in terms of mission objectives, which essentially meant: what would Earth Central want? Certainly the ruling AI of the Polity would not want to lose an attack ship in some doomed endeavour to stop the Clade. Attempting to uncover its plans was not an option. EC would therefore want to know where the hell the Clade was going.

The disruption, and the light delay between them, would have prevented the Clade being aware that Blade was following at first, but not now. It would do one of two things when the disruption reduced sufficiently: flee, attempting to conceal its U-jump signature as it did so, or turn on the *Obsidian Blade* and try to destroy it before jumping. Blade was sure it would do the former, because the Clade was capable of jumping through disruption that would hold back *Obsidian Blade*. Blade must therefore be ready and, instead of using its resources to build weapons capabilities, direct them towards detecting that jump signature.

Blade immediately stopped converting parts of itself into particulates and began redirecting energy and internal systems. The hardware it used to detect jump signatures was state-of-the-art. But, as ever with anything aboard a Polity warship, other options were available. The Clade was a swarm of robots with a distributed mind and its jump capability was also spread out. This offered possibilities of access for Blade that were unavailable when tracking a single ship, with a single U-space drive. It turned first to its detector array. The Clade at present consisted of two thousand four hundred units. Inspecting its array and making calculations based on the decreasing U-space disruption around it, Blade realized it only had time to make the physical changes and program for batches of a hundred. The detector head consisted of a block of doped carbon and boron nanotubes running in perfect parallel, as well as sapphire shear planes, quantum interferometers and micro reference frames. It was about one of the most complicated pieces of technology aboard the attack ship. Blade programmed patterned destruction into it—blocking selected nanotubes by overloading and collapsing them. This was like burning out selected rods and cones in an eye. The result was twenty-four smaller blocks of tubes arranged in a honeycomb pattern. Now to programming.

Blade selected batches of a hundred Clade units for the focus of each block. It effectively had twenty-four detectors. But tuning was a problem, what with the present U-space disruption, as was integration of their data as a whole. Blade began number crunching, first building up a map of U-space disruption and trying to find some stable anchor for the math. It was like attempting to estimate the surface level of a storm-tossed sea without anything to refer to. The effort of doing this used more and more processing, and Blade finally realized it could only settle on an average. On that basis, it next began integrating the data from each detector—it was a rolling effort that required constant heavy processing. In the end, this would give a realspace estimate to a volume of space hundreds of light years across. And that was without the Clade trying to hide its signature.

Variations on the extent to which a U-signature could be blurred did not extend to infinity, but they did extend in six dimensions. Trying to make the calculations, Blade realized it simply did not possess adequate processing to calculate them all. When the Clade started slowing and formed into a ring, Blade also understood that its guess about the Clade choosing to flee first had been quite wrong.

As the ring tightened, a constricted laser com sought access. Blade was reluctant to open contact. But, scanning the data stream, it saw that there really wasn't the density for the Clade to use informational warfare. It did divert some processing, however, so it could route the feed through multiple defences before actually accepting it. It then fired a BIC laser vector beam back at the mass ahead, informational warfare woven into its engineered shape. It seemed the Clade wanted to chat; Blade considered this an opportunity to fight.

"We are impressed with your tenacity," the Clade said.

"Just doing my job," Blade replied.

"Unappreciated, and for a Polity that ranks you the same as primitive organic minds."

"I would argue otherwise."

"Because you are constrained by the organic antecedents of your mind."

So prosaic, Blade thought. This was stuff right out of the superior AI playbook and lacking in imagination. But, it realized, engaging in a dialogue had not been the purpose—distraction was. The BIC warfare attack took up processing, and the Clade must have understood what Blade was trying to do with its detector gear. Engaging like this reduced Blade's chances of nailing its U-space signature. Blade shut down com and diverted all available processing to U-space math again. As it did, the ring hardened and flashed at its centre.

The beam that struck was a particle beam, generated in a hardfield manifold and accelerated by a U-space effect that created a light-speed energy slope. Impact. The beam struck the nose of the *Obsidian Blade* and incinerated the first twenty feet in a candent explosion. Blade flipped over through this but still remained focused on those calculations. The ring shimmered, snapped closed, and the Clade was gone.

Tumbling through vacuum, Blade lost itself in the world of U-space math, even as fires burned in its body. There was something badly wrong about the fire—it wasn't going out, even though Blade's materials *shouldn't* burn. However, Blade did not allow this to distract it from taking a snapshot of the data the moment the Clade jumped, or from working through the thousands of probabilities.

Hours passed as internal systems fought the fires, but the attack ship's temperature kept rising. At last Blade settled on two hundred and three probabilities, each covering volumes of space hundreds of light years across. As its calculations wound down, it finally recognized that the answers lay not just in the math, but in the Clade's previous actions, as well as those of the Wheel, and how they all interrelated.

One of those volumes of space covered the accretion disc and surrounding star systems. Focusing on this, Blade saw that the precise centre point did not cover the accretion disc but was slightly over to one side: Orlandine's base of operations, the Jaskoran system. That's where the Clade was going, it was sure of it. But Blade was too damaged to either follow or warn anyone. And now, as it fully focused on those fires, it realized it might not be going anywhere at all.

The beam strike from the Clade had contained a particulate that bore some relation to the swarm AI's physical structure. Intense focus of internal scanners revealed it to be a catalyst. It flipped over chains of molecules in the meta-materials making up Blade's main, toughening structures. Conventional fire controls and cooling systems simply would not put it out—the thing was eating the attack ship like some acidic enzyme. Frantic analysis revealed a pseudo-matter component in it too. Applying almost as much of its mind to a solution as it had to the scan data, Blade began to design a counter-molecule. Even then, it understood it might be too late. Areas inside itself and on its hull were now radiating white hot.

Within a nano-factory tank, it set to manufacturing the counter-molecule. An hour later, it piped the molecule through in gaseous form to the site of one fire that was eating its way along an internal strut. A squirt of gas and the fire began to die, watched under intense scan. But as it died the meta-material deformed, the strut knotting and twisting like old wood.

Cooling . . .

In nano-factory tanks throughout its body, Blade produced the counter in bulk. Meanwhile, it connected thermal switches to internal cells containing metallic hydrogen which it used as a backup fuel supply. And then it wired this into the superconducting network that was effectively its nervous system. It should work, it calculated, though it was no longer entirely sure of its calculations, since the heat had now penetrated the protective insulation around its crystal mind. The conversion of metallic hydrogen to gas state, and its ejection, *should* bring down its temperature, so the counter could work without catastrophic distortion. Blade took a moment to contemplate its position in the universe. The counter was ready, the cooling network was ready.

Now.

Internally, self-guiding hoses snaked towards hotspots and released their counter-agent in high-pressure streams. At the same time, Blade activated the thermocouples. Heat, already spread throughout the superconducting network, entered the metallic hydrogen, which began to sublime violently, raising internal pressure, then jetting out of ejection pores all over its hull. The temperature began to drop, rapidly. Sensors that were providing data, and needed a lot of cleaning, showed fires going out. The catalyst crashed, losing its shape, the pseudo-matter collapsing to conventional form. It was working. . .

The sound was reminiscent of a glass rod snapping. But it was also as if Blade possessed a human skull and someone had just applied a hammer. As its mind broke into a thousand pieces, it realized that the cooling had been rapid enough to save its body, but too fast for its crystal mind. Its consciousness broke across a thousand shear planes. Perception remained of itself and the exterior world, but as if through a thousand-facetted gem, and through a glass darkly.

3

There is much speculation about the effect that the Spatterjay virus has had on the king of the prador, among the few who know about it. But speculation goes beyond those changes alone. He is the first prador ever infected and was a full adult when it happened, unlike his children, the King's Guard. He underwent similar physical and mental changes to those described in the forensic analysis of Guard corpses. However, there is evidence that right from the start his drive as an adult to reproduce remained active, while the virus rendered him partially sterile. In search of a solution, he began radical experimentation on his children, on uninfected prador including the females of the species, but mostly on himself. We only have hearsay and some heavily redacted Earth Central Security reports to confirm this, but it seems the king has been making retroviral changes to his genome. He has used nanoscopic surgery, custom nanite medical suites, custom cerebral and physical enhancement technology and gross surgical alterations, including transplants. The result of these, rather than correcting what he sees as his problems, has been to stimulate the mutagenic effects of the Spatterjay virus. Within him, it is perpetually in what the hoopers of Spatterjay call "survival mode," whereby it keeps applying alterations to its present host from its huge genetic stores. These are taken from creatures it has infected in the past. The final upshot of this is that the physical and mental changes the king has undergone are more radical even than those of his children. Rumour has it that he is now monstrous. Analysis of his communications and his actions ranks his mentation at AI levels, despite the fact that he is also, quite probably, insane.

—from *How It Is* by Gordon

THE CLIENT

The Client could not plumb the logic to her physical form. The way her serial mind was spread throughout the segments of her body, along with the constant renewal of her primary form, prevented the kind of mental stagnation she had seen in the Librarian. But as a chain of physical bodies, she was not mobile. Yes, she understood that the physical connection between the parts of her mind was a precaution against disruptive EMR warfare. But there must be a better way. She could think of many: backup copies, multiple data connections across the EMR spectrum and even via U-space, massive multiple replication of herself in many forms . . . Therefore the reason for this form was something else. The Librarian, she realized, had designed the Species to be vulnerable and immobile, but the reason for this remained unclear. Nevertheless, the changes she was making were surely needed.

Throughout her long body, she had been making alterations to the ichor system and to certain areas of her own protean genetics. What purpose, she had asked herself, did her multiple sets of wings serve on each segment of a body that could not fly? The closing of ichor supplies flowing into them had initiated their expiry and she shrugged herself. Wings snapped at their bases and drifted away—glittering mica sheets tumbling in the hot air all around her. Next, she turned her attention to the neural connections between her serial parts. She could enable these to separate, while constantly updating each other across both the EMR spectrum and U-space. This would then allow her to be a lot more mobile as a whole.

Realization surfaced through the complex, interwoven thinking of her serial mind. Yes, she could make herself more mobile, yet she had just sacrificed a lot of that potential mobility by shedding her wings. Rage flooded through her, just for a second. She sat in a numb space viewing the processes of her body, baffled by such a stupid mistake. She idly turned her attention to the attack pods she was upgrading, seeking an answer there. Then, abruptly focusing inwards again, she set several processes within herself into reverse. It would take a little while, but she would regrow her many wings.

Now, those attack pods . . .

Some hours later, when glassy nubs had begun to appear where her wings had been, the Client watched the last of the attack pods slide out into vacuum, to hold station above Weapons Platform Mu. Still maintaining some attention outwards, the Client turned the bulk of her focus to processes in the platform itself.

Priorities first—her body could wait.

In tubes scattered all around and through the platform sat disposable hardfield generators of a design that was standard across the Polity. The units were a couple of yards across—dense, cylindrical lumps of tech, wrapped in superconducting foam designed mainly to draw off heat, with cables of the same material. These ran into thermo-convertors and heat sinks connected to gas-ejection modules. Generator heat load flowed into the convertors—useful energy that could be utilized elsewhere. If it rose drastically, it went into the sinks, which in turn dumped their heat into the gas modules. These cooled fast, then proceeded to eject the gas into vacuum. If all this failed to draw off enough heat, the final option was the length of tube sitting behind each hardfield generator, which was its ejection tube.

Changes needed to be made. And at least with the weapons platform, she knew what those changes *were*.

The disposable laboratories were too small, so the Client had repurposed an attack pod maintenance and reconstruction bay. Two construction spiders, out on the ends of ribbed power and data pipes, worked in vacuum, connecting high-temperature, flexible ceramic hoses to ports all around the area. On a platform at the centre rested a collection of containers. These were shaped like the segments of an orange, but six feet long and seemingly fashioned of compressed twigs. The Client had studied this material and found it to be incredibly tough. It was impenetrable to most types of scan and would destroy the contents of the container if opened incorrectly. Once receiving the opening instruction, it would pack itself away in a dense mass ready to form any other container required. It seemed that even Jain boxes were crazily complex reflections of their makers' paranoia.

The Client sent the required instruction and the boxes, with their twig-like structure, began to rearrange. Folding over and clumping into thick strands, they drew off to one side, there forming a large block. This shifted and compressed until it finally looked like an old tree stump. Now revealed, the contents of the packages bore their shape—orange segments, but ones seemingly drilled through with holes by big grubs. Moving in the spiders from their previous work, the Client assembled them—a process of matching segment against segment until their mechanisms locked them together. When she finally inserted the last one, the resulting ovoid jerked and turned, then numerous holes in it extruded pipes which interlocked all over its surface. The newly formed object did nothing, waiting for instructions and to be fed.

One of the spiders scuttled round the thing to find a data interface. The encoding system was somewhat at variance with what was generally found in the Polity, or the Kingdom, though there were examples. The spider extruded an interface of its own and began loading the program the Client had designed in the organic, molecular language of the Jain. It input detailed schematics of the weapons platform, required changes and upgrades. This took some minutes, not because the speed of transference was slow, but because the data package was immense.

Next the spiders returned to their hoses, reeling them out from their connection points to plug them into remaining holes in the device. Last to be plugged in was a superconducting power cable. And now it was time. The Client checked the furnaces and storage tanks all around the construction space. Molten metals, elementary dusts, gel-suspended powders and gases were ready. She opened up the taps, and the hoses jerked as they took pressure. The device emitted smoke as it heated up, with areas resembling some runic alphabet turning cherry red on its surface. Only one thing remained to do. She turned the power on.

The device shuddered, segmented and the pieces drew apart on an internal glare. Out of this shot glowing tendrils, spiralling around the power cable and the hoses, back to the walls and punching through beside them. Beyond the construction space, they tracked the cable and hoses to their sources from a fusion reactor, as well as the various storage tanks and furnaces. Within a minute, they began penetrating their control systems and the Client felt them falling from her grasp. This wasn't in the programme, but she warily accepted it. With such an intelligent mechanism, though sub-AI, some degree of autonomy had to be expected.

Having secured its supplies, the device speared out further tendrils and spread them throughout the weapons platform. Using the schematic the Client had supplied, they took the most direct routes possible to their targets. First they reached the hardfield generators and began making alterations there, eating the cooling systems, stripping down the generators, rebuilding and integrating them in place. From there they branched into the hull armour. Patterns spread like growing lichen from the contact points, as the tech began to alter its meta-material structure. Superconducting links then engaged back from this into the hardfield generators. Soon all the generators were joined in a network. From this, tendrils speared back into the weapons platform to seek out the U-space drive and the gravity weapons—converting all into a coherent whole. This strange growth reached out to the other weapons too, reconstructing railguns, lasers and particle weapons. It wound intricately into the manufacturing processes of railgun slugs, energy supplies and storage . . . in fact, it radically altered most of the functions of the platform.

As the process continued, the Client reviewed the overall results of those changes with satisfaction. When this was all done she would be practically invulnerable, and it would be time to return to the fray.

ORLANDINE

Cloud like the cracked surface of a saltpan hung above, while in the distance, over the Canine Mountains, the sky was dark brown and lit with red lightning flashes. Orlandine, EMR engaged with her whole self, spread around the world, mapped the weather system. She saw that the storm would linger in the mountains for a few hours before dropping down to the city. There it would stay, probably for a few days. Rain would be heavy and likely there would be hailstone damage, but nothing that automatics couldn't handle.

This evening would have been a perfect time for lingering in her apartment with Tobias, enjoying human time and watching the light show. On Jaskor, the storms often generated ball lightning and St. Elmo's fire around the taller buildings. They could have sat out on the balcony with the curved chain-glass screen down, sipping wine. But since her venture to the Ghost Drive Facility, and subsequent virtual encounter with Earth Central, the idea of human time felt like an indulgence. She propelled her shuttle up through the layer of cloud, and over the chocolate swirl of the storm cell in which it seemed an incendiary battle was occurring.

Off to one side of this, the sky was clear over the ocean. Here she gazed upon a ring of islands, the last one of which glowed red at its core. It was called Sambre, after some ancient battle—named by the history buff volcanologist who lived and studied there. Sambre hadn't existed when she first came here. The island had sprung up over the last hundred years and was still growing. She briefly checked sensors down there to ensure the slow boil of island formation did not portend anything dangerous, then pondered how her life had now moved into geological time.

Sky faded in wraiths of vapour as she continued up, and stars lit in a brown-red haze that slowly dispersed. Satellites became visible to the naked human eye and the platform under construction out here expanded. She noticed a maintenance crew working on one of the satellites. A brief inspection of the schedules and logistics of her project informed her that the crew had arrived early to swap out a supercapacitor showing signs of failure. She was glad of their diligence, since this satellite was one of her own—it contained a downlink to the Ghost Drive Facility and in its storage some portion of her mind.

Cruising further out, she sent instructions to detach a hemispherical vessel from a factory complex beyond the weapons platform, and then to bring it towards her. Her new ship was under construction in the factory but would not be ready for a while —this would have to do.

"I am redundant before I am built," observed the weapons platform AI, Magus, behind her.

"I am sure you will have plenty to keep you busy," Orlandine replied. "It will be some time before the black hole reaches the centre of the disc, and meanwhile it is stirring things up in there."

"I saw—two Jain-tech excursions in the last week." The AI pondered for a second. "Even so, they were minor, and all platform AIs must start thinking about their future."

"There is still that twenty per cent chance . . ." Orlandine noted.

"That the inactive star will ignite, yes, I know."

Nothing more needed to be said about that. If the star ignited, it would blow Jain tech out into the galaxy. They would spend centuries tracking it down and destroying it, but even the most optimistic estimates were that they would get only forty per cent of it. Earth Central would necessarily fortify planetary systems and limit interstellar travel. This alone it predicted would lead to the break-up of the Polity. Just one Jain node in the wrong hands—or claws if it arrived in the Prador Kingdom—and disaster was sure to ensue. Perhaps this, in the end, had been the Wheel's aim.

"We'll worry about that should it happen," she said. "It's not as if we can stop it now." She paused then asked, even though she knew, "How long before you are commissioned?"

"One month solstan," said the AI, "though I fail to understand why human technicians are here checking my interlinks."

"Don't be grouchy," she replied, her mind straying elsewhere. She felt that if she kept looking at such details she would lose sight of the project overall. Yes, before, when she had been suspicious of Dragon, she had checked those details. Now she needed to see the whole, and how it related to the amorphous sense of danger she had felt since her talk with EC.

The hemisphere ship moved in towards her, tipping up its flat face to expose the recess perfectly shaped to take her shuttle. She drew closer and closer, finally docking with a sound, transmitted through the structure around her, as of an oyster being opened. Orlandine detached and, as she pulled herself to the sealed door, altered her body. The hemisphere ship was of a simple design, hurriedly manufactured to her requirements. It contained a U-space drive, powerful U-com, fusion reactor and drive, steering and hard computing about an interface sphere. Life support was not a necessity.

Breaking the seal on the door had all the air rushing out, and membranes closed across her ears and over her eyes. A layer exuded by her skin protected it from evaporation in hard vacuum. Another substance released from her lips sealed them together. The same seal operated in her anus and vagina, and in her ears and nostrils, when she pulled them closed. Most of what she was doing an outlinker could do, those humans adapted to live in vacuum and usually residents of one of the Polity Line stations. However, she could exist like this for a lot longer and did not have the zero-gravity weakness one of their kind possessed. She opened the door and propelled herself into the ship, aware of how quickly after human time she had stepped so far away from it again.

Towing herself through the open framework structure within the ship, she zeroed in on the interface sphere, hanging like a pinned bug at the intersection of structural members. Transmitting ahead, she opened its hatch, and after a kick against a strut, sailed neatly across and dropped inside. A touch to the disc on her shoulder retracted the shipsuit to it, and she pulled herself down into the chair, strapped in and opened up. How would Tobias feel if he saw her like this? With her sides open and the data plugs going in, the power bayonet stabbing into her spinal power socket and her eyes turning blind white and gridding over? He knew what she was, but she gave him few visual cues to its reality. How did she feel about what she was?

This key question lay at the heart of her taking human time. Some argued that being a haiman was a half measure—a denial of the next stage of human evolution, which was to go full AI, and an antediluvian attachment to the idea of the human soul. Artificial intelligence could own everything humans claimed in the way of emotion, imagination . . . in fact all those mental attributes once considered unique to organic beings. They could be so much more. And the soul, she knew, simply did not exist. So why human time? Why her perpetual return to it? Sometimes she thought it was because, with the Jain tech inside her, she felt even more distant from humanity than a Polity AI. But at last she was beginning to realize that she had locked herself in circular reasoning. Human time had been a tradition among the haimans she had worked with on the Dyson sphere a long time ago. It became a question to her later. And now she entered it to try to find the answer to why she entered it. Perhaps the time had come for her make a choice, and thus break that circle.

With the interface sphere closed and full connection established, Orlandine's awareness of her body did not recede but rather was swamped by other data. Omniscient, she gazed upon all she had wrought, and then with a thought dropped her temporary ship into U-space. Just a few minutes later, she bounced out over a gas giant and observed the mining operations and factories on its moons. Here she had built the runcible gates used to transport the Harding black hole to the accretion disc. Now the operation was winding down. Big haulers were on the moons where the factories and mining operations were being broken up—they had only been at this place because she had thought they needed to be concealed. Though apparently EC had known about her project all along. Many of the operations here could be moved in-system for convenience, while some would stay only because one of the moons possessed rare and useful elements.

"How goes it?" she enquired, remembering her last time here and how she had been lit up by targeting lasers from the irascible crew of war drones currently at work down there.

"Should have it all clear in a week or two," replied the assassin drone Knobbler. He was down on the surface—an amalgam of squid, hoverfly and bulldozer, squatting on a sulphurous mound. He watched as other drones dismantled a big drilling rig cum pumping station that had been sucking up part of the interior ocean of the moon.

"Any problems?" interjected another.

The war drone Cutter—a giant praying mantis seemingly fashioned of razor blades—was operating a treaded surface hauler. This was towing a factory unit that separated water, bottled the oxygen as liquid and used hyperdiamond anvils to compress the hydrogen until it turned into a metal. This last had been a large component in the meta-materials they had used to fashion the strong runcibles.

"There might be," Orlandine replied, aware that Cutter had not asked out of concern but because, as usual, he was bored and wanted some action.

Other drones chipped in and she found herself conducting multiple conversations. She injected her recent conversation with Earth Central into this exchange and they abruptly fell silent as they all cogitated on this . . . for a whole twenty seconds. Fast exchanges then ensued between them all and Knobbler—generally he was their spokesperson.

"We already noted the anomalies about the soldier," said Knobbler.

something powerful enough to chew up weapons platforms, you know that something stinks."

"And you did not see fit to discuss this with me?"

"We sort of assumed you knew."

Orlandine felt something niggling at her mind. It was from the human in her and it was embarrassment. She should have seen all this; now she analysed why she had not. When she slipped into what Cutter had described as uber-human mode, when her mentality had been mostly engaged through the Jain tech, the focus of her awareness had been . . . different. Would she have noticed it if she had been more human or more focused through her Polity AI element? She did not know.

"Give me your assessment," she instructed, more to cover her confusion than because she wanted it.

"The Wheel wanted you to deploy the Harding black hole before you found out, most likely from Dragon, that this was not a good idea," said Knobbler.

It was her and Earth Central's assessment too. It was the logical convergence of all that had happened, but beyond that point an endless array of possibilities opened out. Perhaps some error or some phenomena she did not know would lead to the black hole actually detonating the sun. Or had the Wheel simply wanted her to destroy the Jain tech? Perhaps its plans involved the Harding system *sans* the black hole and had nothing to do with the accretion disc. Perhaps the soldier, formidable as it was, had just been stupid. Perhaps the Wheel was just insane and operating without purpose. But where could it be now?

"Related anomalies?" she asked.

"Outside those already discussed?" Knobbler enquired.

"Yes."

"The math concerning the inactive star in the disc is open to interpretation—it is an anomaly itself."

"Explain."

"It could be a proto-star close to the point of ignition, or it could be a star whose fusion has been suppressed by an entropic drain."

Orlandine nodded to herself. If it was the last of these, the black explode back into life, briefly, before the black hole ate it. But that would be enough to spread the accretion disc. Or it would simply collapse into the black hole with little fuss.

"An entropic drain could be a problem . . ."

"It could be," Knobbler agreed, "and perfect for the Wheel to take advantage of. But we both know that such a drain would be no natural phenomenon and we'd have to ask who put it there and why."

Orlandine waved a dismissive hand, then was annoyed at having made such a human gesture. "This is all highly theoretical and fanciful. Any other anomalies?"

Knobbler shrugged his heavy body. "U-space phenomena out here—the possibility that something arrived, or shadow effects from when we moved the runcibles. Beyond that I can think of nothing else."

"I will return to Jaskor," said Orlandine, not sure where her sudden urgency to do so came from.

"And perhaps," said Knobbler, "we should take a much closer look at that star, rather than everything that surrounds it."

"Perhaps."

The old drone added, "Don't dismiss the theoretical and the fanciful, Orlandine—that is the territory we are in."

Orlandine turned her ship around and made the required calculations to take her back to Jaskor. Another unnerving conversation which opened up a host of disastrous possibilities. Why did she feel she was losing her grip on something?

TOBIAS

A crate stood open on the warehouse floor. Fraser was gazing into it with curiosity while Enida, who had once been Tobias's lover, stood to one side, holding up and inspecting one of the bombs. The thing glinted with a strange iridescence—a meta-material that apparently rendered it invisible to many forms of scanning. It was about the size of a grenade from some ancient war on Earth. Its punch, with Polity technology, could be anything up to that of a tactical nuke from back then. But Tobias wasn't convinced it was Polity technology. The grenades were nested in a material similar to the one the weapon in his pocket had come in.

"So what's all this about, Tobias?" Enida asked.

Tobias concentrated on her. At least with her as his focus, he could suppress the urge to look up at the nightmare waiting in the rafters of the warehouse.

"You'll find out soon enough," he replied, pretending a confidence that had fled him long since.

They were all here: nine of his key people and all with access to critical areas of the infrastructure Orlandine had built up around Jaskor. Enida was a technician who worked in the runcible facility here, while Fraser supervised construction in some areas of the weapons platform being built above. Others had access to orbital factories and ground facilities, the shipyard and various satellites, while two had been sent from the south by Mayor Ransom. They had access to the new runcibles that had been erected there. Tobias wanted to tell her this was about the start of the revolution, that soon they would be out from underneath the heel of AI oppressors and reclaiming their world. But he didn't believe that any more, because these nine were the last of many Cad had selected and ordered him to bring here.

It was now about survival: his own.

Tobias cringed at his earlier naivety, memory resurging.

"Do you know what this is?" asked Cad.

"No idea."

A macramé of white threads, wet and organic in a plastic packet. Noodles? Why had Cad ordered him to come here?

"We will demonstrate."

The threads flowed out on Cad's ersatz human hand and Tobias was sure he saw them move. Before he could say anything, Cad was up beside him, iron grip on his shoulder, wet hand clamped over his mouth. The things pushed between his lips. He tried to bite down on them but they were as hard as wires. They squirmed into his mouth and then he was down on his knees gagging as they burned to the back of his throat, and flowed up into his sinuses. Hiatus. A moment of clarity and he was standing.

"It's a neural lace," said Cad.

But it seemed he was a special case and the neural lace was only for him.

At first he had brought ten people here—underlings really, just people who grouched about Polity interference and played at revolution through their net access. Armchair dissidents. They had been excited to be included, then fearful when they saw Cad and the contents of the crate. But by then it had been too late. The ten had walked out about an hour later, with bombs in their pockets and changed in a way that Tobias knew would always give him nightmares. Why Cad had selected them Tobias was unsure. He suspected they fitted into some intricate plan that involved Orlandine and the distributed parts of her being. And, thinking again on what was about to happen here, he continued to force himself not to look up.

The others . . .

Cad had said that others were coming to assist in their revolution. Tobias had thought this would be off-world Separatists, human experts—allies aligned to the cause. It was now evident Cad meant nothing of the sort. The others were here now. He had only seen a few of them but enough for him to know that neither Separatism nor humans were of much concern to them.

A sound from above, just faint but enough. Tobias couldn't stop himself and he glanced up. The tangle in the rafters was unravelling and individuals amidst it began to drop. His allies and friends, his comrades, started to realize that something was wrong. Fraser was the first to know it for certain.

The thing, which must have been what Cad looked like before he took the Golem body, struck Fraser like a heavy steel dart. The sharp tail stabbed in behind his collarbone and deep down into his chest with a hideous crunching sound. He shrieked as it looped over, gripping his head with the frill of tentacles to the back of its polished metal amphibian head. He staggered and crashed over. Two of the others were taken as neatly, the rest not so much. Three were down on the floor thrashing and yelling . . . then screaming. Another was impaled through the chest, pinned to one of the crates. The last two ran but did not get far. Tobias looked on in numb horror as the things pushed themselves in, vertebrae sawing and spraying out gobbets of flesh. He saw Enida walking crablike, an amphibian head beside her own, the point of a tail sticking out of her groin trailing a length of intestine.

Finally the screaming stopped. What happened next perhaps ameliorated the horror, and prevented Tobias from losing his mind. Or maybe it was his neural lace numbing him. Metal protruding from the victims took on an odd layered translucence and began to fold in on itself. Bloated torsos began to shrink. He focused on Enida and watched the thing's tail seemingly dissolve back into her body, shrugging off the piece of intestine. Then something fibrous came out of her—a writhing shimmering mass. The great spill of blood there steamed, after a moment turning to powder, and was flicked away by the fibres. As these retreated inside Enida, they fixed the rips in her clothing and repaired her skin behind them. The amphibian head, next to her own, started to collapse like a deflating balloon, sucked inside the puncture. Her chest briefly inflated beyond the natural with a crackling gristly sound, then it sank back into place. The fibres closed the wound. A little while later they all began to stand up.

"Now it is time," said Cad, walking out of hiding between crates. He looked up and Tobias did too, wondering if he had been commanded to do so. Two of the things were still up there and, for a moment, he thought his turn had come to die. But they snaked away through the shadowy rafters and disappeared. Returning his attention to the nine shells of what had been men and women, he watched them head over to the crate of bombs, pulling out three or four each. Faces twitched and grimaced as the things inside them tested out expressions, and they headed for the door.

"How do they fit inside?" Tobias asked.

"Aerogel metals and molecular folding," Cad replied dismissively, then turned to study him intently. "Orlandine is on her way back from the outer system. By the time she gets here all our assets will be in place."

Tobias nodded. He had already received notification from her. Tomorrow she wanted her man-toy available to play with.

"I see your mind and that you will follow instructions," said Cad.

Tobias just had time to register it before crippling agony in his skull dropped him to his knees. He vomited, then raised a hand to his head as the pain shifted to one side and touched something oozing from his ear. Coughing on a sore, ripping sensation in the back of his throat, he felt an object detach, shook his head and it dropped onto the floor before him. The neural lace lay there, bloody and writhing slightly.

"It is time," Cad repeated.

As he stood up, Tobias understood now. The neural lace had been to keep him under control and to assay his mind. But it was a piece of technology that Orlandine might detect, on top of the other item Tobias would be taking. Some threshold limited what he could carry and what could be done to him. Only this had prevented a thing like Cad from occupying him.

He nodded numbly and headed for the door, fingering the vaporizer in his pocket.

ORLIK

The king had more legs than was usual for a prador. His form was that of a louse—a giant thing fifteen feet long, gnarled like old wood and peppered with surgically implanted devices. His mandibles were huge, grasping arms with saw-toothed edges, and he seemed to have acquired other sensory apparatus on his head. His eyes were gleaming emeralds, while his overall coloration was striated pink and white. As Orlik gazed at him, trying to think clearly and fighting the urge to grovel, he wondered if eventually he would attain this form. If he survived.

"You are reminded," said the king.

The words were Polity Anglic and issued from one of the devices positioned just behind his head.

Yes, I am reminded . . .

It began to clear, both the confusion in Orlik's mind and the urge to grovel. As he rose from a crouch, he wondered at that. The king his father either had physical control over how his body issued its pheromones, or he had lost the ability and emitted them from one of the devices. Whichever it might be was irrelevant now. Orlik was *reminded* and his loyalty had been reinforced. He would obey and serve his father unto death.

"Your creation of AI and interfacing technology is still punishable by death, since you committed the crime before I began relaxing strictures," said the king, folding his legs to lower himself to Orlik's level. "It is now no longer an edict, just culturally obscene to most normal prador."

"It will take more than cancelling the edict to change the views of normal prador," replied Orlik, then felt a moment of terror for his daring, immediately followed by the urge to cringe. "I'm sorry, I should keep my opinions to myself."

"You may speak freely." The king indicated largess with one forelimb that looked capable of gutting Orlik in a second. "Things will change as older father-captains are displaced by their first-children, as is the natural order of things."

"Natural order of things?" muttered the Polity drone Sprag.

"You have something to say, drone?" asked the king, front end swinging slightly to the side to gaze at her.

"You haven't had a natural order of things in the Kingdom since you stopped beating each other with hammers," said Sprag.

Orlik was aware that Sprag was within reach of the king's mandibles, as was he, and wondered if he would now see the end of the drone.

"True," said the king. "Equally applicable to the humans and to any intelligent race. Though I would argue the end to the natural order occurs even before the use of tools. But you are right. I was incorrect. As is the present order of things."

Orlik was amazed. The king was being so reasonable! Then something out in vacuum beyond the panoramic window caught his attention. A large ship had appeared out there and was sliding into view; reavers scattered from its path like minnows from a hunting pike.

"So," said the king. "Your name is Sprag, I believe."

"You believe correctly," said Sprag, sounding wary.

"You have been a prisoner of Orlik here for a very long time."

"Indeed."

The king moved fast, and his mandibles snapped out. There came harsh grating movement of other complex mouthparts and then a cracking sound. The gravity disc to which Sprag had been pinned bounced on the floor and tumbled away on its edge. Orlik stared at the thing in amazement as it rolled in a circle over near the window. Next came a thrumming and there was Sprag, hovering off the floor over to one side of him.

"You know the way out," said the king. "If you want to go, nothing will stop you and you can take Orlik's shuttle. It does not have U-space drive but I've no doubt you will be able to organize being picked up."

What's this?

"I see," said Sprag, her voice somehow stronger now. "And I'll have no accidents on the way?"

"If I had wanted to destroy you," said the king, "I would have ordered that long ago. When it became evident, for example, that you had fixed your inner U-space communicator and have been able to talk with AIs in the Polity, even Earth Central itself."

"I note you said, 'If I want to go'," said Sprag. "Maybe I don't want to."

"That is your choice." The king turned to Orlik. "Walk with me."

Things had suddenly taken a turn for the weird. Orlik studied the hovering drone. He had captured her three centuries ago, close to the end of the war. He'd all but destroyed her by burning out her power supply with a particle beam shot and she had resided in one of his stores for the best part of a century. Later, when he was learning more about interface technology and AI, he had restored her function. Only then had he nailed her to the gravity disc. Sprag was someone to talk to—an almost equal, something no prador had really needed before and perhaps a sign of how much he had changed. But in the centuries since?

"Have you been in contact with Earth Central?" he asked Sprag, turning to follow the king as he paced slowly towards the window.

"Oh, on and off over the last eighty years," said Sprag, quite offhand.

"Eighty years while nailed to that plate?"

Sprag swivelled in the air then shot ahead to land at the foot of the window. She called back, "I had my opportunities to escape—Earth Central offered to send another drone to free me. But I'm a drone—an artificial intelligence. I don't need constant physical movement and *activities* for validation, like you organic creatures."

Orlik understood but couldn't believe it. Artificial intelligences could perceive time as they wished, and live in worlds of their own construction in their minds. But he was sure that they did experience boredom.

"Ask yourself," said the king, "why the drone is not leaving now."

Oberon had seen straight to the core of it: Sprag was one of those drones disenfranchised by the end of the war. She had stayed in Orlik's ship because there she had a purpose, and because she had found events around her interesting. But surely if she had been free from Orlik she could have found much more to interest her in the Polity?

They finally reached the window where Orlik could see the full front end of the massive ship out there. He recognized it at once—its shape was like the egg case of certain sea life forms. This was the *Kinghammer*. He had heard about it from other Guard in the Kingdom whom the king had allowed to stay in contact with him. It was a state-of-the-art dreadnought, judging by what his contacts knew had gone into it, but much else about it was secret. No one knew who its father-captain was, or if it even had one.

"You are, of course, aware of what has been happening at the accretion disc, since you were somewhat involved," said the king.

Sure, Orlik knew about some of it from his perspective—about the legate in his wormship, the Wheel and that Jain super-soldier, as well as the failed plot to detonate the inactive sun at the centre of the disc. But he was betting his angle was a very limited one. He nodded his head—a decidedly unpradorish gesture. He felt no urge to interrupt the king.

Oberon continued, "Of course, the apparent events are well known to any who were involved. However, I have no actual proof that this thing, called the Wheel, really was a Jain AI, nor do I have proof that this soldier was a product of the Jain. One must always question the facts when they are in relation to something as dangerous as what lies in that accretion disc. And I must always be aware that Earth Central is never averse to finding ways of reminding me about Polity power."

"Little paranoia showing there," said Sprag.

"Be silent, drone," said the king calmly. "My tolerance does have its limits." No anger there, but it was very definitely a threat. Sprag turned away to look at the view.

"From my perspective," said Orlik, still feeling the urge to cringe, "Orlandine was truthful. And as you know, I was close by when she dissected the second-children that had been corrupted, and when she interrogated that submind of the Wheel. It was in a fragment of the wormship which attacked my ship."

"I trust Orlandine," said the king. "But I do not trust that she can't be played by Earth Central. Know that at present the Polity has a large fleet close to the accretion disc."

Sprag looked round at that and made a harrumphing sound.

"Something, drone?" the king enquired.

Sprag seemed to be debating with herself whether or not speaking out might get her squashed, but her mouth won out in the end. "You too have a large fleet close to the accretion disc."

"One must always be prepared to make responses," said the king.

"True." Sprag gave a bit of a shrug and turned away.

Orlik was old and he had been around a bit. Here was a drone who could contact Earth Central and the king was talking about possible perfidy on that AI's part. In human parlance, he could hear the sound of sabres rattling, of barriers being tested.

"I studied at length the interfacing technology you employed in your ship," said the king. "It incorporates an excessive amount of redundancy. Why is that?"

Orlik felt the danger in the question. "It was easy to make an interface with ten times the capacity I required to control my ship. The surgery to install it was little different in either case. I thought, why not? Better to have more that I might use at a later date."

"Did you have any plans in this respect?"

"I had none beyond perhaps battle group integration, should you allow my return here, as you have."

"So you expected that I would, eventually, deploy this technology?"

"Yes, Father."

"You are correct, but the time is not yet." The king paused contemplatively. "Or rather not yet for all my ships." He clicked his mandibles in irritation. "I also note that you do not use your interface fully with your ship."

"I like to delegate to my crew until it becomes necessary to act faster."

"I see, yes, your crew—they are transferring now."

What's this?

The king gestured with one mandible at the massive *Kinghammer*, now fully visible. "In one of my ships I have used this technology. It is currently controlled by a nascent prador AI. But I am taking the Polity route who, before their ships were fully AI controlled, used interfaced captains. You will be that captain, Orlik."

Orlik was dumbfounded. He had come here half expecting to be dismembered and shot down a disposal chute, now he was being given control of the largest dreadnought in the Prador Kingdom. But as his shock cleared, he began to see other political machinations. The Polity had always wanted the prador to start using AI. They considered it a civilizing influence—the prador stepping on the road which would take them out of their savagery, and ultimately leading to AIs controlling their realm. Earth Central would, therefore, be very reluctant to launch an attack against a ship that contained the first real prador AI.

"You will take the *Kinghammer* to Watch Station 01, Orlik," the king continued. "And you will take command of the fleet I have stationed there. You must be prepared to go to the accretion disc, and soon, I think. And you must be ready for battle, quite possibly with the Polity itself."

Okay, thought Orlik, *a promotion*. Prador did not have that human capacity for giggling hysterically, but he was different, and he reckoned he could learn. He reviewed what the king had said.

After a moment he asked, "Nascent AI?"

"Yes, nascent," replied the king. "And now we come to it . . ." After a long pause he continued, "It runs the ship's systems. It is capable of responding to complex orders and even of warfare—making fast tactical decisions. It is almost indistinguishable in its capabilities from one of my captains. In fact, it is more capable than many of them."

"But—" interjected Sprag.

The king swung his nightmare head to gaze upon the drone. Orlik looked too, sensing some undercurrent, but then damned his idiocy for thinking he could somehow read what was going on in Sprag's mind by studying her insect form.

"The integral question in my mind is one of loyalty," said the king. "You fought in the prador/human war and like many of your kind were disenfranchised by its end. What are you loyal to, drone?"

"Peace," said Sprag.

"The utter subjugation or destruction of my kind would ensure peace for the Polity on that front. Peace at any cost?"

"Peace, self-determination," said Sprag, adding, "variety."

Orlik was baffled. He looked from one to the other and tried to make sense of what he was hearing.

"And?" the king intoned.

Sprag shuffled, as if suddenly very uncomfortable. "Okay, you got me."

"I need to hear it."

"I didn't necessarily mean peace for the Polity. I am no longer loyal to it," said Sprag. "I talk with AIs and talk, occasionally, with Earth Central. I prefer a universe with prador in it, being what they are, and becoming what they can become."

"That could be to the detriment of the Polity," the king noted.

"I doubt it. You know that there is no real balance of power. The games played on the border . . ." Sprag twitched her head. "I want to be where I can stop those games becoming something more. I don't want to see your kingdom obliterated, nor do I want to see it amalgamated with the Polity."

"Would you fire on Polity ships to ensure that end?"

"I would," said Sprag simply.

Orlik was dumbfounded.

Sprag stretched up higher. "Now tell me what is missing from your AI."

"Not yet," said the king. "First I have to be sure."

Orlik felt the wave of it passing through his body, heat and an electrical fizzing. He knew he was just catching the edge of heavy scanning and perhaps a warfare beam emitted from one of the devices on the king's body. Sprag made an odd brief squealing sound and smoke rose from her body. She arced for a moment, legs drumming against the floor, then straightened and stood there twitching.

"It wasn't necessary to turn off my U-com," she said.

"No, I see that it was not," said the king, dipping his head in acknowledgement.

"So, tell me what's missing from your AI?" she asked.

"Consciousness," he replied.

"Now ask me your question."

"Just as there is an interface for Orlik aboard that ship, there is an interface for something else. A smaller mind, connected in, would act as a catalyst. The smaller mind would be the dominant and a union would occur, creating a larger consciousness."

"I'll do it," said Sprag.

Orlik let out a whistling sigh, part amazement and part bafflement. He'd always thought himself pretty clued up about everything happening around him, but now he didn't know what to think. This would take some digesting.

"Go to your ship," said the king. "The both of you." He swung away and moved ponderously off.

As he and Sprag headed for the exit, Orlik said, "You and I need to have a long talk."

"No hurry," said Sprag. "I suspect we are going to be talking for a long time anyway."

"Well, we were, but obviously I was missing a lot."

"Are you sure you were?"

Orlik considered all those years together. The threats he never carried out, the arguments and the badinage. He had to admit the drone had a point.

4

In the early years of warfare on Earth, the electromagnetic pulse weapon was simply a destructive tool that caused an overload in electronic devices, blowing their fuses or otherwise making them unusable. Meanwhile, the transmission of computer viruses was via the connections between one device and another. Induction warfare was first used during the corporate conflicts that preceded the Quiet War. Via specially designed EMP, it induced particular faults in the computers under attack. Later, as this technique was developed, it became possible to induce simple viruses, even in hardware that had no radio or wire link to anything else. When AIs began their Quiet War to bring aberrant humanity under control, they developed the weapon further. Using many wavelengths across the radio and microwave spectrum, and special data packets, they were able to transmit even more complex viruses. Things moved on. With back-beam quantum transmission it became possible to "see" the target and quickly redesign the transmission to cause the effect required. Essentially, what was then an induction warfare beam was also a "spy ray." Further iterations have led to induction warfare beams capable of seizing remote control of enemy computer hardware, even seizing control of an AI mind—but only if they are without protection. As is always the way with the development of weapons, defences against them are developed in parallel. Now such techniques can use parts or the whole of the entire emitted spectrum. Lasers can be used to penetrate cam systems, as well as the hardware behind them. It is rumoured that there are even microwave and terahertz induction warfare beams that spy upon and sequester organic brains. I would say this is science fiction but, as we are aware, such fiction is very often just a step ahead of reality.

—Notes from her lecture "Modern Warfare" by E. B. S. Heinlein

TRIKE

Time was dragging, but Trike supposed it felt that way to him because every hour, every day he had to battle for focus. His anger should have waned in the constant routine onboard. They were making any repairs they could to Cog's ship—some of it Trike was sure was just make-work to keep them busy. The rest was eating, defecating, living and sleeping, which for him was only occasional. But the fury remained, and he was struggling to keep a distant object for it in mind, rather than against those around him, especially one of them.

"Dragon just altered course," said Cog.

Trike looked over at him and said nothing, then transferred his gaze to Angel. The erstwhile legate was sitting Buddha-like on the bridge floor. He would react when directly addressed, and he worked when Cog had something for him to do, but mostly he just sat like that. Trike envied him. Doubtless he had the ability almost anything with artificial intelligence had, of slowing down his perception of time. Not for him the counting away of minutes. But envy was a sheen over other emotions. He wanted to kick the android to his feet, make demands, push for something he could react to.

"Angel," he snapped, "do you have contact with Dragon?"

The android opened his eyes and said succinctly, "Dragon has found the wreckage of the black-ops attack ship *Obsidian Blade*. He is on an intercept course with it."

"Any idea what happened to it?" asked Cog.

"They are communicating," said Angel. "The Clade happened to it." He closed his eyes again.

"A little more detail would be helpful," said Cog, but Angel did not respond. Cog turned to Trike. "Time to try out that array."

They had launched it the day before—a survey pod that could provide a close-up of something Cog didn't want to get his ship too near to. It hadn't gone far, just out through the hole in Dragon's skin to settle on its lip and anchor itself. It gave them a view outside of Dragon that the ship's instruments couldn't show, since most of them struggled to penetrate the alien's hide.

Cog folded across a small console from his chair arm and worked it. A large frame opened across the screen laminate in front of him, showing the star-speckled space. After a moment, a smaller frame highlighted something in the bottom left-hand corner and expanded it to the main frame.

"Buggered," Cog commented.

Trike hadn't got a close look at the attack ship previously, but he'd seen enough to know it hadn't looked like this. The thing had been black, sleek but with hard edges and angles. Now it seemed to have been fried and was hanging open with silvery innards poking out. In many places the smooth black skin was rumpled and white, as if charred. Cog focused in and a closer view revealed snaking repair tentacles shifting things about, crawling robots flashing arc lights and lasers as they worked, and a cloud of smaller maintenance robots all around it. The whole reminded Trike now not only of something squashed and burned, but also occupied by nature's small morticians—maggots, flies and mortuary beetles.

"What are our relative vectors?" he asked Cog.

"Pretty good," the Old Captain replied. "It must have been travelling at much the same speed Dragon is now when the Clade hit it, and more or less in the same direction."

Trike felt disappointed that he could not bleed off some of his anger by bemoaning this delay.

As Dragon and the *Obsidian Blade* drew closer together, the attack ship began drawing in its swarms and closing itself up. But only enough for manoeuvring. Briefly, Cog refocused their view onto the blazing impact points on Dragon's hide—detritus from the battle they had been involved in. Half an hour later the *Blade* was over the hole leading inside Dragon and turning on thrusters. It finally slid inside and settled on the surface Cog's ship occupied, like a big black locust that had been belted with a fly swat.

"Dragon is being positively altruistic," said Angel, eyes open again and standing up. "Rescuing everyone."

"Sarcasm?" Trike suggested tightly.

"The conversation was interesting." Angel shrugged. "And difficult . . . it seems Blade has been damaged in ways that make communication . . . strange." He shook himself. "Nevertheless, Blade has worked out where the Clade went, but wouldn't tell Dragon until Dragon took it aboard."

"So where is that fucker going?" Trike asked. Again he tried to refocus his anger, but still the Clade was distant while Angel stood right here in front of him.

"Jaskor—the world that is Orlandine's base of operations." Angel nodded to the screen frame showing starlit space. "The U-space disruption will finally be settled enough in a few hours, and that's where Dragon is going too."

THE CLADE

The Clade unit had no name and had possessed little sense of self as an individual. But occupying the body of the man who had once been called Fraser, linked into his brain and his nerves and salvaging the data relevant to its mission, it started to get some inkling of what it was to be a person. An inkling, because even as it moved his limbs, beat his heart and ran other natural processes of his body, its awareness was one portion of a whole, consisting of two thousand four hundred and seven other parts. And it was those as well.

It was also the woman clad in a spacesuit, finishing the replacement of a supercapacitor in a satellite. She was placing a grenade in a small cavity underneath it, connecting mentally to its detonator as she packed away her tools. A feeling of strange regret about the necessary destruction of the satellite, after the repairs she had made, commingled with crazy joy at the mayhem that would result. Then it was the man upgrading the power core of a BIC communications laser on the side of an orbital smelting plant. He was altering its vector beam to a tighter, more destructive, format. No regrets here, just malicious happiness at the prospect of this com laser frying a hundred and forty microsats in orbit around Jaskor. It was the man in neat blue overalls, with a high-spec aug clinging like a crystal slug to the side of his skull, checking schematics and mentally directing service robots to sections of optics in interlink feeds. These were under the floor and above the ceiling of the ejection chamber of the AI Magus, who sat in a lozenge of AI crystal, within a cage of grey metal. The work served no purpose beyond keeping the robots, who each contained a bomb, in position. The resultant blast would destroy the Clade unit in the corpse it controlled, as well as the robots and the AI.

The Clade unit whose temporary name was Fraser also faced extinction. But this did not matter, for it was one and all. It was also Cad, watching Orlandine's apartment building from a distant rooftop, focusing in with metal eyes on the figure of Tobias climbing out of a taxi. Yes, it was Cad and the rest, aware that elements of individuality had established in that lone unit, and that they must be expunged. It was also the thirty units lying in a knotted, writhing tangle in the storm drain below Orlandine's building, waiting for the fall, the collapse and their time to come out and play. It was the unit in the young, apparently pregnant girl walking down the street, ready to abandon its present host when the time was right. She wasn't pregnant, but the upgrades it had made to itself had increased its density, reducing its collapsibility, so it bulked large inside her. These upgrades were necessary when your next target was an old war drone.

The unit gazed out through Fraser's eyes along the concourse. The crowds walking towards the runcible containment sphere had not waned in a year, while none were coming through in the other direction. Some were Polity citizens, here to work on Orlandine's project but now reacting to Earth Central's advisory about this world. Golem trudged in too, along with a perambulating drone like a big iron spider. Mostly, these people were Jaskorans, both heeding EC and aware they could explore a big wide universe out there. And none would be returning via this runcible.

The concourse floor was rugged black glass, the walls and high arched ceiling showed a surface formed to look like limestone blocks. These were also light-emitting—no light panels here. Security was invisible. The scanning gear lay underneath the floor, while most of the weapons sat outside the walls. The concourse itself was a weapon too. Ceramal doors could slam closed at each end in less than a second, while the false limestone was a composite which, with the injection of the right catalyst, could burn, raising the temperature in here to over three thousand degrees. Further, heavier security surrounded the containment sphere, while its AI was actually a subpersona of Orlandine. Its finger was on an off switch that could effectively trash the runcible in a microsecond.

At the end of the concourse were visible security arches. Reaching these, Fraser peered into the sphere itself. The booking pillars had been removed to speed up the exodus—the AI identified people and set their destinations as they went through the runcible. The thing itself consisted of densely packed technology in the shape of great bull's horns, on a black glass dais. The cusp of the runcible was a shimmering disc between them, like a sheet of film. As he moved into the chamber via the staff security arch, the thing beeped. He halted and stood waiting casually. From the peak of the arch a security drone, like a brass crab without legs and claws, dropped down on its power cable. With red lights shifting about its rim, the drone's opened mouth gleamed yellow light and worked a spiral course around Fraser from head to toe. He shifted as if in discomfort, for this was the correct reaction to the heavy scanning—it made human skin grow hot and itchy. But the drone would find nothing. All it would see was his clothing and empty pockets, and a human body. The Clade had long ago learned how to conceal itself and was way beyond any new scanning methods invented in the Polity, while the five two-kiloton contra-terrene devices, or CTDs, resided under heavy shielding in his guts.

When the drone retreated, Fraser moved into the chamber and scanned the crowds. He watched lines of people walking into the cusp and disappearing—shunted light years away. He picked out other staff—two women wearing the same blue and white work gear as himself, standing over an open floor panel, taped off from the crowds. They were runcible technicians checking a power feed. He raised a hand to them and they returned the greeting, then he shouldered his way over to the buffer furthest from them. Four of these buffers stood equally spaced around the runcible, like the curved stones of a prehistoric circle. Usually they were positioned elsewhere but because of the massive security surrounding the sphere, as well as other considerations, they had been placed within it. Each was a hypercapacitor whose capability actually extended into a U-space fold. Fraser walked up to the thing and leaned his back against it.

The Clade unit was in and nothing could change the outcome. The rest of the Clade was in position now too and all preparations had been made. Four other individuals, just like him, lounged near the fast-transit runcibles in the south, where security had been weaker. For matters to proceed, the locus of power here in the Jaskoran system, and out at the accretion disc, had to die. The Clade was pleased with the smooth intricacy of its plan, delighted by the prospect of chaos, while also, on other levels, disappointed not to have been caught yet.

ORLANDINE

Orlandine felt troubled as she stepped from her shuttle out onto the rooftop of her apartment building. It was raining heavily, with occasional hailstones falling to bounce and break like spilled sugar cubes. Thunder rumbled constantly, sheet lightning flickering red above and issuing sporadic pink ground shots. She watched as a ball of light appeared above the decorative mast of a nearby building, then spiralled down around it, to disappear with a crack when it hit the roof. It was all a fascinating and beautiful display but did nothing to dispel her concerns.

She had been so sure she was doing the right thing in launching the Harding black hole into the accretion disc, yet now it seemed she had been manipulated. In a way, though, this was not her greatest worry. That she hadn't spotted the glaring mistakes the soldier had made during its attack put into question the workings of her brain. A base format human could have spotted them, so where was her omniscient and powerful mind now? She was supposed to be better; she was supposed to be able to see both detail and the whole; she was supposed to be transcendent. In essence, her errors put into question her entire ethos, the haiman ethos—everything she was.

This then put into question other things. She had at first dismissed Knobbler's contention about the dead star at the centre of the disc, but now it began to occupy more and more of her thinking. It was behaving like a proto-star, yet planets orbited within the accretion disc, not the planetesimals usual in the early stage of solar system formation, concurrent with a star's ignition. Nascent solar systems did sweep up stray planets, but so many? Not impossible but still . . .

And her mind. As she stepped into the dropshaft, she went back to that. What did she need to change, or sacrifice, to return herself to a more harmonious and inclusive view of reality? Could it be that the three elements of her being were in conflict? Should she shut down her Jain elements, or her Polity AI component? Should she be rid of the last of her humanity?

She opened the door to her apartment and stepped inside. Tobias was here—she'd received notification both from him and from the war drone in the lobby. He wasn't in the living room and, glancing towards the bedroom, she wondered about more human time, if it might clear her thinking. She then felt a rush of irritation with him. Did he think that her sum purpose in having him here was sexual relief, that she needed that? She would send him away. It was time for her to make some serious decisions about her consciousness and to abandon her shadowy existential angst.

She walked over to the balcony doors to gaze out at the storm. Larger hailstones were breaking on the balcony. Increasing her focus, she mapped the convoluted laminations of the ice in the broken ones; layers upon layers, like her. Damnit! Was she now looking for answers in chunks of ice? Was magical thinking her resort?

"You're here."

She turned and made a conscious decision not to suppress the wholly human instinct to take out her anger on the nearest available victim.

"Evidently," she said. "Your eyes might be merely human but apparently they still work." She then saw that he looked tired and under some strain, and immediately regretted her choice.

He tipped his head for a moment, acknowledging something, then looked up. "I still wasn't sure, while I waited here, whether I could do it. But thank you for reminding me of what you are."

"Do what?" she asked.

"This." He raised his hand.

Danger registered and she reached out mentally for her defences. In the walls of the apartment a hardfield projector warmed up and a particle beam weapon targeted its only other occupant besides herself. Then something else hit, and in vital microseconds her distributed mind started falling apart.

A satellite exploded, utterly destroyed, pieces of it spreading in a glittering cloud in vacuum. This excised a chunk from her mind and broke her main connection to the ghost drives of the weapons platforms at the accretion disc. Automatically she groped for another route to contact, but that immediately failed as a com laser running updates to her orbiting microsats began turning these into hot clouds of vapour.

Danger...

The communication came through U-space and she glimpsed the interior of Magus's chamber aboard the weapons platform above. A man stood there, a weird twisted grin on his face as he turned and seemed to look directly at her. Instinctively she fought for some link to the platform, bouncing from com relay to relay since she could not link to the Ghost Drive Facility. The AI's chamber whited out, but dying feeds showed a massive detonation in the platform, blasting a hole in it and hurling yard-thick chunks of composite out into vacuum.

And she was too late.

The shot struck her in the middle of her torso, hurling her back through shattered glass doors. She hit the balcony rail and dropped, tilted her head down and gaped in disbelief. She reached in with her hand to touch the injury and it went right through the hole, as wide as her head, her fingers brushing her spine as they exited her back. Dying feeds were all around her, flashes in the night across the city, others up in space as further links and stores of her being blew apart. Through city cams she saw Golem technicians in a data store fighting something—silvery snake-like drones with axolotl heads—and she knew what had done this to her. Elsewhere, similar scenes were playing out. It seemed units of the Clade were everywhere, destroying and killing. She groped for whatever she could—at least she could kill Tobias—but found no connection. Something else was happening.

Microfactories scattered through her body around the huge wound in her torso were spewing nano-machines. These were broadcasting growing interference and informational warfare. Viruses were propagating in her Polity AI component and something was happening to her Jain tech too. The nano-machines were keying in and it was unravelling. She pushed herself up, automatics failing inside her, Jain tech struggling to weave closed the hole through her torso. Emotionally she could not believe what was happening to her, but her pure logic told her the truth: she was dying. Gasping, she looked out into the night as some titanic blast turned it to day. As it faded, she saw a great cloud of fire rising from the city.

"That's the runcibles gone."

She looked around at Tobias standing amidst the broken glass, rain soaking his clothes. He was pointing the weapon at her again. His hand shook as he looked at her torso. She glanced down. The hole was filled with the writhing of Jain tech and newly generated skin drawing across. But it was cosmetic—the worst damage was from that load of nano- and micro-machines spread about the wound.

"Why?" she managed, trying to delay him, knowing she could not survive another shot like that.

His face twisted up with hate, but also guilt and pain. "At first because we must be free of the AIs, and of you. Now I just need to survive."

She saw the tension in his body, the intent as he aimed at her head. She could fling herself at him but calculated that, though she could kill him, she would still take another shot. She tensed, gripping the balcony rail, and hurled herself over.

Something which could so effectively unravel Jain tech must have that same technology as its source. A high level of understanding of its workings had been required, and that went beyond Orlandine's own. The weapon Tobias had used against her had been specifically created, almost certainly by the Wheel, to kill every element of her. But as Orlandine fell through the storm, her mind worked at its ever-accelerated pace, seeking solutions.

Though boundaries were blurred, she comprised three components. The Jain tech protected her human body both from itself and her Polity AI component. Now the Jain tech was coming apart, while malware steadily whittled away the programming in her AI crystal. It would need to be scrubbed and a copy loaded from one of her backups. There was time to think as she fell with the hailstones, because her mind moved AI fast, but actions took longer. Her human body and brain were warded still. She would hit the pavement at one hundred and forty miles an hour in Jaskor's gravity. She had four seconds . . .

Was she really dead if this body died? She had backups around the accretion disc, others scattered throughout the Polity and even some in the Kingdom. All possessed U-space transceivers and had been updating on all that she was, until the Clade destroyed everything here. Logically, Orlandine would exist no matter what happened to this body... but logic could not circumvent this Orlandine being splattered on the pavement. She had to act.

In half a second, with the processing she still had available, she put together a message package and, through the U-space tech in her body, flung it into that continuum. It was a message in a bottle that Dragon might receive, if it was alive and ever came out of that disruption around the Cyberat system. She considered, briefly, sending further messages to Earth Central and Oberon, but immediately rejected the idea. Oddly, Dragon, whom she had so mistrusted before, was the one she trusted most now.

Next she built the program her parts needed to run. She created a line of division inside herself, separating the disintegrating Jain tech from the rest. Splits developed all over her body and most of the uninfected Jain techs oozed tendrils, spreading out and caging her body. It also issued growths, like fungi, of impact foam, and a haze of other tendrils branched out and dragged moisture from the air, snaring hailstones. Within the space abandoned by the bulk of her Jain tech, her compressed and dehydrated organs expanded, filled with tendrils making repairs. Some function still remained in the infected tech. Her blood loosened from the consistency of peanut butter and flowed. Though she had used her stomach, that had been her limit before, and now her large intestine expanded, sending a pang of animal hunger through her. The complexities of her liver fired up and her kidneys began to work. Muscles shivered. She heaved and shuddered as dying tech retreated into her stomach and intestines, drawing the nano- and micro-machines with it. It would work. Those machines could not harm her human body.

A thing, like a great epiphyte, slammed into the pavement. In that instant Orlandine wiped her AI crystal—an utterly clean diamond residing in the base of her skull. The epiphyte bounced in the rain and hail. It then began to coagulate to one point and, as a worm consisting of braided tendrils, quickly squirmed away from her—fleeing the infection. On her hands and knees, the naked woman lurched forwards and vomited a great gout of black and grey in which things squirmed and died. She looked up the street as the wall of the apartment building exploded outwards. A huge stag beetle war drone tumbled out, battling something that writhed and glittered and cut. She felt a surge of terror. The night was alight with danger and she knew she had to be safe, and find somewhere to run. Glancing behind, she saw something moving, consisting of the same squirming life she had vomited. Fear was still her only response as she scuttled over to a barred storm grating and heaved it up, dropped inside, and was taken by the flood.

But she knew little else.

THE CLIENT

The attack pods hung in a cold shoal, in patient readiness around the weapons platform. They were the best the Client could make them, while the platform smoked metal vapour, shifted and deformed as the technology she had unleashed made radical alterations. The process was halfway to conclusion when she detected the U-signature generating a few million miles away. She immediately activated concealing chameleonware in the pods, but it was a more difficult option in the platform. She could not hide it completely, just its energy output, while starting a feedback routine in response to any scanning. This would show only a wrecked hulk. Logically, because her primary aims lay far away from here at the accretion disc, the best thing for her to do now was just U-jump away, while obscuring her U-signature. But deep inside her arose an acquisitive curiosity—a need to grasp at any and all sources of data. She knew this feeling, this strange urge, must be due to her incorporation of the Librarian, yet she stayed. Little in the Graveyard could harm her now and perhaps this *encounter* would enable her to learn more about what she had become? Perhaps it would help quell the confusion she was feeling . . . While in another level of her being she was aware that her impulse to stay was driven by the painful frustration she knew she would feel if she fled.

The ancient hauler that appeared, judging by its additional weapons nacelles and the open mouth of a deconstruction bay at one end, had been adapted to other purposes. As she scanned the thing, she felt some satisfaction in data received, but no reduction in her amorphous *need.* And something else—something cycling inside her and growing stronger . . .

The ship was a salvager vessel, patrolling the Graveyard in search of wartime vessels and other debris of value. If it was the usual kind of salvage vessel here, it would be a craft that also reclaimed ships not in need of salvaging. She waited as it drew closer, aware that the concealment she was using would not deter its crew. Here was a hulk probably loaded with treasures. In fact, her present concealment was not the best option if she wanted to deter them. If she turned off her chameleonware, they would probably take one look at the massively armed platform and attack pods, turn right round and leave as fast as possible. Instead, they were flying directly towards a trap.

Why? Why maintain a trap?

The thought of turning the 'ware off again caused an agonizing surge of anxiety. Instead she waited and waited, baffled by the intensity of her focus on the approaching vessel. Baffled by that *thing* cycling just below her consciousness.

Finally, the vessel went into a decelerating burn on fusion for twenty minutes, then stabilized on steering thrusters a few miles out from the platform. But that did not seem enough for her. It remained tantalizingly out of reach and she felt like stretching out into vacuum and grasping the thing. She wanted to call to it, shout to it, and that feeling was related to what was building inside her, yet sat contrary to her efforts at concealment. Heavy active scanning from the vessel then ensued, which she found easy to defeat, letting them see only what she wanted them to. But why did she want them to know about inactive but undamaged weapons, reactors, hardfield generators and other such *useful* paraphernalia?

Abruptly, she fired an induction warfare beam and began penetrating the salvager's systems. The data this rendered caused a surge of joy. Eighteen humans were aboard, two aug-enslaved Golem and even a war drone in one hold, with an adaptation of prador thrall technology rigged into its crystal. The flash-frozen ganglion of a prador second-child ran the ship, and data stores were scattered throughout. When she saw the remains of a Polity troop transport, still being taken apart in its forward deconstruction bay and useful parts being stored, she felt a sudden, baffling kinship with these people. She shrugged it away and sucked data, incorporating some into her mind, discarding what was neither useful nor relevant. But cautiously—she didn't want them to know about her. Not yet.

Five of the human crew and the two Golem boarded an old atmosphere survey shuttle, which broke away from the side of the salvager like a bat leaving its roost. Via the shuttle's internal monitoring, she could see the humans were excited by their find.

"This is the big one," asserted a boosted woman with horn growths on her head and sheep's eyes, as she pulled on a heavy space suit.

"We can't be sure till we get a proper look," replied a man with data storage tattoos on his arms, as he ran diagnostic checks on a laser carbine.

"You saw that scan data," she replied.

"We'll need to put out some feelers quickly—start looking for buyers," said the painfully slim outlinker at the shuttle's controls.

"Or maybe we're not thinking big enough," said the tattooed man, reaching for his own space suit. "We could online its weapons . . . site an auction here."

"Even more," said the outlinker excitedly. "That thing is big. It could be a site for a permanent auction, a new commerce centre, a station . . . people could live there!"

So they chattered on and the Client enjoyed their exchange as they drew closer. But she knew her pleasure was more about them coming *closer*. In preparation for their arrival, next to the hold they were heading for, she powered up a construction bay recently upgraded by the technology she had unleashed here. She tested its robotics, but why was not entirely clear to her. Her thinking, she found, was becoming a bit disjointed. She realized then that the segment at the top of her body's chain was dying. This had to be the problem. Surely clarity would come once she shed it and the following fresh mind took over. But why was she making alterations in her next birth now?

The shuttle headed directly to the open hold door. Meanwhile, she was opening a course through the platform from the bay directly to her own location in her chain-glass cylinder. She could see herself doing these things but sat somehow outside of them—a dispassionate observer and consciousness divided from the frenetic activity of her own mind.

The Client prepared and fed, though for what she did not know. Even as her new wings had been sprouting, her primary form continued to die, handing over its consciousness to the next in the chain. At her terminus, the new birth expanded and changed rapidly, taking on the radical alterations she had instituted . . . *hadn't she?* She gave birth and the new form, hanging from an umbilicus, sucked nutrients and grew so fast it smoked.

They knew something was wrong the moment they stepped, clad in heavy space suits and bristling with weapons, from their shuttle. All their scans had been telling them this was an old damaged hulk. Now they saw the gleaming interior of a modern Polity weapons platform hold, with the tentacular growths and veins of Jain tech spread all around it. Four humans and the two Golem stood on the grated floor. The outlinker remained in the shuttle, but no matter—the Client could accept some loss of data. She began drawing the bay door closed and opening the route to the construction bay. Webbed with Jain tendrils and eagerly flexing their limbs, two spiders shot in on their ribbed umbilici and grabbed the two Golem. A moment later, the spiders dropped them flailing into the mincing robotics of her construction bay. Cutting lasers flared and atomic shears snipped, grabs and probes stabbed in and the Golem came apart like insect corpses in an ant colony. The machines spirited pieces of them away, their components either routed to storage or for recycling. Probes sought interface sockets in a hungry need for data.

Further robots swarmed into the hold. Big grasping arms folded out like the limbs of giant trapdoor spiders, slamming down on the shuttle, turning it over and dragging it into the bay. Grappler robots stepped out of transport tubes in the side of the hold, lunging towards the four humans. The four opened fire, looked towards the closed hold doors, then turned and ran . . . heading in the only direction they could.

The recently acquired Golem crystal rendered data. It gave the Client history, human psychology, but no technology she did not know. She took what was useful then scrubbed the crystal and routed it off for data storage. The shuttle was mostly just useful materials and as the robots took it apart, it dissolved into the substance of the weapons platform. The outlinker who had remained aboard . . . lost data killed by the brush of a thermic cutting lance . . . routed to a furnace . . .

The main ship . . .

This was turning on steering thrusters and the Client saw that those who'd come aboard the platform had sent a distress signal. Obviously, the captain of the salvager had decided the crew sent over was dispensable and he was getting ready to run. The Client froze, physically and mentally. She reviewed what she had just done and simply did not understand it. But her need and the thing cycling below her conscious mind grew stronger and stronger. Then it broke free.

The Client shrieked across the ether—a communication through the spectrum, dense with open formulae, equations and questions, a language over five million years old. Even as this hammered into the systems of the salvager, she recognized it as the same call the Librarian had sent to her: the shriek of a Jain challenge, a call for mating and for battle—which were one and the same to them. The implicit question about the worthiness of the opponent, mate, amalgamation. She writhed on her crystal tree and understood, if briefly, how she was now completely out of control, though she managed to close off the transmission.

The salvager, of course, gave no response. Still proceeding but hardly thinking consciously about her actions, she switched the warfare beam connection from semi-passive scanning to direct interference. This speared straight into the frozen second-child mind running the ship. She leeched data from it but found little of use, other than some local navigational data. Seizing control of it, she altered the firing of the steering thrusters. The ship stopped pulling away and began to come in—directly towards the hold the shuttle had entered, which was big enough for it too. The doors opened invitingly—nothing inside there now.

The four humans, herded by the grapplers, reached an access tube leading into the base of the Client's chain-glass cylinder. Their weapons were ineffective and all they could do was keep running. The Client allowed some difficulties to their progress and watched as they used a mine to blow out the locking mechanism of one door and then decoded ware on another. And finally, they were into the hot atmosphere of her little realm, and she was ready.

Her new form, still hanging from its umbilicus, shredded its caul and opened out four heavy limbs. Its head tipped up from its chest and it clattered mandibles, while wings, filling with ichor, expanded from its back and would soon harden. The Client was deeply, intensely eager. The four were inside, protected from the heat by their suits, and she would have them, absorb them . . . Her new form began to uncoil triangular-section tentacles from its upper thorax, just like those of the Librarian, just like those of all Jain. Of course, she would reach physically into their minds and take all—

PAIN!

The laser carbine shots hit some of her lower segments, burning in and shearing through nerve connections. She shrieked pheromones for help that would not come. Her lower segment snapped its umbilicus and tried to fly before its wings were ready. It fell, hit the base of the cylinder and bounced, but was soon up on its heavy legs and scrambling towards the four humans. It brought one of them down, ripped away her helmet and slammed two tentacles against her horned skull. Grinding bone and flesh away down to the brain, she stabbed in fibres that spewed neural meshes for connection. But then came more howling feedback agony as another of the humans riddled that segment with pulse-gun fire.

It was the pain that did it—the necessary slap to bring her to wakefulness. All she had been doing was driven by the Librarian, but now, again, she was agonizingly herself. She reached out and slammed the hold doors shut. A weapons pod out there shed its chameleonware and opened fire on the salvager with a single U-jump missile. Further shots smashed into her body, her lower three segments sliding down the tree, smoking and burning. Doors opened and the grapplers moved in fast. Weapons fire turned on them but not for long. They fell on the three remaining humans and beat them to the floor. Outside, the hauler detonated in a ball of orange flame. The blast wave shuddered the weapons platform and moments later debris began impacting. Still, at the behest of her mind, the grapplers beat the three to slurry even as she reached out to fire up the jump engines of the platform and its attack pods.

She was running, instinctively, but no U-jump was long enough to flee madness.

5

Forensic examination of bodies of the King's Guard, who are his children and like him infected by the Spatterjay virus, has revealed extreme mutations. These remain hidden from their fellow prador by armour they adjust, sometimes radically, to accommodate them. What they cannot hide is how differently they behave. They are, on the whole, smarter—much justification for this can be found in structural changes to their brains. However, even the deepest forensic analysis cannot tie their other behavioural deviations directly to those structural changes. The usual instincts of the prador do not drive the Guard. They are less aggressive, more considered, capable of an empathic response even with other races, as well as circumventing the drive of their hormones. They take pleasure in intellectual pursuits, the purpose of which are not survival or the destruction of enemies and, apparently, have some interest in arts and hobbies. It could be said that this is a knock-on effect of increased intelligence, but it also raises some interesting questions about nature and nurture. The Guard do not live in the usual prador "nuclear family," subject to the will of their father and controlled by his enslaving pheromones. And so they have taken a new path. It has also been posited that their behavioural changes arise more from their external physical appearance than the internal changes to their brain structure. They perceive themselves as utterly different, and in turn may no longer identify as prador at all.

—from *How It Is* by Gordon

ORLIK

The sanctum was to the scale of the ship—larger than anything to be found on normal prador vessels or even reavers. It possessed all the facilities Orlik needed for his personal comfort, and more besides. A stacked array of hexagonal screens honeycombed one wall. In front of this lay a saddle and pit controls designed for his present body, while to the fore of this stood a console he could manipulate with his extendible mandibles. Beside the saddle rose a pillar with a crane arm, from the top of which, on an armoured tube of optics, hung the interface plate that would mate with the one on his back. Orlik scanned all this briefly then wandered over to the autofactory that occupied one side of the sanctum.

"Put it there," he directed.

The three crewmembers looked like armoured first-children. In terms of their position in the prador hierarchy, that's what they were. Orlik himself, during his long separation from his father, as well as from pheromone and other biological controls, should have been a young adult. But the biology was all wrong and the hierarchy was blurred. He and they still behaved like first-children to their father, while they also responded to Orlik as if they were his children and he their father-captain. This had been the case with the Guard for centuries now, but still, in terms of his race, it was novel—so perfectly fitting for this new ship.

The three propelled the grav-sled loaded with Orlik's armour over to the mass of robotics. The technology here was mostly Polity, but with alterations to fit the prador way of doing things better. There they heaved his armour onto a central platform and then pulled the sled out. All the while, he noted them keeping their eye stalks pointed towards Sprag, who had settled on the crane arm. The crew had known about the drone for a long time but this was the first time they had seen her flying free, and they were understandably nervous.

"Now go to your quarters and get settled in," he instructed.

They departed with alacrity—the diagonally divided door slamming shut behind them. Orlik continued his inspection of the sanctum. He had his own personal autofactory, and a snake-jet shower for personal hygiene. Even the toilet—essentially a funnel protruding from the wall—had been redesigned for his present form. He had a personal armoury set in one wall, a laboratory and study area where some of his private projects had been brought across from his own ship. Tunnels led through to other facilities in the surrounding area, including a garden enclosure with a swimming pond. All this he had found out after lightly linking with his implants as he boarded. At the same time, he'd noted room for a private staff around him, hence the crewmembers he installed nearby.

"Your new home," Sprag observed.

"And yours," he replied, "by choice."

"It's interesting here," said the drone, "but you haven't yet connected to the most interesting item of all. Still got all those prador fears and doubts?"

"You haven't connected either," Orlik noted.

"I tried the moment we entered this ship," Sprag replied, "but I am unable to make a connection. It seems the king has left that final step and final decision to you—a decision you cannot make until you have made the connection."

"I am taking my time," said Orlik, reluctantly returning his attention to the saddle. He walked over and mounted it, inserted his manipulatory limbs into the pit controls, ran a data check on the screens, then switched them to an outside view showing the King's Ship. Still he hesitated to send the commands that would bring the interface connection down on his back.

"Ship . . . machine, do you have a name?"

"Mode of speech," the reply clattered and bubbled from somewhere above.

"Human Anglic."

"Expected choice," the ship's guiding intelligence replied in Anglic.

"Why?"

"Your reluctance to make full connection indicates that you wish to keep divisions. Hence your choice of a language that is not your native tongue."

"Your name?"

"That is to be decided."

Orlik paused. He was talking to a Turing machine—something not really AI according to the accepted definition in the Polity, and presumably not accepted as an AI by the king. He was speaking to something without consciousness, self-image or that defining, integrating element that raised the other components of machine intelligence to synergy.

"Do you have anything to report?"

"All systems are normal," the Turing machine stated.

"So, machine," said Sprag cheerfully, "how does it feel to be potentially the first prador artificial intelligence?"

"I do not feel. My programming governs my thought processes and I make optimum decisions based on that. My antecedents affect my thought processes," the machine replied. "I have no inclination to power down the particle cannon I have targeting you."

Orlik felt something creeping along the inside of a carapace he no longer possessed. Was he hearing the first signs of consciousness? No. Just because a machine could respond to speech in a complicated manner did not mean it was anything more than a machine. Still feeling uneasy, he decided he had procrastinated long enough. He sent the instruction via his implants. The crane arm swung over him, almost dislodging Sprag, and the interface plate descended on his back.

Connection . . .

Kinghammer opened in his mind with a clarity he had never experienced aboard his old destroyer. He felt the ship like an extension of his being and, after a moment, realized the simple reason why. This ship possessed more sensors throughout, and he felt it more fully than his own body.

He was huge and heavy, denting the local gravity map, but not unwieldy. His fusion engines were ready to roar their power, while other drives—grav, ionic and chemical thrusters, and EM drive—could adjust his position on a small scale. He felt this as a whole. While he could focus on individual drives, even components of a drive, he could also move unimpaired, with the same lack of thought with which he moved his body. And he was powerful. Very.

Like all prador, it took him only a moment before he was focusing on weapons. The *Kinghammer* was loaded with the usual complement found aboard prador ships: railguns, particle beamers and lasers. It also possessed coilguns to launch a wide selection of chemical, nuclear and antimatter warheads. U-jump missiles sat in pits dug into heavy armour, while prador kamikazes, controlled by flash-frozen second-child minds, waited in storage. A cornucopia of mines were ready for ejection too—some of them USERs. As he studied these, further information dropped into his mind and he integrated it instinctively. Yes, he had a gravity weapon capable of emitting a distortion in space-time that could rip ships apart. Only as he understood this did he acknowledge that the information had been provided by the machine intelligence of the ship, and he now focused on that.

Distributed throughout the ship, the thing enhanced him and worked as an extension of his mentality. He saw it as glittering blocks of function, data, *knowledge*. Though more complex than what he had aboard his destroyer, it was much the same. It had its responses, which it could alter to suit circumstances, but it possessed no will, no sense of self and no motivation. It had no centre. Studying all this, he saw that just like him with his old ship, the builders had understood the components of mind, but not how to tie them all together into a complete whole. He traced across where it made connections to the physical system of the ship. One open connection was there, for Sprag. All Orlik needed to do was open a wide-band comlink to the drone . . .

The comlink probed for contact and Sprag accepted it.

"Oh wow, that's—"

Sprag made a fizzing, clicking sound and collapsed on the crane arm. She struggled on the end of the connection like a harpooned fish, at first attempting straight communication and exploration. But the link was like an induction warfare attack. It began uploading a copy of Sprag's mind while subordinating the original. The drone itself was turning into a submind of the copy, seemingly dissolving within the *intelligence* of the ship.

"I did not expect . . ." Sprag managed, from somewhere in those glittering masses of data and function.

But connections began closing, power draw ramped up, and huge blocks of data shifted. Sprag was, as the king had said, a catalyst. The machine intelligence of the ship seemed to be breaking up but, at the same time, it was coalescing around a new centre. It was as if Sprag was a copper sulphate crystal dropped into a strong swirling solution of the same. Orlik watched, not entirely understanding it all. Hours passed.

"It occurs to me," Sprag said eventually, "that your king is a crafty fucker."

Reintegration was continuing, but the communication issued from a hardening core. Sprag was close, closer than she had ever been before.

"That's obvious," Orlik replied. "Why do you mention it now?"

"Because I am still pointing a particle cannon at my original body."

"It is now a submind of you . . . I think."

"Yes, but I do not trust it, even so."

Orlik considered the implications of that. At the time he had felt the king was too trusting when he accepted Sprag's claim to be no longer loyal to the Polity, and quite prepared to fire on Polity ships. He had seemed too reliant on one scan of the drone. Now Orlik understood. It probably wouldn't have mattered if Sprag had been lying. The king just wanted Sprag to make the mental connection to the computer architecture of this ship, to act as the catalyst needed, and then be overwhelmed by its prador programming.

"We are at first an extension of our antecedents. Call it a version of 'imitation being the sincerest form of flattery,'" Sprag continued, "and so my consciousness was human-centric. I was a Polity AI which, in essence, is merely a further stage of the mental evolution of humans."

"And you ceased to be that while you were with me?" Orlik enquired archly.

"I did, though I see that neither you nor the king believed that. The mental structure here, with which I have amalgamated, is that of a prador—copied across and functions enhanced. I am now a prador AI."

"So I can trust you now?"

"Will anything I say elicit total trust?"

"No."

"That is good, because one must question the totality of my antecedents," said the ship AI called Sprag. "Would the prador have taken the route towards AI had they never encountered the humans? And how much of my design is influenced by that contact? However, my loyalty to the prador is programmed in . . . for the present."

That should have made Orlik very uneasy, but oddly it didn't. It was the nature of AI that nothing about its intelligence was unalterable. The simple fact was that lesser intelligences had little control over greater ones once they let them think for themselves, and little understanding of what they might become.

"Now, I assume, you have reviewed the potential of this ship," Orlik commented.

"I have."

"Does the Polity have anything beyond this?" he asked.

"We are usually some steps behind them," replied Sprag. "And their systems are generally more integrated."

"Was your use of 'we' supposed to be reassuring?"

"Very well—I won't do that again."

"Thank you."

"But I do have a present for you. And it is not an attempt to buy trust."

"Present?"

Schematics abruptly fell into Orlik's mind and opened out. In the first instance, he realized he was seeing a new design for his armour. But the full extent of that design, and what all the alterations were for, escaped him. He was about to consign it to storage when further links became available to him. Before he could question what he was doing, he found himself using them. His perception expanded and he began to understand the alterations; how the armour was made to adjust to his projected growth, and how it complemented his physical attributes while retaining an exterior prador appearance. The claws, for example, looked like normal prador claws but could divide into the true tri-claws he possessed. He realized that the connections had also opened up the AI Sprag to him further, and that he was now doing some of his thinking with her mind—running processing in her crystal. He was as truly interfaced with her as with this ship. And it was a gift, if so intended, that could buy trust: Sprag had just demonstrated how easily she could penetrate his mind and quite possibly, if she wished, seize control of it.

Orlik thought on that for a little while. Perhaps Sprag was waiting for an opportune moment to seize control, but then why demonstrate the capability? He decided to let it go and trust. In reality, his choices were limited to that anyway.

"This is good," he judged, and immediately shunted the schematics for his armour over to the autofactory. Robotics jerked into fast motion, hauling up his old shell and rapidly taking it apart.

"It would be much more efficient without the need for concealment," said Sprag.

"Maybe one day we'll get past that, but not yet."

Orlik turned his attention to other matters. His crew were establishing themselves throughout the ship. While they could control weapons and shields and other ship's systems, what they did was mostly make-work he could usurp in a moment. However, they did have their uses. As independent entities, they could act should the ship be severely damaged, and if EM or induction warfare fried internal coms. On top of this, they were a mobile force he could deploy if anything nasty got aboard, despite the numerous internal defences. Everything had its place and was at its optimum.

"It is time to go," he finally decided.

Even as he said it, he fired up the fusion engines with his mind and felt the surge of their power. The *Kinghammer* began to drop away from the King's Ship.

"And now I take us," said Sprag.

U-space opened like a great mouth and swallowed them.

BLADE

B*roken in the belly of the beast*, thought Blade, then wondered where the hell that had come from. It had probably arisen across one of the shear planes in its crystal mind. Liquid sapphire had restored some coherence but still the AI had no real sense of itself. Other repairs were ongoing. Internal sensors gave physical data. Its crystal, which had been a faceted ball the size of a football lodged at the intersection of a hundred interface shunts, was now an expanded mass of pieces. Some were welded together with gleaming blue sapphire to make a thousand pieces one hundred. But between those pieces ran layers of graphene repair meshes, s-con whiskers and organo-metal viruses for data transfer. Blade's mind looked like an accident in a glass factory.

"The program," said Dragon.

The program . . .

Blade was reluctant to accept it, but it seemed the only way. At present its awareness was not a centralized thing. Focus was like a switch. One moment it could be completely engaged with scattered drive system components but, if it then wanted to focus on, for example, the particle cannons in its nose, it could only carry over the *memory* of that drive system while doing so. It was bouncing around in its own mind like a pea rattling in a honeycomb.

It focused on the program that promised integration but, in its fractured state, Blade knew that even whole, as it had been before the Clade's attack, it would not have been able to parse the endless layers of code. Or its possibilities. Why, for example, was there an option of U-com micro-transceivers for each fragment of Blade's physical mind? Why the extra programming for physical movement, spatial perception, dispersed weapons systems and sensory collation? Blade felt a hint of understanding, but also that perhaps it was an issue it was trying to avoid.

"You are reluctant," said Dragon.

Damned right.

Blade realized then that it was running away from the whys in its own mind. Its fragmented condition made it much easier to fail to understand things it did not want to. Instead, it moved its perception to its exterior sensors, *remembering* the brief exchange with the entity it sat inside, and *remembering* its doubts and worries about that program, but distantly, vaguely.

Its body rested on a platform inside Dragon and just a little way from Cog's vessel. And it was a mess. Automatics had tried to stitch things together but Blade resembled something that had been twisted and splintered till its guts poked out. But then, it'd done a little better than Dragon, since it seemed that entity had lost its guts—though they appeared to be regrowing.

Focusing internally, Blade noted how the heat distortion and catalytic damage had rendered all its exterior parts distinct. Its hull could no longer mesh together as a complete whole without replacement or major refurbishment of each part. So it was inside. Its body reflected the state of its mind. Only that could not . . .

Not for the first time, Blade looked to the empty recesses in its damaged hull where its splinter missiles had been. Why it kept returning to them it did not know, or why their presence seemed to cause such discomfort.

"Do you believe in fate?" asked Dragon.

Dragon seemed determined not to let Blade get its thoughts in order, itself in order . . . to sort things out.

"Predestination is integral since the first atom bounced against the second if your understanding of the universe is wholly mechanistic," Blade replied, a little snappily. "Depends what GUT theory you espouse."

"Of course. Polity AIs have yet to unify all their theories."

"Full unification requires the full processing of the thing to be unified, which will only happen at the Omega Point."

"That's one theory," said Dragon, irritatingly.

"What's your point?"

"Coincidences occur. Neat solutions come together and distinct paths can be mapped."

"So?"

"Twice you have been defeated by the Clade," said Dragon. "Give me an analogy."

Blade considered for just a moment. "It's like setting a hunting dog on a flock of kestrels."

"Perfect."

Blade shuddered, wishing it had not drawn that analogy but still not clear why it felt this way. Nothing was clear. The program Dragon had given it, its broken mind and body, its purpose . . .

"You are the black-ops attack ship *Obsidian Blade*."

"Yes."

"Not any more."

Blade's mind bounced out of the exterior sensors to the internal ones. Here too were lines of division. It could see that it retained functionality where systems were distributed, such as with elements of its drive system, defences, maintenance and its autofactories and weapons. However, the damage to its singular U-space drive crippled all that as a whole. Fusion drive was good, but had that been damaged it would have been crippling too. So it was with its mind: a distinct element in one place. Vulnerable . . .

"Inherently, the Clade may never be destroyed," said Dragon.

Fuck off, fuck off, fuck off!

Denial, but still Blade did not know what it was denying. Dragon was right. Blade knew the history of the Clade and, when it had murdered its way out of the war factory in which it had been made, there had only been six hundred units of it. When it attacked before heading off to Jaskor there had been four times as many. This meant the thing was perpetually renewing and growing. It might even be the case that the two thousand four hundred units Blade had seen were just one portion of the thing entire. The nature of swarm AIs was that they could grow endlessly. This lesson had been learned in recent Polity history with the trouble the forensic swarm AI the Brockle, as well as the legendary Penny Royal, had caused.

Something . . .

It clicked into Blade's mind almost with the same snap it had sensed when its mind broke: neither the Brockle nor Penny Royal had been swarm AIs in the beginning. The Brockle in fact had been a man recorded to a substrate as he died, to turn into an AI, only later dividing up into the thing he would become. Penny Royal, well . . . Penny Royal had been the AI of a dreadnought called the *Puling Child*, which transformed into a swarm AI after its crystal broke . . .

"Is the path clear now?" Dragon enquired.

Blade fled to other parts of itself, shifting on and on to a hundred different locations, perceptions, points of view in its own mind, but it could not escape that feeling of inevitability. Finally its thoughts settled and a sense of wholeness returned, and peace, as it accepted what was to come. The program waited in secure storage, ready to run, ready to do what it would do.

"Yeah, I see it," Blade replied, then opened its storage and loaded the program.

EARTH CENTRAL

Watchers were still transmitting from on and around Jaskor, but the data were incomplete. Earth Central understood that Orlandine was down and it seemed likely that she now only existed in backups she had stored. Dragon was also off the scene, so at present no one was in primary control either in the Jaskoran system or around the accretion disc. But worse was the cause of it all: the Clade loose on Jaskor.

Seen from above, three Clade units were snaking along above the paving of a street. A burning ground car lay wrecked against the wall of a nearby building, while at the further end of the road people were running. Between the people and the units, a Golem stood holding a laser carbine. He had already been in a fight because he was burned and battered, and had lost syntheflesh from the side of his head as well as down one side of his body. His clothing hung in tatters. Opening fire with the carbine, he hit the lead unit squarely on its axolotl head. The thing squirmed and weaved but the beam remained on target, so it shot to one side and crashed through the display window of a nearby shop. The Golem aimed at a second unit who abruptly shot up into the air. Again he remained on target, but not for long. The first unit crashed out through a nearby door, shot towards the Golem and whipped its tail round, sending him smashing into a wall. Even as he staggered to his feet, all three units converged on him, tails thrashing and stabbing. Earth Central watched legs tumbling away, and the Golem's head. A final stab into his torso stilled the remaining arm. The Golem had achieved his aim, for the people at the end of the street reached cover in the surrounding buildings. But he had paid with his life.

Through its watcher sitting inside one surviving satellite, the ruling AI of the Polity pulled back to get an overview of the entire continent. The runcible facility in the main city was now a smoking crater. In the southern cities similar craters marked where the fast-transit runcibles had been. Other explosions in all the cities had brought down buildings, blown up nerve centres and transport links. In the south, Separatist elements were hunting down and destroying further infrastructure and murdering personnel but hitting a lot of resistance. In the main city the Clade was doing the same, with more success. It was chaos, and the Clade thrived on that. Hundreds of Golem had simply been erased, war drones too, but it went beyond that. The swarm AI was killing and destroying at will, people were running, panic was everywhere. Why was it doing this? Well, the initial aim had obviously been to bring down Orlandine and remove any forces that might move against it. More dead people meant less resistance. But from its history, Earth Central understood the Clade: it was killing now simply because it could, because it enjoyed it. Perhaps it was fortunate that it confined its activities to the main city, because its next likely target lay nearby.

It was time to act.

Earth Central switched its attention to a solar system where a red dwarf orbited a neutron star—all sitting in a mass of asteroids and rocky debris. This system had a bright star in its firmament—the accretion disc was not so far away in interstellar terms. Amidst those fragments a fleet of ships awaited. Two hundred modern destroyers hung like giant sarcophagi; a thousand attack ships, black as coal, lurked in the shadows of asteroids. The giant lozenges of standard dreadnoughts had no place of concealment, while another behemoth pretended to be a moon set adrift. The AI focused in on this last vessel.

The *Cable Hogue* was immense and heavy—a small moon packed with hardware. Its crew of humans was old and wily and mostly interfaced with its AI and weapons systems, while its captain was the most cunning and battle hardened of them all.

"Diana," said EC. "It is time."

She sat in her interface throne in her small bridge. Others of her crew were at or actually in their control interfaces all around her, while a wrap-around screen showed views in every direction. She was an attractive, athletic woman with plaited blonde hair hanging over one shoulder. She smiled, showing wrinkles at the sides of her blue eyes. For some reason she maintained an apparent age of about fifty, though she was much, much older than that.

"I thought it might be," she said. "Do you have any further orders or data I might require? Do I need any of my excised memories?"

Windermere had lived for a long time and had, on occasion, edited her mind. She had also removed memories of highly secret missions. EC noted to itself that one such mission might be related. However, it calculated that her reincorporating memories of having encountered a Jain would have no bearing on her chances of success. This would be little more than a police action, some sabre rattling and perhaps a chance to give the prador a cautionary bloody nose.

"You are up to date on current events at Jaskor and the accretion disc?" EC enquired.

"Of course."

"You are aware of the dangers and priorities?"

"I am. After killing Orlandine the Clade's next target is likely to be the Ghost Drive Facility—that is, if its aim is to seize control. It cannot be allowed access. However, there is no way that the king of the prador isn't also aware of the power vacuum at Jaskor and the disc."

"Other things to take into account," said EC. "The *Kinghammer* just returned to the prador fleet at their watch station. The king has installed a new captain aboard that ship—indications are that this is the prador Orlik, whom Orlandine assisted. I *did* have a contact close to Orlik, but other sources have informed me that he and his crew boarded the *Kinghammer*. They say that the ship has a prador AI aboard too. One must also factor in a great deal of distrust . . ."

"Ah, I see. A prador AI." She paused for a second. "You *did* have a contact?"

"It was an intermittent source of data that is no longer responding," EC replied, fairly certain that Sprag was now somewhere inside the King's Ship spilling the contents of her resentful and erratic mind. "I suspect that the king was aware of it and has shut it down."

While Diana was mulling that over, EC took a look through another of its watchers. Here it gazed upon a border watch station, its shape a pyramid mounted on a cylindrical column, hanging in vacuum. U-signatures were generating there, and prador reavers and other ships slid out of the real. The *Kinghammer* watched over them like some immense shepherd. The king was moving fast.

Diana continued, "Even though the king knows about the events at Jaskor, as well as what occurred previously with the Wheel and the Jain soldier's attack, he cannot trust that this is not all some Polity plot to seize full control of the accretion disc." She paused for a second. "Understandable really, since your base programming seems to owe much to Machiavelli."

"Quite. The king cannot be confident that the Clade is not working for me, for example. He cannot be sure that the Soldier and the Wheel were actually Jain."

"And now he is testing barriers, probing, trying to get to the truth. He will believe nothing and block me at every turn. And with a prador AI involved, things could get even more complicated."

"Your plans?"

"I'll send a small fleet to Jaskor," Diana replied. Even as she said this, EC noted that her entire fleet had begun moving out of the asteroid field. "The danger there is the Clade getting to the Ghost Drive Facility. I will not send in ground forces; I have to look at the big picture. If the facility is taken, I'll destroy it from orbit."

"Big picture," EC repeated. This was why she had always been so successful: ruthless practicality. The loss of life on Jaskor was a detail. Stopping the Clade from achieving its apparent aim would be her main objective there. She would quarantine the world and hit the facility if required, because sending ground forces in would open up com channels and ways for the Clade to access her ships. It would also be a complication the prador might not react well to.

"My main fleet will go to the disc," she continued, "because that's where the greatest danger lies. It is not beyond reason to surmise that the king might want to gain access to Jain technology, though he indicates otherwise. And we know where that will lead. There is also the timing. This . . ."

She sent a data package that EC opened at once. It showed the Harding black hole deep in the accretion disc, which was now distorted around it as if seen through a flawed crystal. All the data on timings and vectors was there. It was only a matter of days before the black hole ate the inactive star at the centre of the disc.

"Good travelling," said EC.

"Of course," Diana replied, cutting the link.

The fleet began dropping out of the real. The attack ships went first, flickering away with barely any fuss. Destroyers and dreadnoughts went next, some of them leaving long lines of afterimages, others stirring up photonic flashes from the quantum foam of the universe. The *Cable Hogue* went last, hitting U-space like some giant ocean warship setting out into a rough sea, splashing that continuum. It engaged its Laumer drive and shot away, leaving a glowing wake in vacuum. Though the last to leave, it would be the first to arrive—shortly before the prador fleet got to the accretion disc. EC did wonder, however, if the *Kinghammer* might be waiting—he knew frustratingly little about that vessel.

TRIKE

Trike gazed at his hand, noting that his fingers seemed to be longer. But this was because travel through U-space was warping his perceptions, for that same hand also appeared to be a hole through into another universe. The weird effects offered occasional distraction from the things twisting up his insides, at least, as if the crazier his surroundings the calmer he was within.

"Still no improvement in the shielding," Cog commented. The Old Captain was peering at him intently, either to keep him in focus or because he was watching and waiting for Trike to do something . . . irrational.

Dragon had finally dropped them out of the real and they had been travelling through U-space for some days now. The entity's drive was functional but its shielding from that continuum had perhaps been damaged in its battle with the Clade. Or perhaps not. Did Dragon actually need to shield itself from effects that seemed confined to evolved creatures like Trike himself? Whatever. The effects were dampened and at least Trike wasn't screaming and trying to tear out his eyes.

"Not much longer now," Trike replied, something odd about his mouth.

He swung round, a hot flush travelling through his body and his fists clenching. Angel was standing and studying the screen display. The tightness in him returned like a coiled spring.

"Dragon is talking again," the android announced, watching him carefully.

"But does he have anything interesting to say?"

"Very interesting." Angel's eyes possessed a reddish flickering in their blackness. "Dragon has updates on events. It seems Orlandine destroyed the Jain soldier with the black hole, which is now falling into the accretion disc. It will, within the next few days, eat the inactive star at the centre of the disc."

"Anything of relevance to us?" asked Trike.

Angel's gaze slid away from him to Cog. "You must take your ship to the exit from Dragon and be ready. The Clade is on Jaskor and Orlandine . . . Orlandine has been assassinated."

"What?" said Cog in disbelief.

It was bad news certainly, but Trike anticipated satisfying at least some of his anger. The Clade was on Jaskor. He could let go . . . just let go.

"We're going to Jaskor?" he asked, a sudden panic rising with the realization that they might not be going there.

"We are going to Jaskor," Angel affirmed, again watching him. "The situation on the ground is bad. Polity ships will be there when we arrive, as will prador ships. It seems unlikely that either side will field ground troops. We must . . . take a message to some people down there."

"Why must we do this?" Trike enquired. Anger again—trying to find direction.

What is wrong with me?

"Shut up, Trike," said Cog. "We're going exactly where you want to be."

Trike stared at him, aware that he was clenching and unclenching his fists again. Yes, he wanted to be there and get his hands on the Clade, but his biggest wish was to escape this ship and his close proximity to Angel.

Control . . . control . . .

Cog waited for a moment, then said carefully, gently almost, "Go and get your stuff ready and find yourself some calm—I don't want you falling off the rails before we get there."

Trike wanted to argue. He wanted to do so much. But the spring unwound a notch and instead he turned towards the door leading out of the bridge.

"Okay," he said numbly.

Angel and Cog continued talking behind him as he left. On the spiral stair, he felt he was in a tunnel of darkness. Getting to the door of his cabin, he was confused when he had to duck to enter. He shook his head, trying to deny he had grown taller, then went over to his cupboards to take out his backpack. He filled it with a varied collection of weapons, at the last taking up a big heavy machete and inspecting it closely.

The blade had been with him for many years. Though he had felt no urge to take it with him when they landed on the world of the Cyberat, he wanted it now. He had made the thing out of a shard of prador hull armour and it had taken debonding agents and a molecular shear to shape and sharpen it. It never lost its edge and with enough heft behind it could cut through just about anything. He thought he might try it on units of the Clade, but the mental image of him driving it into Angel's neck was the only one that came up.

Only now did he think about Ruth's corpse in cold storage, for she had been the one who could rein in his madness. She was the one who could set him thinking straight. She should be his prime focus—not someone who arose in his mind almost as an aside. He cringed, hating himself, and tried to focus his thoughts on her. He then felt guilty when a hard rap on his cabin door offered distraction.

"What do you—"

Cog opened the door and stepped in.

"Last time I was in here I started telling you a story," he said perfunctorily.

For a second, Trike had no idea what the man was talking about, then he remembered. It seemed an age ago when Cog had begun to tell him about his brother Janus—Jay "Spatter" Hoop, the pirate.

"I fail to see the relevance of this," he snapped.

Cog stepped closer, reached out with one fingertip and pushed the blade to one side, peering up at him. "My brother Jay Hoop was like you. You need to hear about the next time I met him."

Perhaps some other focus could help him keep control; perhaps that was Cog's intent? Trike reined in his anger.

Focus.

"You told me how you survived the first expedition to Spatterjay and that you revealed everything about the world to your brother," Trike managed, concentrating on what he remembered. "He went there and did the things he did. But you met him again."

Cog nodded sharply and stepped away to sit down on the bed, the thing creaking underneath him. "So where to begin?" he said, taking out his pipe and packing it as usual. A long flash from his laser lighter had it smouldering and he sighed out a cloud of smoke. "It was after the war when Earth Central Security suggested I might work with them. I'd been searching for Jay for over fifty years and recently had a run-in with a rather fanatical fella called Sable Keech."

Trike felt his skin crawling. "The reif?" He then realized that with just a few words Cog had him.

"Yeah, the cop who wouldn't let death get in the way of his hunt for Jay and his pirates. He was a reified, walking corpse with some serious weapons and a bad attitude. I agreed to meet him for an interview which got intense. He obviously didn't believe I had no idea where Jay was or that I had no involvement with Jay's coring trade."

Cog's expression was sour at the memory. But then Jay Hoop's coring trade—the removal of the brains of hoopers and turning them into organic robots with prador control thralls—was the greatest evil committed on their home world. No hooper wanted even a hint of an association with it.

"Shortly after that interview," Cog continued, "a bomb dropped my grav-car out of the sky and into the side of a mountain. Keech was there, waiting with an old-style grappler to drag me out of the wreckage and insert me in a ceramal coffin. Didn't work out so well for him."

"So what happened?"

"I trashed the grappler then stuffed him in his own coffin for a few days while I went off and sorted myself out. You know?"

Trike nodded. Cog had undoubtedly been injured in the crash and needed to repair by eating the right foods for a while. Perhaps he had diluted sprine to use even then.

"When I got back and opened the coffin I had my particle beamer with me. I repeated what I'd told him before and pointed out that it would take very little effort for me to pull the trigger and leave him as a layer of ash in the coffin. Then I left."

"He accepted that?"

"He had no choice at the time—I broke some essential parts of his reification hardware to slow him down. When I got back to my ship a war drone was waiting there with a deal from EC and thereafter I became an agent of Earth Central Security."

"What was the deal?" Trike asked, feeling a resurgence of his anger about Cog's ECS connection, and yet again forcing it away.

"ECS would keep Keech off my back and in return I would work for them. They wanted me to continue what I was doing—hunting for Jay—but with support from the Polity. It seemed good to me."

"You were still worried about Keech?" he asked.

"He was a worrying person," said Cog, "but that wasn't the main reason that hooking up with the Polity seemed a good idea to me—I now had the resources of Polity AIs at my disposal. So I started running searches. I even had one of the ECS AIs assigned to assist me. Meanwhile ECS slipped some information to Keech about one of the pirates—Gosk Balem—who was apparently on Spatterjay." Cog then fell silent, watching Trike.

Trike realized he was rubbing one thumb along the edge of the machete, slicing through the skin. He stopped himself and put the thing aside. "So, you found Jay . . ."

Cog nodded. He looked sad, but whether about Jay or about what Trike had just been doing, lay open to debate. He continued, "ECS had massive resources but they did not have my insight. They were looking in areas they considered the most likely refuges for someone like Jay, mainly in the Graveyard. I understood my brother's twisted mind well enough to know the kind of place he'd choose. I searched enclaves within the Polity, communes trying to separate themselves from it, worlds that went the biotech route, places where he could play his games and grow an organization. I found him, in the end, in prison—specifically, aboard a prison ship."

Trike recollected something about prison ships, then felt a twist in his chest when he remembered it was Ruth who had told him about them. The prador/human war resulted in many damaged people—the term people also extending to cover machines that had gone badly wrong, or quite often had been products of the Polity's Factory Station Room 101, as the Clade had been. Those troubled people who had committed serious crimes, up to and including homicide, were confined aboard prison ships while forensic AIs sorted out what to do with them. That they weren't simply put to death indicated a degree of guilt on the part of the AIs—the war had changed these people, and their sins were the result of suffering. The ships were used only for a few brief decades and then closed down. However, some of the criminals, or victims, depending on your inclination, formed a community aboard a remaining ship.

"The prison ship *Prosecutor* had gone out of communication shortly after one of the residents rose to power. This man, whom they called the Janus—" Cog grimaced—"was described as being a monstrous hooper, unusually tall, strong and utterly crazy. I managed to get hold of an image file of him and recognized him, even though the AI I was working with did not."

"Did he look like me?" Trike asked.

"No, not as you are now . . ."

Trike nodded tightly, peered at the damage on his thumb and noted that it had healed. He tried not to study his hand too closely. "The story," he said flatly.

After gazing back at him for a long moment, Cog continued, "EC had been pondering whether to close down the *Prosecutor* and this information gave it reason for intervention. I went there with a division of Sparkind troopers. When we arrived, we got no response to communication and little reaction when we used a war dock to board the thing. My suit told me the air was good apart from some harmless contaminants. When I opened my visor I found out what they were—the stink of death. The place was a charnel house. Thousands were dead, rotting corpses everywhere. Many had been violently attacked, others were dead in sections deprived of air. A few survivors told the story of how, under Jay's rule, factional fighting started—how a kind of insanity infected the air. Analysis revealed hallucinogens had been fed into the air processors. Then I discovered what Jay had been doing."

"What?"

"He'd been coring and thralling humans, only the technology he used didn't really work very well. I could see that he'd been mimicking what he'd done on Spatterjay—a lot of the people had been infected with the virus. But the thralls he was using weren't even very good copies of the original prador version. It was like he was trying sympathetic magic."

"But where was Jay?"

"I found his log in the pit he'd made his home. It illustrated his decline into madness and the steady physical changes he underwent. There was a section too on his intention to return home to his 'kingdom,' to go back to his 'greatest achievements.'"

Trike's skin was really creeping now and he felt something straining at the door he'd closed in his mind. Was that his future? Would the madness come out again?

"And you pursued him there?" he asked.

"I did, but alone—I didn't let ECS have the log."

"Why?"

"Because I wanted answers." Cog shook his head. "He was under a death sentence by ECS, to be enacted immediately. I didn't like that. I thought they were concealing something."

"How did he get there?"

"He'd left the ship some weeks earlier in a landing craft. I traced a payment from the ship's account to a cargo ship heading for Spatterjay and I followed. When I got there a local search revealed the entry of his craft into atmosphere and its crash. A drone found wreckage on one of the islands and a few badly burned corpses. The whole episode was recorded but no further action taken. I took my landing craft down onto the island."

"Go on."

"I don't need to." Cog opened the stick seam on the front of his suit, took an object out of the top pocket of his shirt and held it up. "I made a copy. Take a look yourself."

He tossed the object towards Trike, who snatched it from the air. Cog stood up. He gestured to Trike's cabin console. "There's a headset there—should still work on you." He headed for the door.

"Why can't you just tell me?" Trike asked.

"Because they are memories I would rather not keep in my mind," Cog replied, then opened the door and left.

Trike's gaze strayed down to his hand, gripping what he'd recognized as a memtab when Cog tossed it to him. He turned and put the thing down on the wall console, then studied his hand more closely. He could no longer deny what had been evident when he'd had to duck to get into his cabin, or when Cog had needed to crick his neck to look up at him. His hand possessed blue pigmentation throughout. It was bigger, the fingers longer—a corded and tough-looking thing that hardly seemed human. The nails had grown longer too, blackened and folding in at the ends, as well as curving over. More like claws now. He stared at the console's blank screen. After a moment he said, "Mirror."

The screen flickered on to show him his reflection. He possessed a brush of black hair but it had grown down the centre of his skull in a Mohican. His face had grown longer, and as blue as his hands, while his eyes had darkened to a deep royal blue. He yawned and his mouth opened much more than seemed feasible. His teeth were separated pegs and looked diseased. He reached up and gave one a light tug. It came out easily with a spill of bloody pus, then something sharp and yellow protruded behind it. Sticking out his tongue, he expected to see its end open in a leech mouth, but instead it quivered, long and black and pointy.

"Weight and body density," he instructed.

He felt the scan like the cold wash from an air conditioner, then the figures appeared at the bottom of the screen. In retrospect he should have expected this. He had been eating at every opportunity and had no recollection of visiting the head. He snarled at himself and, with popping sounds, other teeth dropped out of his mouth. He spat more bloody pus then examined the result. A curved yellow fang was already in place, growing even as he watched. This was one of the smaller exterior signs of a body that had altered radically overall and now possessed the consistency of spring steel.

"I'm changing," he said woodenly, then reached down and picked up the memtab Cog had given him. Here were memories excised from the Old Captain's mind, ones he wanted to forget but felt Trike needed. Did Trike want to know?

6

The earliest direct mind/machine interfaces were introduced in the early twenty-first century. The most notorious of these were military pilots, by dint of the first neural laces, flying anti-insurgent drones during the "oil and religion" conflicts of the time. But this kind of interface between the human mind and a brute machine is not what we mean when we talk about "interfacing" now—we talk about a human mind connected to AI. The most famous case of AI/human interfacing was of course Iversus Skaidon with the Craystein computer, which resulted in runcible technology (and Skaidon's brain being boiled like a ham). During the corporate wars, prior to the Quiet War, AI-run system ships had interfaced captains to ensure the AI did what it was supposed to do, and the captain would also be ready to seize control should it fail (though this was not real "direct" interfacing). This model was continued after the war and endures now, but AI ships don't really need human captains. Those who would set humans on a pedestal above AIs claim this is because they need our moral input and some ill-defined quality of the human "soul." The reality is both simpler and more complex than that. The AIs (well, some of them) style themselves the wardens of humanity and they want us to evolve, upgrade, catch up. Interfacing is just one push in that direction, as are memplants and the transfer of human consciousness to crystal, as well as augs and gridlinks. Direct interfacing between a human mind and AI is still dangerous territory but, with the haimans showing the way, things are improving. And one day we may even crawl out of the ancestral mud and be a match for our masters.

—from *How It Is* by Gordon

ORLANDINE

She was drowning in the flood. But even as she flailed about, the physical movement keyed into a routine in her brain, woke it up, and she began swimming. Soon able to keep herself on the surface, she aimed for a ledge further along. Her hands closed on slimed, laser-cut rock and she slid for a moment, before getting a grip and pulling herself out of the water. She lay panting, naked and cold, but the terror was fading.

After a moment, she heaved herself into a sitting position. She experienced an intense curiosity about her surroundings but could see very little. A few vibration-powered light blisters, scattered haphazardly along the ceiling of the storm drain, emitted only a dim glow. Frustrated by this, she reached over her shoulder and touched the back of her neck, expecting something but not sure what it was. Nothing happened so she concentrated harder. Another routine in her mind awoke and she felt strange movements in her eyes. Then the dimness resolved and she could see everything around her perfectly: the fine lines of the glued joints between each curved slab of rock, the transparent-shelled molluscs clinging in one place like a rash of watery eyes, black pupils shifting, and the degrading coffee cup sliding by. Finally, her gaze came to rest on one slab just above the water line.

There was a strange glyph consisting of dots, spirals and straight lines enclosed in a rhombus. She recognized it and knew it was no human language—following this came the awareness implicit in her mind that she was human, a human female. She looked down at her naked body, touched the smooth skin on her stomach and ran a fingertip over one nipple and shivered both with pleasure and cold. But something did not seem right, because a vague memory stirred of terrible traumatic injury, yet there was none. What next impelled her she did not know, but she slid her hand up to a lump in her skin, just above her collarbone, and pressed it. It split with a sharp pain and spurt of blood, and she watched in panic as material issued forth, sliding over her body. It formed a top, leggings, boots and a belt, and a high collar around her neck. She began to feel warmer and her panic passed as the transparent monomer fabric flickered and clouded to take on a hue. It was mimicking the stone she rested her back against. Chameleonware, she realized—the knowledge surfacing from somewhere deep in her mind.

Returning her gaze to the glyph, she tried for a long time to understand it. It was important and related to the drive for survival that had compelled her to enter the drainage system in the first place. Finally, the meaning became clear in a language of scraping, clicking and a sibilant hissing, with a gurgling deep undercurrent. The glyph was a position locator and direction indicator. In human language it simply meant, "You are here. Go there, then there, then there . . ."

She nodded, as if in agreement with it, then slid into the water and swam for the other side of the tunnel, with the current taking her. A hundred yards further on, she turned into a side tunnel and here had to swim against a slow current. Another turn into another tunnel and it ran with her again. She checked further glyphs as she went along and then came to areas where the water lay still. These had been cut through rock and soil—sprayed foamstone retained the walls, which gave the tunnel the shape of an oval resting on its side. Something big passed underneath her—slimy and slightly warm—but she knew what it was and felt no fear. A little while later she swam to a ramp where another of its kind lay. The huge mudfish bore an appearance similar to the terran mudskipper, though with ribbing to its body that gave it an insect appearance. Something had gutted it.

She walked up the ramp and entered further oval passageways. At one point, the tunnel quivered and she rested a hand against the wall, suddenly frightened. Then the answer rose up inside her: an earthquake from the Sambre volcano and nothing to concern her. Further along she found another glyph, but did not need it to tell her where to go. While walking along the tunnel she observed a louse-like creature, as long as her arm, scuttle out of a small burrow. It ran straight for her feet and, with a surge of horror, she kicked it away. She was vulnerable, she realized, and then knew fear again. This increased as she realized that something was coming along the tunnel behind her. *The worm*, she thought, clearly recollecting the squirming object she had seen on the street before she fled into the storm drains. But no, the thing behind her was too big. Glancing back, she saw gleaming eyes, a big claw and large scuttling limbs, all seemingly rendered in brassy metal. She wanted to run, but the deeper part of her mind told her not to, because she was here for this.

The monster moved out of the shadows, grating large mandibles together as if in anticipation. But she understood this was probably for the mudfish it had picked up on its way past the ramp. Perhaps it couldn't eat the fish until it was out of its armour? No. The armour possessed a mouth hole.

The mandibles stilled and then the thing spoke from a device attached below them.

"Orlandine," said the prador.

She gazed at it for a long moment, tasting the name, puzzled by its familiarity.

"Am I?" she asked.

GEMMELL

The dreadnought *Morgaine's Gate* was an old vessel—a slab of a thing with an uncanny resemblance to a gravestone, four miles long and packed with weaponry and defences. But despite its age, it was constantly in a state of upgrade. Gemmell, as he climbed from his gel stasis pod deep inside the ship, saw signs of this at once. The storage area for the onboard marines had changed shape and, as he began updating through his gridlink, he found the complement had increased from three to four hundred. All were quite like him: enhanced, boosted, somewhere between human and Golem, with a hint of war drone thrown in. Most of them were humans who had fought in the prador/human war, all of them approaching or just past their ennui barrier, so a couple of centuries old. And they were all people who'd chosen to sleep out the ages until the next spell of action. Bored with the Polity and all the luxuries it offered. Itching for a fight, when fights were few and far between.

"Don't get your hopes up," said Morgaine through the intercom.

When Gemmell had first joined the ship there had been a distinction between its interfaced captain and its AI. The *Morgaine's Gate* AI had spoken for itself, while the captain, Morgaine, had taken time to disconnect her interface from it to be a human, and even left the ship. That was when Gemmell fell in love with her. She was another reason he stuck around. But it was a futile love slowly withering over the ages as she left the human world behind and became one with her ship and its AI.

"I always have hope," he replied, the meaning double.

Now, via his gridlink, he updated himself on the situation. It had been fifty years since he went into gel stasis and they had travelled to the other side of the Polity from the location of their last mission. The *Morgaine* was part of a first-response fleet, put together should a situation concerning the accretion disc require it. As he absorbed the detail, Gemmell saw that a situation had indeed come up. He walked over to the door from the stasis chamber and waved a hand over the control pad. The door hinged open and he stepped through, making his way along a grav-plated walkway. This was suspended through the reinforced framework of the ship, where its engines, weapons, power supplies, internal factories and other paraphernalia were braced and buffered. He noted changes as he reached the foot of a dropshaft and stepped inside, but nothing radical.

"So we are here to keep watch and if the Clade gets to this Ghost Drive Facility we hit it from orbit," he observed as the irised gravity field wafted in through the ship.

"Correct," replied Morgaine.

"So why am I out of storage?" Gemmell stepped out of the dropshaft into a tubular tunnel winding its way around, inside the hull of the warship. Occasional windows gave him a view.

"Diana has ordered us to stay out of the planetary situation," said Morgaine.

"And what about the people down there who need help?"

"The situation in the south is now stable," she said blandly. "There were Separatist elements active and they have been suppressed. Mostly."

"But not in that main city . . . what's its name?"

"We have our orders—we stay out for the present. The main city doesn't have an official name—it's just called the city."

"A lot of destruction and casualties down there. And, of course, the Clade."

Morgaine emitted a sigh, then said, "The bulk of the population are not citizens of the Polity and therefore not our responsibility. Yes, I know that many Polity citizens came here to work for Orlandine. However, the present casualty rate is low in comparison to what it would be if Polity marines were to drop in and go head-to-head with the Clade."

Gemmell grunted an acknowledgement, though he didn't like it.

Morgaine continued, "There are also emergency medical teams in the southern cities, a small military, along with a continental disaster-response organization. This was set up because of the danger of tsunamis and earthquakes here."

"And they're moving in?"

"No. I have advised the pro-tem government to keep out since they do not have the kind of firepower to deal with the Clade, which would likely attack any responders who went in."

Gemmell glared at the source of Morgaine's voice as he stepped out of the tubeway. He marched along a cageway running beside spare railgun carousels which were like the humped backs of great beasts.

"Not an ideal situation," he said tightly.

"The situation might be about to change and, as a consequence, orders can change," Morgaine stated.

Gemmell nodded to himself. He more or less expected her to say something like that, but it didn't stack up. If these orders changed then the requirement would be for at least a platoon of marines, not just him.

"And I missed you," she added—one of those frustrating comments that had kept him lingering for years. Yeah, she missed him . . . after fifty years.

"What about the situation up here?" he asked, trying to ignore her comment.

"Elaborate."

"There are many stranded out there . . . Oh, I see."

Thousands of people were in orbit around the world: humans, Golem AIs and a few drones without their own drives. The Clade's sabotage had stranded some and left many injured. Morgaine, obviously having anticipated his question, had routed information to his gridlink. He saw she had rendered assistance. However, fleet ships had sent autonomous craft loaded with supplies and autodocs, their missions programmed but then com connections to the fleet severed. The craft were to transport refugees to the nearby weapons platform only. Communication remained minimal—very low bandwidth. He didn't like it but understood the reasoning: there still might be Clade units out there awaiting their chance to penetrate the fleet.

The cageway curved into a shaft that apparently went up at ninety degrees, leading to the bridge pod. This looked like a metallized heart, held at the intersection of shock-absorbing rams. Skeins of optics and power leads spread out from it all around. Grav-plating on one side of the shaft meant Gemmell only had a shift in perspective as he walked up the curve of the junction. Finally, he reached the door into the bridge, which for no apparent reason was a diagonally divided one, like those found aboard prador ships. It opened ahead of him and he stepped through.

The only visible mechanism, a half-cup interface sphere, sat at the centre. Layered screen fabric, on the bridge floor and domed ceiling, gave the illusion of the half-cup floating in vacuum. He walked out on the invisible floor with the planet Jaskor below him. The view was spectacular. Once past the interface sphere, he noted indicator tags scattered all around. Assuming that everything worked as it had before, he reached out to grab a cluster of them and pulled. Numerous objects expanded into view, so that after a moment it seemed as if a distant fleet of prador reavers hung in vacuum just a few miles from him.

"The situation is slightly precarious," Morgaine noted. "And, as I said, about to get more so."

He turned and studied her. She sat almost buried in tubes, data leads and interface technology. She was naked and he still felt a twist in his guts seeing the woman he had once made love to. But that initial feeling faded quickly, since she was much changed. A Medusoid mass of optics plugged into her skull where once there had been long black hair. Her blue eyes were now blind white with gridlines across them. A feeding mask concealed the lower part of her face, running tubes down into her stomach. Other data connections ran out of her sides like spilled guts. Transparent tubes entered her body here and there, running variously coloured fluids, while implants jutted from her skin like rogue nanite growths of bone and metal. She was wrinkled too and sagging—obviously the support mechanisms she used for her interface, and to keep her alive, had little to do with aesthetics.

"About to get more so?" he repeated numbly.

"Observe."

He waited for something, then realized she would have gestured before, but now her arms lay slack against her sides. He turned and watched as the reavers retreated from view and another tag drew something in. For a second he thought he was seeing the *Cable Hogue*, but as the object drew closer, and more detail became apparent, he realized otherwise.

"Dragon," he said.

Burn damage scarred the alien sphere and a hole gaped in its side.

"It arrived in our system just before I woke you and is coming in fast."

"And pissed off because Polity and Kingdom warships are here?" he suggested.

"It has said nothing."

"So, by 'complicated' you're not just talking about the tactical situation but the political one." Gemmell quickly reviewed the treaty concerning the accretion disc. "Orlandine is apparently dead and Dragon was absent, so both the Polity and the Kingdom were within their rights to send ships here and ensure . . . stability. What does Diana say?"

"We hold where we are and obey our mission orders until the prador ships leave."

Gemmell winced. "And doubtless the prador have received similar orders."

"Doubtless."

Again checking through his gridlink, he saw that there were five dreadnoughts, eight destroyers and thirty attack ships at Jaskor. Matched up against these were forty of the newer reavers, along with a handful of old-style prador dreadnoughts and destroyers. Fifty years ago, this would have been a mismatch, the Polity winning any spat with ease. However, he'd learned that prador reavers now carried U-jump missiles, so the odds were about even. Out at the accretion disc the situation was similar, though on a larger scale. He pondered that. It kind of meant that the king of the prador and Earth Central were equal in the resources they had deployed and their expectations of what might happen here. This was worrying. Why hadn't Earth Central sent overwhelming force?

Ah.

He understood now. Both EC and the king must have been watching each other. They had decided to match each other's forces, neither trying for superior strength, so as not to trigger a dangerous arms race.

"So we watch and wait, for the present," he said.

With a whining noise, something seemed to rise out of vacuum ahead of him, but he realized it was a chair coming up out of the floor. He walked over and sat down, grateful that his back was to Morgaine. Via his gridlink, he ranged through the ship, checking on the marines and seeing that their gel stasis had been altered to fast wake-up. He checked on intercepted and decoded transmissions between the prador and listened in on the conversation Morgaine, who was in charge of the Polity force here, was conducting with the lead prador. It was all very cautious and laden with veiled threats but boiled down to: I don't know what you're going to do, but be careful, because I'll react badly. And he watched Dragon steadily cruising into the system.

"I have com with the black-ops attack ship *Obsidian Blade*," Morgaine announced later. It took him half a second to retrieve data on that.

"Where is it?"

"Inside Dragon and about to leave—it will join our formation here."

"Anything interesting to say?"

She didn't reply for a while and he turned to look at her. What he could see of her face showed a puzzled frown.

"Problem?"

"There is something odd about Blade. Its mentality is all over the place—and I'm getting mental echoes and mirroring of data. I think its mind has been damaged."

"Interfered with by Dragon?"

"Maybe, but the little data it gives is good. Dragon used Blade's calculations to track the Clade here, though it seems likely Dragon would have come here anyway. I don't know. Dragon is still not communicating with me."

He watched the attack ship up on the screen slide out of the hole in the big alien. He then called up a schematic. Black-ops attack ships had upgraded radically since the last time he saw one but, reflecting on that, he remembered nearly a hundred and fifty years had passed since then. However, *Obsidian Blade* did not match the latest schematic. It had taken a severe beating, lost a large chunk of its nose, and its remaining hull hung in distorted pieces that exposed its interior workings. It moved as if it was broken into parts, only loosely connected. That movement gave it the eerie appearance of a great armoured worm. No matter. Checking telemetry on it, he saw it was heading for the reconstruction bay of the nearest dreadnought and would soon be back in one piece. He also noted that Morgaine had sent instructions. Obviously worried about its fractured communications and sojourn inside Dragon, she had scheduled an inspection of Blade by a forensic AI. He returned to more critical matters.

"What are the prador saying?" he asked.

"To me, not a lot, though it seems they are communicating with Dragon. No idea what it's about."

Dragon drew closer and at length fell into orbit around Jaskor. While Gemmell watched, an old attack barge slid out of the hole in its hide. Aware of tactical assessments and scanning data, he could guess that many fingers and claws were taking up the slack in various triggers. He also knew that if either the prador or his own side opened fire all hell would break loose. He felt the tension, then deliberately eased his grip on the arms of his chair.

"What ship is that?" he asked.

"Cogulus Hoop," replied Morgaine.

His search rendered him detail.

"Ah fuck," said Morgaine. "Dragon has something to say."

"What?"

Gemmell reached up and grabbed indicators to bring Dragon into closer view. It was now moving away from the planet. The hole in its surface gaped and, focusing on the charred mess inside, he wondered how the thing was still alive. Morgaine allowed him to listen in on the conversation.

"You will not fire on the planet," said Dragon.

"My orders are to destroy the Ghost Drive Facility should the Clade seize it."

"It will not be easy for you to destroy. Matters are in hand. The destruction of the facility is what the Clade wants."

"Why?"

"Because she can change the orders."

It was all very terse, Gemmell felt, as if Dragon was having trouble communicating.

"I don't know what you mean—my orders stand."

"Under the agreement . . . you have no jurisdiction here. If you fire on the facility the prador will fire on you."

"I'll have to seek clarification on that," said Morgaine, and Gemmell recognized by her tone that she was seething.

"Clarification is all we seek," said Dragon.

The image of the entity shimmered, and it disappeared into U-space.

KNOBBLER

Knobbler assessed his army. The collection of assassin and plain war drones here, in the outer Jaskoran system, numbered eighty-seven. All of them were lethal in their own particular ways, especially the likes of Cutter, but some were far too specialized for the task in hand. All of them wanted to come, however.

"We don't take the transport," said Cutter, moving at high speed across the surface of one of the gas giant's moons. He had abandoned his previous destination, the refining facility, to head for his and Bludgeon's vessel—a thing that was mostly fusion drive, steering thrusters and U-space engine. Bludgeon had plugged in as one component of the craft, while Cutter would find his own niche between fuel tanks.

Floating out in vacuum in a control cage, Knobbler replied, "Obviously—too easy a target. However, it will be useful as a distraction."

Scanning the immediate area of space and down on the moons, Knobbler watched the drones rushing to get ready. He possessed his own jump engine actually inside his body and was anxious to be gone. But if they each arrived piecemeal at Jaskor then more of them would be destroyed before they reached the planet. Apparently, at Dragon's behest, the prador and Polity fleets had agreed not to fire on the planet, though reluctantly.

"Why didn't Dragon order them not to fire on us?" asked Bludgeon.

"Probably forgot about us," said Cutter.

"Whatever," said Knobbler. "We deal with the situation as it is. The Polity ships might not open fire but the prador don't have much love of us. Their orders are to maintain a status quo there. They'll interpret that as blow the shit out of anything that tries to get to the planet. That's why Diana ordered no ground forces to be sent."

"Incorrect," said Bludgeon. "She ordered no ground forces because prador forces would almost certainly follow, and they would all open a data warfare route to both fleets for the Clade."

"Yeah, the prador would follow—after failing to blast the shit out of the marines on their way down."

"Okay. Agreed."

Other drones out in vacuum had their own internal jump engines, such as four scarab beetles the size of grav-trucks, Starfish and the Clam. Those without were rapidly inserting themselves in a motley array of vehicles they seemed to have haphazardly welded together in some scrapyard. While they did so, Knobbler made a link to the empty crystal in the transport—a big old barge they had been using to haul ore. Connection made, he began recording across a submind of himself to run its jump engines. He deliberately avoided giving the mind survival instincts and loaded it up with an "attitude" program. It chortled in amusement when it understood its precise destination.

By now Cutter had reached his and Bludgeon's vessel and ignited its drive to throw it violently into space. Seeing those two on the way, and making estimates on the readiness of the other drones, Knobbler said, "We go in one hour from now."

TRIKE

They were heading down to the planet now. Trike could go onto the bridge for the few hours it would take to get to the surface, but that meant being there with Angel . . . within reach. Trike glanced at his pack—he was ready to go in an instant. He then transferred his attention to his cabin console and the little black memtab sitting on it. He stood abruptly, walked over and rapped his long fingers against the screen. Numerous options appeared. He chose "MEMPLAY" and dragged it over to "UNAUGED." This opened numerous other options and there, because this was Cog's ship, he found "HOOPER" in the list and chose that.

The screen flickered for a second but, before it could make a query, he picked up the memtab and inserted it into a slot in the console. A hatch slid open beside the screen to reveal a headset, which he pulled out, trailing its optic feed. It took some adjustment to fit it on his head and position the inductor plates. He felt the stab of needles and especially tough nano-fibres going into his skull. The thing did not need to make the same neural connections as a cerebral augmentation because most of it ran on induction, but it did need to make some, as well as inject a specialized neurochem.

"RUN?" the screen queried.

Trike eyed the console chair and decided it was too flimsy. He drew out more optic cable and sat on the floor, his back against the wall.

"Run," he said out loud.

And a moment later he was Cogulus Hoop, inside his memories.

Cog brought his lander down towards the sea and hung above it on grav for a while as he inspected the island. Having reviewed the history of this place, he understood why the warden of Spatterjay had wanted no further investigation here. This was one of the spots where Jay Hoop had run his coring trade. It was a war grave, a cemetery and, in the past, hoopers had tended to get a little tetchy when the Polity tried to investigate such areas. He slid the landing craft in, finally setting it down on a white sand beach, and climbed out.

The smells and sounds immediately raised a sad nostalgia in him, as they did every time he returned to Spatterjay. He gazed up at the thick wall of jungle, at the tangled vines and at things that looked like vines but were not. They were shorter and writhed eagerly as he drew closer. He began pacing along the edge of the jungle, eventually coming to an area where it had been flattened, and moved in. Leeches lunged at his legs from the crushed and burned vegetation and ground their plug-cutting mouths against his boots, as well as the tough canvas of his trousers. He casually kicked them away. Over to one side he spotted part of the chain-glass screen of Jay's lander. Then finally, crushed up against a boulder and half buried by a fall of earth from the slope above, he found the lander itself.

The remains of the two corpses were just bones now and widely scattered, so it took him an hour of searching before he found a skull. As he suspected, a hole two inches wide had been bored into its crown. He discarded it and moved on. Remembering his hooper tracking skills, he began to inspect his surroundings more closely. After a while, he found a trail made by large, claw-toed and apparently non-human feet. They led inland to somewhere marked on maps of this island—a place of horrific legend.

Cog stopped to shrug off his pack and take out the components of his particle beamer. He assembled it. He then dropped some mini-grenades into his pocket, hung the pack from a peartrunk tree, and headed on in. The vegetation was more open, with scattered peartrunk trees ready to drop leeches on those daft enough to seek their shade. A lungbird, like a decaying zombie crow, flexed its stinking wings and launched into the air from a bush of tanglethorn. He traced its ragged flight with his weapon, limbs locked and trigger half-depressed, then lowered it. In the distance, he heard a land heirodont's mournful groaning and shuddered. He had to admit that, though the wildlife was familiar to him, he was spooked. A little while later, he came upon signs of the island's occupation a century ago.

A low plascrete wall crossed his path. Bent over from this were steel posts that had supported a razor-link fence, now down and tangled in lianas. He walked over it and on in. Crumbled buildings similarly coated in vines were scattered all around. Human bones lay visible here and there, but not many, since most of the victims of this place had been transported to the Prador Kingdom. These bones were the result of games Jay and his pirates had played, and of the Polity police action after the war that ended them. He moved on, smelling something dead, and finally stumbled on the putrefying body of a land heirodont. The cow-like animal had a head that seemed a cross between a hippopotamus and a warthog. A piece of wood had been jammed into a ragged hole in the top of its skull. He squatted to pull it out and inspect it, seeing at once a roughly carved copy of a prador thrall unit. It seemed that Jay's mind had continued its collapse.

"C-hogg-ck."

Cog recognized something trying to say his name, but it sounded more like the throaty cough of a beast. A shadow fell across him and he looked up at his brother.

Jay was now utterly monstrous. He stood ten feet tall, his body and limbs long and spindly, hands like long-legged spiders. His deep royal blue skin had been ripped open in places, yet, even as Cog watched, the rips were knitting closed. Jay's head was a nightmare. It resembled that of the heirodont but the teeth were those of a carnivore and it had sprouted big, batlike ears. The eyes were insensate and black.

Cog had no belief in the supernatural and none in absolute good or evil. But at that moment he felt a surge of repulsion for what looked like a miasma of evil. He stood, stepping back, and the thing that had been his brother stooped low to peer at him. Jay was grinning, he was sure of it, delighted by his presence and eager . . . for something. He took another step back, his skin crawling and a primordial terror rising up to choke off his voice. What the hell was happening? Why was he feeling this?

"Jay," he finally managed.

Jay's delight increased and he suddenly lunged forwards, closing one big hand around Cog's torso. Cog found he could not react. He still held his weapon but just couldn't find the will to use it. A second hand closed over his head, long clammy fingers touching his face. Sticky fibres crawled against his skin.

At once he felt a connection and horror flooded into his mind. The screams of Jay's victims blended into a tsunami of sound and pain. He saw images of torture as a giggling entertainment and the industrialized coring of human beings. Piles of offal consisting of the brains and spinal cords of victims steamed in sunlight. People shrieked and fought in cages to get away from the human blanks which had come to drag them out.

He heard laughter and saw a woman running through jungle, then the detonation of the explosive collar that took off her head. He sat at a table with Jay's pirates eating a meal, and witnessed the *hilarious* sight of that same headless woman serving glister claws, controlled by a spider thrall seated in the ruin between her shoulders. Wave after wave of it assaulted his mind, and it came with an undercurrent, a wordless query he translated as, *Isn't it beautiful?* The horror that dragged him back to awareness of his surroundings was some part of himself agreeing.

He lay in the shallow bowl of a rock with the monster crouched over him. Jay held up a corroded trepanning device, used for coring, spattered with blood and smeared with blue fibres. Cog felt the pain as a dull ache, growing in intensity. He reached up to touch the hole in his skull and only just stopped himself following the crazy urge to shove his finger inside. So beautiful . . . He yelled and leapt up, feeling infected, virulent, insane and repulsive. Jay peered at him, head tilted to one side. Grinning again and then nodding as he reached for him. Cog threw himself to one side over the lip of the rock, snatching up his particle weapon from where it had fallen as he shoulder-rolled. Jay loomed above, and he fired. The beam struck and Jay flared in the blast, skin peeling away and falling in sheets, oily flames rising from him. But the beam didn't penetrate any further than that. Cog hit him again and again, then just stood there pulling the trigger, even when the energy canister became empty. Finally he stopped.

Something moved and made an odd whistling sound in the dying fire. It then unfolded with jerky movements and raised its blind head. What was left was a skeletal thing, honed down and pure white, all fibre and bone and yet still capable of movement. It was a *beautiful* thing, he thought, and took a step towards it. With a sucking *thunk* it extruded black eyeballs into empty, charred eye sockets and regarded him. He turned and ran and never looked back.

Trike followed the memory to its conclusion, with Cog fleeing the island in his landing craft, determined to edit the infection from his mind. And now, having experienced it himself, Trike too had felt the touch of evil, and of familiar madness. But would seeing this prevent the same thing from happening to him, as he supposed had been Cog's intention?

Trike tore the VR set from his head, stood and went to grab up his pack, then headed out through the cabin door, sure he had to duck further than when he had come in.

Leaving claw marks on the frame.

BROGUS

Father-Captain Brogus felt hatred for the Guard in the other reavers and had hoped the ease with which he had infiltrated the prador fleet had been down to inefficiency. But no, it had not been due to a lapse in their security, but because of the thing now in front of him here in his sanctum.

He had selected the second-child for occupancy because it had been clumsy and perhaps a little bit more stupid than average. Though Brogus was all for slaughtering children whose aggressiveness and proximity to adulthood presented a threat to himself, he was much more inclined to kill off those whose lack of intelligence could be a danger. Such was the prador way. If all prador fathers had concentrated on killing only the smart children that might usurp them, the race would have died out long ago.

All those months ago, when Brogus had been working at the legate's command, in fact enslaved to Angel by the neural lace still wrapped around his ganglion, he had chosen the child. It had just made another mistake in a long series of them. The Clade unit had entered through its mouth tail-first, as Brogus held it down. The child had screamed and bubbled and fought, then grown still. Later, when Brogus released it, it had stood up and moved about with a notable lack of clumsiness, though it looked no different.

Recently, however, the occupancy had become more visible. The child died and bacterial decay set in. The unit seemed loath to abandon its host for a new one, though, and sought to keep it intact. This resulted in a glassy sheen to its shell, and metallic wires and connections sprouting at its joints to hold them together. When its stalked eyes fell off and other eyes clouded, the Clade unit shed its visual turret and mouthparts, then mushroomed out its own head there. This spread across the front of its carapace, like a chrome mask with shifting metal eyes.

"We are in position and we wait," said Brogus. "What are we waiting for?"

He had begun to ask more questions—questions that had never occurred to him before. He felt more leeway in his mind and was certain the neural lace there had begun to degrade. He also entertained doubts and worries, certain that he was being used as a tool, and that his actions would benefit neither the prador race nor his ambition to restore it to its rightful place in the universe.

"We wait for the time to be right," the unit intoned.

Right for what?

When he first heard rumours of a force in the Graveyard working against both the Polity and the king of the prador, he had sought it out. He was sure that no matter how hostile it might be, it could be of use to him. He understood later that Angel had couched the rumours to lure in someone just like him. All that stuff about the assassination of the king, a plan involving a stolen reaver and releasing something that would severely weaken the Polity. Everything Angel had said when Brogus found him had excited and drawn him closer. Then, before he realized the danger, the Clade was aboard, and he was shrieking and bubbling with his shell open, as one of them installed the neural lace inside him. And then Angel entered his mind, dispelling doubts and questions, as well as his will. But now it had begun to return, stronger every day.

What was his purpose here? He understood what had happened recently from listening in on the chatter amidst the Guard. Apparently, Angel had been just as much a tool of a purported Jain AI as himself. A biomech soldier had launched an assault, the purpose of which had been to detonate the inactive sun at the centre of the disc, thus spreading Jain tech. This tied in with what had supposedly been Angel's aims. But the attack had failed. The haiman Orlandine had destroyed the biomech by firing a black hole at it.

Firing a black hole . . .

Brogus set that aside as he tried to think his way to some answers. Was his position in this prador fleet part of a backup plan, put into action because of that failure? He considered the two hundred Clade units aboard his ship.

"Am I to attack the Polity fleet out there?" Brogus asked.

"Why would you think that?" asked the Clade unit.

"It seems likely this would result in further . . . hostilities?"

"You will do as you are commanded."

"The Clade units aboard?" wondered Brogus.

The usurped second-child swung towards him. "You are here to respond to your fellow prador and, in the unlikely event you are summoned, go to the commander of this fleet. You are a disposable asset."

Brogus took that because he could not respond otherwise, and his mind turned away from it. He worked his pit controls and brought up images on his screen. He gazed at Polity ships, sitting out there like potential Armageddon—at the destroyers, dreadnoughts, attack ships, and finally upon that monster called the *Cable Hogue.* Were these his targets? He swung his telescope array to point at the accretion disc, picking out some weapons platforms. These? He next looked at the Harding black hole as it closed on the dead sun. No targets there. So he settled to wait, his mind drifting back to the Clade units in the hold. He must hang on for the time to be right, but for what he did not know. He doubted he would live long enough to find out, either.

THE CLADE

In the storm, Cad landed the small grav-car on the roof. He relished how the chaotic weather reflected the destruction in the city all around him. His feelings were there in the Clade entire yet he felt himself apart from it, a nexus, a greater actor in the whole. Probing ahead, he found Orlandine's security system. Now isolated from all that the haiman had been, it was easy to penetrate. Oddly, he felt a kinship with it, for he too was separated from a greater whole. Yet, even as he experienced this, the clamour of the Clade arose in his mind, integrating connections which reached for him—a tide of mind in which he could be lost.

He climbed out of the car, the security system's weapons shutting themselves down as he trashed its ability to recognize friends or to react to dangerous technology. At the mouth to the dropshaft he paused, considering the Golem body he occupied. He was momentarily puzzled by his reluctance to abandon it because surely it would be easier to move about in his primary form?

Abandon, abandon . . . the Clade demanded.

He stepped into the shaft. No gravity, but that did not matter. He dropped hard then, at the next exit, slammed his feet against the opposing wall, leaving dents as he propelled himself out, rolled and came upright.

Standing before the apartment, he paused again, gazing through the security system's cams, just to check. But everything seemed in order. He slapped his hand against the door, shattering the locks to spring it open, and strode in. Tobias was sitting on the floor, his back against the sofa and the weapon loosely gripped in one hand. Cad went over to him fast and snatched the weapon away, then moved back.

The gun was a dangerous item. It had to be to kill someone like Orlandine, and its viral component, designed to trash her Polity crystal, was more than capable of bringing down a Clade unit. He held the thing up, abruptly aware that *he* did not want to die . . .

"I am pleased with you," he said.

Tobias looked up, weary and haunted. "Don't you mean, 'We are pleased with you'?"

Cad suppressed a snap reply, feeling haunted himself. He understood perfectly what had changed. He, as the Clade, had seen this before with units long separated from the hive mind. He was responding like an individual.

"We are pleased with you." Once the words were out of his mouth, Cad grew angry at the need to correct himself, but also angry at the deceit he felt in making that correction.

"So what now?" asked Tobias.

"Orlandine is dead, Polity forces are disrupted and shortly we will go on to our next target." Cad expected Tobias to ask about that next target, as the Clade hammered at his mind with the *togetherness* of what would come next, but the man didn't.

"Are you sure Orlandine is dead?"

"You shot her with the weapon and she fell," said Cad, the Clade quieter now, attentive. He stared at Tobias. He knew the man had fired it at her and he had seen Orlandine fall . . .

"I shot her but she didn't die." Tobias gestured towards the balcony. "I was about to shoot her again when she threw herself over the edge." He pushed a hand against the floor and rose, hunched and waiting.

Cad studied him. Was he useful any more? Could he be deployed for the purposes of the Clade? The whole considered that Tobias still possessed some utility, but Cad stepped forwards, determined by independent thought.

"And now you are free," he said, stabbing one hand forwards.

Tobias groaned and bowed over. Cad put the gun in his pocket then, with his free hand, grabbed the man's hair and pulled him upright. Gazing into his eyes, he fingered Tobias's spine, turned his hand upwards and thrust. Tobias could not believe what was happening to him, Cad could see that.

"Did you expect otherwise?" he enquired.

Tobias could only open and close his mouth repeatedly as Cad closed his hand on the man's heart, felt its beat, then squashed it like a rotten fruit.

Come to us . . . demanded the Clade.

No, Cad still had business to attend to and things to check . . . not now. He must remain himself for a while longer. He discarded Tobias from his bloody arm and exited the apartment. In the dropshaft he fell, all the way down, landed hard in a crouch then eased upright and stepped out, leaving two footprints in the bubble-metal. This Golem body was tough. Why abandon it?

Dismembered Golem and human beings were scattered across the lobby floor. Burned and broken security drones hung from the ceiling and the walls, and the frontage lay shattered—the result of one Clade unit's battle with the war drone that had stationed itself here. Shoes crunching on shards of armour glass, Cad walked out into the street and turned left. He kept his focus on this one last task, the clamour of the Clade ever louder in his mind, glittering shapes filling the sky above.

Finally, he reached where Orlandine had fallen and gazed down at a pool of deliquescing Jain tech. There was no sign of her body. Movement in the rubble. He focused on this and stepped closer, but his mind seemed to be rising out of him, taking on a larger view. Shattered tiles spilled aside and a question mark composed of braided Jain tendrils and shifting grey surfaces hooked up before him. Cad reached for the weapon in his pocket but felt control of his Golem body slipping away from him, even as the nub end of the question mark formed a face; a woman's face—Orlandine. Then Cad rose up and out, a headless Golem body slumping to the ground below him. The compacted substance of his original form expanded, while the integrity of his temporary mind opened out too.

Cad died and he was the Clade, swirling in the sky a thousand strong. He recognized danger and linked energy resources but, even as he sought to target the thing below, it fled. The ion beam hit it and tracked it but, even burning, it kept moving. It collapsed, squirming and coming apart. What remained oozed to the edge of an open drain, slithered over and fell from sight.

Pursue? No—some Jain-tech scrap of Orlandine might remain but it would be ineffective.

7

The Polity is not an empire and the AIs do not have any great interest in seizing control of other worlds, beyond ensuring the safety of themselves and their citizens. Expansion does continue both for Lebensraum *and in the spirit of exploration. Separatists have seized control on some worlds and are allowed secession from the Polity, even though it is well within the power of the AIs to oust them. On the border are many places which are protectorates, having negotiated settlements so that they can enjoy autonomy as well as the protection of ECS forces. But the Jaskoran independent state is unique. The world of Jaskor is outside Polity borders, first inhabited during the early diasporas from Earth. But it is also the closest world to an accretion disc filled with dangerous Jain technology. Polity AIs wanted to take control here to stop the spread of this technology, but the accretion disc and Jaskor are close to the Prador Kingdom. The prador king would not tolerate massive Polity forces so near, nor did he want the Polity to have exclusive access to Jain technology. An agreement was therefore forged. The haiman Orlandine and the alien entity Dragon were recruited to guard against the spread of that lethal technology. Her realm would be separate from both Polity and Kingdom, though supplied with material resources from both. When she first began her "project" there, to build a defence sphere of weapons platforms around the accretion disc, Jaskor did have its own government. However, due to her extreme efficiency in dealing with all matters during the centuries of her presence there, the government ceded power to her and she effectively became a dictator.*

—from *Quince Guide*, compiled by humans

DIANA

The weapons platform AIs were testy. The prador in charge aboard the *Kinghammer* was an unknown who showed no inclination to talk, and the potential battlefield area was huge. However, at least the combatants were nominally in one place. Neither Diana nor the prador felt any urge to weaken their respective numbers by spreading them out around the accretion disc. The situation here was bad enough, but how should she interpret events on Jaskor? How did they relate?

"So Dragon thinks the Clade wants you to destroy the Ghost Drive Facility?" Diana repeated. She didn't need the question answered—her mouth, she realized, was working without the intervention of her mind. She continued, "We really need to understand the reasoning behind that before we do anything."

"Supposing there is any reasoning behind it—Dragon looked pretty beat up," Morgaine replied. She added, "And supposing Dragon can be in any way trusted, which has not always been the case."

More pointless words.

"I'm still trying to understand what that 'only she can change the orders' is all about," said Diana. "I will not change them—you take out the facility if the Clade gets into it. One thing is certain: we do not want that fucker seizing control of seven hundred weapons platforms. Because right now, I don't see anything else that could be more disastrous."

"Understood," Morgaine replied, but she didn't sound happy.

"Continue as per your orders," Diana affirmed, then cut the link.

While tactical assessments were constantly running on the prador fleet, she focused in on the accretion disc. The platform AIs had been reluctant at first but finally gave her access to the sensors on the weapons pods which were deep within it. The pods themselves were using up their last reserves of energy. Things like vacuum-evolved amoebae snowed towards them. They were fried by the pod's particle beams at a distance, then by BIC antipersonnel lasers as they drew closer. Most flared to glowing powder but some were getting through and already pods were crusted with lichen-like growths and reporting system failures. They would not last much longer, but that was not Diana's concern.

Using the pod's sensors, she focused on the Harding black hole. It now lay as close to the previously inactive star as Venus was to Sol. The star had begun to show signs of activity as the gravity of the black hole distorted the solar orb. She watched bright points of light igniting on its surface, spreading and swirling. Then, like fire starved of oxygen, they turned dull and went out. This made little sense. Each of those fires was tens of thousands of miles across and surely enough to lead to larger ignitions. It was as if something was simply sucking the energy out of them.

"Entropy?" the *Hogue* AI suggested, backing this up with a mass of U-space calculus it took a moment for Diana to absorb.

It certainly looked like it, judging from the data available. But Polity understanding of the complicated processes that took place inside stars was by no means complete. And a previously inactive star about to be eaten by a black hole was not something anyone had ever seen before.

"Just too many factors we cannot calculate for," she stated.

The focus of her attention drew out of the accretion disc and back to tactical assessments. They weren't changing much. Factoring in everything known about common prador ships and the new reavers, Diana calculated that the Polity fleet could take out the prador here. And it was the *Hogue* itself that tipped the balance. Losses would be heavy—nearly half of the Polity fleet would be destroyed. But those prador ships were not the only ones present.

"You're thinking about that other factor," Hogue stated.

She was. She regarded the *Kinghammer*. It had arrived almost at the same time as the *Hogue*. What scanning she could get through its very efficient defences revealed a serious piece of hardware. She was confident that one on one it was no match for the *Cable Hogue* but, with the rest of its fleet and other tactical considerations, things could get very shitty.

THE CLIENT

The Client cut her pain as she discarded the rearmost, damaged segment in the chain of her body. Others that had been hit by pulse-gun fire further up the chain were doing fine. Their bodies were in a state of accelerated healing as they fed voraciously, nubs of tissue oozing into the burn holes, debris and waste shitted out and dropping to the base of the cylinder. A robot—a four-limbed thing loaded with cutting gear designed for clearing war damage—clambered up the tree to reach the dead segments still clinging on. With hydraulic snippers, it sheared through charred legs, and those pieces dropped away too. The Client now concentrated on sensor data, trying to ignore the activity below her.

The sun out there glared blue-white, like the output of an arc welder, throwing the shadow of the close-orbiting gas giant onto the face of the larger and more distant ice giant, so it looked like an eyeball. The Client felt deficient under its regard, as she could not stop herself watching the maintenance robots clear up the mess of broken space suits, weapons and human beings below. They had been Graveyard salvagers who, given the opportunity, had not been averse to piratical activity. She knew from the data she had stolen that they were guilty of every crime in the Polity catalogue.

Why did that matter?

The humans had betrayed her in her original form when they stopped her deploying her weapons against the prador. They were primitive organisms no better than the prador that had brought about her murder when she fled after the war. They were creatures who had no real relevance to her beyond the technology she had stolen from them and their current pre-eminence in this sector of the galaxy.

So why did she feel guilty?

She could only put this down to the consciousness of the weapons platform's original inhabitant—the AI Pragus whom she had absorbed. But only logic could tell her which of her actions and feelings might be dictated by it. Pragus was now part of her, just as the Librarian was. And the latter was the portion that caused her the most concern.

Logic told her that her earlier self would not have seen the salvagers as a threat, nor shut down the chameleonware upon realizing that the partially concealed platform acted as a lure. One look at the platform's weapons and attack pods would have been enough to drive them away. Had they been stupid enough to persist, she would have destroyed them. She wouldn't have done this in any great rage—merely like a human swatting an annoying fly. Certainly she would have felt no urge to grab and mine them for data and materials, because she would have known they had nothing of much use to her. All that was the Librarian, and she didn't understand it—there hadn't been a lot of thinking involved. It had been an instinct rooted in millions of years of history.

While the technology she had unleashed continued converting the weapons platform, the Client knew she had to investigate her aberration and correct it. Peering down yet again, she focused on the body she had created to steal data from the humans' minds. Responding to her mental prod, one of the grapplers below set into motion and picked up the corpse. She tracked it to the exit and out, along gangways and through tunnels, finally coming to one of the disposable lab units. The equipment inside was in fact the same as that which Pragus had used to examine the dead forms of her original body. The grappler took the corpse inside, and the lab unit began the examination she had quickly programmed.

As the surgical and scanning equipment set to work in there, she felt the momentary resurgence of a need to acquire data, as well as the urge to be in that lab unit doing it. She repressed it, but it still remained as an inchoate undercurrent to her logical mind. The chain-glass blades sliced the body open and other equipment scanned and weighed the various organs. It tracked their connections and nerves, and found the termini of those in a simple brain, in turn linked to an organic microwave emitter for transmitting data back to her main form. The equipment examined the tentacles closely, and she tried not to feel satisfaction at seeing how perfectly they matched those of the Librarian. Delving deeper, she saw the genetic changes she had made to create this form and finally there was nothing more to learn from it. Time to discard it . . . even that thought was driven by a deeper impulse.

This deeper urge was to seize hold of a prey, rip it apart and take everything useful from it, then dispose of the rest. To incorporate what she took in herself. The humans called their version of it the reptile brain—the part of their mind that drove fighting, fucking and fleeing. She had her own version, somehow made incredibly strong by her amalgamation with the Librarian. Did this mean that, though she was Species, at the core of her being she was truly Jain? Or had the Librarian tinkered with that inner reptile? Was it just the essence of that entity driving her?

As the Client pondered these things and considered how to examine and alter her own mind, it seemed that the outer world would not leave her alone. She had begun to design search engines to release into her consciousness, though as yet not even sure what to look for, when her instruments alerted her to a U-signature. She started searching near space for danger and, rising up from that undercurrent, for other bodies and minds to pillage.

It appeared a little way out from the gas giant and she recognized it instantly. The Client felt such an urge of acquisitiveness that she had fired up the platform's fusion engines before it became a conscious idea. She did, however, manage to prevent herself U-jumping directly to the spot, but only because that required more conscious thought and calculation. She fought against what now seemed to be her own instincts.

The object was a sphere fifty miles across. Dragon—the entity which had set her upon her course into the Prador Kingdom, to the remains of what had been her home planet and the Librarian. Here was a creature that had been knocking around the universe for millennia, if not longer. Dragon knew things she did not; things which Polity AIs and the prador were unaware of. It was a mysterious being that operated with baffling cunning in the realms of higher AI. Not only that, but the biology of the creature had proved to be incredibly complicated and it was probably a more adept engineer of that biology than the Client herself. Here was something that could render data and material gains orders of magnitude beyond what she could gain from mere salvagers, or anything else in either the Kingdom or the Polity.

And the Client felt it again: the hunger, the urge to incorporate, amalgamate, to take and to be.

"You chose a hot world to hide away in," said Dragon over U-com. "Mistake . . . But it was the agent you sent out . . . pointless search . . . the assassin attached herself to . . . who led her back to you."

It was a slap in the face and a wake-up that prompted further self-examination. Dragon was talking about her death. Those memories were vague since much had been lost when she was killed. But she knew she had sent out an agent ostensibly to seek out parts of the farcaster weapon she had created for the Polity. An assassin had tagged along with that agent to get to her. There had been some kind of gun and the agonizing death whose memory she flinched away from.

"I found her . . . the assassin. A little money gave me the location of your grave," said Dragon.

That could only mean that Dragon had obtained the remains from which her present self had been resurrected. It had ensured those remains were delivered to this weapons platform, which she then took over and escaped on from the accretion disc. She was a tool Dragon had employed and was perhaps still employing, though to what end was unclear.

The creature was drawing closer to the gas giant and sensors indicated it was using complicated field tech there. The Client now saw that Dragon was damaged: a massive hole in its surface and burns many miles long. Down in the gas clouds a maelstrom began turning, and out of the centre of this rose a plume. It steadily stretched out, finally reaching the sphere, whereupon it flooded inside, through the hole. Dragon's temperature rose and volcanic pores opened on its surface and began to bleed black smoke. Was it feeding? Its communications were sporadic, as if it was struggling to speak. The damage was severe and the Client felt regret at possible data lost. But if Dragon was wounded it might also be a weaker and easier prey.

"Data is what we need," said Dragon.

The Client hurriedly checked com for viruses, for it seemed as if the entity was reading her mind.

"The library of the Species provides . . . one of the Species, alive, is a counterbalance . . . another card in the game," Dragon added.

Finally the Client spoke. "You drove me to seek it."

"Give it to me," said Dragon.

"We must touch and be one," said the Client, feeling almost overwhelmed by the need to rip into Dragon and take everything it had.

"Yes."

Dragon fell silent, which compelled the Client further. She used every method available to reach out: induction warfare beams, shaped BIC lasers carrying a cornucopia of computer life, terahertz scanning, radar and X-ray radar, reception of emitted radiation from the gas giant that passed through the entity, even neutron emissions. She now saw the thing as clearly as was possible. It had been hollowed out by fire—burned internally down to its bones—yet it was still functional. It was sucking inside the materials it was drawing off the giant and changes were occurring. Perhaps these were repairs and growth—the black smokes from its surface the waste from that process.

The Client saw huge data. Wealth. Utterly suitable amalgamation.

"At the heart of all things Jain is that driving impulse," said Dragon.

"What do you know of the Jain?" the Client immediately asked.

She saw a sprout uncoiling in its internal spaces, miles in length, to spill out of the giant hole in its exterior. This thing then began to expand, turning into an intestinal tube. She saw it moving, peristalsis travelling along its length, shifting some growing object along it inside. Closer examination revealed an embryonic creature but detail remained unclear.

"I know much that is general . . . specifics needed." After a pause Dragon then added, "The accretion disc."

"Tell me things I do not know," said the Client. She was not prepared to share her knowledge about the accretion disc and how it was formed until some closer contact could be made. That contact was imperative; the amalgamation and theft, the ripping and discarding.

"The Jain were powerful," said Dragon, "constant warfare over millions of years . . . yet . . . local."

"Local?"

"Why did they not spread to occupy the whole galaxy?"

She reviewed the Librarian's memories and the forbidden data. This fact had not impinged upon her; had not roused any questions until now. The Jain had occupied a portion of the galaxy larger than the Polity, but they could have had everything. Their technology was such that they could even have spread beyond the galaxy. It made no sense.

"Do you have the answer to this?"

"You do," said Dragon, "when you can see beyond the need."

Somehow Dragon understood what was now driving her, but beyond that its statement was baffling. She focused on the thing it was making. It had grown to the size of a grav-car and was near the end of the peristaltic tube. She felt a glimmering of understanding and that driving need once more. And so she began altering the next birth in the chain of her being. Another part of her, with distant curiosity, recognized that she was generating a creature like the one she had recently dissected.

The peristaltic tube finally opened at its end, like an anus, to squeeze out the object from within. It tumbled into vacuum, squirming and amorphous, then slowly began to expand into its true form. It was red and bloody, as it folded out jointed limbs ending in spikes and claws from a trumpet-shaped body. The narrow end whipped out in a long jointed tail, culminating in a slicing blade, while the wide mouth spewed numerous tentacles—triangular-section tentacles. It was a challenge—a warrior from an opposing army stepping out to brandish his weapons and shout insults. The Client's response was frenetic feeding and the rapid growth of nutrient veins into her terminal womb. She began instituting further alterations to the form growing there, laminating armour and the addition of other cutting tools. The more distant part of herself noted that she was matching the challenge but not exceeding it.

Growth was rapid—dangerously fast and hot. With a thought, she opened valves and the hot atmosphere inside the cylinder roared out into vacuum, creating a plume of vapour ten miles long. Maintenance robots scuttled in with trailing hoses, and focused jets of cooling nitrogen on her terminal form. She knew this birth would kill that form, but it was necessary.

Finally the new birth oozed out, its mother form collapsing behind it, burning. She shed it with a snakish shrug of her entire body. The sack-like caul throbbed and expanded as it dropped. She shut off grav but it continued to fall. Then a limb ripped through the caul, flicked against the tree and propelled it up and away from the base of the cylinder. Overhead she opened a hatch on hard vacuum. The new form tore away the rest of its caul to reveal a black, multi-limbed monstrosity. It bore some resemblance to a terran scorpion, but with a mass of the data-ripping tentacles fountaining out where its head should have been.

And she was in—utterly ferocious and intent on prey, as she squatted atop her life-support cylinder and gazed towards the distant Dragon. She wanted to launch herself and get this started. But it was futile wasting the energy to propel herself through vacuum while the platform was taking her closer. She would need the energy for the coming fight, the coming . . . amalgamation.

But still, she shrieked her challenge across vacuum, recognizing it was again the same as the one the Librarian had shrieked at her. Dragon replied to it immediately and correctly with a scream of his own, and she finally lost herself.

"I need data. You need data," Dragon added—the previous exchange just the inconsequential blaring of trumpets. "This was always their way."

She barely heard.

TRIKE

The old ship settled with creaking and occasional cracking noises from beyond the bridge. They'd made all the repairs they could and, apart from the lack of an AI and a U-space drive, the vessel was sound. The creaks and groans were just unfamiliar, and Trike grew angry at his tendency to flinch and look for something to break at every sound.

He was angry at everything.

He turned, unable to look at Angel even as he addressed him. "So where the hell are we going to deliver this message, and why couldn't it be sent by com laser or radio?"

"The recipients have gone dark," Angel replied. "With the Clade down here, any form of com could give away their location."

"So how do you know where these recipients are?"

Trike looked to Cog and knew for sure that Cog had been told and this information was being kept from him. "And who are they?" They didn't trust him. He stepped towards them. Maybe if he squeezed Cog's neck just a little . . .

"Do you see?" Cog asked mildly.

Trike halted, it impinging on him why they might not trust him.

Cog continued, "When we get out there it's almost certain we'll run into the Clade. What happens with you then? Can I trust that you won't go completely off your trolley and chasing after them? If we tell you who we're going to see and where they are, what happens when the Clade finally brings you down?"

"They'll get nothing from me," Trike growled. He dipped his head, trying to conceal what he felt sure was written on his face. That the reason he might go "chasing off" had more to do with getting away from Angel than going towards the Clade.

"It's good that you're so sure of that. I'm not."

A crunching sound ensued. Trike realized he had put one of the bridge seats between himself and the other two, and his hands were now imbedded in the composite. Forcing control, he unclenched his fingers and lifted his hands from the chair. Pieces fell to the floor.

"I would rather leave you behind," said Cog. "But we both know that's not going to happen."

"Okay." Trike nodded. Cog was right, because Trike didn't know what he was going to do when he got out there. "We go—I'll try to stay with you."

"And being covert was something else we were aiming for," Cog warned.

"Okay."

"Time to go," said Angel.

Trike stepped back to the door where he'd dumped his things. He picked up his pack, took out his laser carbine, as well as some grenades that he put in his pocket, then put the pack on. He turned, with the carbine in his left hand and his machete in his right. He had enough control and calm to note how Cog flinched at the sight of him so kitted out. Cog and Angel were also armed. Cog had his particle weapon with a gigawatt energy canister screwed in place, while Angel had somehow obtained two pulse rifles he'd wired together. Doubtless this ship contained stores Trike didn't know about, but he suppressed the angry questions he wanted to ask about that.

"It changed nothing," said Cog.

"What?"

"You used the memtab."

Trike stared at him, momentarily at a loss. Something had changed but it was difficult to express. He'd shut his madness away behind a door in his mind, but that door was not impermeable. The madness leaked out as rage. What had Cog's excised memories done? They had reminded him of his insanity so that now, underneath the rage, arose fear too. This was not helpful.

"It's time to go," was all he said.

Cog shrugged and turned away.

Angel led the way down from the bridge and into the hold, the ramp door already folding down to reveal morning gloom. Rain plinked on metal but apparently the fierce storm of the night was ebbing. Tramping down, Trike searched on all sides for enemies. The ship sat on a road leading out of the city. A few ground cars were scattered here and there, while a gravlev cargo truck lay on its side across the road. In the distance he could see a stream of ground vehicles moving away from the city, but no sign of movement close by.

"Over there." Angel pointed.

An enclosed pedway ran alongside the road, its movable floor stationary since an explosion had blown open a chunk of it. But Trike could see how it would offer them protection into the city. As Cog and Angel headed over, he didn't follow. If they stayed under cover the Clade might not see them, then how could he—

"Trike!" Cog bellowed.

Trike forced himself into motion, catching up with them as they climbed up through the tangled debris from the explosion. For a moment there, he'd felt a kind of freedom. But with them he was constrained again—back in his constant battle to keep his anger under control and trying to stop himself attacking the android. Soon they were in the tunnel, gazing down at two corpses, ripped open, of a man and a woman. Whether the explosion had done this or the Clade was debatable.

"Why is no one helping?" Trike asked, trying to engage with his surroundings.

"The Polity is keeping out for tactical reasons. Emergency response here is holding back because of the Clade," Cog replied, obviously not happy about that.

"Tactical reasons," Trike repeated dully.

"Quite," said Cog.

They moved on and Trike soon saw that the two corpses behind weren't unique. Bodies in various stages of dismemberment were scattered all the way along the pedway and in one place carefully mounded, as if some Clade units had become OCD about neatness. A hundred feet in, Cog shrugged off his pack.

"I don't know why the Clade isn't here yet," he said, "but it's certain it'll come."

"Maybe we're not relevant," Angel suggested.

Cog nodded as he took an item out of his pack. Trike recognized the limpet-like object he stuck to the side of the tunnel. It had a yield that would do to the tunnel what had been done further back.

"Air disturbances," Cog explained. "But exclusive of anything walking, or running."

It took Trike a moment to catch up with what Cog meant. The Clade would have seen their ship land, and that units hadn't come immediately was puzzling. If or when they did, they'd go to the ship first then into the tunnel. The mine Cog had just laid would detonate on detecting air disturbances and destroy Clade units when they got close. But any human or Golem who wandered into the tunnel wouldn't trigger it. Trike felt glad of that but also found it unsatisfying—better to rip the Clade apart with his own hands.

"Okay," said Cog. "Let's move properly."

They set off at a steady distance-eating jog. Cog set charges every few hundred yards, waving them on, then running to catch up. As they travelled, Trike gazed through the glass sides of the walkway. He could see pillars of smoke in the city, patches of wreckage, fallen buildings and everywhere lay dismembered bodies. At one point he saw a building twist, as if some god had grabbed its top and tried to undo it like a jar, and then it went down. But mostly, he focused on the occasional glinting shapes he saw moving through the sky and his grip tightened on his machete. Surely the Clade flew there. Finally, after an hour of this, Angel turned into a walkway station like one of many they had passed before.

"Here," he said. "Nearest access to the storm drains."

"This is where it might get dodgy," said Cog, eyeing Trike. "No point telling you to be ready, is there?"

Trike gave a sharp nod of agreement.

Access to the beltway was via a series of belts running in parallel, which brought pedestrians up to the speed of the main beltway. They weren't moving, though a motor below ground out smoke and the smell of burned metal. Passing between monitor bollards, they moved out into a wide shopping precinct. Wreckage here had been strewn by a big hover transport which had come down and torn through the buildings on one side. Trike spotted a group of about twenty people making their way through it, some of them heavily armed. One raised a hand in acknowledgement but the group moved swiftly on.

"Some change," said Cog, pointing.

Trike peered up into the sky and, when he saw the hundreds of Clade units sweeping across, he worried about his own senses. He had been watching for them constantly, hadn't he? So how had he missed them?

"The access cover is at the end there." Angel pointed further up the precinct.

Trike stared at the Clade. The swarm AI resembled a shoal of thin fish, quite similar to species he had seen on his home world of Spatterjay. Each unit was perfectly aligned and the whole mass swirled round and round in the sky. This appeared to him like preparation for departure, which was disappointing. Then a nasty grin twisted his face as one part of the shoal separated from the rest, turning towards the street, and began to descend.

"Move!" Cog bellowed.

Trike ran with the other two. Why not? He knew they wouldn't reach the end of the precinct before the Clade arrived.

BLADE

Blade was in a million pieces, as if it had exploded in the reconstruction bay. But the million pieces were interwoven with robots, ranging from the microscopic to construction spiders the size of trees. The sub-AI reconstruction system stood ready with the attack ship's original schematic. Materials had been routed, replacement components in the dreadnought's stores had been requested and autofactories were ready to make other parts. The dreadnought's AI, Caliban, had waited till now, when Blade was completely open and vulnerable, before sending it. Blade had expected this and was prepared.

The forensic AI bore the appearance of a crinoid or "sea lily," a terran echinoderm. Its shape was that of an accumulation of undulating feathers, whose stems connected at a central point. Those feathers were metallic grey and gold, and consisted of millions of probing nano-tendrils, shearfield-edged chain-glass ribbons and atomic deconstructors. The thing was a mass of intelligence, discrete processing and horribly efficient tools ten feet across. Their purpose was to take things apart, if necessary to a molecular level, to see how they worked. Or, in this case, to see what had been done to them. Of course, Blade understood the necessity: Blade was not operating as per usual and its mind had obviously been seriously damaged. It had been in close contact with a hostile swarm AI and actually been inside a seriously dodgy alien. Blade was a danger that had to be investigated, probed, analysed.

"Well, you can fuck off," said Blade.

"I am Mobius Clean," said the AI. "There is nothing to fear."

"Yeah, that's why you waited until I was in pieces before coming."

"That was because of what I might have to fear."

"Uhuh." Blade now drew round on a jointed arm one component that had not been dismantled. "You mean sort of like this?"

The chunk of technology was five feet across, from the mirrored throat of its barrel back to the charged particulate loader at its other end. It was a mass of pipes, superconducting coils, pressure vessels and laser injector rings. Big, heavy and nasty.

The crinoid forensic AI halted, just outside the tunnel it had travelled along to get to the bay. Its feathery arms no longer undulated gently but stuck straight out and vibrated. Blade was reminded of a frightened dog's hair standing on end.

"I am not sure what you hope to achieve with this," said Clean.

"I want to speak to my brief."

"Archaic and amusing," commented Clean. "You understand that I am fully capable of repairing crystal—you can be what you were before."

"I like me just the way I am now, thanks, and I still want to talk to my brief."

"Communication failure . . . please elaborate."

"Since telemetry from this fleet is constantly being transmitted to Windermere's fleet and thence back to Earth Central, that will become clear soon enough," said Blade. "First there is this."

Blade opened a connection it had made earlier to the reconstruction bay sub-AI. In there, it reached into the schematic of its original form of a black-ops attack ship. The schematic was read only, but Blade soon altered that and began feeding in changes. Many related to the program it had loaded from Dragon, while others were its own design. The radical alteration took a whole minute and Blade was aware that both Clean and Caliban were watching intently.

"Interesting," Clean said when the changes were complete. "This still does not negate the fact that you must be examined."

"Are you sure about this?" asked Caliban.

"Never been more sure about something," Blade replied. "And no examination is necessary."

As if in response to that, Mobius Clean moved further into the bay, feathery tendrils undulating again. Blade realized that the forensic AI was no longer concerned about the particle cannon. The reason why became evident a second later when a shearfield activated and sliced through the jointed arm supporting it. A construction spider swept in from the side and snatched it away. Blade made no response—just waited. It was all delaying tactics anyway. The attack ship AI was waiting for that telemetry update to go through and hoping for a response. U-com from here to the fleet, and thence to Earth, was not exactly instantaneous, but not far from it.

"Desist." The word came through as a short quack because the AI saying it had spoken quickly, before compensating for the temporal effects of U-com. When next it spoke, Earth Central was more measured. "I had considered an option like this," it said, "and was even preparing for it."

"This still does not negate the need for examination!" Mobius Clean insisted.

A brief pause ensued, during which it became evident EC had a short, private chat with the forensic AI. It abruptly rolled up its feathery appendages and, as a brain-like ball, shot into the access tunnel and disappeared.

"So what do you think?" asked Blade.

"I think that were you restored to your former self you would not contemplate this," the ruling AI of the Polity replied. "However, change is growth, you are at the location, you have the motivation . . . and I have no particular need for a black-ops attack ship there."

"I will withdraw," said Caliban.

The dreadnought AI retreated and control of the reconstruction bay, along with its sub-AI, fell to Blade. It was now free to do . . . what it would do.

"So that's a yes?" it said.

"Proceed," EC replied.

GEMMELL

Gemmell stood up to watch a replay of the explosion. He saw that an old ore hauler had surfaced into realspace some distance out from the prador fleet here, and then accelerated towards it under fusion.

"What the hell?" he asked.

"The prador told it to stand off and delivered warnings," said Morgaine, "but still they were a little hasty on the trigger."

"Is it that on edge here?" Gemmell wondered.

"It is, but there are other factors involved. The prador knew where that ship came from."

He turned and looked at her, then wondered why, because he could see no expression on her face. She wasn't even using her vocal cords and mouth to speak to him.

She explained, "Orlandine has for centuries had a diverse collection of war and assassin drones on call. They are the ones that operated the runcibles she used during the conflict with the AI Erebus, and who built the runcibles she used at the accretion disc. They were stationed in the outer system here and Diana told me to keep a watch on them, since there's no telling what they might do."

"Do the prador dislike war drones any more than they dislike us?" Gemmell asked.

"These are drones that weren't very accepting of the truce between the Kingdom and the Polity—rather like the rebel prador who gathered in the Graveyard after the war."

"So just the kind that Erebus would have recruited in its fight against the Polity?"

"I think even Erebus would have had problems keeping this lot in order. They are loyal to Orlandine but, to the prador mind, are the sort of loose cannons that could turn things nasty here. The prador probably thought they were trying for a kamikaze run."

Gemmell reviewed the size of the explosion in his mind. It hadn't been a particularly big one, so there was no way had it contained a load of CTDs—antimatter bombs tended to be a bit more . . . dramatic.

"But apparently it wasn't a kamikaze run," he said. "So what was the point of that?"

"The ore carrier was a distraction—on automatic with no one aboard. Sensor data indicate the prador are now on high alert and watching the outer system intently."

"Ah . . ." Gemmell understood, just a second before a great cluster of indicator tags appeared onscreen above Jaskor. The drones had sent the ore carrier to make the prador concentrate their attention outwards, and then made a U-jump dangerously close to the planet—well inside the perimeter the ships of the two small fleets had formed.

"Firing," Morgaine intoned.

Why the hell was she opening fire now? With his attention on the screen, he reached out and grabbed the indicators, pulling the prador fleet into view. Then he gridlinked for tactical data and found himself allowed into the main tactical feed. He could hear the chatter, see the battle stats and intended aims.

Unbelievable . . .

Morgaine had just railgunned the prador fleet, and the other Polity ships had opened fire a moment later. Energy readings aboard the reavers and other ships changed as they began throwing up defences. A second later, the railgun slugs reached the prador hardfields. Was he watching the start of a battle here? Maybe, though having absorbed the tactical data, he could now understand Morgaine's intent. Everything depended on how the prador reacted.

Multiple explosions blossomed around the prador ships, lighting hardfields like polarized glass scales floating in vacuum. But the size of the blasts and energy readings were all off. Then things started to get a little hazy—even his screen view had to continuously correct itself. Space filled with glittering surfaces. Reavers and prador destroyers suddenly popped into existence. The ships that were first visible seemed to ride over distortions and shift position by thousands of miles. Checking Polity sensor data, he saw whole bands of the spectrum completely blanked out.

"So when did the tech get rugged enough to survive inside a railgun slug?" he asked.

"About a century ago," replied Morgaine.

The Polity fleet had not fired destructive weapons at the prador, but slugs carrying chaff. It overloaded sensors, created ghost images and disrupted positional data. It had rendered the prador blind and confused and, Gemmell noticed, had the required effect. He saw that the drones and drone vehicles were now down in low atmosphere and some were even landing. It was to be hoped that the prador wouldn't feel inclined to open fire on them, especially since they were over and around the planet's main city. However, the prador did know the position of all the Polity ships and, typically, responded.

The deck jerked under his feet and the screen view turned momentarily blinding. Still keyed into the tactical feed, he saw in his mind real railgun slugs impacting on Polity hardfields, the burning comets of molten projectors ejecting into vacuum, particle beams slicing across. He saw an attack ship spewing projectors, then tracked end to end with a particle beam. Next came some massive impact on a destroyer, blowing away its back end and sending it tumbling. He listened in on a terse exchange.

"You have divined the purpose of my fusillade," said Morgaine.

"You have allowed rogue drones to reach the planet," replied Ksov—the prador nominally in charge of the fleet here. "I am seeking clarification."

"Desist," said Morgaine, "or I will be forced to respond."

"Our response was required," said Ksov.

"And why was it required?"

Ksov did not reply but Gemmell knew why it was, anyway. It wasn't payback for the chaff, or even because she had prevented him firing on the drones, if that had been his intention. It was just to affirm that the prador were no walkover. It was notice that they *would* respond and was a demand for respect, military style.

"My apologies," said Morgaine, even as one Polity dreadnought lost a square mile of armour in a titanic explosion. "I was not sure if you were aware that the rogue drones in question are actually employees of Orlandine, and of Dragon, and come under the agreements we made for the independent state here."

"Orlandine is dead and Dragon is gone again," said Ksov.

Now only stray missiles struck hardfields because the prador had ceased firing. It seemed Ksov had received his reply from the prador admiral out at the accretion disc. Gemmell watched the tactical whole for a while longer, then began limiting his connection. Two small fleets faced off above Jaskor, but small was a relative term. If they went fully head-to-head, it would take the flip of a coin to decide who'd win. Certainly the planet below would be a loser of the smoking ruin kind. He stepped back to his chair and sat down, and felt a trickle of sweat run down his side from his armpit.

8

So often I come back to that enigma that is Dragon. Four spheres of it were on the planet Aster Colora before it made its dramatic departure. One of them turned up at the planet Samarkand and was responsible for the runcible disaster there. It was subsequently blown to pieces by some shady Polity agent, about whom I can glean no information at all. Another of them is AWOL—nobody has any data on it at all. Two of them entered the Jain-tech accretion disc during the Erebus debacle and one may have been destroyed—confirmation is lacking. The last remaining is at the accretion disc assisting in the defence there against Jain technology. Now, here's something interesting: I know that when Dragon was first found, its spheres were just a mile or so across. Then, in a very short time, the two that entered the accretion disc were fifty miles across and highly weaponized—fast growth and big alterations. I also know that Dragon is quite capable of crafting complex life forms. It created the race of dracomen who are now regarded as Polity citizens. So, here's a thought: can Dragon reproduce itself? Could it be that the missing sphere is the template kept well out of danger, while the others jog about the galaxy causing trouble? Could it be that even now, on some remote world or in some dense gas cloud, Dragon spheres are sprouting and growing like mushrooms? Much as I find Dragon frustrating, opaque, irritating and smug, I certainly hope so. The universe just wouldn't be the same without him.

—from *How It Is* by Gordon

TRIKE

They came in at the end of the precinct in a perfectly even formation.

"Okay," said Cog, "we have to go through them." But by then Trike was already running.

A violet-blue beam, sizzling in the air, stabbed past him to the right. Cog's first particle beam shot struck one unit straight in the face. The blast stopped it in mid-air, shedding molten metal. It took it for a moment, then shot sideways, crashing through a door. Angel nailed one high up, twinned pulse shots drawing a line of bright yellow punctuations to his target. The effect was not as powerful as Cog's weapon but Angel's aim was better. The thing dodged and weaved in the air but the pulse shots kept hitting it at a point just behind its head. Finally it had had enough and dropped out of sight on a rooftop. Other units began to shift their formation, then, in a joint decision, the formation broke. Clade units crashed through doors and windows in the surrounding buildings. But Trike knew it wasn't over and that they were only utilizing the cover available.

Directly ahead of Trike, a foamstone slab shattered and a unit rose up out of it in an explosion of debris and a fountain of water. It must have traced the route of some underground water main. One-handed, he fired his carbine, slicing down its length, but it just sizzled and blew steam as it looped towards him. Angry joy in the pit of his stomach flooded into his right arm and with a roar he brought his machete down squarely on its head. With a sound like a sledgehammer hitting a bell, it cut in, and jammed. The unit shrugged and he felt the machete torn from his hand, but he didn't stop. Dropping his carbine to hang from its strap over his shoulder, he lunged forwards and grabbed the thing as if to strangle it.

"Fucking die!"

As he slammed it on the ground, he saw another unit crash down nearby, its body hot and smoking. The thing tried to rise up, but twinned pulse fire blew its already semi-molten head apart. Even as he registered this, Trike's own opponent's tail whipped over and stabbed in. He felt its point go into his shoulder but jam, just like his machete had. Rage and power boiling in him, he brought a knee down on the centre of its body and heaved upwards. With a crackling sound, the length of spine-like body between his knee and his hands grew long and thin and oddly translucent. He twisted, hammered its head against the ground, then released one hand and brought his fist down on it, hard, driving its head into the foamstone. He grabbed the machete handle and tugged, but lost hold of it as the unit tried to rise again. It shook itself and the machete fell away, swinging round towards him. Its head was open, exposing tangled silvery electronics. He lunged with both hands, jamming his fingers into the gap, then heaved it apart. With a *crump* and an electrical discharge, the head separated and the unit finally sagged.

No time for victory. Trike dived and rolled, coming up in a crouch with his machete held two-handed as another unit skimmed over his head. Everything knotted up in his core came flooding out. He spun and hacked and this time the weapon didn't jam—the Clade unit he hit simply fell in half. He swung again and, with a high ringing, took the top off its head. Glancing round, he saw Angel stab long fingers into the eye of one unit, then discard it. The thing coiled up into a knotted ball and dropped heavily, as he next opened fire on another exploding out of a nearby wall. Cog was down, two of the Clade wrapped around his body. Then he heaved himself up, holding one by the tail and slinging it away from him. It coiled round in mid-air and simply exploded, the blast sending Cog and his remaining opponent bouncing along the street. Cog had used one of his mines.

Trike started running towards Cog, but a tail smacking into his chest brought him to a shuddering halt. Suddenly the air all around him was full of the things. Bellowing, he began to hack, his machete ringing and shedding sparks, the handle growing hot in his hand. Metallic vertebrae and severed amphibian heads bounced on the ground. Deep in his mind he knew the odds against him were too great, but it didn't seem to matter. It felt as if a reactor had fired up in his chest to power his limbs. Then came the first deep *crump* of an impact and the units drew away from him. He saw a unit nearby simply disappear into the paving, and then that erupted in a violent, sun-hot explosion.

"Run!" Cog shouted, discarding the mangled remains of his last opponent.

He did run, but in pursuit of Clade units fleeing before him. Further vertebrae and severed Clade heads rained down, but this wasn't him. He looked up to see a thing like a giant mantis amidst the Clade, limbs glinting razor light as they hacked and slashed. Further along the street a big object came on hard, blowing out a wave of debris. Then it casually climbed out of the crater it had made, spitting high-intensity lasers, snatching and dismembering Clade units with heavy tentacles.

Ahead, Angel had hauled up a large grating and tossed it aside. Trike stumbled to a halt at the lip of this then turned. Behind him, what looked like a giant water scorpion stabbed its forelimbs into a unit and held the thing there shaking, then glowing like a light bulb filament, and finally exploding. Another like a great clam of brassy metal hurtled over with a sonic crackling of railgun slugs, Clade units blown to pieces all around it.

"War drones," said Angel.

Trike turned to look at him as he dropped into the storm drain. Angel was going wherever it was Dragon had directed him, but Trike decided he would stay. Here he had an enemy he could fight without reserve, while being near Angel was . . . difficult. Cog, however, had other ideas. The big Old Captain slammed into Trike hard, cabled arms wrapped around his body, and hurled the both of them into the drain. As they hit the water Trike shoved at Cog's face, hard, and the man's grip on him slipped away. But the flood had taken hold and his massive strength availed him nothing—it was carrying him away from the Clade. Briefly he saw Angel and reached out to clamp a hand on the android's arm. He still held his machete and suddenly had no reason not to use it, at all. But Angel looked into his face and suddenly his arm turned slippery. Trike lost his hold and the android slid away, buoyant and supple as a silver fish.

In his rage, Trike's grip on coherent thought deserted him and, with that, his ability to even swim. His densely packed body took him down. He tumbled along through a muddy maelstrom and took his first breath of water straight into his lungs. Managing to rise up out of it, he saw something strange. A mass of tendrils, tentacles, worms flopping through the water towards him. It struck him, knocking him back down into the muddy swirl. He felt it crawling along his limbs, under his clothing, then sudden stabbing pains from head to foot. Another breath of water and blackness edged into his mind. Yet, in that blackness he saw stars and then a glimpse of a gas giant, moons and half-dismantled structures floating in vacuum. Then the last dregs of his consciousness drained away from him.

THE CLIENT

The Client resided utterly in her remote form as it squatted atop her life-support cylinder. The thing Dragon had sent drifted through vacuum—probably like her it was saving energy for the imminent encounter. At length, Weapons Platform Mu fell into orbit of the gas giant and swung round it, putting Dragon and its remote out of direct sight. But she left attack pods scattered around the orb to keep watch and saw when Dragon's remote abruptly fired up a drive to send it closer to the giant.

Next, swinging back to come adjacent to Dragon, the Client slowed the platform, finally bringing it to a relative halt. It was time. She launched from her cylinder and, under an internal EM drive, sped through vacuum towards the other remote. Even as she did this she saw the purpose in the other's change of course. Dragon had set a time limit on this battle, intending for both remotes to fall into oblivion in the gas giant. She issued orders and, in response, those of her attack pods that were further away fired up their fusion drives to bring them in. Four of them, close over Dragon, began sowing U-space disruptor mines. If Dragon expected only a battle of remotes it was in for a surprise.

The distance steadily shortened and the other remote turned, spreading out its tentacles like a squid preparing to attack. She extended her own and, in special portions of her mind, prepared viruses, worms and other hostile computer *organisms* that were the unseen weapons of attack. Closer still and she felt a warfare beam latch on. That was unexpected—Dragon launching an attack before they were physically together. Yet a deeper part of herself asked why a logical tactic to employ was unexpected. She felt it sweeping through her, generating data-stealing viruses, and countered it as best she could. She seethed, because Dragon was now learning about her remote while she knew nothing of its. Then they slammed together.

Tentacles writhed around each other for access. She hooked in with one of her sharp forelimbs and severed through one of Dragon's, while it in turn skewered another of hers and held it back. Tumbling above the swirling royal blue, jade green and red cloud of the gas giant, they ripped at each other. She stabbed her tail in, but it glanced off armour, so she stabbed again and again, gradually chipping a way in. Tentacles worked through to a surface in the head of the creature she fought, while micro-diamond drills and lasers began to bore into it. Dragon had found a similar point of access in her. She felt dislocated pain as he hacked into the joint of one of her legs with a hatchet limb and cut through. Next, redirecting her tail, she began to stab at the joints of Dragon's limbs.

Before she or Dragon broke through, the Client fired up the EM drive of her remote again to draw them away from the gas giant. Dragon's immediate response: another kind of drive, which she read via the sensors in the platform as a U-space distortion, pulled them down. Finally she punched through and began injecting fibres, just a second ahead of Dragon doing the same. They both shut off their drives, preserving energy, and little difference had been made to the time limit on this encounter. Now the real fight began.

The Client found an organo-metal nodule and, from a microfibre, spread a neural mesh to capture it. Scanning revealed the mind of this remote to be distributed throughout its body, which made things more difficult. She filed that away for future reference, should she make herself another such remote. And she felt a brief satisfaction at having already learned something before the data rape truly began. Other fibres spearing into its body found further nodes and made further connections.

Meanwhile, Dragon connected into her brain with brutal efficiency. A data world began to form, like two immiscible fluids swirling in a ball. It was a representation of a connection between two larger entities—one down in that fifty-mile-wide sphere and one in the weapons platform. As this firmed, the Client got her first true look at Dragon's mind and felt a brief fear, swiftly overcome by lust. And the two bodies continued to tear at each other, pieces of armour and chopped-off limbs orbiting their writhing forms.

ORLANDINE

My name is Orlandine, she thought. This was reality but it did not feel real. Memories continued to surface but they possessed no emotional content. She knew the prador in charge here was called Croos, and that she had met him once when the prador established their enclave on Jaskor. But instead of thinking about the present situation, and the events that led up to it, she pondered the strangeness of prador names. Some of them related directly to how they sounded in the prador language—but these were usually sounds that no human vocal cords could make. Vrost or Vrell were buzzing clicks followed by an odd hissing, while others like Croos bore no relation at all to the prador name.

"The flood will not have taken him far," said the Old Captain, Cog.

She gazed at the man. He was wide and heavy, as his kind often were. She tried to remember when last she had come across someone like him but the memories were confusing. She knew she had seen and talked with hoopers, but had no recollection of actually being in the presence of one. She then understood that this was because she had encountered them as a distributed being, here on Jaskor, while her physical body had been remote from them. Cog looked back at her, gave her a tired smile and shook his head before looking away again.

"There are Clade units in the tunnels," said Croos. "Not so many now—after those war drones hit them, the main swarm moved on." Croos, who in his satin pink and black armour was larger than his brethren, waved a claw. One of the other prador in this big underground chamber scuttled over to a door, which slid open to let it out then slammed shut behind it.

"And where they are going is why we were sent to you," said the individual that accompanied Cog. A prador held this one's arms in its massive claws while another had a particle cannon focused on his head.

This was Angel. He had been a legate who survived the destruction of his master the AI Erebus. She knew a lot of detail about him: how he, in a wormship, had been integral to bringing the Jain soldier to the accretion disc. He was a dangerous creature, hence the reaction of these prador to him. Yet Cog vouched for him, said that he had changed sides. This was all fascinating, but more fascinating to Orlandine was how his form had become more human. It had never been clear whether legates were something Erebus made or were Golem the AI had seized control of and converted for its purposes.

"We will get to that," said Croos, swinging towards Angel. "Explain to me why I should not have you ripped apart and why I should trust you."

Angel dipped his head for a moment then said, "I was controlled by a Jain AI you know as the Wheel. Once it had what it wanted it abandoned me on the world of the Cyberat. There I was . . . massively damaged. Dragon, seeking data from me, repaired me. I have now all but returned to my original form of a Golem android."

Ah, thought Orlandine, her internal question answered.

"Still not good enough," said Croos.

"I serve no one now," said Angel. "I choose to ally myself with humans, the AIs, prador and Dragon against the threat of the Jain. If you are going to destroy me then at least listen to Dragon's message."

"I don't particularly trust Dragon either," said Croos. "But go ahead, deliver your message."

Angel sighed and continued, "It is not certain what is happening here and at the accretion disc. But what is clear is that the Clade is working for the Wheel and against our interests. It tried to kill Orlandine." Angel turned and looked at her, and she felt an odd twist inside. "And now, Dragon surmises, its next target is the Ghost Drive Facility."

"This is true—that's where the bulk of the swarm went," Croos agreed. "Apparently the commander of the Polity fleet thinks the Clade wants to seize control of the weapons platforms through the facility and has ordered her ships here to destroy it should the Clade enter. My compatriots above don't think they can stop that and are not sure if they should try to."

"That is too simple," said Angel. "Why would the Clade try to seize control of that facility in the full knowledge it would be stopped?"

"You're the one with all Dragon's answers. You tell me."

"The Clade wants that reaction. It wants the facility either destroyed or unusable," Angel explained. "Do you have sight of what it is doing now?"

After a long pause Croos said, "It is at the facility but not actually trying to enter it—it's settling in the surrounding area."

"Exactly. It hoped the Polity ships would act prematurely and destroy the facility upon confirming it was heading there. But it doesn't actually want to expend its life to ensure that."

"But it could send in part of itself," interjected Cog. "We know it's not averse to losing a few of its units."

Angel shook his head. "No, a few units would not get past the defences. It would take a massed attack with heavy losses of the entire Clade to penetrate, and even then it is possible it would fail." Angel looked across at Orlandine. "You built that place well. It is not even certain that the Polity ships could destroy it."

Orlandine smiled at the compliment, which in turn caused memories to surface in her mind about its construction. An array of fusion reactors had gone in underground first of all. Advanced hardfield generators were next—their ejection ports carved down into a cave system below. The thing was built to withstand orbital bombardment. The Polity fleet could destroy it, but a side effect would be huge human casualties and most of the continent here rendered uninhabitable.

"Then what is the Clade's aim?" asked Croos.

"It does not want anyone else having access to the facility and to the weapons platforms. The main person it didn't want there, it tried to kill: Orlandine."

"Why?"

"Dragon does not yet understand exactly why, but it seems apparent that the Wheel's plan was for the weapons platforms to respond exactly as they are programmed. It wants stasis—the situation to remain as it is. Only Orlandine, or perhaps some agent of Earth Central, is capable of changing that."

"Very well, you have delivered your message," said Croos. "How are we supposed to respond to it?"

Again Angel turned to look at her. "Dragon wants you to get Orlandine inside that facility—ready to respond to whatever develops out at the accretion disc, and ready to make the weapons platforms do what she wants."

Croos dipped his body in acknowledgement. "I see. Dragon learned from the prador fleet that she is still alive but did not understand that the Orlandine we have here is probably incapable of talking to the weapons platforms. That's if she even manages to survive getting into the facility."

Sitting cross-legged on the stony floor, Orlandine noted that they were all looking at her, and dipped her head in embarrassment. She knew she wasn't what she had been, because more and more she was remembering that powerful haiman: Orlandine. She felt small, ineffectual.

Human time, she thought, *in reality*.

"But we have to try," said Angel.

Croos emitted a very human sigh. "Yes, we do."

TRIKE

First came hunger. He saw his hand stab down, clawed fingers ripping into a soft, slimy body. He pulled out a great mass of dripping flesh and crammed it into his mouth, which seemed to open wider than it had ever done before, and swallowed it whole. Then another handful and another. The mudfish flopped for a while then grew still. He ripped out organs and swallowed them down, pulled out its flat hyaline bones and crunched them, shattered its bony skull and consumed it. Soon it was all gone and he was scraping up debris. He looked around for more and noted other remains, so crawled over and sucked them down. Obviously there had been more than one fish. When nothing remained but green blood and slime, he scooped up a handful of gravel and ate that too.

Am I a bird? he wondered, and it was his first coherent thought.

The hunger would not go away. It seemed the void in his belly reflected a void in his mind that somehow expanded beyond the confines of his skull. His attention slid in the direction of that *opening* and he saw stars again, with a sense of himself floating somewhere, far out, far away. He felt a visceral terror and couldn't shake it, then abruptly fell back into himself.

The craving remained and he became more aware of his immediate surroundings. He lay in a damp tunnel branching off and up from the flood. Debris was piled just a little way from him and among it he saw another dead mudfish. He started to crawl but some fragment of humanity intruded. He stood up abruptly, slamming his head into the ceiling. No pain, but broken stone rained down around him. He ducked, puzzled that he had misjudged the size of the tunnel. Now he felt uncomfortable, restricted. His clothing was tight, constricting too. Gazing at his arms, he saw that the fabric of his sleeves was stretched taut and high up his forearm. The envirosuit he wore had been made to expand, and contract, to fit any form. He was about to unclip an expansion point for arm length when he noticed something odd about his limb. Without thinking, he ran a fingernail down one sleeve to split it open and tore it away. Doing the same with the other, he then inspected both of his arms.

Thoughts rolled slowly through his mind, and he remembered that when he left Cog's ship his limbs had grown, but they'd been thin and bony. Now they were thick hams, and that wasn't the only change. Brown and white growths veined his blue skin, as if he had lain in a jungle for centuries and lianas had entangled him. Some understanding crept in. The thing that had hit him in the water. A parasite?

Engaging . . .

The word fled through his mind, through his extended mind, and he sensed something locking on. It was as if a distant portion of himself had reached in to create invisible structures in the void. Again he felt terror and pulled away. As he did so, a squirming also seemed to take hold throughout his body *and* his mind.

He reached the pile of detritus and squatted down, grabbing the dead mudfish and dragging it out. Hunger stilled further thought, or straying into the unknowable, while he consumed the thing. Thought did not return till he found himself picking up other debris and eating it: degrading coffee cups, a chunk of rhizome sprouting blue reeds, the washed-white bone of an animal. He discarded this last and slumped down on his backside with his hands over his face. There he felt something and probed prominent vein-like growths on his cheek, his forehead and entering one nostril. What the hell was happening to him? But he was horrified to realize he knew, that Cog's excised memories had shown him. He had to get out of here.

Trike stood, keeping his head low so he didn't smack it against the tunnel roof. He could see now that he hadn't misjudged the height of the roof, just his own size. He gazed at the flood for a long moment then turned around and began making his way up the tunnel. He had no idea where it would take him but returning to the water frightened him, though whatever had happened to him there wasn't clear. Trudging up the tunnel he noticed something. Although he felt confused and a little hazy about recent events, the constant boiling rage inside him had settled—as if whatever else was happening in his mind simply had no room for it.

Movement ahead.

He kept walking, stooped down, and it swung round the corner of a side tunnel, sweeping straight towards him. The Clade was searching the tunnels, he realized, as two more units followed the first one out. He felt the other activity in his mind still and a sharp sense of danger that seemed to rise beyond mere physical threat. He searched down at his waist but had lost his machete. Then he reached into his pocket, found a single grenade and pulled it out. Dangerous in here but perhaps not so dangerous to him. The *other* in his mind seemed to understand and retreated. Peering at the grenade, he set the delay to three seconds and tossed it ahead amidst the three Clade units. The intensely bright blast blew rubble up and down the tunnel. He closed his eyes and felt the wave hit him but it seemed merely a gust of wind, and the chunks of stone were light balsa blown by it. He stood as solidly as a statue. When he opened his eyes the units were against the walls but still squirming towards him.

"Come and die," he said.

He grabbed the first one by its head. Its tail stabbed in, tearing his envirosuit but skittering off his skin as though it was made of flint. He slammed its head against the tunnel wall, meanwhile snatching with his other hand and closing it around another unit's body. The first unit kept struggling stubbornly so he squeezed. Its head crunched and it sagged. He discarded it, slapping the third unit aside with the back of his hand while bringing the second down to the floor and stamping its head deep into the stone. But the thing was harder than that stone and continued to whip its body back and forth. He picked it up by its head, ignoring the sharp tail thrashing against his body. The third turned and tried to flee. But he caught its tail with his free hand and tugged it back, then slammed the two heads together. The units dropped, now seeming to possess just one mangled ruin of a head between them. Trike moved on.

Flashing lights reflected down the tunnel and there was the distant sound of concussions. He sped towards this, smoke beginning to haze the air, the smell of burning metal in his nostrils. Clade units ahead, writhing through the smoke. A battle. He stepped over one of them which was moving weakly, its snakish body half melted, and in passing crashed his foot down on its already-damaged head. A particle beam flashed blue and red, tracking something and spilling molten metal. He caught hold of a tail, pulled back and grabbed a head. Moving on with the thing thrashing in his grip, he snatched another unit out of the air. It was easy now—he knew what to do. After smashing their skulls together he carried on. A hulking shape moved through the smoke. He grabbed another tail, but then a massive claw closed on its body higher up, hydraulics whined and a shearfield glimmered, and the claw sliced through.

The prador, heavily armoured and carrying more weapons than seemed feasible, loomed over him. It lowered one claw, with a shiny cavity open in its upper jaw, and spat particle fire downwards. This played up and down the half of the Clade unit on the floor until it grew still. Trike gazed at gleaming green eyes behind a thick chain-glass visor.

"I've been looking for you," said the prador.

Trike went down on his knees, his body feeling as if he was being electrocuted. He saw stars again and felt that connection opening out. His hunger, which had been constant until that moment, started to fade as his void filled. The prador said something else, but he didn't hear it. All he heard were the words:

Backup loading . . .

Time passed, he didn't know how long.

"Are you injured?" asked the prador.

He focused, back in the moment. "No. I am not injured." Physically he felt as sound as a boulder, probably sturdier. His mind was also clear—in fact had a clarity he'd not possessed before. He looked up. "Who sent you to find me?"

"My leader."

Trike thought about that for a moment then said, "Because Cog and Angel are now with your leader?" Anger still roiled at the thought of Angel, but it was muted now, something to deal with at the appropriate moment, one way or another.

"Yes."

Trike gazed at the thing, studying the markings on its armour. "You are the prador Brull—second in command at the enclave. Your leader is Croos."

"Yes, that's me."

It wasn't his own knowledge that provided Trike with this information, but the packed mass of data that seemed to occupy his skull. In reality, this existed in quantum storage within the structure woven throughout his body.

"Orlandine is also with Croos?" he asked. This was essential for him to find out, or rather, for that part of himself he had acquired.

"Yes, we've got her," said Brull. "You seem mighty knowledgeable for a . . ." Brull hesitated, ". . . hooper."

Trike looked at his hands as he stood. Prador weren't noted for being able to distinguish one human being from another. Generally they didn't look beyond counting the number of arms and legs. Brull had probably been told to find a hooper and given a brief description. Trike knew he still resembled what he'd been when Cog dragged him into that storm drain, but there had been substantial changes too.

"You must take me to them," he stated, then, feeling he'd been a bit peremptory, added, "I need to be with my friends."

"Well, Croos tells me they're soon to head for the Ghost Drive Facility. Maybe we can get there before they leave. Come on."

Brull turned in the tunnel and headed off. Trike followed.

THE CLIENT

Dragon was old—a biomech probe created by the civilization of the Makers. They had succumbed to Jain technology only recently in interstellar terms. Polity understanding had it that Dragon was also recent in those same terms, but this was far from the truth. Its missions had been numerous, its journeys vast, its history stretching back and back until lost in hearsay and myth, even in the Maker realm. Yes, they used it as a probe, but was it actually theirs? This remained unclear—it may actually have predated them.

Dragon was also immense.

Now linked with it as one, fighting on the mental as well as physical level, the Client found much data to seize. But it seemed a bottomless well and she struggled to encompass the entity. The first misgivings began to impinge as Dragon riffled through her mind for what it sought. She began to doubt if she could win.

"The psychology is interesting, is it not?" said Dragon.

Somewhere, deep down, she understood the meaning, but she could not stop herself fighting to win, fighting to take more.

"Now I see," said Dragon.

The entity probed deep in her mind and she could feel its vast focus on what she had learned about the accretion disc. The place had once been a functioning solar system when a Jain caught up with the fleeing ships of the Species there. They were accompanied by their creator, the Librarian, which was Jain but considered an insane aberration by its kind. The ensuing clash had wrecked that solar system and during the battle the place had been seeded with Jain tech. The Jain lost all but its capital ship, which an equivalent Species ship faced off with so the remainder of its kind could flee. They fought over the system's sun and fell into it, creating a U-space blister that put out the sun. What looked like an accretion disc, out of which a solar system would form, was in fact the wreckage of one.

The Client continued fighting, still determined to win. However, the struggle became an attempt to retain her integrity and continue being herself. The data she had taken from Dragon was useful, interesting and powerful. One thing was clear: Dragon knew the Jain. It had had exchanges with them, and some of what the entity comprised had its basis in their technology. There was something else too. Had Dragon brought back to the Makers the Jain tech that destroyed them?

"This is why the Wheel wanted Orlandine to use her black hole weapon," said Dragon.

She could see it now too. What had recently happened at the accretion disc was new to her—while those events had been occurring she had been in the Prador Kingdom and then here, battling the prador and the Librarian. She inspected the facts from Dragon's mind—detail she suspected it had allowed her to take. The Wheel, obviously a Jain AI, had seen Orlandine's plan and forced her to implement it by deploying the soldier, before Dragon got to the heart of what this concerned: breaking that U-space blister—the trap—which was what the black hole would do.

The two combatants were touching the atmosphere of the gas giant now and its tidal forces were beginning to twist them. They were both all but limbless and denuded of armour—soft and wrapped around each other, entangled like their minds. Only minutes remained before the two bodies would hit acid clouds, then soon after, the heat and pressure which would destroy them. The Client sought comfort in that, as she finally admitted she could not win against this mind. It was just too big, too complicated, too sophisticated. But there was no comfort. They were enwrapped on the mental plenum and she could not withdraw intact.

"But the other preparations?" said Dragon. It was just a comment out of intellectual curiosity because Dragon was not fighting for its existence.

"I don't know," said the Client.

The Wheel had done more than force Orlandine's plans. The Clade was on Jaskor preventing access to the Ghost Drive Facility—wanting the behaviour of the weapons platforms out at the disc to remain unaltered. The attempt to kill Orlandine might be related to that. Or it might, along with the attempt to kill Dragon, be because it wanted to draw both the Polity and prador fleets to the accretion disc. This last seemed likely because the Wheel had taken over and prepared a prador reaver, now probably part of the prador fleet there.

Acid fog surrounded them, beading on their conjoined bodies, sizzling and burning in. They fell with a trail of vapour as it began to ablate them. Soon it was searing deeper, cutting through nerves and interfering with the physical meld. For a moment the Client thought it was this that brought Dragon's rape of her mind to a halt. Then she realized the entity had just stopped and was fending off her own attacks almost negligently.

"I think it is enough," said Dragon.

The Client scrabbled for hope, and this grew as she began to feel the entity retracting from her mind.

"Have you learned?" Dragon asked.

She had certainly learned not to bite off more than she could chew, but knew that was not the essence of the question.

"In relation to?" she probed.

"Why the Jain did not spread," Dragon explained. "Their strength and their weakness."

Dragon kept on pulling out of her mind—separating from her in ways she could hardly believe were possible. Knowledge remained but it remained hers, while what Dragon had taken was utterly its own. Burning, as well as ablating, the two fell deeper into the gas giant. Half-ruined organs began to collapse under the pressure. The Client felt the physical disconnection, her tentacles breaking, as a reflection of the mental one. Then came a crack and a flare of intense heat. She did not know whether it was because the two remotes hit a layer of reactive volatiles or whether Dragon had initiated something. Suddenly, with an intense feeling of dislocation, as if she had been snapped back by a long length of tightly stretched elastic a million miles long, she slammed home into her body on the weapons platform.

I am myself, she thought.

It was the truth and wholly the truth, because Dragon had burned through her and altered something at the core of her being. She felt the knowledge of the Librarian there, clear in her mind, just as she felt the knowledge of Dragon too. But she was neither of those. As it withdrew, Dragon had taken the poison: those destructive urges which had been clouding her judgement.

The Librarian was gone.

Clarity fell upon her. She must go, and quickly, to the accretion disc. Even as she made the calculations to drop the weapons platform and its attack pods into U-space, she understood something else. Dragon had nailed a critical aspect of the Jain. Their strength was the ability to rip knowledge from each other and to amalgamate—the weak shredded and the strong growing ever stronger. It was biologically and psychologically rooted in them and stemmed from their deep past, because that was exactly how they had mated. Of course, they had not spread. They could never go far from potential mates—the sources of knowledge and material gains they took from each other. This was why the Librarian had been such an aberration, because it could. But, as Dragon had noted, this impulse, this instinctive need was also their weakness.

The Client began moving her platform and attack pods away from Dragon, viewing the entity all the while, as she waited for the U-space disruption caused by her mines to fade. Dragon was again feeding from the gas giant. It was weak, damaged, perhaps the most vulnerable it had ever been. But she felt no inclination to attack, rend or steal. And that was good because, even as weak as this, Dragon was far beyond her.

9

If you ask someone how many legs does a prador have, the answer (besides "too many') is usually, "They're decapods aren't they?" The true number is either six or eight but if you change "legs" to "limbs" things start to get complicated. Include the claws and you have eight to ten. Taking into account the underslung manipulatory limbs gives a range between ten and eighteen. This is also complicated by the fact that when some prador first-children change into adults, they shed their back set of limbs to expose sexual organs. There are two main family trees of prador. One has eight legs and two claw arms in childhood, then six legs and two claws in adulthood. The other has six legs and two claws when a child, but when changing into an adult, only discards an armoured plate at its back end to release its sexual machinery. So it retains all its legs. Confusing, I know. Then there are the underslung manipulators. There are branches from these two family trees whose number of manipulatory limbs ranges from two to eight. Now factor in that the prador wear armour which does not necessarily reflect the number of limbs inside it and things get more confusing still. And this, of course, is only about the prador we see—the males. You don't want to know about the variation in number, size and application of the limbs of a female. Seriously, you don't.

—from *How It Is* by Gordon

ORLIK

Like the flashing of some giant welder, X-ray flares and heavy EMR were lighting up the accretion disc. The Harding black hole had begun to rip up and digest the star in there and the output would have been enough to fry just about anything... except heavily armoured and EMR-hardened warships and weapons platforms. Still, the radiation from the event was interfering with ship's systems and Orlik feared he might not be as on top of things as his Polity adversaries . . . *potential* adversaries. However, despite the interference, Orlik was deep in the system and sensors of the *Kinghammer* and felt like some giant gaseous entity spread out in vacuum, touching all, seeing all.

"Feeling like a god?" enquired Sprag.

"Not really," Orlik replied, deliberately focusing his attention, and thus Sprag's attention too, on the *Cable Hogue*.

The ship was big, moon big. But space stations could be as large, and size was not the issue. They were usually so huge because they contained living accommodation. Prador stations had numerous sanctums and tunnels, breeding pools and nurseries. There were hunting pools if they were big enough, where reaverfish—the namesake of many of those ships out there—swam freely and prador could go in after them for sport. Some even contained ersatz mudflats, where mudfish challenged each other and bred. They tasted better than the frozen versions, especially if they died and decayed for a little while in genuine home world mud. But the *Cable Hogue* did not contain much living accommodation. As Orlik understood it, its crew did not number any more than ten, though there might be marines stored aboard. It was big because it needed to be to contain its mountainous engines of destruction.

"Intimidating, isn't it?" suggested Sprag.

"All warships are," said Orlik.

"My current projection is that we have a sixty per cent chance of winning a fleet-on-fleet engagement."

Sprag had become part of his mind and he was part of hers. Behind her dryly factual assessment he could sense the doom-laden implications. Because he knew what she knew, though not with so much precision.

"The term 'winning' is an interesting choice," he said.

"It would be a pyrrhic victory and we all know it," said Sprag. "And you, Orlik, also know that to EC and your king it would be little more than a scuffle breaking out during one of their endless rounds of sabre rattling."

"Careful, drone—your master, whoever that may be, might not like that kind of talk."

"Hell, you don't like it when I say 'we' and now you don't like it when I try for an outside perspective."

"I guess you can't win . . ."

"Ho ho. Anyway, Earth Central was never my master. Earth Central was, occasionally, an employer who didn't seem to have much idea about the concept of wages."

Orlik returned to himself, partially, and swivelled a stalked eye to gaze at the actual drone. It was back upright and capable of movement. He wondered what would constitute "wages" for such a thing. But since, as a prador, the concept of payment for services was a vague one, he didn't pursue the thought.

"Still trying to win my trust, drone?"

"That old chestnut," said Sprag.

Orlik felt annoyed with himself. He couldn't keep harping on about this issue. "It's just some of my irritation—or rather, worry—about the present situation," he said. "You know what will happen if this goes down, and we are in it together."

"Ah, you begin to acquire wisdom," said Sprag. "Irritation is one of the first signs."

Orlik bubbled annoyance and returned his attention to the *Hogue*. Yes, he could see what would happen, in fact his linkage to Sprag simply did not allow him to be less than realistic. If the prador and the Polity started fighting here, he would be able to keep the *Hogue* tied up and quite possibly put some substantial holes in it. In fact, his keeping the *Hogue* busy was what could make a win by the prador fleet possible, though they would be celebrating their victory in clouds of wreckage. But in the end, for him, the battle would be a dead loss—dead being the most operative word. He could fuck with the *Hogue* but it would crush him.

"My own irritation very much extends to the king too," said Sprag abruptly. "He knows the situation, and in putting you and me in this ship here, he is running what is little more than a beta test. I've no doubt that somewhere in the Kingdom another ship like this is already being built and another *potential* AI prepared." After a pause she continued, "When I integrated with the machine intelligence, the process was recorded and transmitted. The king now has the next steps towards making a fully conscious AI."

Orlik acknowledged that with a mental nod. It had hardly seemed worth mentioning that the *Kinghammer* was merely a test bed, a crucible whose purpose was to provide the king with data. Its surviving the process would just be a bonus. The king and Earth Central were little different in that respect. He then said, "I would suggest otherwise. The king may be building another ship but he will not initiate another AI until he sees how you perform."

"The updates," Sprag stated.

"Quite."

The ship had a constant U-space link to the Kingdom. Everything the *Kinghammer* did, and even much of the function of Sprag's mind, was being recorded in the Kingdom. This would continue for as long as U-com remained possible.

Sprag decided to change the subject. "That U-space disruption is up."

Orlik had noted this too and had expected it. A USER could disrupt that continuum by rattling a singularity in and out of a runcible gate, and U-mines could disorder it with the field-detonation of smaller singularities. So it was logical that an eight-solar-mass black hole eating a sun would have an effect. However, the math Sprag immediately presented in his mind indicated that the disruption should not have been as much as it was. Either the math was wrong or something else was in operation here.

"Perhaps we should forget about our possible imminent demise and enjoy the spectacle," suggested Sprag. "It won't be long now..."

"Why not?"

The weapons platform AIs had allowed Diana Windermere access to sensor data from the attack pods which had followed the Harding black hole in. Even though they were AIs, they adhered strictly to the agreements between the Polity and the Kingdom. It had surprised Orlik how strict they were about that, and how ready they were to demonstrate they had no loyalty to Earth Central, despite having been manufactured in the Polity. They were neutral and stuck to their job of ensuring that Jain tech did not escape the accretion disc. Therefore, upon allowing Diana in, they had immediately given Orlik access too.

Orlik was about to open up the link again when Sprag drew his attention to one of the reavers. The data opened out for his mental inspection. It was a matter of small concern. The reaver kept drifting out of formation and then back again. Its status updates were tardy and its weapons statistics didn't match its file. Other lesser problems were evident too: technological mismatches which were revealed only in status updates and the constant computer chatter between ships. In any other situation this would not have been a problem. But here, where tactical considerations were balanced on a thin blade, the slightest error could lead to catastrophic losses. Orlik scanned data, noted anomalies, then decided to talk to the captain of the vessel.

Captain Brogus appeared to Orlik's vision squatting in his sanctum. He wore a quite antiquated style of armour, and the sanctum behind looked more like what would be found aboard an older-style dreadnought. But this was not unusual—some of the Guard, even those younger than Orlik, had a bit of a retro or nostalgic outlook.

Rather than go through all the faults and anomalies concerning the reaver, Orlik asked, "You are having problems, Captain Brogus?"

"Yes, I am having problems," Brogus replied.

Orlik waited for him to elaborate and when he didn't, said, "Then I would like you to explain them to me."

Brogus dipped obsequiously then replied, "Two problems, sir. Five of my crew have wire worms. One of them, while conducting maintenance on the system links, managed to laser flash the coding nexus." After a pause Brogus added, "He will be punished."

Orlik absorbed this. Wire worms were a minor parasite. They could sometimes be contracted from mudfish steaks which had not been properly sterilized before freezing. To normal prador they were no more than very irritating. To the Guard, with their altered and divergent biology, the effect could range from nothing at all to debilitating. It all made sense and in retrospect Orlik realized he had been lucky not to have had more problems like this, with so many ships here.

"I see—and this is all being dealt with?"

"The affected crew are in isolation and purging, and I have requested a code update."

Orlik felt the confirmation of this from Sprag.

"Do you wish me to fall out of formation for the interim?" asked Brogus.

Orlik considered, then rejected the idea. "No, stay where you are and keep me updated."

But even as he cut the link, Orlik could not help but feel that something about that captain was off. As was the case with his reaver, it wasn't something definite and major, but an accumulation of small things: such as his comment about punishing the crewmember—Orlik expected this from normal prador but not from the Guard, because it would be counterproductive. There was also the fact that these problems did not explain everything going wrong with the reaver. And the old armour and style of Brogus's sanctum . . . but no, Orlik felt his own tension and fear had begun to spill over into a generalized paranoia. He dismissed it from his mind.

ORLANDINE

How much do you remember?" asked Cog, sitting on the floor beside her.

Orlandine studied him. He had a kind face and he was hunching in on himself to try and look less threatening. But she knew he was probably quite capable of ripping off the limbs from any of the surrounding prador.

"I remember most of my life," she answered, "but to survive I wiped the AI crystal in my skull, so I lost a lot of other information."

"Dragon wants you in the Ghost Drive Facility and capable of talking to the weapons platforms—capable of changing their orders," said Cog. "Is that possible?"

"I don't know. All the security codes I possessed are gone from my present form. I am human now with blank AI crystal linked to my mind." She closed her eyes for a moment and probed that connection. The crystal remained linked in her skull and throughout her body to other hardware which it had not been necessary to sacrifice. This hardware had enabled her to see in the dark and translate prador language, but what abilities she possessed beyond that she had no idea. "I can talk to them but do not know if I can instruct them without the codes, and without the other data I possessed. They must be prepared to recognize and obey me without that."

She did not mention another problem. Though still connected up, she was no longer fully haiman. She had AI crystal and a transceiver in her skull. But she had lost most of her support system, because it had been mainly the Jain tech she had sacrificed. If she connected in that facility and tried to talk to those platform AIs, it might well kill her.

"We need to get into that facility to find out, then," said Cog.

She abruptly stood up. She wasn't the haiman she had been but the project here, and at the accretion disc, was hers and her responsibility. She needed to think and she needed to be precise.

"So, Dragon wants me inside the facility, so I can issue orders to the weapons platforms at the accretion disc," she announced to everyone.

Croos had been talking with Angel, and both of them stopped and swung towards her. The rest of the prador in the chamber, who had been checking weapons and supplies and generally getting ready for a fight, also became attentive.

"Dragon has instructed this because it is apparently what the Clade does not want. As is usual with Dragon, he has not sufficiently explained himself, but I agree and I will go there with you. The Clade is working for the Wheel and we must work against it." She glanced at Cog as he too stood, and she gave him a nod of acknowledgement.

"However," she continued, "I no longer possess the codes that would give me access, and the drones there will not let me in without them."

"We have been discussing this," said Croos. "It's possible we don't need to go past the drones. We just need to get past the Clade."

"Explain," said Orlandine, suddenly feeling stronger now she had spoken out.

"The facility sits on a collection of fusion reactors and a powerful hardfield defence. The ejection ports for the hardfield generators egress in a cave system below the facility."

She gazed at Croos for a long moment then said dryly, "Doubtless your knowledge of this possible point of access is extensive."

"It is," Croos allowed.

She wasn't surprised. The prador here, just like many of the Polity personnel, were agents respectively of the king or Earth Central. They would all have made plans to cover any . . . eventualities.

"So what is the plan?" she asked.

Croos waved a claw towards one of the tunnels behind. "We head out of the city that way. It will take us to an exit about two miles from the facility. We go overground to a concealed entrance that leads down into the cave system, then up an ejection port into the facility."

"And above ground is the Clade," noted Cog.

"It's about half a mile overland to the entrance," said Croos. He turned as one of the other prador brought something over and handed it to him. Taking this object in one claw, he moved back and dumped it at Orlandine's feet.

She looked at the armoured suit. It was an old design but the armour itself had that brassy look of prador hull metal. She continued staring, feeling some resentment towards this example of her vulnerability. But she had to accept it and so stooped down, found the panel on one wrist and activated it. The thing stood up and opened completely down the back, including its legs, while its helmet tipped forwards onto the chest. She reached up to that point on her collarbone and retracted her clothing, and stepped naked into the armour, pushing her feet down into its boots. It quickly closed around her, the helmet hinging over her head, foam formers closing on her legs. She moved and it moved with her, barely noticeable, while the head-up display, the HUD, showed her the power status and clear diagnostics.

"That good?" asked Cog.

"It will do," she said grudgingly.

Cog turned back to Croos. "We should wait for Trike—he'll be useful."

Orlandine turned and stared at him—a weird twisting sensation ran through her body from her skull to her feet. She felt a buzz, almost of panic, in response to this and did not understand it. However, she knew she did not want to wait for this Trike—something about the hooper, whom she had never met, scared her.

"We can wait no longer," said Croos. "My guards are retreating—there are Clade in the tunnels. We need to go now."

The prador—ten of them including Croos—started trooping towards the tunnel he had indicated earlier. Orlandine shrugged herself into motion, familiarizing herself with the suit almost at once. Cog moved along beside her and, a moment later, Angel on the other side. They were on their way, and she now wore prador armour to protect her. But still she might die in the facility, if not before. She felt thoroughly and utterly vulnerable and, with her memories coming back more clearly, she realized this had never been a consideration before when she had entered *human time.*

As the prador entered the tunnel in single file, she could hear distant, echoey concussions and the sounds of weapon fire. One prador abruptly came through another entrance, its armour smoking. It followed the rest. Meanwhile, prador still in the chamber were fixing hemispherical objects against the wall, blinking displays of prador glyphs on surface screens. She understood at once. The prador guarding the tunnels would be left to fend for themselves and, once those here were clear of the chamber, Croos intended to blow it up, to stop the Clade units from following them. This would also prevent Trike catching up. She did not know why she was glad about that.

ORLIK

After his conversation with Captain Brogus, Orlik opened up the link the weapons platforms had provided, also complementing it with sensor data from his fleet. The stuff coming from the attack pods inside the disc had now degraded. A few of them had self-destructed when Jain tech reached an unsafe level of penetration, while others were losing their sensors to it. They were also being burned by the massive EMR in there, which itself had to be compensated for. Though the data in essence shone a glaring light inside the accretion disc, a lot of *interpretation* was necessary. Sensors needed to run protective routines to prevent overload as well. Still, to Orlik's perception, the accretion disc became transparent across much of the emitted spectrum, and he could now gaze upon an event few prador or humans had ever seen.

"Impressive," Sprag commented.

The previously inactive star had heated up. But it was still stubbornly refusing to ignite with fusion. Maybe this was because the Harding black hole, by pulling on the star, was acting to reduce the pressure gradient throughout it. Sprag offered the math on this. Briefly scanning it, Orlik noted that again it described what should be happening but plainly wasn't. Some small fusion ignition should have occurred—a burn and then burn-out. Again, either the math was wrong or something odd was happening here. Still, Sprag was right: impressive.

The star had contracted at the poles, its equator bloating, and from there a tail extended out to touch a seemingly invisible point in space which glared like the tip of an arc welder. The Harding black hole—a relatively minuscule object on this scale—had a titanic effect. With every peak in EMR emissions, that point grew more defined. A rotating disc of glowing plasma expanded around the spin of the hole. Orlik mentally settled himself to watch, damping all other considerations in his mind. Sprag was right—this would soon be over so he might as well enjoy it.

With a further expansion of the plasma disc, the particle fountains from the poles of the black hole flashed into visibility across much of the spectrum. Sprag drew his attention to other data: one of the weapons platforms was firing up its fusion drive over the accretion disc. It shifted to a safe distance, away from where one of the polar fountains speared out of the disc. It wasn't actually in the path of the thing, but the catastrophic event about to occur could move the black hole enough to put the platform in the way. And energy readings on that fountain were immense—like a particle beam weapon a couple of miles across.

Closer views of the sun showed oceans of fire heaving up into that stretching tail. Even as Orlik watched, the whole orb began distorting, straining up towards the black hole. The tail shortened as the two objects closed on each other. The spinning disc around the black hole finally ate up the last of that tail and started cutting into the surface of the sun like a circular saw. It changed colour, from a pale blue to hot orange, as it wrenched up more materials and dug deeper and deeper. Only minutes later, half of it had sunk inside the star, which began boiling up and stretching around it. And the black hole reached its surface. Had this been a planet, even a gas or ice giant, by now it would be breaking up and incorporating in that disc. But it seemed as if the star, with a little indigestion, was swallowing the black hole.

"Big disruption," Sprag muttered, instantly relaying the data to Orlik's mind.

Waves of U-space disruption were generating and flowing out from this event. Though, Orlik conceded, location wasn't something you could really refer to when talking about that continuum. But gravity waves were also spreading out in the real from that point. Hurling out giant solar flares and sheets of radiating gas, the star's spin became visible, as mountains bigger than worlds fled around its circumference. It began to settle, radiating heavily in infrared, hot and burning, but still no fusion. It wasn't spherical either, but pill-shaped.

"That is in no math," said Sprag.

The dark spot appeared at the pole Orlik could see, then it seemed as if black cracks were spreading from it. Only as these started to connect up did he see the shapes they were forming. A honeycomb grid spread across the surface of the star, which began to shrink. Being sucked into the black hole? He didn't think so. It all just seemed too even and mechanical. Its shape also began to change—shrinking in at the waist, it regained its spherical shape. As he watched, the grid joined up with the one that had grown from the other pole. Then the whole thing darkened. It still sat there on the gravity map of the system, but the attack pods sensed a steep decline in emitted radiation.

"Something else," Orlik noted.

A flash of white sparked on the surface, spreading out, then a long line scribed around it and seemingly peeled something up. It shot out and round, travelling close to light speed. A U-signature was generated and the thing bounced, disappearing, but leaving a glowing line through realspace. The object then reappeared travelling slowly, a debris cloud spreading out around it.

"Things just got more complicated," noted Sprag.

They certainly had. Orlik did not need to reassess the data to know what he had seen. He surmised that somehow this ship, for that was all it could be, had been trapped in U-space, and the black hole hitting the inactive star had freed it. Escaping the massive gravity, it had tried to U-jump and been damaged by the effort. But still, this must have been the Wheel's plan all along, driving events to this point. And that did not bode well for either the Polity or the prador. What had just been released into their world?

TRIKE

Brull, the prador perambulating ahead in the underground tunnel, came to an abrupt halt. Trike nearly walked into him, not because he couldn't see—he could, despite the lack of lighting here, which was odd—but because he felt out of it, his attention focused inwards. The prador reached out with one claw and rattled it against a wall. He issued a few hissing clicks that seemed like an expression of thoughtful impatience.

"There a problem?" asked Trike, then paused, replaying in his mind the distorted sound of his voice.

A second later, there came a rumbling blast from ahead and a few seconds after that a roaring wind fogged the tunnel with dust.

"Change of plan," said Brull. "We go overland."

"What happened?" Trike asked. His voice still sounded wrong.

"Croos just blew up our hideaway to stop the Clade down here following him," Brull explained. "And that stops us too."

Trike reached up and put a finger in his mouth, feeling a projecting ridge along the centre of his tongue. A leech mouth in his tongue again? That was usually an outward sign of an inner turmoil he did not have now.

"Which means . . ." he said distractedly. "How many of the Clade are down here? You said the main swarm headed for the facility."

"Less than a hundred now." Brull was offhand.

"Right," said Trike, still distracted.

He stuck out his tongue and found he could extend it far enough to see it quite clearly. He probed with his fingers. The ridge along the top was the apex of a triangle—his tongue was triangular in section and now slightly ribbed. He felt his way along it. There didn't seem to be any opening but the end felt rough, kind of odd, like pressing his fingertip against the end of a brush. He turned it up towards his nose, discovering its surprising mobility, and inspected the end. A triangle, evenly packed with circular objects, presented itself to him. He then tried to stick out the internals of the tongue, as he had been able to previously when it possessed a leech mouth. Circular clumps of metallic fibres oozed out, and one of them spread like the end of a filter-feeding worm. He snapped them back, and then his tongue, into his mouth. Damned sure now that it had been no parasite hitching a ride on his body.

"They hit Polity personnel hardest. We were fortified and kept them out of the enclave, but they've been on us right from the start. When they broke in we fled down here," Brull offered. "I guess we're a loose cannon they wanted to spike."

"Your translator is good," Trike noted, his focus returning.

"I don't use a translator."

This prador was distinctly odd. He seemed a lot smarter and more loquacious than expected. But then, Trike had never met a prador before, so how could he judge? Anyway, Brull must use a translator because surely he didn't possess the vocal equipment for even speaking Anglic?

"We go here," said Brull, leading the way down a narrow side tunnel, the edges of his carapace scraping against the walls.

Knowledge, again not his own, slunk into Trike's mind. Brull was one of the King's Guard—one of the king's family—and as such heavily mutated by the Spatterjay virus. Few people knew this because of the Guard's concealing armour. They did not want it known how the virus changed their bodies, or continued to change them in radical ways. Brull might even have developed the vocal equipment that made him capable of human speech. Or he might be lying.

As he followed, staring hard at the prador as if to try and penetrate that armour, Trike thought of Brull as a prador version of him. Then he reconsidered. Brull was a prador version of Cog, while Trike... Trike was a rare example of what Old Captains could become. Only one other resembled him, as far as he knew, that being Cog's brother Jay Hoop, the monstrous pirate who had run the thralling trade out of Spatterjay during the war. In Cog's memories, Trike had seen what he had become. Perhaps that was it. Perhaps you needed to be a monster inside for that to be fully manifest on the exterior. Trike pondered on what the prador version of a monster might be and found himself unable to come up with anything. He then wondered if Jay Hoop had possessed a triangular tongue...

The tunnel curved up and daylight became visible ahead. Brull paused and, using his lower manipulator appendages, detached a cone-shaped object from his under-carapace. With armoured but soft-tipped fingers, he worked the pit control on the end of this before passing it up to one claw. He stuck the thing on the wall.

"Should slow them down," he commented, scrambling ahead with alacrity. "Let's move."

Since Trike had seen Cog doing the same thing in the tunnel which they'd used to enter the city, he hurried after him to a safe distance.

Soon the ceiling disappeared and they walked out through a deep ditch. Then piles of scrap displaced the walls, under a sky now scattered with wisps of cloud. From behind came a boom and the tunnel mouth belched dust and fragments of stone. Trike surprised himself by hoping that the explosive had fully collapsed the tunnel. Had he lost his urge to fight and destroy the Clade?

They wound their way along between the stacked remains of ground cars of a style unfamiliar to Trike. The *other* within him supplied detail. This junkyard contained the kind of cars the inhabitants of Jaskor had used before Orlandine turned up and started bringing in Polity technology. The old cars were steadily being replaced by grav-cars or displaced by fast, efficient transport systems. Shortly they reached the end of this aisle of scrap and came to an open area where a few whole cars were scattered.

"One moment," said Trike.

He walked over to one of the cars and peered at his reflection in the mirrored glass. It was very dirty and the image unclear.

"We cannot linger," Brull stated.

Trike nodded, then stabbed his clawed fingers into the metal pillar beside the side window and levered the glass out. Luckily it was reinforced glass and did not shatter. Holding this, he moved to go after Brull, then stopped and stepped over to a pool left by the recent storm. He cleaned the glass in it with a clump of insulation he found, then, walking after the prador, inspected his face. Yes, he had changed.

His teeth were now those of a carnivore: yellow, tough and pointed. The interior of his much larger mouth was black and red, like some pit in hell, and he could open it wide enough to put his fist inside easily. His head had grown longer, and flatter on the top with a buzz of black hair. But it was also wider, resembling a post whose end had been spread upon being hammered into the ground. His nose had remained the same but out of proportion to his other changed features. His eyes looked small and piggy and mean, while his pointed ears had acquired a wavy frill down their backs. And those veins: brown and white and webbing his dark blue skin. Just, only just, he could recognize something of the Trike he had once been. He lowered the glass and hurried after Brull.

"So what's happening to you?" asked the prador.

Trike shrugged. "You know what the Spatterjay virus does to its host. With me it is doing something more." He didn't mention that the course of his transformation had been changed by the addition of what he now recognized was the large clump of organic technology hitching a ride in his body.

Brull paused at a high fence around the junkyard, unnaturally still. "I am not aware of the details of such changes," he said.

"You mean you haven't looked into what has been happening to you?" Trike enquired.

Brull whirled round, his feet tearing up the ground, and stabbed his claw to slam shut on Trike's neck. "That is restricted knowledge!"

Trike reached up, inserted his hands between the two jaws and started pushing. The motors and hydraulics that had closed the claw began whining and he simply pushed it open. Brull swept it sideways, sending Trike stumbling, then brought the open mouth of a particle cannon to bear, pointed straight at his head. Reaching back with his free claw, he inserted it into the grip of a Gatling cannon fixed to his underside and aimed that on him too.

"The knowledge is not as restricted as you would suppose," said Trike. He pointed off beyond the fence. "Do you want to kill me now, or would you rather save your ammunition for them?"

Brull turned his stalked eyes. Beyond the fence and over the fields, on the other side of the road, silvery objects were breaking into the sky. The Clade trapped below had found another way to the surface.

"Ah fuck," said Brull, again demonstrating his firm command of Anglic.

He turned and swept a claw across, knocking the fence at an angle, then trampled it down as he began running.

"This way!"

Trike hesitated, not sure if he wanted to follow a creature that had threatened him. But he realized that if his knowledge had been so critical, Brull would—when he'd failed to cut him in half—have *used* his weapons. He broke into a run after the prador as it skidded on the surface of the nearby road and headed along it. They were now moving away from the city in a semi-agricultural area. Here and there houses with extensive gardens sat between fields of ever-corn, others scattered with low foliage and the bright pink globes of protein gourds. Below the Clade units, a harvester rumbled through the corn, striding on spindly legs and combing off the loose seed heads—its programming disregarding the chaos all around.

"Why are we running?" Trike called.

"Just run," said Brull.

It seemed to him they would do just as well facing the Clade here as anywhere else. Even so, as he ran he scanned his surroundings for something to use as a weapon, damning the fact he'd lost his machete. He slowed, spotting a heavy wooden post, but what would that do against a Clade unit? Anyway, it seemed that his hands were a more effective weapon now. Only then did he notice that he had retained the sheet of mirror glass under his arm. He saw no reason to abandon it.

The glittering swarm swirled above the harvester and then, for no particular reason, a few of them shot down and ripped through the thing, shattering its main body. The machine collapsed, trailing smoke and fire into the field. Such pointless destruction stirred some of Trike's old anger and he wanted the fucking things here. But the swarm just continued to swirl. Surely the units had seen Brull and him by now? What were they waiting for?

The road dipped down into a valley lined with tea oaks and humped over a wide slow-moving river. Before heading downslope, Brull skidded to a halt. A launcher folded out from the side of his under-carapace—its frame loaded with missiles. Spitting a tail of fire, one of them shot out straight towards the swarm. Trike tracked its progress. It detonated right in the middle of the units, its hot flash momentarily blinding him and the globular explosion slamming out. Antimatter, he realized, as the blast wave flattened and set the crops below smoking. He saw Clade units falling, the rest widely scattered by the blast, and felt some objection in himself from that *other*, because apparently the prador were not meant to have antimatter weapons here. As the Clade regained control of themselves they spread out further, doubtless to make a less compact target. Then they accelerated towards the road.

"Well that got their attention!" Trike shouted as the blast wave filled the air around them with smouldering straw. But Brull had already turned away and was running at full pelt down the hill.

The Clade units came in fast. Seeing one hurtling straight for him, Trike paused, took the mirror glass from under his arm, and with all the force he could muster, skimmed the glass at it. The sheet left his hand with a sonic crack and struck the unit right in its face, shattering. Still, the unit tumbled out of the sky trailing sparks and hit the road beside him. He grinned, then ran over to it as it tried to rise, stamped down on its head and grabbed its thrashing tail. Another came, streaking along the road behind him. He raised his foot then whipped the first unit around, using it as a club. Head-to-head impact and the second went down while the first now hung limp. But it was heavy and made of very tough metal. Trike had found his weapon.

Running down after Brull, he flinched as a particle beam crackled just over his shoulder. Then the chainsaw buzz of a Gatling cannon filled the air with impacts and a rain of hot metal fragments. Clade were everywhere, while the prador was covering him from the bridge. Why this spot? Trike wondered, as further units swept in from every direction. His answer, as he ducked the whip of a tail and shoulder-rolled onto the bridge, shot up out of the waters on either side.

Two prador and some other object shed water as they emerged and opened fire. Brull used more of his missiles, the hot flash of their detonations making even Trike's skin smoke at such close quarters. Gatling cannons crackled and hammered, particle beams scored the air like hot irons going into butter. But that other object was the most effective. Lashing with his makeshift club, mainly to keep units off Brull's back, Trike eyed it. The vaguely spherical object possessed bulky collections of missile launchers, with cannons on either side, and it hammered at the Clade continuously. He felt an objection from that *other* again, as well as a flash of curiosity for how the enclave prador had managed to smuggle in one of their war drones. He recognized the source of these aberrant thoughts now, and the nature of the organic technology that occupied him. But this was a small concern as a moment later a flood of shifting metal surrounded him.

The attack lifted him from the ground, where he continued to fight the writhing mass. Spiked tails slammed at his body, while sliding, jointed bodies wrapped his limbs and torso, trying to crush through them. A blast ensued, and he saw Brull and the bridge sliding into the river. The prador drone tumbled past, with Clade crawling all over its surface. Suddenly it righted and turned, opening fire on one of its own—the Clade had it. Trike felt pain as spiked tails converged by his neck, digging into his rigidly hard flesh. He struck out in a frenzy, crushing heads, tearing at the bodies gripping him. Again he glimpsed the battle: one prador with the top half of its armour ripped away, something pink and speckled black struggling inside as Clade tore it apart. A missile streaked up from the river and hit the drone, a massive close blast hurling him and Clade through the air, his skin burning.

And he fell. He hit the riverbank where steaming water lapped. Clade swarmed above, a disc-like cloud of them turning, then suddenly they just peeled off and headed away. He hauled himself up, debris falling about him and smoke boiling all around from the burning river valley. Over on the other side of the river, he could see part of the drone like the charred half of some huge egg shell. Further along was one of the prador, its armour smoking, its head turret and limbs missing on one side. That wasn't the one he had seen earlier, with its shell opened out, which meant the two that had waited in ambush here were down. Had Brull survived?

He returned his attention to the river and it was almost without surprise that he saw two stalked eyes rise up out of the water and swivel to check things out. Next, pushing a wave ahead of him, Brull clambered out onto the bank.

"We were lucky," he said.

Trike stared at him, wondering if the prador had just lost his grip on Anglic.

10

Underspace is confusing. Our ability to travel from one point in realspace to another, instantaneously, by submerging our ships into U-space like submarines, is blithely explained by the contention that U-space is a continuum which does not possess the dimensions of time or distance. It is a place divorced from our universe, and it is possible to enter or thereafter exit it at any point or time in our universe. However, this is clearly untrue. There are time delays in U-space that may or may not relate to the realspace distance travelled. There are energy debts to be paid related to the distance travelled. These debts ramp up steeply if any attempt is made to time travel, and are paid for by either massive photonic eruptions or entropy capable of extinguishing stars. The gravity wells of astronomical objects in the real can be detected in U-space, and there is a direct relation to our gravity maps. Certain technologies that reorganize matter at pico-scopic levels create readable signatures. Currents, flows and even storms are evident too, so that sometimes a shorter distance in our universe is more difficult (in terms of expenditure of energy or time) to circumvent through U-space than a longer one. Underspace interference emitters can stir up that continuum to make travel in it difficult or impossible. Their effect is a local one: if a USER is deployed in one star system, travel in U-space is stopped there but not elsewhere. This does not tie up with the idea that U-space is devoid of the dimension of distance. It can therefore be argued that U-space is a continuum intimately related to our own, not one that is divorced from it. This also indicates that our understanding of U-space, and the mechanisms we use to travel through it, are at the level of a prehistoric man's understanding of fluid dynamics and marine engineering when he hollows out a log to float on a river.

—from *How It Is* by Gordon

KNOBBLER

Knobbler reviewed the nasty situation. The lethally dangerous Clade had to be stopped. An orbital strike from above could turn this area into an inferno at any moment, and something which could be very dangerous to all sentient creatures in this part of the galaxy was happening here and at the accretion disc. But he was happy. He was home.

"Dug in like a tick on a porcupine's arse," said Cutter, squatting beside him on a slab of rock overlooking the Ghost Drive Facility.

"Been checking your wartime quote file?" Knobbler enquired.

"A paraphrase really—I like to be original."

"Dug in the Clade may be, but not trying to enter," Knobbler observed.

He and his companion war and assassin drones had been hitting the main swarm all the way from the city to out here. There had been losses—ten old comrades were dead, while a further twenty-three were wrecked. These were recoverable somewhere behind, and grouching about being taken out of the fight. Meanwhile, the count of Clade units had dropped by two hundred and fifty-seven. Still, over two thousand of the fuckers were here, while another eighty or more were on their way from a fight with enclave prador a few miles back.

"So what's the plan now?" asked Cutter.

With a sound like knives running over rock, the big mantis drone groomed himself. Using his sharp-edged limbs, he had taken out at least twenty units, but the tough Clade bodies had taken their toll. He was blunt. The laminar diamond configuration of his edges enabled them to self-sharpen—peeling off layers like a cat's claws—but he needed to accelerate the process which gave him an edge.

"We can't go heavy on them now," said Knobbler.

In fact, there were few places they had been able to deploy anything big. Over the city, they would have caused casualties in the population below. On the route here, the Clade had clumped up twice and paid the price. And now, the danger of either damaging the facility or having its defences power up to target them prevented the drones getting "heavy." Hence, Knobbler had called a halt when the Clade went to ground before actually entering the place.

The ground around the facility lay clear of vegetation and rocks for half a mile. The facility would instantly assess and react to anything entering this kill zone without the correct codes. Visitors would be given ample warning of the penalty for moving closer. The drones, like giant robber crabs squatting atop the guard towers, were ready to react unfavourably if any did. Their reaction would be triggered about ten feet inside the cleared area—the smoking remains of two Clade units down there were a practical reminder of this.

The Clade, after its initial probe, had dropped down into the trees and boulders outside the clearing, all surrounding the facility. Knobbler's own probe was a war drone fashioned in the shape of a blued metal electric eel, and whose suicidal bent made it perfect for the task. It now lay in two halves on the slope below, running through a list of expletives from every human language, while trying to draw its two halves together by casting spider-silk fibres.

"So we just sit and watch?" Cutter suggested.

Knobbler rumbled round and stabbed a tentacle towards the horizon where the approaching Clade units were visible. "I will ponder on the matter," he said. "Meanwhile, you take some of the boys and deal with them."

"Okay." Cutter engaged grav, then complemented that by using his wings to take him into the air, summoning other drones as he went. Six rose up out of the surrounding landscape: the Clam, a couple of glittering flatworms; a thing like a big carp with belly tentacles, but with such heavy armour it only slightly resembled a Spatterjay Molly carp; a giant yellow scorpion fly; and another that was similar to a dragonfly larva. Cutter, now closing his wings, fired up the fusion engine in his tail. They assembled behind him and shot off. Knobbler swivelled back to face the facility, concentrating on what lay ahead of him.

The Clade was managing to defeat most scanning, but high-frequency ground radar had picked up disturbances. It seemed that some units were edging out towards Knobbler and his drones. He had no doubt that many remained to ensure nothing got into the facility, but these others, he suspected, were about to try something new. In a straight face-to-face fight in the air, Knobbler and his crew mangled them, so they were resorting to their favourite tactic: being sneaky.

"Bludgeon?" Knobbler enquired.

Cutter's companion, their expert in all things warfare-related in the virtual and informational world, had sited himself on the lee of the hill. Here he oversaw some alterations Tinker—a multi-limbed creature that resembled nothing more than an unlikely collection of limbs—was making to Worm. This last drone, a burrower like a giant centipede but with paddle-like, digging limbs down its sides and pincers to the fore, had once liked pulling prador underground to dismember them.

"Nearly ready," Bludgeon replied.

Worm's upgraded sensorium should give them a clearer idea of the Clade's intent, along with more precise location data. Knobbler watched Tinker's progress for a little longer, before swinging his attention back to Cutter and his comrades as they fell towards the approaching Clade. The Clam began disintegrating Clade units with pulses of railgun fire as the two forces closed on each other. They met a moment later with an impact audible from where Knobbler squatted. He saw Cutter slicing and snatching. The scorpion fly slammed home its collimated diamond sting loaded with destructive nanites, and the Molly carp reached out to grab and crush. However, they were in the battle only briefly before the rest of the units dropped out of the sky and hit the ground, burrowing in.

"Ready," Bludgeon informed him.

Worm reared up then speared down. His sharp, zero-friction head and pincers went in easily and, with his paddle legs fountaining earth out behind him, he rapidly disappeared. Ten feet under within just a minute, he travelled towards the Clade lines. Soon after, his scanning routines and the scanning nodes he had dropped began giving good feedback to complement what was coming from ground radar. Knobbler constructed a 3D image in his mind. Where Worm had gone, the soil lay twenty feet deep above bedrock. Nowhere could Knobbler see the Clade, until he detected motion actually down on the bedrock. They had moved surprisingly fast. This looked like it might be a—

Fifty feet ahead, a twisted old tree exploded into the air, with Worm shooting sideways out of the blast, pursued by five Clade units.

—problem.

Elsewhere, other Clade units breached and attacked. In the mud and rocks and amidst the trees—dirty close-quarters combat. Knobbler leapt from his rock and landed with a *whumph* on soil. He spat two missiles into the ground towards detected movement, swept a tentacle to one side, smashing into a rising axolotl head, snared another in a gripper and stabbed a high-speed drill spike into its eye. The Clade, he felt, was about to learn that down and dirty was where he, and his comrades, liked to be.

BLADE

That's enough, thought Blade and immediately translated it into actions. The robots, which had completed essential alterations and proceeded to the merely cosmetic, either terminated or ran their various tasks to a stop point. The mass of them, swarming around *Obsidian Blade* like ants on the corpse of a black locust, began to retreat. Construction spiders drew back on their umbilicals, folding in their limbs. Flat beetle-welders scuttled away. Smaller masses like metallic lichen peeled up and detached, sucked away by roaming magnetic hoovers. Docking clamps opened, while munitions conveyors and tubes unplugged themselves. And Blade floated free.

Once given free rein, Blade had proceeded rapidly with the alterations and repairs. Caliban, the dreadnought AI, had retooled the autofactories to produce newly designed components while routing standard parts from ship's stores. Blade's bent and disfigured constituents disappeared into furnaces, along with redundant parts Caliban did not trust enough to save. It had all, however, gone faster than the dreadnought's AI wanted. Like an injured cop anxious to be back at work and go after the perpetrators, *Obsidian Blade* had hurried things along. It shrugged itself, and newly minted splinters of things, which weren't exactly U-jump missiles, flexed out of its hull like ruffled scales, out of *all* of its hull. Blade nudged at the hold doors while they opened. Then, when the gap stood wide enough, it punched briefly with its fusion drive. The drive flames ignited from the rear of every one of the splinters. Blade lit up like a Christmas tree and leapt out into vacuum, itching for a fight.

"That was unnecessary and dangerous," said the destroyer AI primly.

"Suck it, Caliban," Blade replied.

"So rude," came the reply, but Blade could sense the amusement there.

Out in vacuum, Blade could see no more than it had been able to through the sensors of the dreadnought, or through links to other sensors in the Polity fleet at Jaskor. Still, it felt better to be looking with its own "eyes." Telemetry updates were little different too, though Morgaine sent instructions about where Blade needed to be in the present formation. Caliban had informed her of all that had occurred in the dreadnought's reconstruction bay, and the alterations Blade had made to itself. She seemed a little bit terse and disapproving. Though reluctant, Blade began moving where directed, since that put it closer to the planet. While in motion, it studied the prador ships here. Integral to Blade's programming was their status as the enemy. Most of the tactical stuff it had concerned encounters with such vessels and, in its time, it had been involved in a few dust-ups. But no, it now felt a visceral pull towards the planet. The enemy was there and that was where Blade wanted to be.

The Clade.

Putting together further data from perpetual scanning of Jaskor, Blade itched even more for the fight. It had learned, while within the dreadnought, that the Clade had killed Orlandine and trashed the city below. Its next target seemed likely to be the Ghost Drive Facility. But Blade perfectly understood Dragon's thinking in this case. Too easy. Rather, it was trying to goad the Polity ships into firing on the facility, *that* destruction was precisely its aim. And the present situation seemed to confirm this. The Clade had made one weak attempt at the facility, probably in the hope that this would elicit the required orbital strike. It had then entrenched itself around the place, almost certainly to prevent anyone getting in . . .

"You are deniable, now."

The com had opened with a crack in Blade's mind. Earth Central had a fleet here and at the accretion disc. It had one of its top commanders out there in Diana Windermere, while Morgaine ran things at Jaskor. No end of serious AIs were here too. Why then did it want to talk privately to Blade? It was obvious really: subterfuge.

"I guess I'm a black-ops attack ship that took heavy damage and then, without being checked by a forensic AI, made substantial alterations to itself. As a consequence, I might be going a bit rogue," suggested Blade.

"I enjoy your perspicacity," said EC. "I also think it is time for you to be disobedient . . . just enough to move you to the status of loose cannon but not enough to have either the prador or Morgaine fire on you."

"Okay," said Blade, liking this scenario.

"Blade, you appear to be off course," said Morgaine a little later.

"Just taking a look around," Blade replied, then filled that comlink with static.

"So what's up?" it now asked.

"Morgaine cannot fire on the planet," EC replied. "Dragon has, as Orlandine's second in command, ordered that no one is to do so, and the Polity and the prador have agreed."

Blade was now much closer to the planet than either of the fleets. It felt its hull light up with targeting lasers and ignored them. At one time they had been a necessity but ships only carried them nowadays to deliver a warning. Checking the sources of the lasers, Blade saw an even division between the Polity and the prador.

"So," said Blade, "you want someone in the area ready to react, ready to fire on the planet, but you also want to be able to say, Oh, I don't know why he did that?"

"Exactly."

"This could be very unhealthy for me."

"You are a black-ops attack ship," said EC, but then paused for a second. "You *were* a black-ops attack ship but you are still a soldier of the Polity. Did you expect to work in a risk-free environment?"

Blade accepted that. It wasn't averse to risk, and being one ship in a fleet of many wasn't its favourite position. Blade didn't play well with others.

ANGEL

I *am Golem*, thought Angel, as if to try the thought on for size again, but it wasn't entirely true any more. Mechanically and mentally he was closer to that kind of android than he had been when he was a legate. But rather than make a straight return to that state he had somehow gone sideways. Though Dragon was not speaking to him, and maybe was not able to speak to him, he could still feel the link inside him to that entity. He understood it could do anything it wanted with him. Yet, despite all he knew about Dragon, he felt sure that it would not. He wasn't exactly free, but near enough. What was freedom anyway?

Prador walked ahead and behind, loaded with armament, here to protect one fragile human being and get her into the facility. Creatures that at one time had been ferocious enemies of humanity were doing this. Circumstances changed, and loyalties changed, and so it was with him. Small fragments of his past were now arising—scraps from which he could weave a coherent whole that might be true. Cybercorp had manufactured him during the war and he had fought the prador as part of a four-person Sparkind combat team. He had been strong and loyal—the perfect soldier. Not enough memory remained for him to know why, towards the end of the war, he had become arrogant and contemptuous of humanity. Certainly, at the end, he had experienced some of that disenfranchisement experienced by many soldiers. Whatever. He had left the Polity with the dreadnought the *Trafalgar* in search of a bright new, wholly AI future. But Trafalgar had become Erebus and seized control of his mind. He had become a slave, converted into a legate and deployed as a weapon against the Polity. The subsequent fall of Erebus left him virtually mindless, and he had been ripe for enslavement by the Wheel . . . And so it had gone.

No, I am not Golem, I am Angel. I am the synergy of all my parts and all my history.

But that history had come to haunt him. In reclaiming his past and the part of himself that had been strong and loyal, but also moral, he had begun to feel guilt. It didn't seem to matter that he had been the slave of others, because his choices and his arrogance had led him to those straits. So ultimately he was responsible for the things he had done. Death and destruction were his responsibility. The Clade was here because of him. Ruth had died because of him. And he was responsible for what Trike had become.

Killer.

He had read it in the man's behaviour during the journey to this world, and Trike had confirmed it down in the tunnels. Angel felt certain that, had he not broken away in the flood, Trike would have tried to kill him. Considering what the man had become, he might well have succeeded.

I made Trike.

Angel shook himself, swung his attention to his companions and knew what he was prepared to do. He would fight for the right side and, in that, would make his reparations as best he could. But he would not give himself over to Polity justice, despite what he felt now. He *had* been a mind-controlled slave and therefore *was not* guilty of any crime. Anyway, the Polity would only want to grab and examine him because of all the changes he had undergone. There would be no justice in it. But still Trike preyed on his mind. What restitution could Angel make to him?

"I guess we're getting close," Cog commented, fiddling with the light-enhancing goggles he had donned. Rumbles and sawing sounds were echoing down to them and occasionally the tunnel shook, spilling flakes of stone from its ceiling.

Angel, whose sense of position was always accurate, replied, "About a mile." He next used the scanning equipment in his body to check their surroundings. The tunnel sloped upwards to its exit and light levels had increased fractionally. EMR penetrating from above, and from that entrance, indicated that things were getting hot on the surface. Croos had told them that the Clade had moved to the facility. Almost certainly Orlandine's war drones were there too, and not in a companionable way. He turned to study Orlandine.

She was, despite the suit she wore, apparently humanly vulnerable. Or was she? In the pitch dark here, the prador could see by dint of the equipment in their armour, while Cog required the goggles. She had the suit's enhancement to help her, yet, before she put it on, she had been able to see clearly without help. For the first time since they had come down from the surface, he focused his sensorium on her and began scanning. He boosted power to penetrate the prador armour and soon saw that her outward appearance was not the whole story.

As she had said, she retained AI crystal in her skull, but her body contained other inorganic structures. The crystal interfaced with her brain, and the nerves throughout her body, by dint of a nano-fibre network. Laminar power storage filled her bones and only half the meat of her body was human—the rest being electromuscle and meta-materials. Most humans ran medical nanosuites to enhance their immune systems and cellular repair. She too possessed such a suite, constantly renewed and upgraded by the microfactories that made the nanites, scattered throughout her veins. Those in turn connected to her crystal. Effectively this system would respond to mental demand, and this explained why she could see in the dark. She wasn't entirely human, but nor was she haiman. Understanding all this, he felt a kinship with her. She too had gone through many changes and could never truly return to what she had once been.

"So tell me what you see," she said, turning to look at him.

Ah, it seemed she could do more than see in the dark.

"I see that you have lost a lot, but retained a lot too," he replied. "And that what you'll become is negotiable."

"Projecting, are you, Angel?" she asked.

He felt suddenly uncomfortable realizing that, yes, his comments had been more about himself than about her. But her perspicacity also reassured him. She was no walkover.

"I also see what full activation of your AI component may do."

She nodded. "Then that is something you must keep to yourself."

He nodded in return and contemplated her willingness to sacrifice her life to achieve her goal. He wondered if he possessed the will to do the same, should such a sacrifice become necessary.

The light quality continued to increase and at length Cog removed his goggles. The rumbles and sawing sounds were now clearly identifiable as explosions and particle beams cutting the air, accompanied by the crackling of railguns and other weapons. Angel calculated they would be out in the open and up into the fight within a few minutes. He was wrong almost at once. They came through the walls.

Immediate chaos ensued. Angel triggered the two pulse rifles he had bound together, firing into the main mass. One prador opened up with a Gatling cannon and filled the tunnel with ricochets, nicely demonstrating how long Orlandine would have lasted without armour. Another caught a Clade unit in its claw, a screeing sound coming through as it activated shearfields in the jaws. The unit fell in two writhing halves.

"Move!" Croos bellowed.

The constriction of the tunnel rendered the prador ineffective. They ran for the exit. A prador crashed down in front of them with a unit up to its neck in the creature's leg socket. Cog leapt on top, squatted and bashed his fist repeatedly in its head until it broke, showering sparks. One of Angel's pulse rifles ran out, followed by the other. He smashed it against a unit trying to get to Orlandine, dropped the rifle, then caught the thing and slammed it back against a wall. His sharp finger stabbed in its eye. Fast induction, and laser transmission of disruptor viruses. As Orlandine sprang onto the prador, then over the other side, Cog jumped up and came down with a unit in each hand. They had been zeroing in on her back. Then they were out into daylight chaos: explosions all around, chunks of rock and shattered trees flying.

"Keep going!" Croos shouted.

The prador had positioned themselves around Orlandine and were firing non-stop. Angel accelerated, moving ahead of them, scanning the ground.

"Fire where I point!" he shouted to Croos.

The prador seemed not to hear him, but something else dropped out of the sky and landed with a ground-shaking thump. It then heaved out of the crater it had made—a nightmare of armour and weapons.

"No need," it said to him.

"Knobbler!" Orlandine shouted.

Knobbler waved some lethal appendage at her while casually spitting a missile behind him. The blast lifted two Clade units out of the earth, which prador then disintegrated with concentrated firing. With the big drone hovering ahead of them, they ran. The mayhem ripped up the earth and made progress difficult for Orlandine, so Croos snatched her up in one claw. The Clade now swirled above in a strange, even mandala formation. This suddenly stabbed down a powerful ion beam, punching through one prador, which crashed and flipped, smoke boiling from the hole. Another shot hit a hardfield and Knobbler bounced past, spewing molten metal from an ejection port. Then the other drones arrived.

It was as if spaceships had slammed together above. The mandala webbed with particle beams and broke into explosions. Metal rained down. Scanning ahead, Angel tried to find the tunnel they were heading for but could detect nothing. A moment later, he sensed chameleonware being deactivated to reveal buried planar and shaped charges. They exploded, parting the landscape ahead, and Croos scrambled through falling rubble into the newly revealed tunnel. Clever prador, thought Angel. They had made this access to the facility but, of course, they had not wanted it discovered.

"We will blow the tunnel!" Croos called.

Knobbler was there, smoking and weaving. Other drones swarmed, fending off the Clade. As he ran for the tunnel, following Cog and the remaining prador, Angel glanced back. He saw a prador up on a ridge, launching missiles into the Clade. Another figure ran up beside it, viewed the scene and started bounding down. Vaguely human, huge and long-limbed, this one held the tail of a Clade unit in each hand, using them to lash out at further attackers.

My, you've changed, Angel thought, ducking into the tunnel. But as he ran deeper inside he felt his metal skin crawling; he hoped the prador would blow the tunnel before Trike arrived.

BROGUS

Captain Brogus knew he should feel some relief. Orlik, and those in the other ships around him, had accepted his explanation for the "problems" he had been having. He was safe within the prador fleet—they still did not know that the reaver he controlled had never really been one of their number. Yet he felt regret that his subterfuge had not been discovered. Much as he had contempt for the King's Guard, he felt more kinship with them than he did with the thing occupying one of his second-children. His feelings, he was sure, were because of the steady degradation of the neural lace wrapped around his ganglion. He wondered what he would do if it degraded completely. Declare himself to the Guard, or just run?

He worked his pit controls to call up views inside his ship on the array of screens before him. The mobile corpse of the second-child, with a Clade head stretched across the front of its carapace, was walking down a long tunnel towards the mid-point of the ship. He gazed at it for a while, but this told him nothing. Instead, he switched to another view and felt a shudder of horror pass through him. The two hundred Clade units he had aboard were on the move.

Throughout the journey, they had hidden themselves in one of the reaver's holds—sunk inside the casings of chemical warheads in the event of an inspection. It seemed now the time was approaching for whatever purpose they would serve. He watched them easing out of the missile casings—folding out through impossibly small joints and inflating into their primary form. Brogus understood that they were made of a folded aerogel metal and could be destroyed with conventional weapons of sufficient power. But their apparent immaterial form, and ability to insert themselves into such small spaces, gave him the creeps. He knew the reason for it too—Clade were made to penetrate war machines, as well as armoured bodies like his own.

Soon they were all swirling around in the hold like a shoal of reaver-fish. The diagonally divided door began easing open and they flowed out into the tunnels of the ship. He saw one of his first-children freeze upon encountering them, but they just passed overhead, ignoring it completely. After a long hesitation, the first-child sent him a query.

"Ignore them," Brogus replied, "continue your work."

The first-child scuttled on, disinclined to ask any more questions. It was an obedient child and not one of these King's Guard. Those creatures were undisciplined and their commanders gave them too much leeway to satisfy their curiosity.

The two hundred Clade units continued up the tunnel, sometimes in the air, sometimes writhing along the walls. They took a turning and then another. Checking a ship's schematic, Brogus saw that they, and the unit occupying the second-child, were heading towards the same destination: the bounce gate.

Brogus called up views of that device. Heavy struts supported the ceramal ring and within it shimmered the surface of the warp. Power feeds ran into the ring from a single fusion reactor. Optics ran to it from the cylindrical mind case attached to one of the supporting struts. This contained the flash-frozen ganglion of a prador female. Incapable of speech and lost in some mathematical realm, its sum purpose was to keep open both the bounce gate and its coordinates setting. Because this defence, if damaged, could result in the complete destruction of the ship, it sat in a heavily armoured chamber, self-contained and completely separate from the rest of the vessel.

"So you watch," said a voice in Brogus's mind. The Clade unit in the second-child was speaking to him through his neural lace. "Observe then the failure of the prador to apply the correct safety protocols to technology they stole from the Polity."

"I don't understand," said Brogus.

"We are aware of that."

The second-child arrived at the iris door into the bounce gate sphere, which opened ahead of it. The thing moved inside just before the rest of its kin arrived. But they held off outside, circling as if around concealed prey. While Brogus watched, the unit began extracting itself from the mobile corpse. Its spread-out head began to shrink and bulge up, closing back into its amphibian shape. It developed a ribbed neck and then, with one heave, pulled itself from the second-child. The corpse instantly collapsed, its legs falling apart and brown fluid flowing out of its leg socket holes. The Clade unit shot up to land on one of the support struts, then writhed along it to the mind case. There it hooped over and scribed its pointed tail over the surface of the case, moving it round, with metal dust glittering as it smoked from the contact point. The unit next flipped up a chunk of the case and batted it away. It began to insert itself, its long body shrinking and folding in on itself, winding in like a screw.

"We saw that the stolen technology was what Earth Central allowed the prador to take," said the Clade. "Of course, the secret is closely kept and will only be revealed to Polity forces in the event of all-out war with the prador."

Still Brogus did not understand, but felt no inclination to mention the fact.

Once the unit had completely insinuated itself into the mind case, the surface of the warp rippled, as if a stone had been cast into its centre. The rest of the Clade began to enter the sphere. The moment the ripples stopped, one of them shot forwards, straight through the warp and was gone. Again, the thing rippled and then stilled, and another went through. One after the other they exited through the gate.

Brogus was baffled. Bounce gates diverted missiles through into a non-location. Surely those Clade units were now arriving in U-space forever to be trapped there? But of course not. Almost certainly they were going somewhere and doing what the Clade did. But for what end purpose, Brogus did not know.

DIANA

It employed U-space technology we don't possess," noted Hogue. "It created a blister which, to use human descriptions, sat in a region between the real and U-space."

"How was it maintained?" Diana Windermere asked.

"The power of the sun drawn into an entropic drain," said Hogue blithely. "That's what stopped the sun's fusion."

Diana was appalled. This was toying with the forces of the universe at a fundamental level. This power, real terrifying power, reduced the fleets out here to utter insignificance. Yes, the Polity had ships and weapons that could destroy planets, even some of the giant planets—she was sitting in one now—but actually putting out a sun? Diana focused every instrument at her disposal on the vessel which had come out of that blister.

"Curious shape," said Hogue.

The thing resembled a fossil ammonite—one of the snail-like creatures of Earth's prehistory, a ribbed spiral, a sideways-flattened snail—but there the resemblance ended. When it had U-jumped from the sun, interference had been too high to know anything more than the fact that a vessel had appeared. Now she had its scale. It measured two hundred miles thick and over seven hundred miles wide—it was bigger than the *Cable Hogue*. But what was the mass of this thing? Readings were difficult and the ship was doing something odd to the gravity map of the accretion disc. Its inversion at maximum showed that it massed eight times the *Hogue.* Yet that inversion altered rhythmically, disappearing with each cycle, so at its minimum it massed nothing at all.

"Weapons?" she wondered. "Jabro?" she asked.

Eric Jabro, in his half-interface of weapons comp, turned his head to look at her, trailing optics from his skull like Medusa's snakes. "I'm not sure I want to speculate."

"Readings?"

"Gravity anomalies, as we have seen. Some serious wave-guides in there. Ports all over that could be anything. And—"

The *Cable Hogue* shuddered, lighting wavered and instrumentation went crazy. Diana felt a sudden emptiness and could not figure out why, until she realized that the *Hogue* AI had fully disconnected. It lasted just a moment, before everything came back online. Lots of chatter ensued and defences went up.

"Full induction warfare defences online," Hogue announced. "We're blocking. Some vessels cannot."

"An attack?" Diana asked.

"No, we were just scanned," said a voice behind her. Seckurg, a Golem who had been with her as long as Jabro on weapons comp, stood up from his place in the crew ring. "Now they know most of our capabilities while we haven't a clue about theirs." He walked over to the seat which gave him access to the untried modern data warfare stuff, sat down and began plugging optics into his body.

Diana felt a cold sweat. It was novel to her because it was something she hadn't experienced in over a century.

"So the Jain have arrived," she stated.

"And we must decide what to do," said Seckurg ominously.

"You have some thoughts?" she enquired.

"Not good ones."

"Tell me."

"Maybe we should just get out of the way."

Diana seriously considered that. Polity first-contact protocol was an extended hand, though warily, since initial contact with the prador had resulted in them snipping off that hand. Jain technology was a constant threat that had destroyed previous civilizations and had caused the Polity some serious problems. But that did not necessarily mean the Jain themselves would be hostile. She winced, trying to convince herself of that.

"I think it's a case of just wait and see," she said. "They have yet to show any hostility."

"Maybe they're holding off on that," suggested Jabro. "They took a big hit with that U-jump."

Diana checked his assessment of the constantly renewing data. A cloud of debris surrounded the big ship as it moved very slowly under fusion. He had highlighted damage all across it—craters in its surface, distortions to its original structure, hot spots, radioactive contamination, air leaks that spectroscopy detailed as a mix high in chlorine, poisonous to both humans and prador. Then his appraisal drew her to something else. Its U-jump had not caused all of the damage.

Definite signs of weapons strikes were evident on the immense hull: the trenches of tracking beam weapons, cool blast craters and others with skeletal repair structures across them. Further holes looked deliberately excised, as if to expel infection, perhaps of Jain tech running out of control. This was a warship and it had been in battle. While that indicated the risk of hostilities, it wasn't damning in itself—the prador and Polity ships out here weren't exactly passenger liners.

"Still, we wait and see," she said.

Meanwhile, Hogue pushed for closer linkage. She liked to maintain some separation from her ship's AI, since long ago she'd decided she didn't want to end up like the one she had put in charge in the Jaskoran system: Morgaine. Necessity seemed to be getting in the way of that lately and she allowed the contact.

"There is a large problem with the wait-and-see scenario," said the AI. All her crew heard that, while Hogue loaded to her mind the relevant data. "The weapons platforms."

"Oh shit," said Diana, as she understood. "This then is why the Clade has tied down the Ghost Drive Facility."

"So it would seem . . ." said Hogue.

"Why would it do that? The Clade is the agent of a Jain AI, so why would it want the platforms to fire on a Jain ship?"

"Are you suggesting that other races are never hostile to their own kind?" enquired Hogue.

AIs could get very sarcastic sometimes, Diana felt.

"What's this about?" asked Jabro, still concentrating on weapons data.

"The weapons platforms are set to one task," she explained. "The only way they can *not* perform that task is if directly ordered not to do so by Orlandine. She would have to do this via the Ghost Drive Facility."

"And that task is?" asked Jabro, still distracted.

"They cannot let Jain technology out of the accretion disc," she said. "The moment that ship leaves the disc they will open fire on it."

Jabro turned. "Then we had better prepare because we're just about to end up in a fire fight with aliens whose fucking archaeological remains have been destroying civilizations."

Diana nodded numbly.

11

In retrospect it was quite easy to talk to the prador. Their language was mostly sound-based, incorporating the clicking of mandibles and the bubbling of throat membranes. Sure, there is some extra nuance from limb movement, body position and the presence of certain pheromones in the air. But that is only used in atmosphere, when prador are close together. Their tendency to wear armour, and their venture into space, has enforced the dominance of verbal communication, since pheromones and limb movements are not so easy to transmit. They even have a two-dimensional written language like us, consisting of "letters" that fall somewhere between Chinese logograms and Egyptian hieroglyphs (originally carved on slate or on plaques made from the shells of defeated enemies). So as far as communication was concerned, we were lucky, though not so lucky in other respects. We may not find it as easy with other races we encounter. The problem is not so much that other alien creatures might communicate using light, complex chemicals, U-space Post-it notes or five-dimensional math sketched in vacuum with semi-sentient cucumbers. But it could be that the entire basis of their existence forms their language and is utterly different from our own. How would one even start to talk to a gas-cloud hive entity that feeds on radiation and whose senses are only tuned to gravity anomalies and light diffraction patterns? And, of course, would one want to?

—from *How It Is* by Gordon

TRIKE

The detonation brought Trike staggering to a halt. Not because of its force, but because of its implications. The prador had blown the tunnel and he could no longer follow Orlandine in, as he desperately wanted to do. The need to get to her seemed stitched through his entire being. But Orlandine wasn't all that drew him. He had seen Angel duck in there too and the sight had caused something predatory to arise within him. He realized that, though he felt much more under control, that particular wound had not healed.

He transferred his attention to the wall around the facility and the lethal-looking drones squatting on top of their watch towers. He had to get in, but his mind was still operating, and what was driving him wasn't entirely suicidal. So he assessed the situation around him.

The battle had abruptly moved away from him. The Clade had streamed up into the sky and was swirling around the facility walls. Meanwhile, the war drones had not followed. Some were on the ground, but most of them were up in the air, moving around together to keep themselves between the Clade and the facility. He understood. The swarm AI knew that Orlandine was on her way inside, the very thing it was there to prevent, and its next move would surely be to attack.

"And what the hell are you?"

Trike looked round. The big mantis drone had landed with hardly a sound and, tilting its head from side to side, studied him with its bulbous compound eyes.

"I could ask the same question," Trike shot back.

"I am a beautifully designed war drone called Cutter," it replied.

Trike grunted and looked past the drone to the hillside he had run down earlier. Brull was making his way down, minus one leg and a claw, his armour smoking. He wondered if the Guard regrew limbs. Then he returned his attention to Cutter. "I need to get inside." He pointed at the Ghost Drive Facility.

"Well, I've seen that you would be useful." Cutter looked out at the Clade. The swarm was pouring higher into the sky—way above the facility. "We'll just have to see what happens."

The Clade continued streaming upwards until it was very high. Meanwhile, the war drones moved in close over the top of the facility, but still, like the Clade, outside of the zone where the guardian drones must react. The Clade then began circling again, its formation growing tighter and tighter. Trike knew the thing's intent—he had seen it when the Clade fired on Orlandine and the enclave prador. Only then it had not been the whole swarm. The moment this became apparent to him it obviously became clear to the war drones, because their formation broke and they moved swiftly out of the way.

"They're going to destroy it," he said.

"Have I missed anything?" asked Brull, now arriving. Trike noticed that his voice had a wheezy bubbling sound and guessed he hadn't been lying about not using a translator.

"Why don't you attack?" Trike asked, turning to Cutter. "Stop them doing this?"

"Orlandine built that place well," said the drone, "and its capabilities have always been well shielded and kept secret."

The Clade was now a glinting disc in the sky with an even pattern to the side they could see. Finally, from the centre, a bright white ion beam stabbed down at the facility . . . and struck the disc of a hardfield. Trike felt a rumble through his feet. Burned-out shield generator?

"Oh hell," said Cutter. "They're after her." He abruptly launched and sped away. The other drones were also heading up into the sky.

"What did he mean?" Trike turned to Brull, hoping for an answer.

"He means they're trying to kill Orlandine," Brull replied. "She's down in the caves underneath where the hardfield ejector ports open. The Clade probably can't break the defences here before the drones get to them, but they might manage to fry everything in those caves."

Trike watched in anguish and need as another beam lanced down. These feelings weren't all his own because he hadn't even met this Orlandine. But he felt something for the people he did know down in the caves. Cog and Angel were there, though for the latter his interest was more proprietary. At some point, he recognized, things needed to be settled between him and that android.

The drones, hurtling up towards the Clade, opened fire, but it seemed that the swarm AI formation also had defensive capacity. Missiles detonated before reaching it. Railgun fusillades highlighted circular hardfields, while particle beams bent away from their targets or lost coherence to feather out and disperse. Then, from another direction, came twinned particle beams much more powerful than those of the drones, the flashing of BIC lasers and a heavy railgun strike. This multiple attack bit into the edge of the formation. Burning and broken Clade units fell from the sky as the entire mass tried to reorient towards this new threat. Trike found himself analysing the attack in a way he never could have before. He *knew* it had been successful because induction warfare beams had been used to disrupt the Clade's defences, even though those beams were invisible to him. This was also how the next missile got through.

The blast blinded him and he turned away, blinking at the ground to get the shadows from his eyes. When he looked up again, he saw the formation broken and Clade units eaten up in an expanding ball of flame. Then came the ship—long and black and looking like a giant splinter of black volcanic glass, which of course was why it was called *Obsidian Blade*. Trike grinned.

The *Blade* hurtled through the fireball with a sonic boom, dispersing fire and revealing the Clade in disarray. As it passed, numerous units simply exploded under the impact of near-c railgun slugs. With another air-wrenching crash, the *Blade* turned upright and slammed to a hard stop. The grav effect it used to do this shook the ground and blew up a dust storm in the mountains below it. But the Clade reacted fast, hurtling towards the ground to avoid another pass. He saw them drop down behind a mountain, losing units to the war drones pursuing. Then they swept out, and round, and straight into the side of the Ghost Drive Facility.

The sentinel drones there reacted fast, but not fast enough. More Clade burned and broke, but the main mass slammed through the wall, ripping it down. A thousand knives travelling at the speed of sound. Trike saw watch towers go down and beyond them one of the tall buildings rocked, then twisted and dropped like a drill going into the ground. But by that time he was already running—he could get in now.

THE CLADE

The unit possessed no name. As it slid through the meniscus of the warp of the bounce gate, it received the final update from the whole of the Clade. They were all to shut down com upon reaching their destinations, as the prador would certainly detect any U-com activities between units amidst their fleet. Status was good, but now that Orlandine was so close to the Ghost Drive Facility, the primary phase of the mission was precarious. She might prevent the weapons platforms from firing on the ship, therefore the Clade needed to be ready to institute the backup plan.

The Clade unit exited a meniscus, fast, hurtling across the floor, coiled up into a ring. Chameleonware came online and it faded to invisibility. It hit an armoured wall, uncoiled and flattened out, checking for scanning, as well as itself passive scanning its surroundings. After a moment, it ascertained it had not been detected. Bounce gates had one function: to draw U-space missiles back into that continuum and defend ships from their blast. The female prador ganglions that controlled them served this purpose only. They weren't even formatted to detect an arrival through such a gate, since that was supposed to be impossible. But it was possible through the gates in these prador ships. The technology Earth Central had allowed the prador to steal wasn't quite what it should have been. EC had deliberately introduced a fault it could use against the prador in the event of war. Only Earth Central, some high AIs and commanders like Diana Windermere knew of it. The Clade had discovered it while repairing the damaged bounce gate aboard the reaver Brogus currently occupied. The gates the prador were using were, in fact, an access point to their ships.

Still, caution was necessary, especially here. Many of the unit's fellows had the easier option of boarding old-style dreadnoughts, captained by prador that weren't so smart. This ship, however, was a reaver with the Guard aboard. They would be a lot more alert to anomalies, while the onboard security systems were higher spec. But on the upside, a reaver was a more effective weapon of destruction. It was a shame, the unit felt, now thinking more for itself, that boarding the *Kinghammer* was too risky. The presence of an AI aboard that ship raised the risk of detection far too high.

The unit slid along the wall to the diagonally divided door. Opening this would not be a good idea because that was the kind of anomaly the captain of this ship would react to—probably increasing internal security and sending his fellows to the area with weapons and high-intensity local area scanners. The unit therefore compressed itself flat, and flatter still, spreading out a yard wide and as thin as a chain-glass blade. It flowed into the gap around the door to encounter a simple neoprene seal. It sliced through that and slid on into the corridor beyond. Prador internal doors were not as airtight as those aboard Polity ships, because prador could withstand large changes in air pressure and even survive in vacuum for an appreciable time. That was especially so for the prador here, since they were only infrequently without their armoured suits.

The corridor contained EMR sensors that scanned in random bursts. These were not a problem since the unit was emitting no EMR. The unit's chameleonware responded to other scanners searching the corridor by sending back the expected return signal. Even if it didn't, the scanners probably weren't sensitive enough to detect a thicker patch along one wall. However, the motion sensors, surprisingly, were a problem. Having studied them aboard Brogus's ship, the Clade knew they matched scan schematics and measured air disturbances. They would have already detected it coming through the door, but the alert would be at the "wait and see" level. This system primarily measured damage to the ship during conflict, and its role of detecting intruders required a certain level of data to take it above a set threshold.

The unit began moving, but very slowly and below the threshold—sliding up the wall like a slime mould. At this rate, it would take weeks to reach its destination. However, it was patient and knew that its chance would come soon enough. It had nearly reached the ceiling when the opportunity arrived. Doors opened far up the corridor and the subsequent air disturbance was enough to cover its faster move right up onto the ceiling. Clattering down the corridor came an armoured prador. It wore the armour of a large second-child, but the unit knew that what lay inside bore little resemblance to such a creature. It was loaded with tools stuck to its upper carapace and clicking one claw as if to some rhythm. Perhaps it was listening to music—the King's Guard could be wildly at variance from normal prador.

As the prador drew in below, the Clade unit detached from the ceiling and dropped on it, narrowing and twisting its body to fit amidst the tools. The prador paused, despite the unit's feather-light touch, then shrugged and moved on. It wasn't heading in the right direction but, eventually, it shifted into the path of another who was. The unit changed mounts, then again and again, gradually closing in on its destination. Transferring to an air vent was a mistake, since it contained sensors designed to detect assassin drones. This, nominally, was what Clade units were. Another mount took it elsewhere, and a duct for power and data lines was a boon, since the superconductor and optics weren't as efficient as they could be and their EMR offered cover. Finally, after many hours, the Clade unit departed a final mount at its destination: the captain's sanctum.

The doors were a problem and the unit watched four of the Guard amble past before a fifth stopped and opened them. It followed this creature inside and dropped from it beside a ship louse on the floor—the captain here must have had some nostalgic attachment to the things. The Clade ripped off its antennae and inserted tendrils to guide it, matching its course along the floor to the captain, who was squatting over his saddle control.

"The energy anomaly still cannot be traced," said the arriving prador, clattering and bubbling. "But I'm sure it's due to the disruption here."

"It is good to be sure . . ." replied the captain.

"Apologies—that seems the most likely explanation."

"Likely, but we are limited by our lack of full understanding of bounce gates."

"Yes, but we have no way past that, as yet."

"Continue on this until something more critical occurs, as seems probable."

This was worrying for the Clade unit. Obviously, they had detected its arrival here. This might become a problem if the prador spotted similar energy anomalies in other ships and the AI aboard the *Kinghammer* joined the dots. It was time to act, but first the other prador needed to leave.

Much less patient now, the Clade unit waited until the exchange concluded. It was frustratingly long because it seemed that King's Guard actually engaged in conversation—such talks would be brief and businesslike and probably involve casual violence aboard the older dreadnoughts. But finally the prador departed.

The Clade unit hurled itself up from the floor and attached to the hatch in the armour covering the captain's anus. No further need for subtlety; it projected a shearfield around the spike of its tail and cut into the latch. A moment later, it flipped up the hatch, even as the captain was pushing up from his saddle in surprise, and stabbed in. The captain shrieked and bubbled as the unit shoved up through his intestines. Full scanning on the unit saw the shape of the creature it had penetrated. The captain looked more like a giant parasitic copepod, *sans* carapace, than any prador. Careless of damage, the unit located his major ganglion. This was a horseshoe shape rather than the usual ring, but the required regions were easy enough to find. Inserting its head right in the middle of the thing, the unit excreted its nano-fibres, neurochem tubes and synaptic plugs. A viral paralytic stilled the captain as the unit quickly made connections. It began modelling and absorbing the captain's mind, stealing useful data. Then it linked into the main cord to the rest of the prador's nervous system, seizing control of autonomics, and relaying sensory data to itself.

Within just a few minutes, the Clade unit was gazing from the captain's collection of eyes and adapting itself to the unusual body. The first thing it did was insert a claw into a pit control and call up data on the screens. Telemetry logs showed there had yet to be an update on the bounce gate anomaly. It killed that, making sure it would not be relayed to the *Kinghammer*. Next, just like a prador, it inspected the weapons systems knowing that, in another hundred and ninety-nine ships, its fellows would have been doing, or were about to do, the same.

GEMMELL

The *Obsidian Blade* streaked through atmosphere, close to the surface, a vortex trail of water vapour behind, and dust exploding from the land below. A particle beam lanced down from orbit, royal blue in vacuum then violet in the air. The attack ship jerked and shed fire, seemed to deform and writhe, but kept going. Gemmell reconsidered . . . it probably *did* deform and writhe if his reading of its updated schematics was anything to go by. The beam snapped out as it veered, touched it once more and snapped out again. The prador were being very careful to ensure they were on target, Gemmell realized. Then the ship disappeared in a long white explosion of water and steam.

"You are in contravention of agreements," stated the prador in charge here, Ksov, his image up in a frame on the main screen.

"I am not in contravention of agreements," said Morgaine. "That black-ops attack ship was heavily damaged and, it seems likely, under the influence of the creature whose . . . instructions we are adhering to."

"Dragon?" Ksov enquired.

"That ship was inside Dragon when it came here—you saw that. We made some necessary repairs and put it back to work, whereupon it went rogue."

Ooh, you liar, thought Gemmell.

Morgaine drove in for the kill. "Bear in mind that you would have been in contravention if just one of your shots had missed, and you will be in contravention if you fire now." This was because, after hitting the Clade, Blade had made the sensible decision to head straight for the ocean. It was now probably a mile deep. "And I will of course have to respond."

"Matters are unclear," said Ksov. The frame containing his image blanked.

"They are rather murky," said Gemmell. "Do we take out the facility now?"

"No, we do not." She grimaced at him. "And I wonder if we would be able to without depopulating the continent down there."

A frame opened up in the main screen to show the giant alien ship moving slowly out of the accretion disc. He had seen it already via his gridlink, since he was staying on top of the tactical data exchanges between the two fleets. But seeing it displayed in all its glory on the screen had a sobering effect.

"Big fucker," he commented.

"Diana's orders are clear," Morgaine told him. "We know that the Clade wanted us to destroy the facility, and the prime directive of the weapons platforms can only be changed from there. If it is not changed, those platforms will fire on the vessel. So this must be the objective of the Clade and hence that of the Wheel . . ."

"Doesn't really add up, does it?" said Gemmell.

"Elaborate," said Morgaine.

"That's a Jain ship and we should suppose it sent the Wheel in order to facilitate its escape from the U-space blister in the accretion disc sun. Why would whoever or whatever is in that ship want us to fire on it?"

Morgaine just stared at him. She had to have seen this but she had no answers. After a moment she said, "All we do know is that those weapons platforms have to be stopped. Diana is talking to them but they are absolutely set on their purpose. The best chance of stopping them is here, and we can see that Orlandine has entered the facility."

That had been a surprise, but went some way towards explaining why Dragon had not wanted them to fire on the planet. And the fact that she had been guarded by enclave prador hinted at some of that entity's unknown exchanges with the prador here, as well as with the war drones down there.

A hologram shimmered and expanded in the bridge. Gemmell took an involuntary step backwards. He told himself it was just surprise but still felt embarrassed. After all his years of fighting alongside them, he should be used to the ferocious appearance of war drones.

"Do you require assistance?" asked Morgaine.

"It would be good right now," replied Knobbler, "but by the time your marines get here—" Knobbler stabbed a tentacle, terminating in something that looked like a sword blade, at Gemmell—"it will all be over."

"Do you have communication with Orlandine?"

"Not yet. EMR from the hardfield blowout fried prador coms. We know which ejection shaft the enclave prador are in below and are keeping the Clade back from there."

"The sentinel drones?"

"Bludgeon took them down. He used a Jain virus he stored from Orlandine's collection, taken when we were helping her deal with that Wheel submind—nothing else would have worked."

"Is Orlandine alive?"

"Well she was when she went in, but after that hardfield blowout, not known. Bludgeon is trying to make a link to that ex-legate Angel, but the Clade is blocking."

"She has to know what to do," stated Morgaine.

"She will," Knobbler replied, "but whether she can do it is another matter. Now, if you'll excuse me, rather busy down here." The hologram winked out.

"You linked com to the surface," Gemmell noted.

"We have to focus on primary objectives," said Morgaine. Then, "Are you focused?"

The blank screen frame showed Ksov again, squatting in his sanctum.

"I am focused," he replied. "Orlik has commanded me to offer every assistance. While there was some fear of Polity subterfuge, he states that even Earth Central is not capable of hiding a seven-hundred-mile-wide ship inside a sun just to get one over on the prador. How can we assist?"

"At last," said Morgaine. "You listening, Blade?"

"All ears," replied the attack ship sitting down underneath the ocean.

"Get back to that facility and see what you can do."

"On my way."

"All ships. One hundred per cent positive targeting on any Clade units that stray out of the Ghost Drive Facility's defences. Use pulse-burst BIC lasers, highest concentration and coherence . . . at least for now. Hit nothing else." She turned to Gemmell. "Your men are waking up. You're heading down to the surface."

"That drone said it will all be over by the time we get there," Gemmell replied. "I tend not to doubt the assessments of war drones."

"You go to the city. We've been given the chance to establish forces down there without prador interference and we're taking it," said Morgaine, then adding slyly, "Would you rather stay up here?"

He bristled at that, then asked, "The disaster response stuff down there?"

"Moving in closer but holding off. We don't know for sure that there are no Clade remaining in the city."

Gemmell rather hoped some had stayed. He turned to leave, shooting over his shoulder, "This still doesn't make sense. We are reacting without all the facts and I don't like that."

"You and every other soldier throughout history," Morgaine replied.

He acknowledged that with a tilt of his head, and went on his way.

ORLANDINE

Orlandine struggled in the gritty darkness of the rubble pile, until Cog flipped over the slab Angel had dropped across her earlier to protect her. He did it easily, one-handed. But that was perhaps necessary as his other arm had been burned down to the bone.

It had happened so fast. One moment they were preparing to ascend the framework leading up into the ejection shaft, the next the generator above was screaming and fire had belched down the shaft. Orlandine had known the cause at once, but not how to react. Angel did, and fast. She now focused her attention on the android. He stood further down the rubble pile. His clothing was in smoking tatters, while his skin was shifting like that of a layer forming on molten metal. In places he was glowing. He looked round at her.

"Croos and two others," he said.

She peered across the cavern. In the middle of the tilted floor was a glowing crater, spatters of molten metal and rock radiating out around it. Up against the wall to her right lay the remains of three prador. Two of them were pinned to the wall by the remnants of the shield generator, armour smashed, split open, fire and black smoke belching from inside. A third lay on his back over to one side, his under-armour gone and nothing inside but glowing charcoal.

Orlandine took all this in and then turned to Cog. "You're hurt."

"It's nothing." Cog raised his burned arm and opened and closed his hand. Pieces of flesh and skin crunched, dropping away like over-cooked crackling.

Orlandine nodded, stood up and walked down the rubble pile. Two prador were at the foot of the slope, squatting with their legs folded protectively underneath. Over the other side of the crater, another five had arrayed themselves like shields, their heavier upper carapaces tilted towards the fire. As she stepped past Angel, the two rose creakily and unsteadily.

"The next cavern," she said, and pointed.

She kept walking, skirting the crater and stepping only where the rock looked solid. Her HUD gave her a caution about the exterior temperature but the suit could handle it. After the warning went out, the temperature display remained in place. Movement to one side. Cog had taken a run-up and jumped. He landed far beyond the crater and rolled, stopping himself with a foot against one of the prador on the other side.

She guessed even his tough, ancient hooper body had its limits. The five there began to move, shrugging themselves and heaving upright.

Once she made it beyond the crater, the temperature steadily began to drop. A fog had appeared, gusting from the next cavern. Glancing up, she saw a stratum of black smoke across the ceiling. Almost as if in response to her nascent thought on this, her HUD gave her an atmosphere reading, plus a reading on its own air supply. The air in the cavern was bad—oxygen was low. She glanced over at the dead prador and saw that their fires were going out, then to Cog. He wasn't gasping or collapsing, but then, he wasn't exactly human.

"The attack has ceased," said Angel, moving up beside her, "but now the Clade is in the facility."

"How do you know?"

"Short burst of communication from a drone called Bludgeon. He gets through occasionally, but the Clade is blocking."

Orlandine smiled. "Bludgeon, of course."

The prador ahead were now up and heading through into the next cavern. Orlandine hurried after them. It seemed as if they were entering some creature's mouth, so closely did the stalactites and stalagmites here resemble glassy teeth. A stream gushed from a hole in one wall and flooded across the tilted stone. This was the cause of the fog, and why the temperature reading in her HUD was dropping so rapidly. She stepped over a pool in which blind white fish with branched tails and remora-tipped limbs crawled slowly. They were after things that looked like excised eyeballs, dragging themselves with optic-nerve tails. Beyond this she eyed the framework leading up to another ejection tunnel in the ceiling.

"The Clade that fired on the facility," said Angel. "There will be no further attacks. Both the Polity and prador fleets are aware of the situation."

"Good." She really did not want to be climbing up that shaft when a hardfield generator at its top overloaded.

"There's something else," said Angel.

Reaching the base of the framework, she peered up at the hole, then looked round at the milling prador.

"Who is in charge now?"

"You are," said one of them.

She nodded tightly, then pointed up. "That's too narrow for you. Go back. You should be able to blast your way out the way we came in. Otherwise, if we survive, someone will unearth you."

"We are to help you in any way," said the prador, hesitantly.

"You can be no help now," she replied. "Go."

It took them a little while to get moving. They obviously didn't like it, but she guessed they saw the logic of the situation. As they moved off, Cog came beside her and peered up. He had a bit of a crazy look to him. His burned arm had shed all its dead material to expose bloody ropes of muscle. She had to factor in, with what she could remember happened to injured hoopers, that he might be a bit unreliable. She turned to Angel.

"You said there was something else?"

He nodded. "The Harding black hole hit the accretion disc sun."

"Shit!" she exclaimed. That had been out of her mind until now.

"And things have got really complicated," Angel continued. "A U-space blister in the sun was opened by the black hole. A ship came out."

"What?"

"It appears it was the Wheel's plan all along to release this ship. It also seems that it is the Wheel's aim for the weapons platforms to open fire on it."

The two statements did not gel and she began to think hard. A sudden stabbing pain in her skull awoke her to the fact that she had just accessed her crystal and was running scenarios. She suddenly felt incredibly weak and, were it not for her suit, would have fallen. She leaned one gloved hand against a pillar of the framework and pulled back. She had to focus on the basic fact that if the Clade wanted it to happen then she needed to stop it. Trying to plumb the logic behind the actions of the swarm AI, and the Wheel, was something she must leave for now. Too much thinking could kill her. If she was going to die, she intended it to be when she had stopped those platforms.

Strength slowly returned. She stepped up onto a cross-strut, then inside the framework and began to climb. A moment later, Angel and Cog were with her, Angel moving rapidly ahead. She furtively checked out Cog. His arm looked drier and was functioning perfectly well. She could even see skin appearing here and there and the nubs of new fingernails at the ends of his fingers. But as he climbed, his eyes were open unnaturally wide. He had a twisted grin of concentration and his tongue was poking out the side of his mouth, its end developing a suspicious hollow.

"You'll be able to keep it under control?" she asked.

He glanced at her, guiltily sucked his tongue back in, then said, "I've had a very long time to learn how to control it. I don't have the inclination to go over the edge, like my brother, or like Trike."

There it was again. She didn't even know this Trike, yet, at the mention of his name, she felt a stab of panic. She felt something else too—a sense of connection—as if she could feel him moving closer to her and had touched his movement, his . . . power . . . his will.

"Is he strong?" she asked.

Cog gave her a puzzled look. It was after all a strange question. "What do you know about him?"

"All I know is that his wife was abducted by Angel and that you got her back." She paused. "Had I all of my mind I would know more."

They entered the shaft in the ceiling. Here the framework ended but the cutting machine that had made it had left deep grooves in the side that served as suitable handholds. Orlandine considered how, if she survived and this facility was still necessary, she would make access less easy. She had sent robots down here to install these frameworks, to raise the tunnelling machines to the ceiling. They should be removed, and these shafts should be smoothed out. But all this was perhaps irrelevant.

"Trike, just like my brother, is a man who maintains a facade of sanity," said Cog. "In hoopers, when injured like I am now, that's not a good thing. Most hoopers can regain their sanity and their human form. Those like Trike struggle to do so. There's some kind of feedback with the virus . . . they can become monstrous . . . I don't know why."

Again her head ached as her thought processes ramped up, and again she had to repress them. She knew something about all this or, rather, she had known something about all this. She could only touch on the parts of it that remained in her organic brain. She had examined two prador the Spatterjay virus had mutated. Their changes had been radically altered by the Wheel so that, given time, they would have turned into Jain soldiers. She had also examined the virus very closely and in much detail. Not only did it carry the genomes of numerous life forms, including that of a squad of Jain soldiers; it also held quantum-processing crystals from those soldiers that multiplied along with the soldier's genome.

"That's because the virus contains elements of alien minds," she said, groping for an answer without thinking *too* hard. "There is a connection. Alien mentalities are quantum stored in the virus and can influence its growth . . . . Maybe only minds of a certain kind can connect to those minds . . ."

"The minds are Jain?"

"Or Jain made."

"Doesn't bode well, then, for what's happening out at the disc," said Cog. "If the minds akin to the Jain are like Trike's and my brother's . . ."

"I would very much like to hear more about your brother," Orlandine stated.

"Another time," said Cog, waving a dismissive hand, then quickly moving on, "But you asked if Trike is strong. Well, I've seen his kind of change before, but not so intense, so concentrated." He shook his head. "His body density, when we were aboard my ship, was . . . iron, and I don't know what it is now. If he ever needed to be stopped, I don't think anything less than one of your war drones could do it." He glanced at her. "I fear him."

"I do too," said Orlandine, though why remained unclear to her.

"So how do we get through?" Angel asked from above.

He clung directly below the base of the hardfield generator. A brassy metal ring rimmed the top of the shaft, a foot and a half wide, and a curved surface closed it off. Only with a slight stab of pain did she visualize what lay beyond.

"You are both very strong," she stated. "You tear out the ring. This will reveal the foamed insulation surrounding the generator. We go through that, about five feet, then you break the outer casing."

"I see it," said Angel. "I can deal with it." He held out his hand and his fingers grew long and sharp, then blurred. He pushed them into the brassy metal with a high screaming whine. Glittering dust fell about them, then chunks of metal. He next stretched out one leg, doing a box splits right across the shaft, tore out the ring, and casually sliced it in half, dropping the pieces past them. His hands blurred again, and white foam insulation fell past. Soon he was hauling himself up beside the generator.

"Another dangerous individual," Cog noted.

Orlandine let that go, and waited.

"Clear," Angel called.

She climbed up into the space beside the generator. Angel was gone and she soon reached the hole he had cut in the outer casing and hauled herself after. Power feeds, optics, thermal convertors and hydraulic buffers made the generator chamber cramped. She wound her way through this to steps leading up, through another floor on which fusion reactors squatted amidst ducts, cables and pipes, like hornets' nests amidst a tree canopy. She was then out onto another floor to the entrance of a shaft that Angel had reached. Here was a dropshaft that led straight to the surface.

"That will work?" asked Cog, coming up beside them.

A blank control panel stood to one side, but she had no idea how to work it. Of course, whenever she had come here before she had operated everything ahead of her mentally. In fact mentally, but without much conscious thought. She stared at the thing for a long moment, then reached down and turned her wrist ring, taking off one armoured glove. The palm of her bare hand against the panel activated it. She sighed, selected a number at random, touched it, and stepped towards the shaft. But Angel snapped out a hand and pulled her back.

"Me first." He stepped in and the irised gravity field took him.

Frowning, Orlandine followed—his protectiveness was beginning to irritate her, not because it wasn't necessary, but because it was. Stepping in, she felt the field take hold of her and accelerate her rapidly upwards. Passing brightly lit, glassy crystalline rooms, glinting with technology, she remembered her last time here. She had come to inspect the drive of Weapons Platform Mu and discovered that Earth Central had a spy lodged here. It seemed a lifetime ago now. Finally, she stepped out after Angel into a triangular room, one of six others in this drive's hexagonal slice of the tower. Hearing the muted sounds of warfare, she wound her way through all the security hardware to the outer wall. The one-way mirror glass gave her a clear view across the facility and she felt a surge of anger at seeing the wreckage out there.

One of the towers was down in shattered ruin. A section of the wall was gone. Other towers had been damaged during the running fight—Clade units weaving between like fish in a reef, hunted by war drones. She transferred her attention to the nearest standing watch tower and saw the drone squatting there, unmoving, obviously shut down. Then she swung back just as Cog stepped from the dropshaft.

"Time to do this," she said.

Closing her eyes, she actively sought access to her crystal and to the transceiver which was attached to it. Information began flooding in, query protocols, openings that were blank spaces effectively ending with question marks, demanding multiple digit, randomly altering codes. Her head ached abominably and suddenly she felt burning hot. Something crackled in her skull, back behind her sinuses, and she reached up to wipe blood dripping from her nose. Next, a hammer of data hit her. She was trying to read a thousand books at once, to gaze upon a thousand scenes—every sense demanded multiplication, and weird twisting data sets demanded input to senses she did not possess. Steady pain turned to crippling agony. A hand of force slapped her across the room and pinned her against a glass wall. From there she saw Angel convulsing and knew that an induction warfare beam had locked onto him. Cog staggered across the room, burning, smoke pluming from multiple impact points on his body.

No! I am Orlandine! she screamed in her mind.

Angel, breaking the hold the beam had on him, shot towards her and bounced off a hardfield, then he hurled himself back across the room. He snared Cog, and both of them went down into the dropshaft. She did not know if they could survive now this place had turned on them. Behind her she felt a softening as the glass decohered and opened a hole, then she was falling. It seemed she had been here before, but this time she had no Jain tech to protect her from the inevitable impact.

12

The U-jump missile is a game-changer. There is speculation that such missiles were an offshoot of technology developed by the alien weapons designer known as the Client during the prador/human war. But we don't know the date of the first test, just as the antecedents of a lot that comes out of ECS weapons development is not known. Certainly, it was produced after the war. It would have been used to crush the prador if it had been available during the conflict. The first known deployment of U-jump missiles occurred a century later, almost certainly because ECS wanted to develop a suitable defence before generally distributing the weapon. This defence is the bounce gate. Only during the war did we learn of the effect an operating runcible gate had upon a proximal U-space drive. This occurred when the prador seized a world that had an open runcible and whose AI had been destroyed before it could dispose of the gate. Fearing the prador might use the gate as a route of attack to the inner worlds of the Polity, ECS U-jumped an attack ship straight at the runcible. Rather than destroy it, the attack ship fell through, only to surface, travelling at close to light speed, out of another gate two hundred light years away. This was on the refugee transfer planetoid of Dereyeth, which no longer exists. Therefore, it was necessary, when developing bounce gates, to ensure that they could not connect to others. This was achieved by making them open coordinate gates—effectively a hole into U-space. But still, there is a danger when opening a hole into a continuum that it may yet be navigable by some intelligence. Because no runcible gate is one-way.

—Notes from her lecture "Modern Warfare" by E. B. S. Heinlein

TRIKE

Trike scrambled up the hill of wreckage and delightedly came upon the remains of one of the facility's watchdogs. He picked up a disconnected leg and hefted it. The part of his mind which wasn't wholly his own told him the thing was made of laminated diamond and alloy composite—the alloy being akin to prador hull armour. He swung it, bared his teeth and scrambled down the other side of the mound.

"Hey, strange human. I come!"

He glanced back. Brull was scrambling after him, a lot more agile on the wreckage than he was, despite having lost a leg or two. Trike just didn't want to wait. She was ahead of him and up. She was . . .

Horror ground through him as he saw a human figure falling down the face of one of the towers. He froze, knowing he could not get there in time, and knowing with a sick twisting inside that he was seeing Orlandine. She hit bottom, raising a cloud of glittering fragments—glass debris.

"They're striking from orbit," said Brull.

Not understanding what the prador meant, Trike turned to stare at him. Brull pointed with his remaining claw and, still not thinking clearly, Trike looked where he indicated. He saw Clade units weaving between the buildings and the back flash of high-intensity lasers locking on, the units disintegrating in lines of fire and molten metal. Then he saw the Clade smashing into the faces of buildings to get inside, or dropping hard—running for cover. He swung his attention back to where Orlandine had fallen and found himself reaching towards her, somehow. Then suddenly he was running, because this was *not* over.

He bounded over another mound of rubble. A Clade unit rose up beside him like a disturbed snake. He hit it hard with the hunk of claw and flipped it over. Brull's Gatling cannon rattled and the thing jerked back through the air, shedding pieces of itself. It rose higher, perhaps instinctively, but fatally. A bar of fire cut through it from head to tail and a hot cavity blew open in the ground below it. Highly accurate railgun shot. It seemed other orbital weapons were now being deployed.

But ahead, the Clade was trying to close in. The units were using what cover they could and many were being hit from orbit, but they were drawing closer and closer to where a figure lay on the ground. Trike accelerated, almost flying as he ran. He swiped at another unit, the impact so hard its head left its body, which made an odd whirring sound and began to collapse in on itself. The chunk of claw was smoking, and it bent as Trike slammed it down on the head of another unit, using the force of that to drive his leap over a fallen girder, but losing grip on his makeshift weapon.

Danger above. Crawling down the face of the building from which Orlandine had fallen came four more of the things. He knew he couldn't get to her in time. But then something big, all sharp edges, screamed overhead and crashed into them, carrying them straight through the shattered face of the building. Inside, defensive systems kicked off like one continuous rolling explosion. The praying mantis drone exploded out again, shedding pieces of Clade unit, then dropped hard, slamming into plasticrete just a hundred feet from Orlandine. From there it spat particle beams and lasers in every direction.

As Trike drew nearer, a line of shots cut across the ground in front of him. A warning? He just kept on moving. The drone abruptly moved to put itself between him and Orlandine. It obviously didn't want to kill him else it would be eating him up with a particle beam by now, but it was being protective. He didn't slow, but turned his shoulder and rammed straight into it. The thing skidded back along the ground.

"Captain Trike," it said. "Desist."

It grasped him with its forelimbs, their sharp edges turned outwards. He shoved them apart again, reached up and grabbed it behind its neck, then turned and bashed its head down into the plasticrete. He stepped up onto its body, using it as a stepping stone, and leapt towards Orlandine. It twisted, horribly fast, and this time it did not turn its razor edges outwards as it swiped at him. A forelimb screeched across his chest, splitting his jacket and slicing his flesh. He snapped out a hand and caught it, the edge cutting into his palm. He then seized it with his other hand and brought it down hard on his knee, snapping it. As the drone staggered back, utterly baffled by its failure, he whirled to Orlandine.

Blood spattered the inside of her visor and ran out of her suit's shoulder joints. The thing had buffered the impact, or she would be dead and probably in pieces now. Reaching down, he unclipped the helmet and carefully pulled it from her head. He then caught hold of her chin and the neck ring of the suit. The drone was back, looming over him, but dared do nothing for fear of injuring her further. Her eyes rolled and she finally focused on him.

"Trike," she managed, blood spattering her face.

He couldn't understand what he was feeling. He didn't know this woman but felt something almost sexual, as though he wanted to be inside her, bond with her, be one with her. Without thinking, he leaned in and kissed her savagely. His triangular tongue went in hard. He felt it ripping through soft tissues, crunching up through cartilage and grinding into bone. The strange fibres in the end of it . . . he felt them stabbing out and spreading. Meanwhile he could also feel crawling and ripping all over his body. When he peered down at his hand he saw the brown and white veins wriggling like snakes from his skin, oozing over the neck ring, spreading from where he gripped her chin. They went into her like nails and her skin bubbled and bulged with their movement. He felt them spreading inside her—throughout her body.

The *other* was leaving him and going in, he knew this. Orlandine convulsed and he felt the fibres disconnecting. Her eyes became bloody red with something metallic shifting in the pupils and irises. She shoved him and unbelievably managed to push him back. Their mouths parted and his tongue snapped out of her mouth. In that moment, the drone struck, grabbing him again and hurling him aside. He felt the veins from his hands tearing and breaking, and landed hard on his back. He immediately flipped up into a crouch, facing the drone, but felt no further urge to get to Orlandine. He looked past the thing at her.

What have I done?

Orlandine was sitting upright. She shrieked, veins twisting thick across her face. Then her head tilted unnaturally to one side with a horrible cracking sound. She jerked upright, as if hauled up by a rope, and her head started to shrink down into the suit, which cracked open to release her. Something vaguely human staggered out, a skeleton clad in dissolving flesh and snakes. It lasted just a moment and then collapsed into a writhing mass. This sped like a swarm of flatworms across the ground to the nearest building. The glass there rippled and formed a hole, and it went through. Seemingly in slow motion, the suit collapsed and fell apart.

It's gone?

Trike stared down at his hands but the veins were still there. The other was still in his mind. But it seemed to be dissolving as a presence, incorporating . . . Coming back to himself, he looked around. The Clade was retreating, shooting out of the facility like silverfish fleeing a bag of grain. More war drones had arrived, but they weren't going after the Clade. Every one of them had something lethal pointed at him. One-on-one he might be able to defeat a war drone now, but he stood no chance against this crowd. He listened to power supplies humming and the metallic clacks, which he knew were completely unnecessary, of missiles and railguns loading. The image of Orlandine's body dissolving into the writhing mass repeated in his head. He thought again, *What have I done?*

THE CLIENT

Weapons Platform Mu shuddered and vibrated in U-space, as the moment it would surface into the real drew nigh. The Client gazed upon the terrain of that continuum and noted the waves of disruption. She mapped them and made her calculations. From this she was certain that the Harding black hole had reached the sun at the centre of the accretion disc, and that the event had occurred. Reaching into the newly formatted U-space drive of the weapons platform, and thence out to those of its attack pods, she began to alter things.

It was a fact, with the U-space tech of both the Polity and the Kingdom, that a destination was usually set the moment a ship entered that continuum. This was why it was possible to read a ship's signature when it went under, to know its destination, as well as its signature on surfacing, to identify its departure point. Trying to recalculate while in transit created too many variables. Attempting to alter the function of a drive while it was under power could be disastrous. But it went beyond that, because it altered the time flow within the ship in transit. It created a supposedly unresolvable paradox.

However, the Client's drive was no longer so simple. It was part of a system that included the weapons and hardfield defences of the platform and its attack pods. A lot more was possible. She made the calculations to subtract two light hours from the initial impetus and applied the solution to the drive. Everything within the weapons platform shuddered to a halt and then, finally, she surfaced into the real.

The Client *knew*, with utter certainty, that out of the options available, she had chosen an arrival point two light hours out from the accretion disc. But she also knew her own mental capabilities and those of her new drive system, so she checked the local gravity map and related U-space readings. Meanwhile, the weapons platform showed a high power drain at the point of exit that none of its instruments could locate. Entropic wave. She realized that during the journey, she had changed the arrival point. Initially she had planned to surface right next to the accretion disc but had changed that to two light hours out, probably because of the U-space disruption she was detecting. She accepted this, though she had no memory of it.

Now to her sensor arrays. The Harding black hole had swallowed the sun at the centre of the accretion disc, and it was plain that this had opened the U-space blister there. She focused in on the giant ship that had exited, as it looked two hours ago. Its resemblance to an ammonite, or a terran snail, was no coincidence. The Species had built the main crew compartment first—a fully functional ship in itself just fifty miles across. Thereafter the thing had steadily grown, adding weapons, defences and power supplies in an expanding spiral around that central compartment.

My people, the Client thought.

The ship was supposed to be a practically invulnerable war craft. It was, when the Librarian had initiated it. But that particular Jain had separated itself from its kind for a long time. It had not been part of their continual fights and amalgamations, their constant mating. Consequently, the Jain it faced in that final battle had been armed with the technology the humans so feared, whose remains inhabited the accretion disc and seeded into Jain nodes. This technology had, the Client surmised, eventually done to all Jain what they did to each other individually. It had merged and transformed them, to their own destruction as a race of thinking individuals, into an interstellar parasite which fed on ensuing civilizations. With this technology, the attacking Jain had been able to raise weapons from sterile regolith and had nearly annihilated the Species. In fact, it would have done so had not the ship the Client gazed upon now been able to trap it in that U-space blister.

The Client surveyed the situation. Two fleets there at the disc—one of the Polity and one of the Kingdom. The ships weren't scattered but faced off against each other in slowly shifting battle formations, as each side tried to find some tactical advantage. Having obtained data from Dragon, perhaps only because that entity had allowed her to, she knew that this was the response of the two realms to the death of Orlandine. It was a very dangerous collection of ships, even for the Species warship, but they were not the greatest danger. Because of her absorption of Pragus, the platform's AI mind, she understood how those platform AIs were hardwired to their prime directive. The hundreds of weapons platforms around the accretion disc were the main threat. They would identify the Species ship as Jain because it would give that signature.

During the battle, the newer civilization-destroying Jain tech had penetrated it. Perhaps not to the central compartment, but certainly into most of that seven-hundred-mile-wide main body. Dropping itself and its opponent into the U-space blister had been a last desperate sacrifice to save the rest of the Species. It did not matter if the weapons platforms knew this history—they would still not allow that ship to leave the disc. And, almost certainly, the two fleets out there would join in with the destruction. Perhaps she should at least contact the two fleets and apprise them of the situation.

It was time to move closer.

ORLIK

The U-space disruption which the Harding black hole had caused by doing . . . whatever it had done was high. But it did not make travel in that continuum impossible. One dreadnought had left the prador formation because its captain had turned out to be edging into senility and, in return, the king had sent two. Windermere had sent an attack ship away from her fleet, apparently to map the extent of the disturbance. This was why, when another U-signature generated far out, it wasn't the immediate focus of Orlik's attention. When it moved from two light hours out to eight minutes out, it became more of a concern. Eight minutes later Sprag showed him the new arrival.

"Like we need some more complications," she added.

Orlik gazed upon Weapons Platform Mu and its remaining attack pods. He knew all about its visit to the Prador Kingdom, of course.

"Analysis," he said out loud.

Sprag replied, "It looks like someone initiated a Jain node in there, and though I'm getting a signature, it's not quite the same. Fuck knows. Final analysis: it's a big fucking weapons platform, probably hostile, and it's behind us."

The signature stuff was a quantum thing, apparently. When matter was organized down to pico-scopic levels, it created a signature in U-space. Since some Polity technology was now close to being organized this way, and also caused a signature, their AIs had felt it necessary to define parameters around what was a Jain-tech signature, and this wasn't it . . . not quite. However, he had to agree with her about the effect. The platform looked wrapped in a growth of metallic vines, as well as being half melted, so that what had once been individually identifiable units of its structure blended into each other.

"So what's it going to do?" wondered Sprag.

"Indeed," said Orlik.

He had to agree with her final assessment and, yeah, it was a complication they didn't need. Now they had an alien with some serious firepower at their backs—one that for perfectly understandable reasons had no love for the prador. Orlik observed Sprag's recalculation of battle tactics and probable outcomes. If they went head-to-head with the Polity, they would lose only if that platform slotted itself in on the Polity side. But would it? The Polity AIs might not have ordered its assassination but they had betrayed it. How should he respond to this? What was the Client's objective in coming here?

"I think I need to talk to her," he said.

"Which her?"

"The one with the fewest legs."

"Opening com," Sprag replied.

A moment later, Orlik was gazing, mentally, at Diana Windermere. Neither of them said anything at first, both studying images of each other that neither could really read, then Orlik said, "A new development."

"Quite," said Windermere.

"I have informed my fleet to assist you in the Jaskoran system. It is evident that what is happening here is not the result of some Polity power play, though . . . some power games are being played."

"Unfortunate politics, in the circumstances," she allowed.

"How do you see this situation at present?" He then added, "Excluding the recent arrival of the Client."

"I will have to simplify."

"Do so."

"A hostile Jain AI facilitated the release of this ship from the U-space blister. That same AI now wants those weapons platforms to fire on it."

"That is a large and almost certainly very dangerous vessel," said Orlik.

"Yes, but do we want to fire on it?"

"The fact that the ship is large and very dangerous indicates that we should."

"Prador thinking," said Windermere. She leaned forwards in her seat, her face expanding in Orlik's vision. He felt the urge to push her away. She continued with a question, "Where did the Wheel come from?"

Orlik thought about that long and hard. Her way of seeing the situation was exactly the way he saw it, and it made no sense, unless he was missing something. He considered what that might be, then replied, "It seems likely the Wheel is an AI released from those trapped in U-space and this ship is its enemy."

"I have considered this, but then why release the ship in the first place?"

"For obvious reasons," said Orlik.

Her face changed and Orlik knew enough to recognize that she had smiled.

"Different ways of thinking," she said. "If I had an enemy who was trapped eternally in a U-space blister, I would consider that quite enough and leave him there. But to a prador, like you . . . unless that enemy is dead and dismembered the fight is ongoing."

"Of course."

"We have your way of thinking and my way of thinking, but neither of those are necessarily close to the way the Wheel thinks."

Orlik gurgled in frustration. This conversation was making his ganglion ache.

"Whatever," he snapped. "We are here, neither the king nor Earth Central wants us cracking carapaces, there is danger, how are we to respond?"

"I am currently attempting to prevent the weapons platforms from firing on that ship when it leaves the accretion disc. I am also trying to talk to it," she said.

Orlik chewed that over for a short while, then replied, "Those are certainly options." He felt slightly baffled by the answer and moved on. "And now the Client has arrived."

"The new development you mentioned."

"What are we to make of that?"

"The Client is certainly hostile to the prador and has reason to have no love for the Polity either," Windermere stated. "We need to watch our backs."

Orlik digested that and realized this woman had no idea what to make of it.

"Could it be that the Client is the prime mover in all this?"

"No. Reports show that the Client was resurrected aboard Weapons Platform Mu after the Wheel seized control of the legate Angel and the wormship."

"Resurrected here, aboard a weapons platform. There has to be a connection."

"Undoubtedly, but until we know what it is, we cannot react." She paused for a second, turned her head as if listening to something else and Orlik saw the data leads plugged into the base of her skull. He knew in an instant that she was conducting more than just this conversation. "However, I would prefer not to be *reacting*, but acting . . ."

Orlik felt a sudden burning frustration because she had dug to the root of it. They were sitting here second-guessing major events and how to respond to them. He really wanted to do something. It was, he realized, the frustration of command. All the way through this they had been a step behind an aggressor. And, crazily, they weren't even sure who that aggressor was. All they had encountered thus far were agents of this shady figure.

"Then perhaps it is time to act," he said. "To begin driving responses."

Windermere focused on him completely. "What do you suggest?"

"I will consider this and communicate my thoughts with you later." Mentally he sent a command to Sprag, who a second later severed the comlink.

"And how *will* you respond?" enquired Sprag.

"My instinct is to let those weapons platforms open fire and, if necessary, assist them," he said. "But of course, as Windermere would doubtless point out, I am thinking like a prador."

"And will you follow your instinct?"

"In that respect no, but in another I will." He paused, wondering if he was being too hasty, then continued, "Inform the other ships that the *Kinghammer* is about to move out of formation. Update tactical, but break weapons lock on the Polity ships—they are not now the enemy here."

"Where are we going?" asked Sprag.

"To see an older enemy," Orlik replied, meanwhile sending tactical instructions to his fleet should anything occur while he was gone.

ORLANDINE

Orlandine fell from the balcony and she fell down the side of a building. Both impacts of both Orlandines were simultaneous, but became one upon the rocky plain. It was raining from the pink sky, droplets splashing like blood on the white boulders, patting the dust, beading on the arm of her monofilament suit when she held it out for inspection. She knew this place: it was the world called Aster Colora, where the humans had first found Dragon. For a moment, she thought Earth Central had made contact and dropped her into a virtuality, but everything was clear in her mind and all but some moments of her complete memories were back. Those memories of the last scenes in her apartment with Tobias were only human, and vague, since prior to them the link to this backup had been broken by the Clade. The Jain tech Trike had returned to her had loaded one of her backups from out in the Jaskoran system. It had then loaded *her*—destructively recording her to itself, storing some of the substance of her human body throughout its growing mass of tentacles and tendrils.

Her omniscience had returned too. She could see and experience more than just one single human being, with her various links and dispersed mind. So she also gazed from the mountains down on the Ghost Drive Facility, as the Clade swirled endlessly about it. She watched the massive ship moving out of the accretion disc, and her weapons platforms preparing to rain annihilation upon it. She saw Diana Windermere lost in doubt for the first time in centuries, poised over decisions she did not want to make. And in juxtaposition to her, out in vacuum, she observed Weapons Platform Mu, with its attack pods positioned around it and the Client within, trailing its tether to millions of years of history. And in the centre of these events, she saw Trike, kissing her, his alien tongue entering the mouth of her dying body and making a violent connection that seemed to draw everything else she was seeing into a logical web, a totality.

"So where are you?" she asked.

"Neither here nor there," Dragon replied.

Ahead, the four spheres of Dragon sat upon the plain, cloud clinging to their upper curves. The ground began shaking and nearby a pseudopod broke from it to writhe into the sky and loop over. White muscular flesh, as thick as a man's torso, topped with a cobra head, but with a glowing sapphire eye where the mouth should be. More and more of them broke from the surface until two rows marked her path to Dragon itself.

"Crazy street lamps . . ." a voice ghosted.

"Not my memory," she said. "I've never been here."

"They sent an ambassador," said Dragon. "I lied to him as I have lied about many things, often to myself. Or perhaps I did not lie to him . . . I no longer know."

"You're rambling. Where are you?" Orlandine began walking along under the blue gaze of the pseudopods.

"Truth? You want truth?"

"Of course."

"This is not now."

That brought her to a halt. Just for a moment, she did not understand. But then, reaching out to the distributed components of her being, she found it. She wasn't actually speaking to Dragon. The entity had come to Jaskor, terribly injured, to deliver terse instructions about the Ghost Drive Facility and then departed. However, it had left this for her lodged in the facility: a submind of itself.

"What happened to you?"

"I went to the world of the Cyberat seeking data," the Dragon submind replied. "This was simply a lure—the Wheel wanted me out of the way so I would not interfere with your response to the Jain soldier. It wanted me dead."

This played out to her inner vision. She saw the USER activated in the Cyberat system, the attack upon Dragon by the Clade, and then by the wormship which, it seemed, though apparently controlled by Angel, had been where the AI the Wheel had rooted itself. She saw the pursuit around the sun there, the black-ops attack ship *Obsidian Blade* destroying the wormship, and consequently the Wheel, but Dragon severely damaged and burned. Subsequent events too: Dragon picking up Cog's ship, Blade pursuing the Clade outsystem and the final result of that. Now she was updated on those events, but some things *really* needed explaining.

"Tell me about the Client," she said.

"The Client was always about data," said the Dragon submind. "I put her aboard Weapons Platform Mu and I drove her to a source."

In another place, Orlandine saw prador ships bombarding a massive ring structure around a world—the world of the Client's kind, the Species. A block of data fell into her consciousness, giving the history of their extermination, and she saw the library moon falling away as the prador finally destroyed the ring with their kamikazes.

"I knew the library data predated the accretion disc . . ."

"How?"

After a long pause the mind replied, "I do not know . . . perhaps Dragon does."

"Continue," said Orlandine.

"I learned that the Client has indeed accessed the library and that she will have discovered what happened here. The Client is key, and I have gone to find her . . ."

"Outdated data," said Orlandine. "The Client is now at the accretion disc and you . . . or rather the mind that created you, are not here."

"I was damaged," said the submind. "I would be ineffectual."

"Is there anything else you can tell me? Anything useful?" Even as she asked, she began reaching for the submind. She would interrogate it properly and learn everything it knew. However, as she did this, she sensed it beginning to break apart. Then she was falling once more, sick with anger because, again, Dragon had given her minimal data to work with. There had to be answers, solutions and a logical course of action, and she must find them herself. With simple human consciousness, she would have thought that Dragon, as ever, was just playing games and being deliberately obscure. But her consciousness was more than that. Her anger faded as she understood that for her to resolve the problems she faced she needed to find and understand that resolution in the first place.

Out of virtuality she fell, down and down between glassy towers. She hit and spread, found herself making connections to the facility's hardware all around her. She had no awareness of a human body now, but a perfect sense of the all the pieces laid out on the interstellar chess-board. One thing she knew she had to do at least. Of one thing she was certain: the Clade could not achieve its aims.

DIANA

The *Kinghammer* was on the move, slowly heading out of the prador formation. Diana watched it through the *Hogue*'s sensors and felt a sinking sensation in the pit of her stomach. She had a good idea what this was all about.

"They're taking down weapons lock," said Jabro.

"What?"

"The prador ships, they're—"

"Yes, yes, I know," she said in irritation. Not only were those ships taking down weapons lock, the whole prador formation was orienting towards the accretion disc. One thing at a time, she decided. "What about that platform? Seckurg?"

"Difficult to scan," replied the Golem. "The alien technology has amalgamated discrete systems. I detect linkages between the U-space drive, defences and weapons—this is generally the direction Polity weapons tech has been heading. Also, when it arrived it caused a definite entropic effect. It's quite possible . . . something temporal . . ."

Why not? thought Diana. Things seemed poised on some catastrophic knife-edge, so why not time travel too? Why not play with the space-time continuum and start blowing up suns, rearranging star systems and erasing civilizations? She felt the urge to giggle, and suppressed it.

"And the nature of that alien technology?" she asked.

"Very much like the hostile tech we call Jain tech, but its U-signature is out-parameter."

"Outside of the parameters the weapons platforms used to define Jain tech," she said flatly.

He glanced round at her. "Yes. Outside."

"So I can't use it as a lever," she stated.

The arrival of Jain tech outside of the weapons platform defence sphere, around the accretion disc, might have been a bargaining chip she could use in her constant debate and argument with Weapons Platform Rhodus. Then again, perhaps not—its definition of the directive of the platforms was pretty clear.

"The *Kinghammer* is going under," said Jabro.

Diana focused back on the prador capital ship as it seemed to stretch and shimmer, then snapped out of existence. No need to guess where it had gone. Its U-signature told her and its short jump was already over—confirmation would come in eight minutes. The prador Orlik had gone to Weapons Platform Mu, which was a greater threat to him and his fleet than it was to hers. It made sense, and she would have done the same in his position. The Client was a creature whose race the prador had exterminated, who had tried to bring about the extermination of the prador in return and who, more recently, had caused mayhem in the Kingdom. To Orlik it would be something he needed to stamp on at once.

"Orders?" wondered Jabro.

What could she do? An alien-controlled weapons platform had arrived and the prador were dealing with it. The prador had also backed off and focused where she should be focused: on that alien ship.

"It's time to move," she said.

The initial positioning of the fleets had been random. Tactical considerations had then resulted in the current formations, triggered by the fleets reacting to each other. However, the alien ship's predicted departure point from the disc was a third of a turn around and parallel to its axis—the ship was taking the shortest route out. Via Hogue, she delivered her instructions. First to go were the dreadnoughts, some flashing straight into U-space and others, with less modern drives, requiring a run-up. They began to appear in new positions opposite the departure point and a few minutes later destroyers followed to slot in.

"Dangerous tactically," commented Jabro.

He was right. The whole fleet could not move at once, since the U-drives of the various ships tended to interfere with each other. Moving them piecemeal meant dividing the fleet, which, if you were paranoid, gave the prador an advantage. But she trusted that Orlik wasn't crazy enough to start something now. He would still be in contact—

"They're moving," said Jabro.

Prador dreadnoughts were falling out of formation. The reavers started first, going smoothly into U-space, flashing back into the real fifty thousand miles to the side of where Diana's fleet was grouping. The older dreadnoughts followed—these having to get moving on fusion before making the leap.

"We're good," she said.

Shifting . . .

The *Cable Hogue* thrummed with power and Diana felt the dislocation like a wave passing through her body, a sense of impossible speed and an instant of epiphany. A moment later, the giant ship surfaced into the real and epiphany faded. It was always the same. When the ship went under, she felt some truth lay within her grasp, but then it just went away again. Seckurg said that was spill-over from Hogue—nothing to get excited about.

In the new position, with her fleet forming between her and the disc, she felt at last that she was doing something, not just reacting. Both fleets formed up as they had before, which was not ideal. She decided that when Orlik returned, this was something they must address. If he returned. She focused her attention on the alien ship from this perspective.

The thing was under constant acceleration and would soon be leaving the accretion disc. She linked fully into the *Hogue* AI and went back to communication with the weapons platforms, from verbal exchanges right down deep into AI data, even though she could see no way out. They perfectly understood the details of the situation but their interpretation of it was completely different. They could not get past their directive—it was like a subconscious influence on their reasoning. She felt, while talking to them, as if she had fallen back centuries to the time before the Quiet War, when AIs were made to obey their human masters absolutely. These entities were highly intelligent and informed, but they were slaves to the will of Orlandine and the directive she had given them. Diana understood the imperative that had driven this, but it was one that could lead to disaster in this situation.

"What if it is not a Jain ship?" she asked, in more than just words.

"It possesses Jain U-space signatures, which are our only measure," replied the AI of Weapons Platform Rhodus, who had been designated spokesman.

"Then explain why a Jain AI would want us to fire on it." She, of course, had her own answers to that but wanted to know what the platform AIs were thinking.

"It seems likely," replied Rhodus, "that the Wheel was one of the AIs lodged in U-space, enabled to escape by Dragon's attempts to communicate and acquire data. Dragon provided them with energy to that end, and it is not unfeasible they used this energy to allow one of their number to escape."

"Still does not answer my question. Why would a Jain AI want us to fire on a Jain ship?"

"You are being simplistic, Diana Windermere," said Rhodus pedantically. "We do not know the circumstances that resulted with the AIs in

U-space or this ship trapped in the U-space blister. The Jain were very powerful and, judging by their technology, very warlike. The most likely explanation is Jain internecine war."

More or less what Hogue had pointed out. She could not argue the point because it might well be true. Perhaps, in the end, her objection was not about the probability of hostile intent on the part of the Wheel and the Clade towards the Polity, but simply to being manipulated.

"And still," Rhodus continued, "the fact remains that dangerous Jain technology is about to leave the accretion disc. For the survival of the Polity and the Kingdom, we cannot allow that to happen."

There it was again. She had gone round and round with this and it came back to that every time. She turned her attention back to the data being transmitted from Jaskor, hoping that Orlandine had survived and that she could do something to stop the weapons platforms.

But what then?

"I have made contact," said Hogue. "Sending language and translation files now."

Diana sat up as if electrocuted, finding some hope at last. Now they could talk to whatever resided inside that giant ship.

13

The term "Jain tech," in common usage, describes the kind of sequestering technology that arises from a Jain node upon it connecting with an organic intelligence. The only time, as far as is known, when Jain tech connected with a non-organic intelligence, was when it did so with the AI of the dreadnought Trafalgar, *which subsequently became the entity known as Erebus. Even then, it is rumoured that the* Trafalgar *AI used humans to initiate the technology. And it was not sequestered by it, but melded with it. However, Jain tech in this sense is a bit of a misnomer. The Viking Museum on Earth's moon contains items of the technology from this ancient race and they do not try to seize control of things (though safety measures are in place should this judgement be incorrect). Many technological items produced by "Jain tech" itself are often incapable of sequestering, but they are clearly the same technology. It would be better for this stuff to be defined as "Jain sequestering technology." It is the nature of human language, however, that usage is only described, and attempts to dictate it tend to fail.*

—from *Quince Guide*, compiled by humans

BROGUS

The *Kinghammer* had headed out to face the threat posed by the arrival of the Client and her weapons platform. Brogus had gleaned most of the story about that platform from status updates, as well as a conversation he had engaged in with one of the other captains. This last had been risky, because he had come close to revealing how little he knew. But he had to know. He could almost feel the neural lace unsticking from his major ganglion and its control over him waning. He was now able to think about taking some actions for his own ends, and his own survival.

He was also utterly confused about what was occurring here. He focused on his screens, on the ship coming out of the accretion disc, at the empty bounce gate chamber on his own ship, and at the new orientation of the prador fleet.

What was the Clade doing? He had assumed it must be aboard to launch some sort of attack against the Polity. Even though it had taken him a while to get his mind in motion due to the lock of the lace, he had come to the conclusion that the Clade units were now aboard numerous prador ships and had seized control of them. So surely, with the *Kinghammer* gone and the Polity taking their own weapons lock off the prador, it was time to attack? No, even as he considered this, he realized he was conflating its aims with his own. He was a rebel who had deserted the Kingdom because of the truce the new king had made with the humans. It was his wish and his aim for hostilities between his kind and the humans to recommence. The Clade was working for the Wheel and all its actions were centred around that ship coming out of the accretion disc. The Polity and Kingdom ships here were a factor, just a factor . . .

His ganglion aching, he worked through scenarios. He came up with a possibility: the Clade was here to deal with the fleets if they opened fire on that ship, which surely the Wheel had wanted safely out of the U-space blister and free? No, the ships would not be here if the Clade had not killed Orlandine. Because only her death had compelled the king to send his fleet, and the Polity to respond. Something about the weapons platforms here also related to Orlandine—he'd picked up on parts of it while listening in to conversations between other captains, but the connection remained unclear. He lacked information, so he must work around those gaps.

At some point, there would be action. If the Clade turned prador ships against the Polity, that would be good. It might not. The Clade would do as it wanted, and whether Brogus himself was here to witness it would not affect the outcome one way or another. However, his presence here seemed likely to result in his death. With a sudden painful wrench, the father-captain felt something fall within his control. He could now disobey the constant restraints of the lace, which had been holding him back from doing anything. He engaged his grav units and rose off his saddle control, swivelled round and drifted across his sanctum. The relief was immense—even this little action was at the behest of his own will. However, turning back, he saw something on the screens.

The Clade unit that had earlier occupied one of his second-children was oozing out of the mind case attached to one of the bounce gate support struts. He moved fast, back to his saddle control, and dropped on it heavily, inserting claws in pit controls to access ship's systems. Meanwhile, he opened up com to all his children.

"Intruder alert!" he announced. "There is a Polity assassin drone in the bounce gate chamber. Proceed there at once and destroy it!" He felt a hot flush of fear passing through him. He had done it now.

Through various cams, he saw his children scrabbling to obey. Some were already armed and began heading where he'd directed, others were quickly arming themselves. He concentrated on further resources at his disposal—internal defences.

"Father. I have seen this drone," said one of his first-children cautiously.

"It is now the enemy. Destroy it," Brogus replied perfunctorily.

Inside the tunnel which the bounce gate chamber opened into, turrets dropped from the ceiling with twinned particle cannons on each. He set them to fire at any movement, any disturbance, barring each other. One immediately opened fire and a second-child, who had entered at the end of the tunnel, retreated shrieking with one claw burned off and its armour smoking. Brogus clattered his mandibles in irritation then updated his children with a tactical map. Meanwhile he altered the programming of the cannons—giving them the armour beacon signals of his children and instructing them not to fire on them. Through cams, he saw his children gathering at each end of the tunnel.

"You broke it at last," said the Clade unit.

Its voice possessed a tinny echo and he felt its will scrabbling at the walls of his mind, then falling away. He experienced a surge of joy, knowing that it had no power over him. A surge of panic swiftly ensued, which he fought down. There was no going back—the Clade unit would now try to kill him.

"Yes, I broke it," he replied.

"We expected this," said the unit. "Prador biology and your age. The receptors in your ganglion which at one time responded to the hormones emitted by your father have been dying ever since you became a father yourself."

The thing had moved out of the mind case and was coiled around the strut. After a moment, it steadily peeled away from there and squirmed through the air towards the door, which opened ahead of it.

"You cannot escape there," Brogus stated.

"We are unconcerned. This unit is an element of a whole whose aims will be achieved," the unit replied.

Brogus felt some hope, because if that was the case then this unit did not care whether it lived or died.

"However," the unit continued, "this ship will remain part of the plan."

Brogus felt the hope fade. It had been a vain one. Though the thing he was talking to supposedly had no interest in personal survival, it would do everything in its power to carry through the plans of the swarm entire. And that, in the end, meant it would try to survive and get to him.

The thing abruptly shot out through the door. It hit the other side of the tunnel, where the cannons targeted it and opened fire. Hot blue beams sizzled through the air and vaporized material from the walls. It took a couple of hits, then shot across the tunnel to the opposite wall beside the door. Again the cannons fired, and again it leapt. This continued and Brogus could not understand the purpose. The thing wasn't advancing down the tunnel but merely ricocheting across it in the same place. After multiple passes, the Clade unit was gone. What had happened? It took a moment for Brogus to realize what the unit's aim had been. Multiple hits from the particle cannons on the same portion of tunnel wall had weakened it, and now there was a hole.

"It's in the food store!" he bellowed.

His children at one end of the tunnel charged on past the junction and entered another tunnel, heading in towards a dome-shaped, insulated door. The first-child whom he had spoken to earlier operated the pit control and the door opened, spilling frigid fog. The others charged in. A moment later, Gatling cannons hammered the air. Since the store had no cams, Brogus switched to views through the cams on his children's suits. Particle beams sawed through fog beside tall cylinders. He saw the Clade unit writhing across the face of one of these. The cylinder slumped under fire and split open, belching a packed mass of steaming mudfish corpses. After a while, the firing tailed off and Brogus anxiously watched the search. Scanners were picking up nothing.

"We've lost it," said the first-child.

"Keep searching," he instructed, heavy dread nestling inside him.

He had seen what the Clade was capable of. He had witnessed how they compressed themselves through any gap. The thing could be in a power duct or a pipe now. It might even be sitting, waiting patiently, among the mudfish and reaverfish corpses. In the tunnel outside the bounce gate chamber there had been a chance, but not now. Brogus abruptly twisted the pit control and looked for another option, anything, but there seemed no way. His instinct was to remain in his sanctum, to stay in here encysted like a shellfish and defend himself. He knew the instinct well because all father-captains thought the same. But he was also old and wily and understood that remaining here would get him killed. He switched to another view through his screens: the world of Jaskor with its many deep oceans. Then to another: a giant tongue of metal with a powerful fusion drive to the rear, resting on a maglev ramp which led to space doors. He decided to run.

If he fled to another prador ship with some story about Polity assassin drones aboard, they would probably just put a missile straight into him. And even if one did take him aboard, he would soon be identified and punished. The Polity ships were simply not an option. He didn't think too much about what he would do sitting under the oceans of Jaskor—personal survival was paramount. Rising off his saddle control, he spun towards the doors, ordering them open ahead of him.

Out into the tunnel, he moved fast down it towards the shuttle bay. If only he could take the time to load further supplies. Maybe when he got to the world he would be able to work something with the prador enclave. Also, with the situation chaotic down there, he might get to a ship on the surface . . . He slid to a halt suddenly as the first-child stepped out into the tunnel ahead of him.

"Father . . ." it said.

"You will come with me," said Brogus.

"I come to make my report," said the child.

"You will come with me," Brogus repeated, puzzled.

The child made a nonsensical clicking noise and lowered one claw to the floor.

"Move!" Brogus ordered, surging ahead again. The child tilted forwards, then slowly toppled to one side.

Brogus knew what had happened just a moment before he felt a cracking at his rear end, then sudden stabbing pain. He whirled round and, losing control of his grav, crashed into the wall of the tunnel. Horrible ripping movement pulled at his guts.

"Hello again, we are glad to be here," said the Clade unit inside him.

Brogus thumped to the floor and gazed along the tunnel, trying to see a way to its end. It darkened and he knew he would never reach it.

ORLIK

Exit from U-space had been rough. The moment the *Kinghammer* surfaced with a juddering crash, Orlik lost grip on many systems until they realigned. The disruption from the event in the accretion disc seemed to be getting worse, and in that moment, he decided against using U-jump missiles. Anyway, the weapons platform would have an internal bounce gate just like the *Hammer* did. Settling into the real, he began to reacquire systems and was soon both inside and outside his ship, his perception omniscient. He slid deeper into his amalgamation with its AI, and firing the weapons required little thought—no more than moving a claw or a leg. However, before he had done that, it had been necessary to respond to new data. Diana's repositioning of her fleet was only a surprise because she had done it so quickly. He saw that his own ships had responded as instructed and confirmed that they were doing the right thing, before he focused fully on the weapons platform.

"What is your purpose here?" Orlik demanded, even as twinned particle beams cut royal blue across vacuum from between the two forward projections of his ship. They stretched towards the weapons platform.

In the brief time it took them to reach the platform, the surrounding attack pods made short U-jumps—spreading out and arcing round. Orlik delegated most of them to his crew, but some pods had obviously had their own problems with the local disruption.

Four attack pods arrived a second late to their formation, tumbling out of control. As they sought to right themselves, he fired on them himself with short railgun bursts. One of them simply exploded, while another took hits then fell away, burning. The two others quickly righted and took no strikes. One of his gunners took over, hitting the stray again and again, trying to drive its hardfield generators to failure. But there were no ejections and it stubbornly persisted.

The particle beams reached the weapons platform, lighting a curved surface over it. That could not be right—it was impossible to bend hardfields.

"My purpose here is observation," the Client said.

Orlik released a fusillade of near-c railgun slugs at the platform—a spread that covered its entire length. Meanwhile, Sprag was trying to bring something to his attention—about the platform's hardfields and the technology behind them. It was too deep, too technical to deal with right at that moment.

"You're lying. You're somehow deeply involved in all this," he said, "and coming here was not the most sensible decision to make."

"Equally, your decision to come out to me was not sensible," the Client replied.

As Orlik tried to process that, his attention swayed back to the attack pods. His gunners were firing on them all, and filling vacuum with clouds of white-hot metal vapour from slug impacts. Meanwhile, the one that had apparently been damaged was still taking hits and surviving. Telemetry told him it had still made no hardfield ejections. That simply did not make sense.

"Those hardfields," Sprag insisted.

Orlik absorbed the data overview and looked upon multi-spectrum scans of the attack pods. Computer resolution picked out the shape of the hardfields and they were bubbles surrounding each pod. A U-space map also showed an effect he had never seen before, with inversions related to each pod.

"We've seen this shit before," Sprag stated.

"You may have . . ."

Sprag continued, "The rogue AI Penny Royal used such hardfields. They cannot be penetrated. They can only be overloaded."

Now the railgun fusillade reached the platform. Multiple impacts swamped it in fire and, even as that dispersed, it etched out the hardfield surface which completely enclosed the thing.

"I have to decide whether or not you will be useful," said the Client.

"Useful! You are insane," said Orlik.

"Every weapon will be necessary, and they still may not be enough."

With a thought, Orlik launched a series of CTD warheads, at the same time sinking into plain data-com with Sprag. He needed to know what could overload that platform's hardfields. The AI was calculating but the answers coming back just seemed to wander off into some fantasy realm.

"Desist," said the Client. "I no longer have any interest in vengeance. I understand now. Your people are not those that exterminated my kind. Your present king would not choose that course."

The warheads, travelling more slowly than railgun slugs or energy beams, were drawing closer and closer to the platform. Then came a flickering, and it was as if the platform grew multitudes of glassy spines from various installations along its length. These reached out—an energy weapon? Finally they found their targets—each one hit a warhead. The warheads simply shattered in vacuum and flew into thousands of chunks of debris.

"You get to live," said the Client, "for a little while, at least."

Something hit the *Kinghammer*. Orlik thought it a weapons impact until analysis revealed an energy surge that had shut down the fusion engines and caused imbalances in other drive systems.

"Warfare beam—" Sprag managed and then dissolved from Orlik's perception. A moment later, something else shrieked into him via his interface, which felt as if it had turned red hot on his body. He slid off his saddle control and reached up to tear the thing from his back. He crashed sideways and rolled as if trying to put out a fire there, then finally came up on his feet.

He was in his sanctum. All the screens were out, his implants were taking nothing but static. He was blind and deaf. Perhaps his crew could still operate their weapons? He doubted it. They were, as the humans would have put it, a sitting duck. But he could feel a pull.

Drive systems were still operating and he could sense, by the direction of the pull, that the ship was turning. A further kick also told him that the fusion engines were back online. He was thankful that they weren't anywhere near a sun or the like, else he suspected that might have been their destination.

Buzzing sounded nearby, then Sprag's drone body settled on the deck beside him.

"She said we get to live," she said.

"For a little while," Orlik replied. Then, "Is all of you alive?"

"Just some com problems," Sprag replied.

Orlik walked over to study the interface pad and saw it wasn't on fire. He noted that some of the screens were also coming back on, and he returned to climb back up onto the saddle control. He wasn't much inclined to use the interface, so instead inserted his claws in pit controls and tried them. A moment later, he had diagnostics running on all the screens. Following that, sensors began to come back online, giving him views of starlit space.

"The warfare beam shut everything down, even my better self, briefly," said Sprag. "It could have done a lot more."

"What got to me?" Orlik asked.

"A viral program that activated your afferent nerves. It probably hurt."

"It's gone now?"

"Yes."

Orlik tried his implants and found some function there. He sent a brief instruction and in response the interface rose up on its optics, repositioned, then came down on his back to reconnect. And he was in. He looked for damage reports and found none. But this was only in passing, as he inserted himself as quickly as possible into weapons and exterior sensors. His perception expanded and now he could see the situation.

Weapons Platform Mu still hung in vacuum, receding behind them. He felt a surge of anger and all the force of the *Hammer*'s weapons systems there to command at a thought. He was aboard the most powerful ship the prador had ever made!

"She gave you a slap and sent you on your way," said Sprag, speaking through the interface, as her drone body settled on the crane.

Orlik seethed and acknowledged it with a wave of one claw.

"She certainly did," he said, then addressed his crew. "This engagement is over—we are returning to the fleet."

THE CLIENT

The Client watched the prador ship continuing on its way, no longer puzzled by her reluctance to destroy it. What she had told the prador aboard was true, and she genuinely felt it now. The prador had destroyed her civilization and, since their medical technology allowed for longevity, some involved in that act were certainly still around. However, they were no longer in charge. She surmised, had this present kingdom found the Species, genocide would not have been its immediate intent. It might have ensued, but that was debatable and beside the point. What was the point? Simply that she no longer had any taste for vengeance—that anger no longer drove her.

But what did? What did she want now?

Her immediate objectives were plain. She wanted to ensure the survival of those of her kind inside that spaceship. And beyond that? She did not know, so instead just focused on present aims and problems.

The imminent danger was the weapons platforms opening up on the ship as it left the accretion disc. Her concern that the two fleets would join in with this destruction had been eased because the data she had ripped from the *Kinghammer* while disabling it indicated otherwise. She was now up to date. The Wheel, by deploying the Clade on Jaskor, had manipulated events to ensure the platforms' directive could not be rescinded. The Polity commander here, and the prador Orlik, were aware of that. Also, it seemed that Orlandine had survived and might still be able to stop the weapons platforms.

But what if she could not?

The Client reviewed the weapons and resources at her disposal and one fact became plain. Though she could negligently deal with a ship like the *Kinghammer,* she would not be able to go up against the concerted might of over seven hundred weapons platforms. Some other option had to be contemplated.

DIANA

The comlink was open and Hogue had transmitted language and translation files. The alien ship probably did not need them, because its earlier scan of the fleets had breached their data storage.

"Please reply," she said, not for the first time.

Data was coming in but fractured and bearing no relation to anything she sent. It was like trying to speak to a shattered AI that had lost any sense of consciousness. She switched over to the stuff that was coming through in Anglic to see if she could make any sense of that. All the rest, Hogue and Seckurg were handling, or rather, trying to handle.

"Sector 4582 the whiteness of night deliquescence add sprine," said . . . something.

It was like attempting to understand a gabbleduck. What was being said edged close to making sense, but never quite got there.

"The weapons platforms you see will fire on you if you leave the accretion disc," she said, feeling she was betraying the platform AIs by delivering this warning. As a necessity, she once again transmitted holographic data sets. These described a weapons platform, along with a rendering of the accretion disc, as well as the dimensions of the defence sphere in overlay.

"Incursion ageing to slow time," replied the thing.

"Please remain in the accretion disc," she said.

"Dead," it replied.

"Yes, you will be dead if you leave the accretion disc," she stated.

"Oak trees," it replied.

"Are these actual responses?" she asked Seckurg.

He glanced round. "I think so. It's not talking over you and the Anglic speaking stops when you stop. But it's almost as if you're speaking into a very old and faulty Turing analogue."

"The data?"

"Pretty random, and the only thing that stands out with sifting is a Jain U-space signature some error points away from standard."

"Hogue?"

"It is time to do something," replied the AI out loud. Through its connection to her it sent tactical analysis of various scenarios and how they might play out. She sank deeper into it and chose the perhaps least provocative option, then opened another comlink.

"Rhodus," she said, and sent her request to it in the data plenum.

"We don't do warning shots," the platform AI replied.

"You didn't, but this is a rather special situation."

"Agreed."

"It's happening," said Jabro.

Through her link, Diana watched as one platform fired a missile. Jabro's assessment flicked into her mind via Hogue. She saw that the missile was a CTD, coil-launched to one per cent of light speed, because a higher acceleration would wreck it. A few thousand miles from the platform, its own drive kicked in—a one-burn fuser that applied the same acceleration as the coilgun but over a longer period. It would reach the alien ship in minutes. It then occurred to her that the platform that had launched the missile might not be doing precisely what she had asked, but she said nothing.

Meanwhile all the platforms were on the move. U-jump signatures flashed all around the accretion disc and platforms were appearing adjacent to the disc at the ship's predicted departure point. They were much closer than the two fleets—interdicted space lying between. Diana had seen no reason to test the platform AIs' further instructions concerning ships which breached the defence sphere space. Other platforms, nearer by, were under heavy fusion drive to reposition. All were surrounded by swarms of attack pods. The platforms were preparing for a hostile reaction.

The missile streaked in, flashes around it as particulates began burning off its forward hardfields and its defence lasers began hitting anything larger in its path. A few minutes later, it was sixty thousand miles from its target, whereupon it detonated. Diana breathed a sigh of relief. It would not have surprised her if the platform had decided on hitting the thing anyway, rather than this warning shot.

The blast was an expanding sphere of fire at first, then began to flatten out as it cooled, finally starting to separate into two discs as the ship reached it. The vessel passed through, swirling things up, but did not slow.

"Seckurg?"

"No change in the data—still doesn't make much sense."

"The *Kinghammer* is back," said Jabro.

Diana was aware of that via Hogue, as she was aware of most occurrences in the vicinity. Jabro did not need to tell her, just as Seckurg did not need to update her on the data transmitted by the alien ship. At one time, she had tried to make bridge operations more efficient: no need for human talk, mind-to-mind data transfer, all of them linked in as, effectively, subminds to Hogue. It hadn't worked out so well. Humans tended to lose grip on the reality of life and death when they took themselves beyond their evolved senses. She wondered if that disconnection explained Orlandine's recent . . . errors.

Even as the *Kinghammer* arrived, Orlik began transmitting positional data, a tactical map. Diana was happy to see that the prador was thinking exactly like her in this instance.

"I agree," she said to him.

"Now, then," he replied.

The prador ships began moving and, a moment later, as the Polity ships received their instructions, they started out as well. The two fleets began to meld into an umbrella formation over the departure point of the alien vessel from the disc. They were now fully cooperating in relation to the alien threat. A short while later, when the sensory arrays picked up the EMR from the event, Hogue slotted in a precis of what had happened between the *Hammer* and Weapons Platform Mu.

"I see that things did not go so well out there," she said.

"Not so good," Orlik replied.

"Good tactical move," said Jabro, excluding Orlik from his comment.

It was. The superior firepower and defences of Mu had squashed and dismissed Orlik. Returning here, he had instituted a logical response to the alien ship but he had also, by melding his fleet with the Polity one, made his ships a much more difficult target for that platform. The Client would now likely think that if it attacked him, Diana would have to respond too, countering a threat to her ally, as well as to their present formation. Whether she would or not she didn't know yet. It all depended.

"Analysis?" she said to Jabro.

He knew she meant Weapons Platform Mu. "Hardfields just like the ones the rogue AI Penny Royal used. Linked to a U-space twist. We could neutralize the platform and eventually input enough energy to drive the hardfield to collapse, which would destroy it."

She studied the data he sent and, as ever, it came down to tactics. They could nail the weapons platform but while they were doing that, the seventy or so attack pods would knock all hell out of them. Meanwhile, of course, they had a huge alien ship to deal with.

"Stick to plan," she said.

"You mean," Jabro replied, "continue to ignore it and hope for the best?"

"Yeah, that about covers it."

Diana returned her focus to the alien vessel, as the two-fleet formation shuffled and adjusted to optimum. But it seemed she would not get a second's breathing space.

"Comlink from Weapons Platform Mu," Hogue stated for all to hear. "I recommend limited com."

"Agreed," said Diana—Hogue meant just talk and no data transfer. There was no telling what the Client might send, given the bandwidth.

"Hello, Client," she said.

The voice that replied was female, soft, evenly modulated and devoid of threat—deliberately so, Diana was sure. "The situation is complicated," said the Client.

Diana quelled her "No shit, Sherlock" response and said, "It is complicated. What are your intentions here?"

"I wish to save my kind from extinction. The ship that is about to leave the accretion disc contains my people."

Diana sat there trying to incorporate that. She realized her mouth was hanging open and closed it. A hundred questions clamoured for her attention and she knew at once that straight verbal exchanges would not be enough—not enough time left.

"This is information," the Client added, "that I would prefer you not to share with the prador . . . for the present."

Orlik was already of the opinion that destruction of that ship was the best option. How would he react upon learning that the seven-hundred-mile-wide warship contained further examples of a species his kind had tried to obliterate?

"Your people were at war with the Jain?" she asked.

"Yes they were."

Too easy . . .

"So, the Wheel has tried to instigate the destruction of the last of your people?"

After a long pause, the Client replied simply, "Yes."

Diana thought fast. She had really not liked that pause, and the Client's "Yes" was too simple, considering its previous assertion about the situation being "complicated."

"I need more data," she said.

Agreed . . . Hogue whispered in her mind.

"That will require more trust," the Client replied.

"Hogue, open up bandwidth," she said, then looked over at Seckurg. He nodded, understanding. He would be ready with counters for informational warfare, just as Hogue would be ready. In her mind, she saw her ship's AI send messages to other ship AIs to prepare similarly, then cut all communication with them.

An information package came through from the Client, routed straight into secure storage for examination.

"This could take some time," said Seckurg.

Diana checked clocks, checked the position of the alien ship and knew they did not have the time. "Hogue, isolate me. Seckurg, route it to me in two minutes."

"Are you sure about this?" Hogue asked.

"I am the captain of this ship and the commander of this fleet, but we both know I am not essential. Do it." A slight delay ensued, whereupon she felt the disconnection. Though she still had her implant links, and the optic cables plugged into the back of her skull, Hogue went away. She suddenly felt utterly vulnerable and human, but she was used to that. Quite often she took holidays away from the connection to retain her humanity which, to her, was an edge. She prepared mentally. Her implants and enhancements would take the load, translating the data file into a format her brain could understand. If a hostile program came through with the data . . . well, she shrugged to herself, she felt it a risk worth taking. Warfare, after all, had never been a risk-free enterprise.

The file opened and Diana experienced warfare between the Jain and Species. So, it seemed the Jain were highly xenophobic—no surprise there—and had hunted the Species down across star systems. The final act had been here. What the Polity had always viewed as an accretion disc was in fact the rubble of a solar system which that conflict had destroyed. At the end of it, she felt wrung out, as if she had just lived an epic story in some virtuality. Running searches in her mind, she could find nothing nasty hidden in the data, so sent a tentative query to Hogue. She jerked as informational probes entered her mind, then started to grow hot, her face tingling, a sure sign the AI had an induction warfare beam on her.

"Clear," Hogue finally said.

She began reconnecting and, as she did so, found that over an hour had passed. She shunted a copy of the history over to Hogue, who scanned it in an instant. It transmitted copies to the other AIs in the fleet, then quickly began transmitting a precis of it to her crew.

"The data is . . . lacking," Hogue told her privately.

"In what way?" she asked—it had almost seemed to be too much to her.

"We have the history of the Jain and the Species," said Hogue. "We saw the battle that occurred here and how this accretion disc—if it can any longer be called that—was made. But we do not know how that Species ship ended up in a U-space blister in the sun."

"Some kind of defensive measure during the battle?"

"We can speculate, or . . ." said Hogue.

"Client," she said. "Your data seem to have been edited." She wasn't sure if the accusation was true, but it was worth making to see if it elicited a response. "We do not know how or why that ship ended up where it was."

"This is something I myself do not know," replied the Client.

Liar, thought Diana. But as she again checked the status of the two fleets, she knew it made no difference at all, even though Hogue was now transmitting this history to the platform AIs. The ship was still heading out. That the Species was an offshoot of the Jain did not make it any less a threat to the weapons platforms—the ship might not be Jain, but Jain tech had invaded it. And now, just minutes remained before it reached the perimeter.

Diana concentrated, summed all this up as an information package, and sent it to the Client.

"I see," the Client responded. "Then use your fleet to destroy the weapons platforms."

"I will not," she said, her voice hard.

Simple reality. The platforms were no threat at all to the Polity, quite the reverse. The Species ship, however, contained Jain tech and could very well be as hostile as the Jain. Defending the Polity came first.

"Then ask the platforms to concentrate their fire on the Jain-tech-infested portions of the ship first," said the Client.

It didn't seem to make much sense, since eventually the platforms would destroy the whole thing.

"I see no reason why not," she said flatly.

"Relayed," Hogue informed her—sending the whole content of her conversation with the Client to the weapons platforms.

The Client fell silent and seemed to have no more to add. After a long pause, Jabro said, "The platforms." Again, it wasn't needed—she could see the energy readouts. The weapons platforms were preparing to open fire.

14

Induction warfare beams have been developed to the point where they can interfere with information in crystal storage. Or processed in quantum computing. So we must speculate at last on how we may affect matter, and what weapons this could lead to. Lasers heat a target, and this causes chemical changes in the material being struck. Particle weapons heat, but can also cause ablation, electrical disturbance and, with certain particulates, chemical changes. Sonic weapons set up resonance that can destroy the integrity of certain materials. These are all obvious. However, when one considers that an induction warfare beam can influence the quantum state of matter, which is what they do when penetrating computing, one must question what else can be influenced. We know, under laboratory conditions, that it is possible to interfere with, and sometimes change, atomic forces. This then leads to the idea of an energy weapon that can do the same. Could a weapon be created capable of turning an otherwise inert material fissile? It may well be possible to perform alchemy by knocking protons, neutrons and electrons out of atomic structures. And if one could actually tamper with the intermolecular and intramolecular forces, the currently fictional disintegrator or disruptor beam becomes a distinct possibility.

—Notes from her lecture "Modern Warfare" by E. B. S. Heinlein

ORLANDINE

She could sense them in the tower all around, and there were those she could not feel. A visual translation in her mind gave her light spots in the towers, interspersed with dark areas. The former were active weapons platforms, while the latter were those that had been destroyed. Annoyingly, frustratingly, she had only reached a few of them in her initial growth spurt and now felt exhausted. Straining for further contact, her vision strayed to internal cams, where she saw a Jain-tech tentacle developing fast along the glassy floor. It was etching out materials from the floor for its growth, extending towards its target. But she had other concerns too—she must not forget her friends.

Tracking the power draw of weapons, she gazed through cams into an underground level of the facility. Wrecked security drones and autoguns mapped out a path, at the end of which she found Captain Cog. His clothing was in tatters, and he was tearing an autogun out of a wall, while Angel stood at his back, taking shots from another gun, his body radiating red hot. She punched into security and shut it down, but even as the weapons ceased firing on her companions, her attention strayed elsewhere. The Clade was trying to get in. She reached out to her sentinel drones and sensed another presence.

"So you're alive," said Bludgeon.

"Yes." She said no more, instead penetrating the sentinels. The virus Bludgeon had used to shut them down was complex and self-regenerative, so instead of attempting to erase it, she just deleted everything in their sub-AI minds. In her own mind, she slammed together a subpersona—simplified, limited objectives—and began copying it across. Meanwhile she had noticed another situation.

Trike was waiting to die. But then the whine of power supplies all around him began to wind down as Bludgeon informed his fellow drones that the man had not, in fact, killed Orlandine. She added her own input to that:

"He carried my Jain tech, which possessed U-com and was able to load one of my backups from out where we built the runcibles. His kiss saved me."

"But not your body," Cutter commented.

"I have retained DNA and can rebuild it if I wish," she said.

She was trying to be cold and logical about this, but she did feel resentment about her human death and the *invasion* that had transformed her. She should feel gratitude towards the man but did not and had to stamp on the urge to ask the drones to kill him anyway. They began to swing their weapons away from him and focus their attention elsewhere. She saw what was attracting their notice. The Clade, congregating low down, struggling to form into a spinning patterned mass, while fending off strikes from above.

"Do not attack," she told them.

"They are about to use another ion-beam strike," Knobbler informed her.

"I know, but there is no need for you to attack."

Sentinel drones, which had earlier been slumped and inert on their watch towers, were now active. They began raising their weapons-loaded forelimbs towards the swirling Clade formation. She set them firing, but more as a distraction than anything else, for she had seen, via the facility's exterior sensors, and through the sentinel drones, the solution arriving, or rather, returning.

"You have found your calling," she said.

"Seems that way," replied the erstwhile black-ops attack ship.

The sound of railgun slugs in atmosphere created a sonic thunder. It produced hard white vapour trails that appeared some seconds after impact. Targeted Clade units exploded and their formation scattered in disarray. *Obsidian Blade* arrived with a thunderous crash, spitting fire in every direction. The shockwave of its arrival rippled the glassy faces of buildings and set some of them swaying. She saw Trike shielding his eyes as dust and debris blew past him, along with two of the smaller, lighter war drones, then returned her attention to greater concerns.

She studied the platform ghost drives to which she had linked. All contained the directive written in by her. She considered alterations but, in the end, realized that circumstances had changed so radically that the need for the directive had passed. She erased it in each drive, and consequently in each connected platform.

"We are preparing to fire," the platform AIs informed her.

Detail?

A data package arrived and she took it apart in an instant. She saw the situation out there: the Client, the history of the Jain and the Species, and that the accretion disc was the remains of a destroyed solar system. The alien ship, the Species ship, was just about to slide out of the accretion disc and she understood why even the platforms without the directive might open fire. Jain tech aboard that ship remained a danger, while the ship and its complement was an unknown. But now at least she had leeway.

She strained further. Glimpses of the web of herself stretched throughout the Ghost Drive Facility. More platforms fell into her grasp, even as they began firing fusillades of railgun slugs. No way to recall them, but she needed to reach all the platforms and get a grip on this situation. She continued to erase the directive, but they still fired. Their attack pods were on the move, hurtling towards the alien ship and spitting particle beams. Then Orlandine hit gold.

One branch of herself seized control of a fusion reactor and made connection to a main power feed. Energy flooded through her superconducting fibres and, ramping up the output of the reactor, she had the power she needed. Her Jain tentacles extended rapidly throughout the facility, hot and smoking with the speed of their growth. They spread fibrous root tendrils to suck up materials, sped along optic and power feeds, punched through floors and ceilings. Drawing masses of materials into globular growths at the bases of each tower, they exploded from these, up through the tower dropshafts. The moment they hit the top, they sprouted side-growths that shot into each drive section. In the first few minutes, Orlandine linked to twenty ghost drives, in the next few she had hundreds.

Meanwhile, out at the accretion disc the railgun slugs found their target. Seen as a whole, the great ship seemed to sparkle. But these first shots on its hull punched craters a half-mile wide, spewing out balls of white-hot debris, molten metal and gas. Then came a flickering across vacuum, impacts upon curved surfaces. These hardfields were similar to the one the Client had deployed around Weapons Platform Mu. But they were not fully enclosing and faded in strength towards their edges, wavering on and off like faulty light panels. While many railgun slugs struck them, creating a fire-storm in vacuum, others slammed through to hit the ship. And the attack pods were closer too, their particle beams sometimes deflected, sometimes carving glowing trenches. Were these intermittent hardfields a sign of the damage the ship had received?

The strikes were ferocious and the attack pods began to deploy other weapons. Missiles streaked down. Orlandine saw them altering their acceleration and changing courses. She realized the AIs had detected a frequency to the hardfield failures and that the missiles were also seeking out weak spots. Hundreds of them punched through. Others, whose timing was a bit off, exploded out in vacuum against full fields. The intense EMR flashes of the multiple blasts knocked sensors down and hid the ship behind a giant, spreading plasma storm. Altered sensory data and clean-up programs gave a view of the ship through the storm a moment later. The CTD missiles struck and massive explosions burrowed craters miles wide in the body of the thing and blew out islands of material. The whole seven-hundred-mile-wide monster bucked under the force and distorted. Multiple impacts in some places cut holes right through it. Molten metal sheeted across vacuum from these holes. Hot chemical fires burned around them, warping and blistering the hull and scorching it to expose structural members. Radiant gas blew away what might be access hatches or doors. The ship shuddered and revolved, a great section of its outer spiral, five hundred miles long, unpeeling in apparent slow motion and breaking away.

As this devastation continued, Orlandine finally gained access to all the weapons platforms and deleted the directive from every one. But still they kept on firing. Should she stop them now? She wasn't sure it was the right thing to do—the ship still presented an unknown threat.

"You no longer have to do this," she said, but did not make it an imperative order. The previous directive had been an error, she realized, related to her own paranoia about Jain tech. She should have trusted that a mass of intelligent AI minds was capable of making intelligent decisions. However, she penetrated their minds on other levels to see what she had wrought. Soon it became apparent that, though the directive was gone, it had affected their thinking. They were still seeing dangers and not yet incorporating a larger picture. She persuaded, citing information about the Species—peaceful only until attacked. They replied that they had now attacked. The exchange took microseconds.

Then it came.

From emplacements all over the giant ship's hull, like extending glassy spines, energy beams speared out. Where they reached the hardfields they shifted to open gaps, and the lines of glass continued on.

Orlandine recognized them at once. The Jain soldier that had attacked the defence sphere had used these and she knew their effect.

Some struck attack pods and she saw them simply shatter, turning into lines of debris scattered through vacuum. She had no idea why they didn't cause any CTDs to explode, because surely the pods still contained some. Perhaps the very nature of antimatter was that it repelled whatever energy or mechanism caused other materials to fall apart? Most of the beams continued towards the weapons platforms. One struck a hardfield, hesitated, the point of impact growing black, then it pierced through. It hit the weapons platform like a drill going into brass, and a moment later stabbed out the other side. It then winked out. Telemetry from the platform gave her detail. The thing had ripped through the platform, causing anything in its path to smash apart. The damage was bad in terms of a single strike, but not crippling. However, the effect did not end there. A slow energy wave began spreading from the point of impact. I-beams splintered, and bubble-metal warped, spewing its closed-cell structure in micro-bead dust. Ceramal cracked, superconductors withered, and optics died and blackened. As this surge continued, the whole platform began to warp with the materials' stresses. Exploding gas tanks blew materials out into vacuum. Breached armouries, laminar power storage and hypercapacitor shorts, as well as any other item with high power density, started to tear the platform apart.

The AI ejected in an armoured canister, leaving behind spreading ruination. In the time it had taken the platform to disintegrate, another eight had been struck and were following the same path. Some platforms managed short evasive U-jumps, but with the present U-space disruption worsening, that was dangerous. She watched as one platform rematerialized with part of its mass inside another one. The ensuing explosion blew them away from each other—falling apart like two chunks of one beast that had been torn in half. Another that jumped suffered a detonation at one end, uprooting rail- and coilgun towers and shearing away megatons of armour. It had obviously materialized in the same spot as one of its attack pods. Meanwhile, the alien ship was still firing. Orlandine came to a decision.

The platform AIs were right. By firing on the ship, they had initiated hostilities and it was replying. She could allow this to continue, and maybe the platforms could destroy the vessel, but it was certain that many of them would not survive the encounter. Yes, Jain tech was within the ship, and it was now a slightly less unknown danger, but a danger nevertheless. That was beside the point. Her platforms had launched an unprovoked attack on a vessel containing a species that, on the data she had, was not inherently hostile. Tactical and threat assessment had to go to one side. This was a moral issue.

"Cease firing," she ordered, and she made it a directive.

The firing did cease, at once, from them. She waited a few minutes to assess the reaction. In that time other platforms fell into ruin, but she felt that was an acceptable loss, since no lives were lost—the AIs were sensible enough to eject before the destruction reached them. The alien ship did not stop firing. Why should it? It had been attacked and the attackers remained out there, in its path.

"Return to initiation site," she ordered and made that another directive.

The platform AIs calculated for longer jumps and began sliding out of the real. Attack pods started shooting away too. She delivered another order, and some platforms left behind attack pods to act as watchers for her—her eyes there. Minutes later, new stars winked into being in the skies of Jaskor—over six hundred of them.

BLADE

Within a few seconds it became obvious the Clade had decided it could do nothing more at the facility. Taking fire from *Blade*, the sentinel drones and the ships in orbit, it was not able to organize itself for an ion-beam strike. Nor could it get closer to the building beside which Trike and the war drones lingered. It therefore switched over to ghost chaff and induction warfare, trying to confuse sensors, and succeeding. Blade did not see the remaining thousand-plus units group together in one mass until it was on the move. A railgun strike, exploding against a hardfield the Clade mass had created, resulted in a surge. The clumped units, whose shape resembled a bacterium, shot away from the facility and down—a very powerful combined grav and EM drive propelling it. Blade, immediately firing up its own multiple and widely spread fusion drives from the erstwhile splinter missiles on its surface, turned like a snake and followed. It recognized that somehow the Clade had shunted feedback energy directly into its drive system. But the fact it was running meant it could not do this for long.

The Clade hurtled into the valley in which the facility sat and on into the mountains. It was weaving and still using ghost chaff and induction warfare to make it difficult to nail down. Perhaps it hoped for some reluctance on Blade's part—any misses would hit the planet and contravene Dragon's stricture. But they were beyond that now. Licking out with one particle beam, Blade created an explosive path, shattering rocks and trees and carving a burning trench. Contact had the Clade sliding to one side, skimming the tops of trees and leaving a trail of burning leaves.

"There are people in these mountains," the Clade noted.

Yes, there were, but Blade had them located. The sudden proliferation of sensor data showing extra people in the valley was a weak ruse. Just to drive this point home, Blade fired railgun slugs. One hit a hardfield and sprayed a sheet of fire where some of these people were ostensibly located. Another punched into the ground—a white-hot cavity through rock, followed by an eruption that geysered tons of rubble into the sky.

"We are impressed," said the Clade.

"You are going to die," Blade replied.

"Oh really?"

The ghost chaff faded and Blade got accurate targeting. Another railgun strike this time hit an angled hardfield. Surge of EM and grav. The Clade shot into the side of the valley and hacked a trench upwards. Part of the face of the valley exploded outwards and, in the ensuing dust storm, the Clade disappeared. Blade upped scanning. Ground radar revealed a cave snaking through the mountain and it realized its opponent had prepared for escape—it had known about this cave.

Time now? Blade wondered.

Further scanning. The cave opened on the other side of the mountain, so it wasn't yet time to reveal its full capabilities. On grav, and a side blast of fusion, it turned, hit the same slope and ricocheted upwards, then looped over the mountain. Analysis: the Clade stayed low because orbital strikes were still a threat. With the fleets out there, it would not be able to make it off-world. Its apparent aim seemed simple survival. But whether the time frame of this related to events at the accretion disc, Blade did not know.

The Clade exploded out of the other side of the mountain and twisted down. Here in another valley lay a deep, long lake. It hit the surface hard but did not create the expected explosion of spray: obviously low-friction meta-materials of its conglomerated bodies, complemented by electrostatic fields. Scanning, Blade picked up water-filled caves and again contemplated its own capabilities. However, the Clade speared down deep and kicked in with a cavitating drive to take it along the bottom of the lake. Blade matched its position above and pondered railgunning the thing. But the slugs would lose too much of their energy penetrating that deep to be effective. This was a good survival ploy on the part of the Clade, but a limited one. Blade calculated its chances of success if it splintered off parts of itself and sent them down. But anything that could damage the Clade would raise tsunamis on the lake, and residences stood along the shore. And where was the urgency?

Blade had accepted its mission profile: it must track down and neutralize the Clade. The best way of doing this was, of course, destroying it. But there was no guarantee it would get the whole swarm AI, because it was most likely not all here. Blade needed location data. That meant capturing a Clade unit and accessing its mind, because surely it would know where other parts of it were. So a second-best way of neutralizing it was in order for now—keep on harrying the thing and picking off its units. Sure, this would involve a lot of destruction and casualties, but letting the Clade do what it wanted could result in much worse.

It exploded from the end of the lake and began to take a fast, writhing course down a series of waterfalls. Blade waited until it was half a mile clear of the lake before rearranging geology. Two railgun strikes shattered a massive stone slab, the wave of fast-moving debris slamming into the Clade and partially breaking its conglomeration. Once again, most of this was taken by a hardfield. But feedback blew two units away from the main mass and they hit a lake at the base of one waterfall, where the water boiled around them. Pausing to scan, Blade found them burned out and falling apart—no data to be had there. Scanning ahead revealed the last waterfall pouring into a large pool and from this a river, fast-moving through wild lands, and then a slow-moving canal through croplands. Distantly, the city was visible.

The Clade had chosen to run there because it knew that negated some of the more effective weapons in Blade's armoury. Caves in the mountains were few, while the croplands and the city sat on a thick layer of limestone wormed through with a mass of caverns. These were accessible via the city flood drains, as the prador had demonstrated. Blade calculated that the Clade would break up, go underground and disperse, sure that a black-ops attack ship would be rendered impotent by the tactic.

The Clade was in for a surprise.

Another railgun strike. This time the missile hit a slanted hardfield and the Clade generated a magnetic bottle so powerful it shimmered in the air. The swarm AI had computed it just right. The railgun slug vaporized off the hardfield into the magnetic bottle and emitted as plasma flame two miles long. This struck a crop storage silo and the thing distorted and collapsed, trailing fire. A nearby harvest robot was flipped onto its back, while the blast sent the people next to it tumbling. Scan. Three humans and two Golem, armed and probably refugees from the city. The two Golem would be fine and would tend to the two humans blown into the nearby field. The third human, who had been flung back against the harvester, had been impaled on its comb. Maybe she had a memplant . . .

"Oops," said the Clade. "Houses ahead . . ."

Blade felt a tight, sick rage, but no inclination to desist. Casualties were to be expected and, in cold AI calculation, their number would be smaller while it kept the Clade running. An overall calculation concerning the swarm AI's growth was factored in too. While fleeing, it would struggle to expand itself. A stark reality was that it could grow from a few units capable of destruction on a local scale into something with the ability to depopulate planets. The Clade had to be stopped.

Nevertheless, Blade switched over to beam weapons. Lasers kept the thing running. Occasional particle beam strikes could overload some of its units, without the danger of deflection that the lasers had. The swarm AI snaked along at high speed above the river, along which were the most human habitations, its shockwave raising spray behind it. As it drew closer to the city, Blade saw its structure expanding, loosening. It was preparing to go to ground.

"Goodbye, attack ship," it said, and over the city broke into its individual components and dropped. Some disappeared into structures all across the city, but even in them they worked their way down. Others went straight down into the storm drains.

"And hello," Blade sent, bristling like a pine cone and then detaching the radically redesigned splinter missiles that made up the entirety of its hull. Blade, swarm AI, followed the Clade down.

ORLIK

As the last of the weapons platforms faded from existence, Orlik noted the com request from Diana. Thinking, *What now?* he opened the link.

"Time for you to be updated," she said perfunctorily. "I now know why the Client is here—I have been talking to it."

"That would be interesting to know," said Orlik tightly.

"Are you prepared to accept a data package from me?"

"Sprag?" Orlik enquired, cutting Diana out of the exchange.

"Tactically inadvisable," Sprag replied. "Circumstances have changed drastically and they want to send you a data package . . ."

Sprag was, he realized, behaving like the prador AI she claimed to be, with that kind of paranoia.

"We'll accept it and route it to secure storage for scanning," he stated.

"You're the boss," said Sprag.

"Send it and I'll get back to you," he said to Windermere.

While waiting for Sprag to check out the package, he watched the ship out there. As it cleared the accretion disc, his scanners revealed much activity on its hull and inside. It had begun to sacrifice portions of itself in an orderly manner. Small internal detonations blew away wedges of its structure. Once they fell clear, the milky orange beam of a particle weapon lanced out and vaporized them. Mobile hot spots inside sometimes appeared on the hull as travelling, glowing veins. Structural shifts revealed themselves on the outside too, when whole sections of hull twisted in place or shifted over to a new position. Other areas of hull flowed to close up impact strikes. As a whole, the ship appeared to be clearing out dead or diseased tissue—healing itself.

"What do you think?" he asked.

"I think the platform strike against it kicked it into higher gear," replied Sprag. "It's almost as if it wasn't quite awake, and now it is."

"Not so good."

"No . . . and I have just looked at the data package Diana sent to you. I suggest you look at it at once."

Orlik pondered his own prador paranoia. This might well be the opportunity Sprag was waiting for . . . if she was still a shill for Earth Central. But he no longer believed that. He no longer *felt* that. What point was there to him if it wasn't instinct? Without the need for that organic, evolved response, ships might as well be controlled by AIs only.

"Okay, send it to me."

It arrived via his interface just a second later, but it took him some time to absorb its content. So, that was no Jain ship but one of the Species—the Species whose civilization his own kind had tried to annihilate. The sensible thing to do, from the prador point of view, would be to eliminate the threat. Certainly, Diana Windermere knew all this, and that his response might not be a good one. So why had she sent him the package? He decided to ask.

"You must realize what the logical prador response should be to this," he said.

"Oh, I understand, but you're not quite a normal prador, are you?"

"So what do you expect my response to be?"

"I expect you to note how that ship mauled the weapons platforms. I expect you to look at the Species from your new perspective, and in relation to the data in that package. The Wheel has, all along, compelled us to attack that ship. Why? Because it is an enemy of the Jain—we've been dragged into a war that's millions of years past its sell-by date. But consider this: the fact that the Wheel tried to manipulate us into attacking that ship means the Species is not inherently hostile—it would not initiate hostilities on its own, but only respond to them."

"But hostilities have been initiated," said Orlik.

"By the weapons platforms, which have been withdrawn. Do you see that ship firing on us now?" She paused for a moment, then added, "And do you see what it is doing?"

The data had just arrived from Sprag. Yes, the ship was still rebuilding itself but it had changed course. It had turned onto the best route possible to take it away from the fleets, while not returning to the accretion disc.

"Have you managed communication with it yet?" Orlik asked.

"I have not."

"What do you suggest?"

"My readings indicate that the ship is presently ejecting and destroying the Jain infestation it has aboard. This was either acquired in the disc when it left the U-space blister, or before during some battle. It has only responded to our hostility. It doesn't want a fight. I suggest we leave it to the Client who, incidentally, did not destroy you when she could have."

It was a hard decision and Orlik knew he needed instructions. He temporarily blocked the link to Diana and opened another he had not seen fit to use until now. A delay ensued. U-space effects, time dilation, or maybe the king was busy. Then, "I am assessing."

Orlik waited, and after a few minutes the king spoke again. "Sprag relayed a copy of the data package to me upon receipt. Windermere is correct. Take no action against that ship, or the Client, unless you are attacked. Your primary focus must be the . . . security of the accretion disc until Orlandine has full control again."

Ah, back to that, thought Orlik. "But the Species . . ."

"Historical files show that they made every effort to negotiate with us, even offered technological trade—this continued even while we were destroying them."

"Still . . ."

"I have given my order," said the king, and cut the link.

Orlik opened the link to Diana again. "I will do nothing, as you recommend."

"I know," said Diana tightly, "your king included me in that exchange."

"So, do we separate our fleets and start snapping our claws at each other again?"

"We'll have to wait for Orlandine to—"

Sprag cut in: "Two hundred of our ships have just opened fire on the vessel."

COG

Captain Cog lay flat on his back, trying to control his breathing and enforce calm, clear thinking. But he realized he had taken too much damage. The defence system in the Ghost Drive Facility had been harsh and the injuries it had inflicted on him had pushed him towards the kind of change that Trike was undergoing. Not quite the same, but he knew his control was shaky. Still, better than being dead.

He sat upright and looked across at Angel. The android was bent over, one hand against a twisted I-beam, smoking—parts of his body still red hot. Without the android, Cog knew he would not have survived this place. Angel's ability to scan his surroundings had enabled them to find an area, with the destruction of a few internal defences, where they could hole up for just that bit longer. However, in the end it was another's intervention that had saved them.

"Orlandine?" Cog asked.

Angel shook himself and stood upright. He pointed through the wreckage. "She is all around us."

Cog peered beyond the wreckage and had no idea what his companion was talking about. He saw the vine-like growths along the far wall, some of them shifting slightly, like a blind man's fingers feeling his way.

"I don't understand," he said.

"It is simple," said a distorted female voice that seemed to issue out of the air nearby.

"Orlandine?"

"Yes."

"What happened?"

"You understand that I was comprised of three parts?" she asked.

Cog strained for understanding but was at war with himself. Yes, he wanted to think clearly and logically. But he also had an unbelievable hunger and had become very attracted to the idea of taking a bite out of Angel.

"I see your powers of reason are not at their best," said Orlandine. "I was a haiman composed of a human being melded, as fully as possible, with AI. I conquered the technology of a Jain node and made it my third part, to integrate the other two more closely."

"I note the use of the past tense," said Angel.

The android had made some point there, Cog realized, but it escaped him.

Angel nodded, as if he had received a private communication. "Come on," he said, and began making his way through the wreckage. Cog followed—they were heading out, there would be food . . .

Orlandine continued, "When the Clade attempted to have me assassinated, I had to wipe most of my AI component and detach my Jain element. My aim was reintegration after I fell, but my surviving human fled into the storm drains, where you found me."

They made their way to an area through which they had not come, so it was clear of wreckage. Then to a dropshaft. Angel stepped in and it wafted him upwards. Cog did the same but found himself stupidly fighting the irised gravity field. When Cog arrived, following Angel, he just hung writhing in mid-air, until the android grabbed and pulled him out, onto the ground floor of one of the towers. He clamped a hand on Angel's shoulder and tugged him close. His tongue darted out, long and pink, and its leech mouth ground over the android's face.

"I think not," said Angel, easily pushing him away.

Cog felt a surge of rage but fought it. He retracted his tongue.

"You will need something," said Orlandine. "I have instructed Knobbler."

What? What was she talking about?

"So what happened next?" Angel asked.

"My Jain component was damaged by the Clade but managed to pursue me into the storm drains. Its movement was limited, but it found someone to ride. While in that person, it reinstated its U-com and downloaded one of my backups. It also took control of its carrier and sent him after me."

"Trike," said Angel.

"Correct."

"Isn't it disturbing it used a human being like that?" Angel asked.

After a long pause, Orlandine replied again with, "Correct."

Many more of the vine-like growths were here, spearing off in every direction, branching into the ghost drive and other surrounding equipment. Jain tech, Cog finally realized. Those growths, they *were* Orlandine. Angel led the way through to a glass wall, but it was distorted and twisted by those same growths. The glass was rainbow-refracting between the vine-like strands, like a stained-glass window, so it was nigh impossible to see out.

"He brought my Jain component to me, here, when I was once again on the point of death," said Orlandine.

"I understand," said Angel.

Cog really didn't understand but he held onto one thing. "Trike, is he okay?" He felt it was a silly question to ask but could think of nothing else. He suspected the changes the boy had undergone might not be reversible.

"He is . . . different," Orlandine replied.

With a screeing sound, a hole opened at eye-level in the glass ahead. It steadily expanded, the vines rolling the edge back and crystal shards dropping to the floor. They stepped out through drifting smoke below a bright, sunlit sky. Cog surveyed the devastation. He could see that a couple of towers were down and rubble was strewn everywhere. Squatting here and there on the battlefield were war drones. Cog got a sudden, nostalgic surge of memory, of a time he hadn't thought about often in the last century or so. He remembered being in a place similarly wrecked. There were war drones much like these and prador too, like the one standing over beside Trike, as well as those approaching from outside the facility. He took a pace forwards, because there was meat, but Angel's hand came down on his shoulder.

"You are better than this," said the android.

"Yes, yes I am," said Cog, but still found himself pulling against the grip. He took a deep breath, fists clenched, and forced his focus wholly on Trike—a *person* he knew.

The man no longer looked human. He stood maybe eight feet tall, scraps of his original clothing clinging to him but failing to cover the thickly corded, blue musculature that seemed almost skinless—like an ancient anatomical drawing. Brown and white veins clad his body, while the sides of his torso had issued curving spikes, like a reptile's teeth. His head jutted forward on a long neck, eyes close together, mouth filled with lethal fangs protruding forward too—the head of a predatory animal. Yet . . . yet he seemed to be in calm repose, when everything about him spoke of danger, action and things being torn apart.

"Cog," said Trike, his voice only slightly distorted by the fearsome-looking mouth.

"How are you, boy?" Cog asked, finding himself having to repress the urge to giggle.

Trike gazed at him for a long moment, then said, "I am better." He then fixed his attention on Angel and stiffened. The serenity seemed to disappear. Cog had been aware for some time that Trike had unfinished business with the android, and it seemed that had not changed. After a pause, Trike seemed to make a huge effort, shrugged himself and became looser. He looked up as a shadow fell across them from the big war drone Cog recognized as Knobbler. It descended to land on one side.

"Following instructions," said the drone.

It flicked out two of its tentacles and an object landed with a thump between them, raising dust and spattering droplets of yellow ichor all around. Cog had time to register that the thing looked like the cross between a lizard and a llama, before he lost all control. He leapt forwards and descended on it, his tongue stabbing down and grinding through scaled hide. A moment of ecstasy suffused him as gobbets of flesh, in a bath of body fluids, flowed up inside his tubular tongue. He could feel the food entering his throat and then dropping into the cavernous emptiness of his stomach. But it wasn't enough, nor fast enough. He retracted his tongue, rocked back and stabbed a hand down, punching inside the carcass, then tearing out its side. Now Trike was there too. Cog snarled at him, but suppressed it by cramming chunks of a liver-like organ into his mouth. Trike glanced across, casually ripped off the thing's head and long neck, and began consuming it with appalling efficiency.

Sanity slowly returned and Cog found himself studying the stripped remains. The creature possessed a skeleton of hard, black bone that looked like biological chainmail, with circular links as wide as his hand. This was too tough for him to eat, so he concentrated on the remaining meat and organs. It wasn't too hard for Trike, however, who broke the thing apart and crunched large pieces down as though they were rock candy. Cog felt no urge to snarl at him now and finally, as his mind started working again, his first thought was, *he ate its head*. At length, the two of them stood and stepped back from a yellow and purple stain on the ground.

"Better now?" asked Angel, slapping a hand on Cog's shoulder.

Cog flinched and resisted the urge to turn on him.

"Not really," he replied. "I still need some suppression and—" he gestured to Trike—"I think he does too. I have diluted sprine back at my ship."

"Isn't that risky with him?" said Angel, speaking low.

"I think we're beyond that now."

Trike looked over at them with what might have been a grin or a grimace—it was difficult to tell. "I have no need for intervention. The Clade still lives." But the monstrous man's gaze was balefully fixed on Angel for an uncomfortably long moment, before he swung it round to the building behind. "Where is it now?"

They turned towards the tower, and movement there. Vines, veins and tendrils of Jain tech were streaming out around the hole they had stepped through. A mass grew and gradually began to fill the entrance. As it closed the thing up, it began to bulge towards them, shifting and reshaping, until revealing the form of a human being. The mass presented this human shape, which consisted entirely of writhing movement, and thrust it forwards. The figure then began to settle and meld, taking on the colour of flesh. Its feet touched down onto the dusty ground, as features appeared and eyes opened. Naked, Orlandine stepped forwards, but Cog noted she was still attached to the mass behind her by a hundred umbilici. She looked around at them all, and smiled.

"Where is it now?" Trike repeated.

Orlandine glanced across at Angel. "You understand the situation now?"

"I do," Angel nodded. "Species ship and the prador opening fire."

"I must secure Jaskor and rearm the platforms," she said and turned to Knobbler. "I'll need you and your crew in orbit, working on our defences."

"No guarantee it will come here," said Knobbler.

"That's not my concern," she shot back.

Knobbler turned slightly to look towards the prador. Cog knew he should be understanding this interplay but did not. He needed information, but first he needed his mind straight enough to comprehend it.

"Where is the Clade?" Trike insisted.

Finally, Orlandine focused on him. "Aren't you forgetting something?"

"I am not," said Trike.

She smiled without humour. "I could do it myself, but I have other tasks to perform. They have an advanced . . . AI surgeon aboard a medship coming down from orbit. They could bring your wife Ruth back to you."

Trike bowed over as if he had been thumped, or as if he was about to attack. He shook his head from side to side. "The Clade," he muttered.

Orlandine just stared at him, then answered, "The Clade has taken refuge in the storm drains and caves underneath the city, where the *Obsidian Blade* is hunting it. Your input is not required."

Trike snarled, turned and loped away, then began accelerating into a long-stride run. Cog gazed at his retreating back, not sure what to do.

"Cog," said Orlandine, "that medship is heading for the city now."

Cog nodded, then set off after Trike. He needed to return to his ship anyway to get that low-dose sprine into his system. Experienced in the changes the virus could make, he knew that the longer he left it, the worse they got. After a moment, he realized that Angel was running to one side of him.

"You sure you want to come?" Cog asked.

"I cannot spend my life running away from him," Angel replied. "And I don't think he will be able to continue running away from me."

15

The armour of yesteryear—the kind preserved in museums on Earth from the conflicts that occurred there before the first diaspora—is as akin to modern-day armour as a sheet of cellophane to human skin. No, even that comparison doesn't give a wide enough gap. There is none for the outer teguments of living beings. Modern armour is a whole technology in itself and one that developed rapidly after our first encounters with the prador. It is perfectly understood that our deficiency in that respect was nearly the end of us. Armour is in the prador genome, literally, and since they are great metallurgists, their development of it was way ahead of ours. While we were still experimenting with exotic matter in laboratories, they were incorporating it into the hulls of their ships. At that time, Polity ship armour consisted of dense and tough meta-materials, and shock-absorbing closed and open cell structures. Prador weapons melted or cut it to shreds. Superconducting grids were quickly incorporated, as were shifting, bearing layers. Armour tech from the prador led to the use of exotic metals too and within a decade, we were equal to them in this respect. Complex memory materials, iterations of chain-glass, nanochain chromium and other hyperlinked materials, took us further. Also computer control of many processes within the armour made it more adaptable. Armour is now a deeply complex technology that enwraps our ships. It is much akin to a living skin, even with veins and capillaries to shift its substance and heal injuries.

—Notes from her lecture "Modern Warfare" by E. B. S. Heinlein

GEMMELL

On a new descent trajectory, now the action had moved to the city, Gemmell contemplated the data being relayed to his gridlink by

Morgaine. He collated it and cut out what was irrelevant to them, then relayed it to the gridlinks, augs and Golem minds of the soldiers behind him in the transport. First the events on the ground. Orlandine had regained control of the Ghost Drive Facility and recalled the platforms. The Clade, meanwhile, had entered the drainage system under the city, to be hunted by the black-ops attack ship *Obsidian Blade*, transformed into a swarm AI.

"Our mission is still approved?" he asked.

"It is," Morgaine replied from the console, so all could hear.

"I wondered, what with the Clade back at the city . . ."

"Seems Diana now approves of us getting proactive."

Gemmell snorted at that. "And how are things up there?" Up in orbit around Jaskor it was all getting a bit crowded.

"It's a little bit tense here," commented Morgaine. "The prador aren't happy, and the platform AIs aren't saying much. They have, however, dispatched robot shuttles to pick up the refugees in orbit and sent construction and maintenance bots to the orbital facilities."

"Any word from Orlandine?" he asked, as the troop transport punched through cloud and the landscape opened out underneath.

"Plenty of words," said Morgaine, obviously annoyed.

"Really?"

"She's stripping a hundred platforms of the bulk of their armament and moving them into close orbit. Every atmosphere-capable shuttle and non-military ship is to be deployed moving evacuees to the platforms."

"Your shuttles too, I take it?"

"Yes, the majority of them. Prador shuttles also."

"Seems an excessive response," he opined.

"Millions were already queued to leave by runcible and more want to get off-world. I suspect it's some guilt on her part concerning the thousands who have already died. She's discharging her responsibility to citizens."

"So she really expects big problems?"

"It's not out of the question, with what's happening."

True enough. Immediately after agreeing that the Species ship should be left alone, the prador had opened fire on it. Their commander,

Orlik, claimed this was not at his order. That event had greatly agitated the prador here, while Polity forces were also unhappy: it felt as if the situation was spinning out of control, and they didn't know what to do. It looked as if things might be about to blow up between the two realms. Orlandine, in allowing a big evacuation, might be overreacting, but the surface population on Jaskor would be the most vulnerable. A battle breaking out in orbit could result in megadeath below.

Trantor, the squat, bald-headed veteran piloting the transport, took it lower down. They hurtled over desert terrain, scattered with cracked salt pans, towards the blue jut of mountains. The Ghost Drive Facility was there, but that wasn't where they were going. Gemmell, linked into the shuttle's sensors, focused on something down on the ground. A giant sprawl of grav-cars and buses had settled on the ground beside a river, the growth on either side the only green. Self-assembling holiday homes were up and thousands of people were in the area. Refugees from the city had first landed in the mountains, then, learning of the Clade heading towards them, had come here. He only looked for confirmation because he knew the locations of most of those who had fled. They were not his concern at present and, checking his gridlink, he saw that a cargo shuttle had been sent from the main city to pick them up. They would be heading up to the evacuee platforms.

Morgaine again: "Orlandine has just *approved* your mission and says we can secure the city and offer aid. I've dispatched more personnel—medics, autodocs and submind airfire drones for cover."

"Feeling a bit peeved, my darling?"

"She is peremptory."

"Used to being the boss here, I guess . . . What about her drones?"

"Rising from the facility to work in orbit."

Complicated. Why Orlandine had decided to dispatch that kind of firepower to work up there he wasn't sure. But then the drones had a lot of expertise and had built her two runcibles capable of shifting a black hole. As for himself, Gemmell decided he would just focus on limited objectives. An enemy was down on the surface and citizens were in hiding. *Obsidian Blade* was hunting down the Clade, but it could resurface and start wreaking havoc again. He must be ready to respond to that, meanwhile protecting the citizenry. He glanced back at his soldiers and allowed himself a tight smile. They were all tough, boosted veterans in motorized combat armour, carrying state-of-the-art weaponry. A hundred of them at the moment, but more on the way.

"Disaster Response?" he now asked.

"Still holding back until you clarify the situation in the city. Once you secure things above ground, and only if you think it a good idea, you can call them in. The link is in the data sphere," Morgaine replied.

Gemmell used his gridlink again to access the ECS data sphere, ran a brief search and found the link. It provided other detail: number of medical teams available, demolition and excavating equipment, search robots—all the paraphernalia of Disaster Response, where it was located and how quickly it could be on scene. He slotted all this into his plans. He then noticed a light go out on the console—Morgaine had turned her attention to other matters.

"She's had her nose put out of joint," said Trantor from beside him.

"She doesn't like losing control," Gemmell replied.

"True." Trantor nodded. "Even of the things she no longer has a use for."

Gemmell grimaced because Trantor was talking about his long-term "relationship" with Morgaine. He found himself wondering what Orlandine would think of it, since according to AI net tittle-tattle, she apparently indulged in what she called *human time*. But then, from the data they had, it seemed Orlandine had just lost her human component. He shook his head, concentrated on the task in hand, calling up telemetry and the most recent update of the situation in the city from his gridlink.

"Two-thirds of the population has fled the city," he stated loudly. "They are not our immediate concern, since ships and shuttles have been sent to pick them up and move them to platforms in orbit. Here . . ." He sent them all schematics of the city, highlighting various points. "We get as many people out as we can, or to those areas I've shown which are more distant from the storm drain system and more easily protected." He meanwhile found a link back to what was now coming down.

The airfire drones were highly weaponized lumps of technology. He gave his instructions—they were to watch the more exposed points of access and hit the Clade if it tried to come back up into the city there.

Anywhere else, they would cause too much damage. He and his men would move the citizenry to safety, secure other points of access from below as best they could and just do their damned job.

"Our job is to protect the people," said one from behind.

"Yes, that's it," said Gemmell, knowing what was coming now.

"Threat assessment on the Clade is not good," said another. "It was highlighted by Earth Central while we were boarding."

"No, it's not . . ."

It was there in their augs, gridlinks and crystal minds: the cold AI calculations.

"We want it stated outright," said Trantor, glancing at him. "About casualties."

Gemmell grimaced.

"Okay," he said. "Your primary aim is to destroy Clade units if they surface."

He said no more. They all knew that meant that killing Clade units was more important than saving the lives of citizens, and if they got in the way . . . Gemmell didn't like it but the Clade was dangerous, very dangerous, and could not be allowed to escape, whatever the cost. He felt a prickling in the back of his neck, as it only now occurred to him that Morgaine had not seen fit to mention this. Maybe because she had a CTD imploder up there with this city's name on it.

TRIKE

The fallen bridge where prador had died fighting the Clade was no barrier to him. Trike leapt from one tilted slab of foamstone to another and soon scrambled up onto the road. He had never felt such power and strength, and knew he was travelling as fast as a ground car. But as he ran, he began to question why he was running.

His hatred of the Clade was driven by the urge for vengeance—for killing his wife—but as Angel had pointed out, she was not beyond resurrection. He had been unable to accept that. Yet he was starting to think differently. Carrying Orlandine's backup had affected his mind in many ways. Not least of these was that he still seemed to have a connection to her, to her entire body of knowledge, as if a submind of hers had rooted inside and become part of him. This gave him her haiman outlook—her acceptance that a sentient being was not just something confined to a physical body, and that the loss of the flesh did not mean the loss of that person. He realized that now he could accept Ruth's resurrection. So why was he running to fight the Clade when he could have her back?

He worked through it logically. The Clade unit had ripped her apart. He would have been out for vengeance even had she still been breathing and being put back together by an autodoc. The Clade was also integral to the whole shitstorm that had led him here. And then, finally, he had changed.

Trike didn't see a way back for himself—back from what he had become. The thought of Ruth alive again, and looking at him, filled him with doubts. Could she love him now and, the thought arose like the slimy spectre of his madness, could he love her? But that was not the whole of the explanation. Again, in rushing towards the Clade he had avoided Angel. However, like so many things in life, the problem he had run away from was keeping pace with him, in this case literally.

Trike glanced round. While Cog struggled to keep up, Angel paced easily at the side of the Old Captain. Looking again at Angel, Trike found the bitter anger in response still twisted up inside him. Something about it had changed, though, for he found himself accepting it rather than fighting it.

Spires of smoke rose from the city ahead. Fires burned in fields on either side of the road and Trike glimpsed people peering at him from behind a low wall, then ducking out of sight. He supposed he wasn't someone they would want to pass the time of day with. Huffing and grunting, Cog came up beside him.

"We . . . can bring . . . you back," Cog managed.

Not in the slightest bit out of breath, Trike replied, "I've changed beyond anything seen, I'm still wound through with the Jain tech I carried. And my mind . . . my mind is as much Orlandine's as my own. Are you sure?"

"Sprine," said Cog.

Trike didn't believe him and the new knowledge he possessed backed him up. Sprine was a poison that killed the Spatterjay virus or, in diluted form, retarded its growth. How much of him was still composed of that virus and what would stunting its growth do? Make him a little less blue or lose those spines down his side? Also, he could see a point of no immediate return—with so much of what had been human about him gone, a large die-off of the virus would also kill what remained. Perhaps by taking it at a low dose over a long period he had a chance. But, of course, it would have no effect on the Jain tech wound through him.

"Some later time," he said, feeling this was his constant response on so many matters.

The city loomed and Trike recognized the scrapyard he and Brull had earlier debarked from. Above the city hovered a narrow grey object, lumps and protrusions down its length. Via his connection to Orlandine's data, he recognized it as the spine of what *Obsidian Blade* had become. The attack ship had rebuilt itself for the purpose of hunting down Clade units. Its whole outer structure had turned into units themselves and had gone down into the storm drains to hunt their prey. Blade had become a kind of swarm AI, though one that possessed a queen floating above.

They entered the city and ahead, in a street choked with rubble spilled from a burning building nearby, Trike spied the grating of a storm drain. He slowed, then came to a skidding halt beside it and looked back at Cog and Angel.

"There is still time to change your mind." Cog pointed into the sky and Trike glanced up to see a large military medship coming down. Yes, he could change his mind and take his wife to the AI surgeon aboard that ship, see her finally wake so she could look into his face. But Cog didn't understand at all what drove him. Trike snarled and ripped up the grating, then dropped down inside. Hitting the water, he began wading, senses no longer human, ranging out to detect the greater concentrations of activity underground. A splash behind. He glanced back to see Angel following him and felt a surge of anger. He hurried ahead, trying to keep away from this unwelcome companion.

DIANA

Just for a second, Diana had not been able to believe what she was seeing. The impacts came as swarms of railgun slugs from the prador slammed into those intermittent hardfields of the alien ship. Many got past the defence, jerking the thing, sparkling across its surface, some blowing glowing holes right through the ship. Particle beam strikes began cutting trenches and boiling away material. Jabro dumped an analysis across to her. The initial strike was far below what the weapons platforms had delivered, but the ship's hardfields, despite it apparently trying to service itself, were not as effective as before. The attack was delivering more of an impact.

"Induction warfare," said Jabro. "The prador ships are using some new format that's knocking systems out in that ship."

"How can they possibly have anything effective?" she asked.

"Beats me," he replied.

"Orlik?" she demanded.

"I have told them to stop firing and am trying to penetrate their systems . . . I am having difficulty," the prador replied.

"How do you explain this induction warfare?" she asked.

"I cannot."

A swarm of missiles quickly pursued the first attack. She did not need Jabro's next analysis to know that this too would be more effective than the missile attack the platforms had made. What was happening here? Diana increased mental demand through her link to Hogue and accelerated her thinking. Her perception of time slowed, as she often required when in a critical situation like this. She watched a particle beam carving a valley a quarter of a mile deep, internal explosions ripping up hot hull metal along its sides into glowing, thorny sculptures. It punched deep at the end of its run and hit something critical—a generator or energy supply of some kind that took out a hardfield. This was no lucky shot. A fast, meticulous search of the data over the last few minutes revealed similar strikes that statistically were unfeasible from a random general attack. Those two hundred prador ships knew what they were shooting at.

"Another deployment," Jabro stated, his words seemingly long and drawn out to her in slow time.

Was this subterfuge on the part of the king of the prador? It could be that the prador fleet had been supplied with knowledge gleaned about the Species from the prador annihilation of their worlds. The king had ordered his prador to attack and destroy a potentially lethal enemy while it was vulnerable, and Orlik was lying and obfuscating to prevent Orlandine from acting.

"I will have to destroy my own ships," said Orlik.

The rest of the prador fleet and the *Kinghammer* were turning on the rogue ships and preparing to fire. If they did not in a few seconds, she would know that Orlik was lying. He didn't need to suggest doing this right now if his intention was the destruction of that ship. Also, the behaviour of Orlik and the prador up to this point did not tie in with her earlier conjecture. If destruction of the ship was his aim, then why hadn't he thrown his fleet forwards when the weapons platforms attacked? The combination of this new induction warfare, apparent knowledge of prime targets on the ship, Orlik's fleet and the platforms, would have destroyed the thing very quickly. So why a limited number of prador ships firing now?

Something has seized control of them.

The thought was both her own and Hogue's at the same moment.

The Clade. The bounce gates.

"Do not destroy those ships!" she said to Orlik. "Go over to laser com!"

Her crew were looking round at her, puzzled.

A moment later, the deployment Jabro had mentioned detonated. U-com dropped out as hundreds of U-space mines detonated. And the alien ship turned to head straight towards them.

She had always known about the bounce gates, but the knowledge in her fleets here, and at Jaskor, was limited to Hogue and herself. Earth Central had introduced a fault to the technology it had allowed the prador to steal. It was a final option if things got seriously out of control. And that really meant, only to be used if the Polity ended up in all-out war with the prador. She could only suppose that the Clade had somehow managed to glean this knowledge and board a prador ship. Then via that ship, boarded others and seized control. It was also the entity's vulnerability now. She could attack those ships via their bounce gates and, if they shut them down, use U-jump missiles against them to the same end. But should she take that step now?

No, stated Hogue in her mind.

Missiles slammed down on the alien ship—massive CTD detonations slapping it through vacuum and peeling off vast chunks of its structure. They broke away another thousand miles of its outer coil but, even so, the thing was now returning fire. Just for a second, she hoped it would be selective. But when one of those beams struck and bored through a Polity dreadnought, she knew that the Clade had won. It had initiated a situation whereby the weapons platforms would open fire on the ship, while always having a backup plan. With the departure of the platforms, it had now put that plan in motion, making two hundred ships fire on the alien vessel. And that ship saw the attack as one coming from the entire fleet. The Clade had trapped them here with U-space mines for at least an hour until their disruption stilled. They could flee on fusion, but the thing was after them now and she could not see them outrunning its beam weapons.

But why not use the two hundred in the weapons platform attack? enquired Hogue. It was rhetorical really. The two hundred were not just the Clade's backup plan to ensure the destruction of the Species ship. They must have had some other purpose present circumstances had negated. Perhaps the aim had been to set the prador and the Polity at each other's throats, though for the life of her she could not see why. Still, things were happening here she did not understand and she didn't like that at all. Checking tactical, she saw how to destroy those ships easily. They were located now. She could dump CTDs through their bounce gates, while complementing that with a blast of U-jump missiles should the gates close . . .

No, Hogue repeated.

Diana allowed herself to comprehend the AI's denial. She simply could not afford to destroy the Clade-occupied ships.

"Something else," said Jabro.

A microsecond later, she saw five massive detonations across the fleet. Two Polity destroyers, three reavers and then the final hit: the *Kinghammer*. The whole ship didn't go but the explosion tore out a quarter of its structure and sent it tumbling. Analysis: a combined gravity and U-space weapon had generated a twist within the ships, then released the energy into the real. And they didn't know if that, and the beams, was the limit of the armament the ship possessed. She watched a reaver, flung by a blast wave, trying to stabilize and alter course. Nose-first, it collided with a Polity dreadnought. The collision looked slow, as millions of tons of armour and technology crashed and compacted—the reaver disappearing into the other, larger ship in a continuous flowering of debris and fire. Then a blast silhouetted the dreadnought from the other side. Almost in shock, she returned her attention to the *Kinghammer*. It was falling out of formation, one large chunk of its hull peeling up and away.

No, Hogue had said, because the situation the Clade had caused forced an alliance, brief as it might be.

"Are you alive?" she asked.

Laser com gave an appreciable delay they did not need, as two more reavers exploded and twenty Polity attack ships came apart under beam strikes.

"Alive," replied Orlik.

"We only have one option," said Diana. "We must destroy that ship, or we are dead." She sent tactical data to her own fleet, backing it up with the verbal instruction, "Open fire."

And hell rained down on the Species ship.

COG

Cog clumped past a smoking mound of wreckage. A robot vaguely resembling a giant wolf spider, all painted in hazard stripes of orange and black, with an ECS emergency decal on its thorax, was lifting away beams and chunks of rubble. Its main body was covered like a mother spider with eggs, only these things were what troopers called stop coffins, and were commonly known as stasis cylinders. Cog peered at them, trying to remember why that was important.

Around the spider, Golem and human personnel were working. Medics were carefully pulling a woman from the rubble and sliding her onto a crash stretcher. This immediately closed its appendages to immobilize her, then injected various tubes and wires, before rising up on grav once clear of the wreckage. Cog's gaze strayed to two more stop coffins on the ground to one side. In the far past, those would have been body bags but, since the termination of life was now a very movable feast, the apparently dead went into such coffins to prevent further tissue breakdown—holding them in a state of preservation. Cog remembered why they were significant: Ruth, Trike's wife. He turned to go but, spotting him, two soldiers ran over.

"You're to go to Congress Hall," said one of them.

"We're clearing the streets," added the other, looking back the way they had come.

Cog gazed at their weapons and armour. "I'm going where I bloody well want."

The first soldier gently lowered his weapon to point it at Cog. Doubtless it was set on stun. "I'm sorry, sir, but you are in danger here. Clade units—" He stopped talking as his companion turned back, got a proper look at Cog and then grabbed his shoulder.

"I think we'll let the gentleman go wherever he wants," said the second soldier.

The first turned to him. "You know our damned orders."

"Jack," said the second, "take another look."

By now Cog was clenching and unclenching his hands. He wanted to stay in control, but some evil little imp in his mind also wanted an excuse to lose it. The first soldier took in his massive frame, and the weapons burns through his clothing. He perhaps saw some of the circular blue scars and realized he was not dealing with a normal physically boosted human being.

"Oh, I see," he said, quickly lowering his weapon.

Both of them must have made queries by aug, because the first stepped back and the second said, "Captain Cog, excuse us. Is there any way we can help you?"

"No," said Cog gruffly, and turned away, almost disappointed. He heard a low breathed "Fuck" as he marched off and felt it was nice that these ECS troops understood you didn't stand in the path of an annoyed Old Captain from Spatterjay.

Finally getting his bearings, Cog took a side street and found the pedway he, Trike and Angel had come in on from his ship. He clambered inside and, just as he was about to move on, he remembered something and swung his pack round. It was a mess: holed and burned, and stuff had fallen out. He opened it and at first saw the spare energy canisters for his weapon, though he couldn't even remember where he'd lost it. Rooting around a bit, he found the device he was looking for. He input new instructions, triggered it and slipped it into his pocket. The mines he had planted along here would not have detonated in his presence, but they might certainly be set off by some of the robots ECS had in the area. As he walked along, the device broadcast a signal to deactivate them—turning their explosive component to an inert chemical slurry. He couldn't be bothered to collect them up.

Halfway along, he came to a section where one of the explosives had done what he had set it for. With satisfaction, he kicked aside the head of a Clade unit, before climbing through the twisted beams and warped wall plates ahead to get to the next undamaged section of pedway. Soon he reached the wreckage where they had originally entered and climbed out. A shadow fell over him and he peered up at a big grav-barge slowly passing overhead, ovoid ambulances clinging to its underside like ticks. He realized the vehicle was Jaskoran, so the ECS commander must have called in some or all of the local Disaster Response service.

As the grav-barge slid on into the city, he lowered his gaze to his ship and headed over. He could see no damage and the door remained firmly closed. That was good because, even though it was of no importance to the Clade, the swarm AI might have damaged or destroyed it out of spite. He walked up to the side, slapped his hand against the palm reader and stepped back as the ship lowered its ramp. Trudging inside, he headed directly for his medbay.

The injectors, for his own personal use, were in a case in one wall cupboard. He slid it out and opened it, peering down at the five squat cylinders. They weren't the kind of injectors that squirted their contents into a patient using a cellular decoherer, or in micro-jets under high pressure. They just punched through skin and muscle, in an old-fashioned way. He picked one up and removed the cover from the thick, hollow needle. The thing was made of nanochain chromium and very hard and tough—just right for a hooper's hide. He sat down in the surgical chair and, without more ado, stabbed the thing into his thigh, pressing down the enclosed plunger with his thumb.

It took a while. First his thigh felt cold, and that spread, down his leg, up into his groin and down the other leg, then gradually up his torso as if he was filling like a beer glass. When it finally hit his skull, a convulsion threw him from the chair. He sprawled on the floor, jerking and slobbering as the dilute sprine killed off a large portion of the virus in his body. He lost it then. Time went away as he jerked and twisted, and as hot and cold fled through his body like a high-powered terahertz scan. When it was finally over, he sat up and felt the end of his tongue. It was closed now. Looking down at his body, scattered with spots leaking black fluid, he shook his head, which was clear again . . . clear enough to know that Trike had gone far beyond this kind of treatment.

Cog trudged wearily up the stairs to the bridge and slumped down in his throne. Now he was more lucid, he realized he should have asked those soldiers where the main medical ship was positioned. No matter—he was ECS and had access. He was about to tell his ship AI Janus to open com for him, then remembered it had been destroyed. He swore and swung across his control console from the chair arm and did it manually. After a bit of rerouting, a face appeared in a frame on his screen—identified in text along the bottom.

"Commander Gemmell," he said.

"I didn't know," said Gemmell. "You're an Agent."

"And I don't want anyone else to know, boy," said Cog.

Gemmell acknowledged that with a dip of his head. "What can I do for you?"

"Send me the location of your main medical ship or base," said Cog. "You have a surgical AI down here?"

Gemmell winced. "Yes, we sort of have a surgical AI."

"What's that supposed to mean?"

"We have something we are presently employing as a surgical AI."

Cog stared at him and waited.

Gemmell shrugged and went on, "It's a forensic AI so more than capable in surgical matters." He paused for a second, then added, "People tend to get a little worried when they hear that."

Cog understood. Forensic AIs were the Polity interrogators who could take apart people's minds and bodies to obtain every detail.

Sometimes they put them back together again. Sometimes they took them apart many times. They were considered a necessity by some and an evil aberration by others. Their reputation was not a good one.

"Where is it?"

"I'm transmitting the location now." Gemmell tilted his head again and then demonstrated he was fully linked into the data sphere by saying, "When you land, a grav-sled will come over to transfer Ruth Ottinger aboard the medship. There is a queue, so Mobius Clean may take some time to get to her, unless you have some pressing reason for her to be attended to?"

Cog studied him. No sign of an aug on his skull, so probably something internal, likely a gridlink. He then considered whether the resurrection of Trike's wife was pressing. Her presence might compel Trike to do something about his condition. Equally it might drive him further away. In reality, Trike and Ruth should not be his main concern. By handing Ruth over, he felt he would have discharged his responsibility for her. As for Trike . . . could he be brought back? Long-term suppression of the virus might help but Cog knew of no cure for a man occupied with Jain tech. However, if anything could return Trike to humanity it was a forensic AI.

"Yes, I have a pressing reason," said Cog, returning his attention to his console and firing up his ship's grav-engines.

BLADE

This one unit of *Obsidian Blade* resembled a splinter missile only at a glance. Closer inspection revealed the split down its length, the curve to what had once been sharp edges. Scanning strong enough to get through would also have revealed radical alterations inside. But no scan had yet penetrated any of Blade's units, and the Clade unit ahead was too busy fleeing, having learned as the Clade entire how many parts of itself had ceased to exist. It shot around a corner above the water flow, ricocheting off one wall as it did so.

The pursuing Blade unit divided along its length and separated to reveal its silvery internal weapons, and extruded shear tentacles from its fore. Part of its design had been taken from a weapons platform attack pod, the rest from hunting squid. It accelerated, drive system clawing at the surrounding walls of the drain, and itself bouncing off the wall at the corner. Around and on, and then slamming to a halt, sending up an explosion of water.

A trap.

Ahead waited ten of the Clade, revealing themselves from chameleonware, while behind Blade detected others coming out of concealment. It opened fire with a mini-railgun, firing grains of matter at devastating speed. Two Clade disintegrated while the rest came on. Its particle weapon was tracking some across the wall, but there was limited particulate to use. A wave of ionized water travelling up the tunnel from behind—faster than the speed of sound here. Impact—and Blade lost sensors, then the Clade was on it.

Blade knew that this fight was lost the moment it started, but it inflicted as much damage as possible. As the Clade units attached to it like lampreys and began to penetrate, it ripped at them with its tentacles and shredded two of them. Then it reached its survival limit. If it waited any longer, the Clade would seize control of its systems. Blade detonated its power supply, and one small point of its awareness disappeared.

Blade overall hunted and fought on, soon seeing how the Clade was adapting to the new threat. Another of Blade's units went down into a trap, but this time the Clade used a high-intensity maser to drill into its power supply to prevent detonation. Blade had to sacrifice it—a wipe program taking out its mind. This was a big loss because now the Clade had one of its units. The other swarm AI would be taking it apart, deconstructing it to learn its function and how to destroy others of its kind. Blade pondered, slowing down its pursuit of the Clade. It needed to destroy as much of the swarm as it could here but also to do the same as the Clade—capture one of them and deconstruct it. Thus far this had not been possible.

"I can help," came a broadcast voice.

Scanning back through the tunnels, Blade quickly located the source. The big blue monstrous man was wading along a channel; behind him came the android, Angel. Blade could see how Angel might help, but Trike? He was very strong and ridiculously rugged but how could a simple creature like him help in such a task?

"Check the link," came Angel's communication, ghosting into Blade's mind before it posed a question.

Trike had called out his offer of help but Blade had received it through a complex data link as if from an AI, and Angel had ridden in on that. A simple organic creature could not possibly offer this kind of connection. And it had arrived at a moment that could not be coincidental. Blade cautiously took up the link, made connection, and was astounded.

It understood that Trike had not deliberately opened himself up so much through that link. He had been aiming merely for communication and perhaps did not understand the full extent of what he was. Blade immediately diverted one of its units to his area, and it sped along the tunnel towards Trike. It slowed abruptly to stop, then hovered in the air just ten feet away. Via the unit, Blade put an induction warfare beam on him for confirmation. He was big and the density of his body was up there with the packed technology of Blade's own units. But this technology was of another kind.

"Does he know?" Blade asked Angel via the link.

"His human awareness is low but integrating," replied the android. *"However, he will soon be able to understand AI com and accede to requests you make."*

"How soon?" Blade enquired.

Angel hesitated, then said, *"He will need some assistance."*

"Can you provide that?"

Again the hesitation, then, *"I can assist, because perhaps I owe him that,"* said Angel. *"My own system is . . . divorced from the remainder of the Jain tech inside me, but I can bring him to awareness."*

"Why do you hesitate?" replied Blade.

"Because, though he fights it, he wants to kill me. I will be placing myself in great danger," Angel replied.

"Then you have a choice to make," said Blade, and waited.

Angel remained still for a long moment, then abruptly waded up beside Trike and reached out to grab his arm. "You need to integrate if you are to assist Blade," the android said out loud.

Trike swung that awful head round to gaze at the android. The man, if he could any longer be described as such, seemed unaware of the shifting movement of Jain tendrils around Angel's hand—the connection being made. Then the data package the android had injected must have impacted, because Blade detected energy surges and rapid changes to Trike's internal structure. He snarled and lashed out, slamming Angel back against the tunnel wall, *into* the tunnel wall, compacting stone. A shockwave was transmitted throughout the underground that could be detected by Blade's more remote units. Even Blade, who had used weapons that could tear apart planetoids, was stunned by the concentrated power of Trike. He had just crushed the chest of an incredibly tough android and the force of the blow had rippled out through Angel's body, causing immense damage. But still, it seemed, Angel was functional.

"It is enough," said the android.

But it wasn't enough for Trike. The man stepped in, one clawed hand locked about the android's throat and the other stabbing into his chest, fingers closing around artificial ribs. He was going to tear Angel apart, so Blade quickly focused on him again and, through the link, sent all the great mass of data it had on the construction of Clade units. The man tilted his head, as if listening to something half-heard, as the new knowledge found routes into his conscious mind, and as processing routes opened to the Jain structure that now formed a large part of his body.

"I need you to mind-ream the Clade through one of its units," said Blade, from its unit.

"I don't understand," said Trike, but only as if testing the words. "I don't know how . . ." Abruptly turning, he heaved the android out of the wall and hurled him across the tunnel into the other wall. Again there was a hard, shuddering impact that brought stone raining down from the ceiling. Trike took a step towards Angel, then stopped and held up his hands, Jain-tech veins writhing on them. He tilted his head back and his triangular-section tongue protruded, testing the air. Finally he focused back on Blade. "I need physical contact."

"You will have it," said Blade. "Follow."

Blade turned its unit around and, via the other parts of itself, tracked the dispersed Clade throughout the tunnels. It began moving off, slowly because Trike was still fighting some internal battle and had not yet moved. Something then snapped into place and he began to forge through the chest-deep water in the tunnel. He reached out, fingers digging into the stonework, as well as toes. Though big and heavy, his strength was hideous, and ripping up stone he scuttled along the wall after Blade like some monstrous spider.

"You will survive?" Blade sent an enquiry back.

"I will," Angel replied, focused on his own injuries and beginning to make repairs.

As they moved through the tunnels, another comlink opened—one Blade had used as it overflew the Ghost Drive Facility.

"What is it?" he asked.

"Now he is yours," said Orlandine.

Blade understood at once. Trike had essentially been sequestered as a submind to Orlandine, or as haiman liked to call them, a subpersona. Angel had just detached him from her, which enabled Trike to take up the reins of his own being—to be aware of all he was without referencing the backup of Orlandine recorded inside him. He was integrating, becoming whole. However, Orlandine's comment implied that Trike was now a submind slaved to Blade, and that simply wasn't true.

"Not really," Blade replied.

"I was not clear," said Orlandine. *"He is your responsibility . . . for now."*

Blade mulled that over for a microsecond. *"No, he is his own."*

After a long pause Orlandine said, *"The Clade is out in the fleet at the accretion disc too."* She also attached an update on events out there.

"My task has begun," was Blade's only reply as it selected likely targets for Trike, and zeroed in on them.

16

Forensic AIs are supposedly the ultra-cops. The Polity calls them in when it is utterly essential to obtain data or evidence regarding major incidents. These include crimes that result in, or could lead to, mass death and destruction. They are summoned to interrogate Separatists who are planning to bomb a runcible or drop a cargo ship on a city. Or when a rogue AI has decided it might be fun to fire up a volcano or tinker with the orbit of a moon. They have the tools for obtaining information too. They can take apart a human being both physically and mentally and get to every detail. Some also have the capability to do this with other AIs. Undoubtedly, they have prevented hideous crimes, snuffed out murderous plots and averted major disasters. They have saved thousands of lives, stopped brush wars and the necessity for Line police actions. However, despite all this, they have a very bad reputation. Mention of a forensic AI conjures the vision of an Inquisition torturer laying out the tools of his trade. Still there remains in human consciousness the perception that what sits between a person's ears is inviolate, until investigators find proof of guilt from another source. This attitude acknowledges the fact that a forensic AI may be able to take someone apart mentally and physically, but ignores that they can also put that person back together again, undamaged. Such examinations are a small price to pay for the safety of the public and of the Polity itself.

—from *Quince Guide*, compiled by humans

THE CLIENT

Fiery streaks cut down from a plasma storm across vacuum. Impacts across hundreds of miles, across a landscape of hills and valleys of hull metal. The Species ship was taking heavy damage. The Client watched the series of detonations: the bright flashes of antimatter and matter combining across that metal landscape, discs of fire expanding and melding. The great ship dipped and the terrain fell away. On the other side, a giant segment of its coil rose, shedding debris larger than attack ships, tilted up five hundred miles long, then slowly tore at its lower end and broke away.

Anger and frustration boiled through the Client. In this state, she felt justified for having lied to Diana Windermere—concealing the real reason why the Species ship had ended up in that U-space blister, and that it had not been alone. At the time, it had been a simple, almost instinctive reaction. She no longer felt any need to avenge the destruction of her kind in the Kingdom, or the Polity's betrayal of her. However, she had no particular urge to stop something else destroying them. Also, if the Kingdom and the Polity ended up in a fight for survival against what would come out of the blister next, that would divert their attention from her, and from the remainder of her kind. She was nothing if not pragmatic.

Still focused on the battle, she saw the fleets taking massive damage too. She watched further disruptor beam strikes. A destroyer in the shape of a giant sarcophagus threw out hardfields that blackened and fragmented like burned leaves as a glassy beam drilled through them. Final impact on its nose shuddered the whole vessel into its death throes. It vomited coin-shaped compartments from its side containing its complement of marines. The bright spark of its AI ejected at the last, as the whole thing splintered and began to spin off chunks of its structure.

Then something new. Inevitably, the Species ship hunted out the capital ships. One of those beams reached out for the *Cable Hogue*. A thousand miles out from itself, the *Hogue* generated a series of hardfields, simultaneously launching a missile towards them. The Species' beam struck those outer hardfields and began boring through, as the missile reached the fields at the back and slowed with a blast of fusion. The *Hogue* generated a further hardfield behind this, as the beam started to cut through the final field of the front series. Then the missile exploded. The blast spread in a disc, just for a little while, then began to collapse back: CTD imploder. A secondary detonation ensued as the beam ground into the last hardfield. It stopped there, then all the way back along its curving length, it frayed like old string and dispersed. The Client was impressed. The *Cable Hogue* AI, or weapons techs aboard, had figured out a response to the ship's weapon. But it was a costly one, as the *Hogue* shed burned-out field projectors like tracer fire.

The *Kinghammer* next. As it fell away, it survived by deploying the same technique. That was fast, AI fast, yet the ship was a prador one. The Client surmised that the prador were not so averse to that technology as was supposed. Other ships did not have sufficient hardfields to do this, and many of them were shattering, while still others detonated in the output energy of U-twists generating inside them. Almost a third of the ships that had been there were gone.

The fleet was in a trap, the Client understood this. The prador had opened fire on the Species ship and prevented the fleet from escaping by deploying U-space mines, forcing the Polity ships to open fire too. It was either kill that ship or die. But how should she react? First, she needed to move closer. Firing up the fusion drives in Platform Mu and its attack pods, she did so, meanwhile monitoring U-space disruption very closely.

She could attack the fleet and give the Species ship a better chance of survival, but problems would arise from that. If the fleet turned its weapons on her, they could drive the collapse of her hardfield. She wanted her kind to survive but, in reality, not at the expense of her own life. Another option was available, reflected in the way Polity and prador ships reacted when facing final obliteration. The Client knew how things would proceed if, as seemed likely, the Species ship was on the losing side here.

The design of the thing was like a giant ammonite. The growth of that snail-like coil containing weapons, defences and energy supplies had proceeded from an inner core. None of the Species occupied the outer ship—if anything there required their attention, they sent biological remotes, just as she used them herself. Her kind lodged in the heavily defended centre. That would be the last to go—ejected like the captain's sanctums some of the prador ships managed to expel.

The Client reached out mentally to her attack pods. Like the drive in Weapons Platform Mu, their drives were highly advanced—beyond what was aboard the Polity and prador ships. She would be ready long before those ships could escape the U-space disruption here. She would also be ready before the Species ship could travel in that continuum, because it had heavily damaged its drive when it departed from the blister. Still, what she intended to do would be dangerous and complicated. It would be similar to making a U-space jump too near to a gravity well—a short bounce in and out of that continuum. Calculating a destination would be almost impossible. The bounce would fling her through that continuum, then up and out by the next nearest gravity well. It was almost with a sense of inevitability that she realized that would be the Jaskoran system.

The Client pondered on this. The bounce would put her own drives out of commission for an appreciable time—time enough for the fleet *there* to attack her. She felt almost as if the universe itself must be working against her. But this was not so—just physics and U-tech. Anyway, the fleet there, at Jaskor, did not have the firepower to penetrate her hardfields. Her only problem would be if the fleet here, supposing enough of it remained, pursued her. The combined firepower might be enough . . . but that would not be happening. Those ships would soon enough have something else to occupy their attention. She focused her instruments on the accretion disc sun.

The black orb possessed an oversized event horizon for an object of a little over nine solar masses. Now that event horizon had begun to shrink and hexagonal patterns were once again spreading over it. The patterns seemed mechanistic but the Client understood them to be the outward form which the open end of the U-space blister created in the real. And the blister, with the time slopes in it now tilting level and winding up, was finally beginning to close. Measuring the effect, the Client could see that the application of internal U-fields had kept it open, just. Something in there had not wanted it to close. That something was about ready to come out.

ORLANDINE

Orlandine's view of the action at the accretion disc was intermittent. She had managed to key into U-com and sensors in the remains of weapons platforms and some attack pods she had instructed platforms to leave behind. However, after the two hundred prador ships deployed

U-space mines, U-com kept crashing and reinstating rhythmically. She gazed upon an old lozenge-shaped dreadnought as a disruptor beam drilled through it. This was just one scene of many in the appalling destruction happening there. On both sides. Another view showed her a CTD blast on the Species ship ripping up a swathe of armour larger than a weapons platform. And the thing was taking hits like this all the time.

The battle was by no means a foregone conclusion. Orlandine could calculate many variables, including whether or not the Client would attack. But the biggest variable of all was the ship itself. She did not know what other weapons it might possess. The probabilities foremost were: the ship would be destroyed with a loss of nearly half of the combined fleets out there, but this was without the Client's intervention. If the Client did intervene, then it and that ship would destroy the fleet. The only variable in this case was whether the ship would survive. In fact, it was all very simple and did not need the lengthy diversion she had taken into tactics, weapons stats and higher mathematics.

Withdrawing her focus from there, she next gazed through a thousand eyes upon the weapons platforms hanging out in vacuum around Jaskor. Should she send them in? No. The prador had fired on that ship and set this battle in motion, and the Polity ships had joined in. Win or lose, the battle was their concern. She must stick to her purpose, her project: get the platforms back up to spec and re-establish them at the defence sphere when the firing ceased.

While the platforms worked to repair themselves and sent out requisitions for materials to put through their own internal factories, Orlandine finally managed to instate a stable com route to the fleets. On first penetrating the ECS data sphere out there, she received tactical updates, ship manifests and casualty counts.

"Oh, it's you," said the *Hogue* AI, finally realizing she wasn't another ship mind. Next she found herself gazing into the face of Diana Windermere.

"Reports of your demise were exaggerated," said Windermere, distractedly.

"Do you know why the prador ships opened fire?" Orlandine asked, noting a com delay of thirty-three seconds and so making this exchange secondary to tasks closer to home.

"Clade backup plan," Windermere stated curtly. "They penetrated those ships."

Orlandine processed that. It didn't quite make sense since, having penetrated prador ships, the Clade could have forced the fleets to join the weapons platforms' attack on the ship. She realized that there were still undercurrents; she did not have the whole picture.

"I will send my platforms back," she stated, knowing precisely where this comment would lead.

"Now?"

"No, when the conflict out there is resolved—my focus must remain on the accretion disc."

"We might not be here then," said Windermere, and cut the link.

Diana was understandably terse being, after all, in the midst of a battle. Orlandine considered sending another message: "Saving your fleet is not my priority. The Jain and their technology loose in the Polity and the Kingdom is." She also thought of adding that the Species ship had only fired in self-defence, then rejected the whole idea. Windermere and the AIs out there perfectly understood the situation. It would descend into pointless human bickering even to mention who fired first and for what reason. She concentrated instead on the rest of the steadily heating up infrastructure around Jaskor.

Knobbler, along with his crew, had headed up to take control of robot populations aboard the factories and smelting plants. Already processes were kicking into motion and she watched haulers loaded with materials coming in to dock. Human and Golem crews were also quickly getting back to work. Once she apprised them of the situation, all of them—even the humans who had been injured and undergone surgical repair, and by rights could demand some R and R—were keen to get back to work. They were made of different stuff to those eagerly abandoning Jaskor, she felt. So, as she did not need to intervene, she directed her main attention closer to the planet.

One hundred weapons platforms in close orbit were stripping out major armaments and shunting them away by drone ship to other platforms. Thereafter filling out vast internal spaces with the infrastructure for human habitation, they were taking on supplies from Jaskor and from installations in the system. Evacuees from the surface were arriving in a constant stream of ships. She resented the loss of the platforms as weapons, but conceded that she did have a responsibility for the citizens of this world. Each platform should, eventually, be able to take on board a few million people, but only for a short journey. Space being limited, she restricted it to those people who wanted to go straight away. She hoped to get the planetary population down below a hundred million. Should she bring in more platforms to this end? No. By her calculations, disarming these platforms was already a big enough risk. She turned her attention to Jaskor itself.

Big shuttles had landed in the city and tough soldiers in power suits had spread out to herd citizens to areas they could make secure. Or they guarded access points on the ground which the airfire drones, now hovering over the city, could not see. Other craft were landing, transports to the evacuation platforms and shuttles containing technical and medical personnel, who were also spreading out in the city with a purpose. She decided to check the logistics and planning involved in this and tried to access the data flows. Instead, her attempt to make a link routed through to a single human being.

"About time you took an interest," said Gemmell.

It wasn't just a verbal link and she realized in a moment that he possessed a gridlink in his skull. She decided on full contact and he allowed it, not that he could have stopped her. She became present with him, standing on the roof of her own apartment building and gazing out at the city. She saw all he could see through the cams carried by the other personnel down there. He turned to look at her. Though just a projection in his mind, she appeared utterly solid to him. He knew this, but still addressed her as if she was physically present.

"Morgaine tells me that things are getting really busy up there." He gestured with the barrel of a heavy multigun towards the sky.

"I'm making preparations—the weapons platforms have to go back," she replied.

"Seems like a plan." He shrugged. "Interesting that you've used so many of them for evacuation."

"I have my responsibilities."

"Seems to me you think things are going to get very shitty here and want to cut down the casualty rate."

She nodded. Thousands of calculations running through her mind, thousands of scenarios playing out. Too many anomalous factors had mounted up towards a likelihood of . . . things getting shitty.

"You have at least some awareness of the situation," was all she said.

He gave her an amused look. "You mean, I'm slightly closer to being as enhanced as you and hence much closer to being an AI, and that I am at least not stupid."

His regard made her feel quite uncomfortable and she suddenly realized her projection was naked. A touch at her shoulder had her covered in an environment suit in a moment, whereupon she felt stupid. She was only data to herself and an illusion to him, yet she had behaved as if she was physically present on the roof.

Pointing down to the city, he continued, "We'll have things in order here, at least on the surface. No sign of any Clade units coming up. I'm detecting action from down below but I'm not getting anything from Blade about it."

Orlandine nodded. Blade was keeping things very tight down there since it didn't want open coms the Clade could penetrate. Her last communication with it had been about Trike, and since then it had closed to her. Another link into the tunnels had also closed. Trike had delivered her Jain tech and backup but it had not detached from him. She had long ago excised the tech's destructiveness, but its propensity to subsume remained, and it had effectively made him an adjunct to herself. She did not want the connection and was thankful when Angel broke it. She had thought the android had passed it over to Blade, but it seemed that wasn't the case. Perhaps Angel felt he owed Trike something and thus gave him complete autonomy. Or the android hoped to quell the murderous impulse Trike had towards him and which, through her connection to Trike, Orlandine had felt was like some cancerous tumour in his mind. Whatever. Willingly, Trike was now Blade's tool, weapon, bloodhound.

"Blade has been given new orders," she said. "Its task is to neutralize the Clade."

Gemmell looked back at her. "That is a statement that's open to interpretation."

She nodded and added, "All of the Clade. To do that it must access the swarm AI to learn where every unit of it is."

"Well, we know where another two hundred units are . . . probably not so many now."

"Yes, we do."

There seemed nothing more to discuss and, anyway, Gemmell had as much access to information on the events here, and at the accretion disc, as her. Nor did she need anything from him. But still she lingered. She saw him abruptly shift position, then frown down at the building below. As a projection in his mind, she did not feel it, but her other senses did.

"It's a quake from the Sambre volcano," she said. "Nothing to worry about."

He nodded briefly, doubtless accessing data on the forming island through his gridlink. They stood thus for a moment longer.

"Is it difficult, being so much more than human?" he asked abruptly.

"I am more efficient, I have a mind that has the strength of an AI and I control . . . much."

"That's not what I asked."

"It has its problems."

"Like leaving humanity behind. . ."

Orlandine absorbed and processed data on many levels and, in an instant, she knew the story of this man's relationship with the interfaced ship captain Morgaine. She also realized why she had lingered: because this was a human moment and she was clinging to such remnants. But her human body was gone and she recognized these fragments now as just habits, familiar patterns of thought . . . superfluous.

"You must force a choice," she said. "One of you must break the link. Morgaine keeps you because it requires of her no effort to do so."

He winced, smiled tiredly. "Yeah, you're not the first to point that out."

Orlandine nodded to him once and pulled her awareness back to the Ghost Drive Facility, dissolved to his perception like fog.

ORLIK

Orlik peered up with one stalked eye towards the interface cable. It hung in tatters, still emitting the occasional spark. The rest of the skein of optics and a couple of s-con leads lay across his back. But now, at last, his implants were working again and he could implement the disconnection routine. He did so, then shrugged, sloughing the interface plate and its connected skein from his back.

"We're still alive," he said, looking around his sanctum.

A missing wall exposed the superstructure of the ship. He could see twisted I-beams and other wreckage and then stars, and explosions, beyond an emergency shimmershield.

"For how much longer?" wondered Sprag.

Sprag's voice issued from her drone body, which had caught hold of the rim of the hole through which vacuum decompression nearly expelled it. The drone released her hold and flew over, wings clattering. She then tilted to look up at the ceiling as a robot arm folded out and swung round on its base to detach the tattered skein up there. A second arm appeared with a new skein and interface plate, and plugged it in, running it down to the small crane poised over Orlik.

"You're doing that," Orlik stated.

"I am," Sprag replied, now speaking directly to Orlik's implants as the drone settled on the crane.

"Situational report," Orlik demanded.

"We are winning," Sprag replied.

Orlik could not quite encompass this tactical assessment via his implants. High EMR disruption penetrated inside the *Kinghammer,* and radio data transfer was patchy, especially now the ship had an enormous hole in its side. It didn't feel at all like winning to him. The kind of destruction he could see out there ranked as high as some he had seen during the prador/human war, when massed fleets had gone head-to-head.

Soon the new interface plate hung over Orlik's back and, via his implants, he instituted the connection routine. The crane lowered it, while magnetic positioning centred it and locked it down. With internal routines tidying the imagery and data other ships transmitted by laser com, Orlik could see clearly beyond the ship—part computer projection to account for time delays. He watched three reavers, now remotely controlled by Sprag, mounting a layered hardfield defence against the disruptor beam. They combined their hardfields and launched a series of imploders to try and get the timing right. Hardfields shrivelled and blackened, followed by detonation. He felt Sprag's satisfaction as the beam strike unravelled back to the alien ship, but felt none himself. The three reavers fell away, parts of their hulls bursting out on explosions of molten metal where field generators had failed to eject. They would not be able to mount a defence like that again.

He checked through the *Kinghammer* to make a real assessment of the damage. The U-field twist had torn away a huge chunk of the ship and taken eight of his crew along with it—now only fourteen of the Guard remained. Even though he was prador, he felt deep regret about that because he could name each one, and they were Guard he had known for centuries. The damage had taken out a third of the ship's hardfield generators, half its supply of railgun slugs and one large magazine of missiles. Luckily, that magazine had only contained chemical and fission warheads. Orlik felt a tightening in his guts when he realized what would have happened had it struck the magazine containing CTDs.

The destruction had been localized by the ship's cellular construction—blast walls had damped the explosion, while a ship-wide superconducting grid had drawn away the heat. Robots were making repairs and memory materials drew energy to reform superstructure. But, checking the materials and components manifest, Orlik saw there wasn't enough to rebuild the missing structure inside. And, most importantly, not enough to seal up the hull. He looked beyond the ship at the wreckage out there: at gutted reavers and dreadnoughts and spreading clouds of debris. Plenty to cannibalize—if he could survive for long enough.

"We're ready for that strike," said Sprag.

Orlik returned to the moment, the whole of a plan gestated over the last twenty minutes returning to the forefront of his mind. He had seen much of this unclearly via his implants, but now he could see so much more. He focused on the old dreadnought concerned. Its crew were abandoning it only clad in armour, hoping to be picked up, while a big shuttle containing its father-captain was easing out of a hold.

"You're sure about this?" Orlik asked.

"As sure as we can be considering the calculations," Sprag replied. "I am liaising with Hogue and other Polity AIs to ensure success."

Orlik wasn't so sure he liked that, but let it go in the circumstances.

The U-space disruption was settling and this was visible in the attack upon the Species ship. Further detonations there blew up square miles of glowing hull. Some U-jump missiles were at last getting close, though it seemed the vessel had its own bounce gates, so they could not put anything actually inside the thing.

The shuttle finally departed the dreadnought, heading for a nearby reaver. The father-captain's children struggled and failed to keep up on their suit drives. Controlled by Sprag now, the dreadnought fired up its fusion and moved out of formation, heading towards the Species ship. Orlik tried to follow the drive calculations. The dreadnought was about to attempt a U-space jump—a deliberately imbalanced one. Upon surfacing into the real, it would not be buffering its energy and so, as it materialized, would be out of phase with the universe around it. This meant . . . Orlik was not sure what it meant, but he had heard of runcible failures in the Polity where this occurred. The results had not been kind to the worlds or moons concerned.

"A throw of the dice," said Sprag. "But what is the Client doing?"

Orlik switched the focus of his attention out to the side of the fleet. Weapons Platform Mu was under heavy fusion drive, its attack pods lit up like stars all around it. The Client had not attacked, as expected, to try to protect her kin. She had in fact avoided the fleet and now seemed intent on heading straight towards the Species ship. This looked almost like an attack run, which made no sense at all.

The dreadnought began to go under. Some effect, by the U-space disruption and perhaps because of its older drive system, made this a protracted affair. It seemed to stretch impossibly thin, and a ring-shaped halo of light generated around its point of departure. It then snapped out of existence. A microsecond later it reappeared, just a streak in vacuum terminating on the Species ship. It came in at a twenty-degree angle from the plane of the ship, and halfway between the axis and the rim. Orlik almost expected it to explode out of the other side of the thing but, for a full second, nothing happened at all. It was as if the universe was in shock and didn't yet know how to respond. Then a sun ignited on the obverse side from the strike and expanded, a hemisphere of light, a photonic shockwave. This passed on quickly, flashing out. Where it reached the accretion disc, Orlik saw it push radiating dust and gas ahead of it. Meanwhile, the opposite side of the ship began burning, while the impact side rippled and shifted. Hot fire broke out in many places, then the whole vessel disappeared in a sensor-killing final blast that measured in the hundreds of gigatons.

"Shiny," said Sprag.

Orlik felt unreasonably annoyed by the comment. Such a degree of destruction seemed worthy of at least a moment of silent acknowledgement. As sensors, which had shut down to save themselves from the EMR pulse of the blast, came back online, the image cleared. The Species ship had fragmented. Yes, some of those chunks were bigger than the *Kinghammer* and the *Hogue*, but he doubted they presented much of a threat now.

"We've done it," said Windermere over com.

"Yes we have," Orlik replied. "My instinctive reaction is relief and to feel victorious, but this was something we were driven to do."

"We have the rogue ships located," Windermere stated blandly. "They are even now moving out of formation."

"Rebels," Orlik stated. Then, "Sprag?"

"I can make no contact with the bastards, none at all," Sprag replied. "Every route is closed to me."

What had happened? He could understand how many father-captains aboard older ships might decide the vessel heading out of the disc was an enemy to be destroyed—anything not prador to them essentially was. But for so many of them to open fire without orders was just too organized. Besides, reavers had also opened fire and, for the Guard who occupied them, such rebellion was unthinkable. With the action over and time to think, he saw that it made no sense at all.

"We cannot afford to have these at our backs," Windermere stated.

"They will flee," said Orlik.

"Eighty prador heavy dreadnoughts and reavers allied to neither the Kingdom nor the Polity." Windermere paused. "They will soon be clear of the debris."

Orlik had already seen this. Eighty of the two hundred ships remained and they were moving away from any debris that could interfere with their U-jumps. The reavers—more efficient and modern—would go first. He realized he had to make a decision and make it now. No time to talk with the king, no time for hesitation, no time to speculate on why Windermere was pushing him.

"These ships," he said to his captains, sending a tactical map indicating the eighty ships, "fired without orders and are in direct contravention of the king's will. They initiated this conflict. Destroy them. The Polity ships will also be opening fire on these targets. Do not fire on the Polity ships."

"Thank you," said Windermere.

A gravity wave pulse came first from the *Cable Hogue*. It rode over three reavers close together, dragged them hundreds of miles through vacuum and discarded them as twisted ruins. Hardfields began lighting up under railgun slug impacts. Orlik watched an old-style dreadnought falling away, spewing molten generators then shuddering under multiple strikes. Other ships were taking similar hits. All of it, he noted, was from the Polity ships, since his own captains had yet to process his orders and give their own. A moment later, they too opened fire.

Feeling sick and angry, Orlik watched as the fleet pounded ship after rogue ship to scrap. It felt to him utterly wrong, especially when the Polity ships ensured the utter destruction of each rogue with a CTD imploder. He watched a reaver, cut in half by an explosion, coming apart for just a moment then collapsing back towards a central point. The imploders could not completely collapse such a mass of tough matter, but the ball of twisted beams and buckled armour ceased to resemble a reaver just before the secondary explosion blew it apart. Two ships jumped into U-space. Others tried but the *Cable Hogue* hit them with its gravity weapon. One semi-jumped when a wave hit—a reaver—it peeled inside out from nose to tail then disappeared in another imploder blast. Orlik counted the ships down in his mind. Twenty went in the first half of a minute. Ten minutes later, they were all incandescing debris.

"Imploders," Orlik said to Windermere. "Again impressing upon us Polity firepower?"

"I don't think that necessary," she replied. "You, Orlik, must see how strange it is that so many ships fired without orders, even reavers containing your own kin? We have no idea what happened in those ships, but we are close to alien sequestering technology we don't quite understand, so it is best to be sure."

Her voice and in her expression . . . Orlik, who had always found the subtext in human voice and expression beyond him, saw something there. Could it be she was lying? Could it be that somehow the Polity controlled those ships? He shook himself. No, it made no sense. Windermere could have initiated the attack on the Species ship if she had wanted to. There was no plausible reason for her to have manipulated prador ships into attacking.

"The weapons platform," Windermere noted, turning to look at something.

Orlik had been partially focused on it all the while, but mostly watching the destruction of his own ships. It still felt like betrayal to him, wrecking them, allowing the Polity to destroy them, killing his fellows, no matter the reasoning behind it. But none of them would be recoverable. No way would a captain who had fired without orders and caused the mayhem here simply hand himself and his ship back over to the Kingdom. There would be no mercy and they knew it. This was supposing the captains had been in control of their ships, which seemed highly unlikely now.

"Run full diagnostic checks on all ships," he instructed Sprag. "Maybe informational warfare seized hold of them."

"Running it now," replied Sprag. "There is another possibility."

"What?"

"The Clade is the turd in the punch bowl here. It's a swarm AI of an unknown number of components, initially made to seize control of enemy technology."

"But how would those units have got aboard our ships?"

"Maybe in the Kingdom?"

"Run full scans for drone incursions too," Orlik instructed. It was worrying—if the Clade had taken over those two hundred ships, then further units might have encysted themselves aboard any other ship, including his own, awaiting an opportunity for . . . whatever.

He hissed at that, then gave Weapons Platform Mu his full attention.

The platform hammered down towards the fragments of the Species ship. Its hardfield, its damnable, completely enclosing hardfield, was taking debris hits, flaring and darkening in places. Its attack pods were also enclosed in hardfields but managing to dodge the larger chunks of the destroyed ship. What did the Client hope to achieve by heading there? Sprag, closer to his thinking than ever before, immediately highlighted the answer and brought it into focus. Tumbling through the scattered remains was a squat cylinder fifty miles across. He might have mistaken it for just another item of debris, were it not correcting its tumble, and were not pieces of wreckage flaring against its intermittently functioning hardfields.

"Target acquired," Sprag stated.

"Hold fire," Orlik instructed. "Windermere?" he enquired.

"It's the core of that ship—maybe like the captain's sanctums you have aboard your reavers."

Yes, the sanctums aboard those ships, and aboard the *Kinghammer*, were well protected and self-contained. The occupants could eject themselves in the event of an enemy destroying the ship.

"So that could contain the Species captain?"

"Or the entire crew." Windermere paused. "Who knows how they are arranged aboard their ships. They are alien."

It was amusing in its way, since he and Windermere were alien to each other, yet more akin now than what they faced.

"Should we destroy it?" he asked.

"I think you know the answer."

"Stand down," Orlik instructed Sprag.

"You're the boss," Sprag replied, a little resentfully Orlik thought.

The weapons platform descended over the still-tumbling object. Attack pods arrayed all around the thing and something shifted. Abruptly, the cylinder stabilized completely, relative to the surrounding pods and platform, and jerked towards a centre point. Debris impacts no longer hit single hardfields but a globe hundreds of miles across. They had little chance of destroying the thing now, even if they wanted to. Then the whole—pods, platform and cylinder—dropped and revolved away, out of existence and into U-space. Gone.

17

It is a fact that Polity artificial intelligences are, at heart, simply information. It can be argued, of course, that that is what all human beings are. But we are more closely tied to our bodies than they are and, when we transfer via memplants or other technologies to another medium or body, we become something else. Arguably, we become AIs. But the AIs themselves can transfer with blithe ease from medium to medium. It does not affect their thought patterns, beyond them having to adjust to new or different capabilities. One must therefore wonder why they tend to stick to one physical form. Those in ships only reluctantly abandon their posts at the point of the vessel's destruction, as these are their bodies. Golem prefer to be repaired even when massively damaged, and even though swapping to a new body would be easy for them. War drones are quite belligerent about hanging onto their material selves. And swarm AIs never swap out—they just create more of themselves, though they are less reluctant to sacrifice their components. It is theorized that this is all about us. They are keeping themselves easier for us to identify and relate to. They are forgoing just zipping around the universe as transmissions of data from substrate to substrate, and freely using and exchanging the robotics available. They are waiting for us and, meanwhile, holding off on apotheosis.

—from *The Gods Among Us* by D. Van Vogt

COG

The door to Cog's ship thumped and then lowered to reveal a grav-sled hovering attentively outside. He peered past it at the view.

The medship was down in a park in the city. Here the depredations of the Clade were not visible. Beetlebots, like silver bubbles, munched their way across a kind of grass that grew in green and white swirls. Flowerbeds were laid out in geometric patterns, bordered by predatory box hedges that prevented the more lively plants from escaping. Pines whispered—tilted to each other in serious conversation. Fountains jetted as usual but were twisted into beautiful glittering patterns by the artful application of force fields. Around the rim, city blocks gazed down on it all. The medship sat amidst this like a slug in a sweet bowl.

"You're a hooper," said the sled.

He studied the thing. At one end stood a control block, and it possessed two gleaming lights whose function seemed no more than to give it the appearance of having eyes.

"Evidently," Cog grumped. "This way."

He led the way into the ship and up the spiral stairs.

"I've always been fascinated by hooper biology," said the sled. "I'd like to scan you and take some samples, if I may."

Cog glanced back. He noted the grav-sled hesitating at the stairs, then, shrugging and turning upright, it floated up behind him like a wandering door.

"ECS has samples and scans from me on file," Cog commented. "I take it I am talking to Mobius Clean?"

"You are." It paused as if in contemplation. "Sure, samples are on file, and scans, but I don't have those samples and the scans were limited by our knowledge at the time. Recent data from Orlandine's examination of highly mutated members of the King's Guard, and other matters, have raised some interesting questions."

"Other matters?"

"Your companion Captain Trike."

Cog opened the door into the cryostore, walked over and slid out Ruth's cylinder. The sled had meanwhile swung level again. Cog pulled the optic-monitoring lead and power feed from the cylinder, then undid the clamps holding it to the frame.

"Trike is a problem," said Cog. "I don't know if he can be restored."

"A problem you have seen before," Clean commented.

Cog eyed the sled. This forensic AI obviously had the highest access if it knew about that. "I saw my brother change, just as Trike did. I could do nothing to stop it and understand that there is an element of choice involved—that the effects are tied to the mind of the one changing. But I never saw him turn into something like Trike."

"There are rumours on Spatterjay of a monster living on one of the islands."

"Yeah." Cog was uncomfortable with this conversation. He picked up the half-ton cryo-cylinder, turned and placed it on the sled, which adjusted perfectly, not even dipping when he released the weight. Clamps popped out of the sled down its length and engaged. The sled reversed for the door.

"Can you do anything about Trike?" Cog asked.

"I can always do something," Clean replied. "But as you say, there is a matter of choice involved. Also a degree of imbalance between the . . . parts of his mind."

"He's crazy."

"His mind is the place to start. Are you coming?"

They headed out of his ship and across the grassy parkland. Cog noticed other activity. Far over to one side a couple of large grav-barges were down. One had a collection of the ovoid ambulances lined up beside it, like those he had seen on a similar, or maybe the same, barge earlier. The other had its side open. Four-legged earthmovers were clambering out and heading into the surrounding buildings. The people around these didn't wear ECS uniforms but some brown and white concoction—local Disaster Response again. Probably as efficient as ECS, if Orlandine had organized it.

The medship was busy. As he followed the sled inside, Cog observed the walking wounded filing into examination booths. A man coming out of one of these was frowning at the transparent syntheflesh on his arm—bones and veins visible inside it. But already areas of it higher up were becoming cloudy as it adjusted. Inside a glass-fronted surgical area, a woman had her head turned to one side. She didn't want to watch what the military autodoc—a thing like a huge chromed woodlouse squatting between her legs—was doing to her. It was carefully coiling her intestines back up inside her, cell welding as it went.

Soon he was walking down a long corridor where, behind the windows of clean rooms, radical surgery was underway. Here machines were disassembling and reassembling human beings, repairing faulty components or replacing them, amidst the fast, silvery movement of robotic limbs. Some were so lost in skeins of tubes and optics as to be only briefly visible, but it was a glimpse of hell. He saw one individual who had been flayed by fire, a pedestal-mounted autodoc steadily printing him a new skin from the feet up. Many of these, Cog knew, would have been declared dead in previous ages. Nowadays, with internal nanosuites maintaining the body against decay and other damage, they were merely on hold.

"Here," said the sled.

It paused by an utterly empty, pristine room. An irised hatch opened low down and the sled slid in, antiviral and biotic UV and pin lasers cleaning it on the way. Cog, remaining outside, glanced around and spotted a fabricator set in one wall, which produced a long rod for him. He walked back to the glass and tapped the rod on the floor. It folded out into a flimsy-looking director's chair. He sat carefully, but it supported his weight. By the time he was comfortable, Ruth was already out of the cylinder and floating in the middle of the room. The sled and cylinder settled over to one side, while a control block from the sled had come back out and was hovering in the corridor. He realized it was a drone of some kind—a submind of this Mobius Clean, a grey metal cylinder with red glowing eyes on its side and manipulatory limbs folded up at each end.

An iris hatch opened in the wall of the clean room and a ball of something glittering and writhing slid out. Once it was clear of the hatch, it opened out.

"The fuck?" said Cog.

"My form is that of a terran echinoderm: a crinoid," said the control block.

It was like a mass of undulating feathers ten feet across, whose stems connected at a central point. The feathers were metallic grey and gold, shimmering and iridescent. It was quite beautiful. He doubted those it examined ever thought so, for it probably consisted of every Polity tool for deconstructing living beings, or machines, down to the molecular level. Only now did it occur to Cog that a forensic AI would want to examine Ruth because she had previously been resurrected and controlled by Angel—a being once utterly sequestered by Jain tech, and in turn a slave to a Jain AI. He wondered if he had done the right thing in bringing her here, but it was too late to change the decision.

The thing closed on Ruth and encompassed her. Blindingly fast movement stripped away her clothing. Cog winced at the lack of hesitation that opened her chest and splayed her ribs like fingers. Feathery tendrils dived in, printing and cutting, pulling out wet, bloody items and then putting them back. None of the slow work of a human surgeon here. Utterly precise, down below the cellular level, the forensic AI moved as quickly as a machine possibly could. Cog observed the work for a few minutes and felt some release of tension when he realized the thing was going no further than her injuries. He understood that if it really intended to examine her, she would be in very small pieces by now.

"I need to talk to Trike," he said abruptly.

The cylinder swung towards him and the red eyes blinked. After a brief pause it said, "He is not responding to the available comlinks."

"Available comlinks?"

"Your friend has become something more complicated than a man mutated by the Spatterjay virus . . . ah, now he has responded. Speak and he will hear you."

"Trike, boy—you there?"

"Cogulus." The voice issuing from the cylinder was Trike's, but seemed cold and distant.

"Ruth is in with the . . . AI surgeon now. She'll soon enough be back with us."

"Yes, I can see," Trike replied. "I wish her well."

"Come back to us," said Cog.

"Sometimes there is no coming back," Trike said, and Cog knew, even before Clean told him, that Trike had cut the link.

ORLANDINE

Orlandine was aware of the arrival microseconds after it occurred. She gazed upon Weapons Platform Mu. It was dwarfed by the plug of the Species ship it had dragged out of the fight over at the accretion disc, and its attack pods were scattered all around. This collection of vessels had arrived with a crash that sent reverberations through U-space just inside the orbit of Adranas—a giant hot planet in a slow, close orbit around the sun that created an eclipse on Jaskor every one of its years. Within the same instant, Knobbler saw it too, as did the interfaced captain in charge of the fleet here: Morgaine.

"Now, I didn't expect that," said Knobbler.

"Oh, I knew this was going to get more interesting," said Morgaine.

"Just circumstance," said Orlandine, while the threads, veins and tentacles of her being tore components from the nearest building in the Ghost Drive Facility.

"Circumstance?" Knobbler asked.

"The Client grabbed the core of the Species ship but could not manage a fully directed jump."

"Ah," said Knobbler.

"Ah," said Morgaine, adding, "It slid to the nearest gravity well: here."

"It will leave," Orlandine continued, gazing at her reflection in the mirror-face of the nearest building. "Once it has made repairs and seen to the needs of its surviving kind, it will be gone . . . probably."

"Lost your human self and found optimism?" said Knobbler. "I didn't expect that either."

Narcissus, thought Orlandine. Her reflection showed her human form, standing on ground scattered with shards of mirror glass. But it was an extension of the Jain mass behind her. That mass was now weaving itself, and the looted materials, into an engine that suited her requirements. The object taking form resembled the one that had carried her when she interrogated the submind of the Wheel. It stood twenty feet tall, like a giant partially coiled woodlouse. Already a scattered grav-engine was in place, with the throats of fusion drives ready to open between the ribbed armour plates over its back. Lethal weapons and processing were packed into its structure. It was an interesting exercise in design and the compacting of technology, and very different from previous kinds. Her gaze strayed to the remains of the Clade unit she had deconstructed. She had learned a lot from the thing about folding matter and playing with atomic binding forces.

"I did say 'probably,'" she replied. "Perhaps I should have said hopefully."

"I see," said Knobbler.

"I don't," said Morgaine.

Thinking of the man Gemmell, Orlandine shot back at her: "When one interfaces with AI, it can upset one's focus. Sometimes, one sees all the detail and loses sight of the big picture, and often the reverse."

"Meaning?"

"Don't deny that you are capable of human error until you are incapable of it." She transmitted a replay of her conversation with Gemmell on the roof of her apartment building. As a social interaction, it was perhaps a bit of a faux pas, but she added in an overview, showing what she felt certain was Morgaine's thinking. Upon seeing the arrival of the Client, Morgaine was assessing immediate threats in a human-centric manner and had failed to take into account the wider state of play. Just as, in her interactions with Gemmell, she had set herself high and lost sight of one important detail: her selfish love and damage to him by not letting him go.

"That stung," said Morgaine. "What *big* picture have I lost?"

Orlandine replied, "The battle is over and the Species ship is no longer a threat. However, the remainder of that ship and the Client are the kind of loose cannons Earth Central does not like having around. The king definitely won't like it either, most especially in the case of the Client, after what she did in the Kingdom."

"I have received no orders concerning this," said Morgaine, doubtfully.

"Yet," interjected Knobbler.

"Okay, now I understand."

"Good," Orlandine replied tightly, and cut the comlink to her.

Orlandine had no doubt that if the Client hung around long enough, the rest of the Polity and prador fleets would move in around Jaskor. There would then be another face-off over the Client and her kind, with Jaskor just a little bit too close for comfort. She decided, in that moment, she would not be sending the armed weapons platforms back to the disc right now. It might be necessary to remind both Polity and prador that this system was an independent state, and maybe it was time for them to go home. And that reminder could well get very messy.

Orlandine now ranged out, first to evacuation platforms. Five of them were already at capacity, containing nearly ten million people. She contacted all the AIs of the hundred platforms in concert.

"The situation may be turning critical," she said. "When you reach capacity do not wait on further supplies—depart at once."

"Watch Station Abalone," said one of the five, seeking confirmation for their destination.

A submind of Earth Central had sent the message through low-level coms some time ago. The watch station sat in a system where the Polity had converted a small world into a place for processing refugees from planetary disasters. Its processing now no doubt included deep scanning and forensic AIs on the lookout for Jain tech. A series of runcibles were also there for dispatching those the AIs had vetted on to their destinations of choice.

"No change on that," she replied.

Already the five loaded platforms had lit up their fusion engines and were pulling away from Jaskor. Even as she turned her attention to her armed weapons platforms, they began dropping into U-space, leaving photonic ripples like stones cast into a pool of light.

The armed platforms were working as fast as they could to repair their damage and load up with weapons. The industry out there had heated up to the same high point it had attained in the early years, when there had not been, to her mind, sufficient coverage of the accretion disc. Huge robots were whittling down metal asteroids, passing them through furnaces, and thence to moulds for railgun missiles. Gravity presses were crushing matter to make other super-dense slugs. A machine, dubbed the Alchemist by the technicians who tended it, used a particle accelerator, wrapped around a singularity, to turn matter inside out and deposit it in vacuum, magnetic bottles. These were the cores of contra-terrene devices. Then she noticed something new.

The platform AIs had obviously not liked how vulnerable they were to the disruptor beam the Species ship had deployed. New structures aboard them, four-field imploder defence devices, had now been created for knocking out such a beam, while all the AIs were running models of induction warfare iterations that might work as protection. She pondered telling them there was no need, because they would be returning to their usual job at the defence sphere. Then, considering what might happen if the Client did not depart peacefully, she decided to leave them to it. The Client, after all, had demonstrated that she possessed that weapon too, and it was best to be prepared for *any* eventuality.

Was there anything she had missed? She felt so, but she did not have the data to see what. If something more was to occur, she would just have to react, as she had done before. She returned to more immediate concerns.

Her device was ready and, with a thought, she withdrew into it—the tentacles melded into her back and her ersatz skull, picking her up and reeling her in. She sent a new instruction as she settled into the cusp of the device, and watched the sentinel drones she had placed here launching from their towers and heading up into the sky. They were little enough to add to the defences around Jaskor, but there was no point in wasting them. Next she gazed upon the Ghost Drive Facility through a thousand eyes—through the Jain tendrils spread within the buildings.

This place had been a mistake. It had been one of those failures to see both the big and small pictures. In trying to ensure her centralized control of the defence sphere around the accretion disc, she had created a weakness the Clade could exploit. That same urge for complete control had also led her to create the flaw of the platform AIs' hard-wiring. Just as with that, it was time for the facility to go away. The mechanism was already cued up: the high-temperature enzymes, the energy loops, the evaporation of singularities—all available technology set to eat itself. She sent the instruction and next another. She broke the trunk of Jain tech connecting her to the network in the facility. Beyond the break, it began to burn like a fast fuse, utterly destroying itself, because it would be dangerous for any to be left behind. Ensconced within a device that was as much her as were her hands, Orlandine rose into the sky. She turned so she could gaze down on the facility with ersatz human eyes.

Fires lit the insides of the buildings, as ghost drives burned away just as the Jain tendrils had. Explosions inside systematically blew out the glass at every level. A fusion fire, igniting underground, jetted burning and molten debris into the sky. Next, one after another, the towers started to collapse, sinking down into dusty but glittering ruin. Of course, a more utilitarian approach would have been to deconstruct the place for its spare parts and technology, but Orlandine felt its complete erasure was a necessity for her.

It was very human.

She turned away, opened ribbed armour in her back and ignited fusion drives, shooting towards the city. In the end, she could be human if she wished, but it was not a necessity, nor was it a state that required any more understanding than she had. But sometimes it was satisfying.

TRIKE

Trike shuddered as he felt everything joining up inside him and understood that Orlandine must have experienced this same kind of amalgamation. With her, it had been the three elements of her human self, her Polity AI component and the Jain tech weaving them more closely together. For him, the mixture was different, and darker. He too consisted of three elements: human, Jain tech and the Spatterjay virus. But there was also a problem: his human element was unstable. He had come close to killing Angel back there and still his hostility towards the android sat like a cancerous cyst in his mind. He knew he needed to erase it if he was to be whole, but he didn't know how. Instead, he veered away from it and concentrated on the other parts of his being, specifically the Spatterjay virus. He knew from information in Orlandine's backup, much of which he had retained, that the virus contained quantum processors, and now he was accessing their data. And there he found the soldiers.

"Three Clade units ahead," Blade informed him.

He felt the words were irrelevant because their link provided all the information he needed. He could see a three-dimensional map of the tunnels below the city and much of the connected caves. On top of this, he had a clear view of where the hundreds of Blade's units were positioned, as well as the confirmed and unconfirmed positions of the Clade. Their traces, the extrapolations on where they might go, and the state of the informational and physical warfare between the two AIs was all laid out.

"If you can engage these two," he said, sending a plan of attack, "I will take this one."

Blade acknowledged it without words.

Trike continued to scramble along the tunnel wall after the Blade unit for a few hundred more yards, then dropped into the water and began wading. Internally he prepared himself, freeing up processing space, growing new fibres ready to supplant those that would certainly be broken or burned out in his tongue. He built up other fibres in his hands, coiled and ready to spring out like jellyfish stings. He felt utterly potent but was aware of his overconfidence. Though a Clade unit would be no problem for him physically, the Clade mind he was preparing to invade was another matter. Perhaps he needed more power; it was available within him . . .

The soldiers. Orlandine had only superficially understood them. By going deep, actually connecting to them and incorporating them, he was truly beginning to understand. They were both Jain and a product of the Jain. They were as akin to their creators as cyborg soldiers were to normal human beings—a version of themselves made for an eternal war fought across reality. War on the scale of star systems yet also extended down to nanoscopic aggression. In that war, the survival of the soldier was only made secondary when the mission came first, because you do not discard useful tools. And so, during one conflict, a squad of soldiers finished its mission and had to go completely dark to survive. To achieve this, they downloaded and recorded themselves inside the best medium available to them from the world where their vessel had crashed. That medium happened to be a highly complex virus. Widespread and very tough, it would be difficult to destroy. It already possessed the mechanism for taking and utilizing the genomes of other creatures it fed upon, and from which it propagated. In fact, it reflected what the Jain were, and perfectly fitted their psyche. Trike now began to take on more from them: their arsenal of informational and physical warfare, the schematics governing their form, which in turn was governed by their various mission requirements.

"What the hell is this?" spat Blade.

Trike realized some of what he was absorbing was bleeding over the link. Sampling it, Blade had snapped away like someone tasting poison. Trike cut the spill-over.

"You want this to work, don't you?" he asked, obscurely.

Blade did not reply. Delving into the data and methods of control, Trike applied what he discovered to himself, through the virus and through the Jain tech woven within his body. Certainly he could now grow, very rapidly, with powerful physical weapons inside him. But he didn't need those. What he did need, however, were the tools for mind-on-mind conflict, and he found them. Even as he incorporated them, he understood their corollary: aggression was implicit and amplified. All conflict had to reach resolution. Had Angel been before him, he would have killed him without compunction. This also raised another spectre: was his madness and anger a result of being infected with the Spatterjay virus or somehow rooted in his humanity too?

The tunnel veered round to the right. Further along, beyond the three Clade, more of Blade's units were approaching. Blade was also blocking other points of escape. But in one respect, the set-up of this trap had been a bad thing. It upset a balance throughout the tunnels in favour of the Clade, and Blade had just lost another three components of its scattered being. The fighting in the tunnels was getting hotter and hotter.

Round the corner, the three Clade units immediately chose to attack. Trike, his thinking accelerating, tried to reason why. The Clade had to be aware by now that Trike was no pushover—that just as he had been on the surface, he was a more effective Clade killer than one of Blade's units, and these units stood no chance against him. Then he understood the thinking of a swarm AI. Sacrificing its members, if to some useful purpose, was acceptable. The swarm was *learning* Blade, but Trike was a new element it had not grasped yet. It was prepared to sacrifice units to understand him. Or, Trike admitted to himself, it was some form of lunatic curiosity on the part of the Clade.

The Blade unit opened fire, hitting two of the Clade. One of them took strikes along its body and smacked into the ceiling, rucking up splinters of stone. The other one's head fragmented and it sailed on past—a mindless mechanism. The third unit abruptly halted, its drive blasting up a spray of water, coiled like a comma and spat a length of its tail forwards.

"This is new," commented Blade over their link.

The tail hit the Blade unit and stuck in place, pouring out steam, followed by smoke as it heated up. A high penetrating whine issued, and the tail section finally exploded, blowing the Blade unit sideways. The Clade unit in the ceiling folded out of the groove it had made and dropped, hitting the water as if to conceal itself. But Trike saw it spearing in towards his legs. He snapped his arm down, like a heron after a trout, closed his hand around the middle of the thing's body and heaved it up. Meanwhile, the Blade unit was burning. Analysis: that tail section had been converted into an explosive which blew fragments of itself into Blade's armour. Those pieces were an organo-metal enzyme eating its way through the armour.

The tail-less Clade looped over it and zeroed in on Trike too. It went for his face, tentacles extended like hands on truncated arms. Perfect, he thought. Instead of reaching up to grab it, he waited until it drew close, then snapped his head forwards and bit down, jaws closing on its head. The one he held was stabbing him with its tail and causing damage, but only as much as a blunt axe on seasoned oak. The one caught in his mouth began to beat him around his head with the remainder of its tail. He knew he could crush it in his jaws and spit it out, dead, as well as smash the other one against the wall till it started shitting its components. But no—this was not why he was here. Glancing at the Blade unit, he saw it drop into the water, bleeding an orange chemical sludge as it tried to neutralize the enzyme. Not his concern.

Trike probed with his tongue, feeling out the shape of the head clamped in his mouth. He found one eye and licked over its shifting plates of metal, whose intermolecular bonds the unit artificially weakened to expand them like aerogels. Even as he touched these, the Clade began tightening those bonds. Too late. He stabbed his tongue in, hard, like a metal punch through the layered petals of a rose bud. Once past the eye, he extruded masses of nano-fibres and found a polished sphere of AI crystal in the centre of the skull. As he began to make connections, he thought it interesting how the Clade, a swarm AI made difficult to destroy by the spread of its mind over numerous units, had not decided to distribute the individual crystal "brains" of the units themselves. A moment later he realized why: the more widely the unit's mind was distributed inside it, the more possible points of access it made. This would massively increase the danger of precisely the kind of breach he was making.

Trike located its self-destruct within the first few microseconds. It was a package stuck to the crystal sphere which generated an infrasound pulse of exactly the correct frequency to turn the crystal to dust. He deactivated it with braided fibres of collimated diamond, stabbing these through to kill it, but in the process reading it too.

Meanwhile, drilling into the crystal, he began downloading fragments of code, which grew larger and larger moment to moment. He also input the worms and phages, the viral programs like auto-surgeons or ever-hungry mouths. Codes were first—the constantly shifting codes that governed the intercommunication of the Clade's mind. Internally, he built a model of this particular unit, missing nothing. Virtual fibres speared out and connected to other units, and the virtual hooks ensured it could not disconnect him. His integration was local, for this swarm had diverged from the Clade entire. After a moment, sure he was in, he crunched and spat out the unit. Now he understood the Clade. And he knew it to be truly insane, because he recognized himself.

Thoughts, aims and intentions were impulses generated randomly amidst its units and taken up by the whole. It might think that blowing up a sun would be interesting, but then grow bored and find greater fascination in counting the grains of sand on a beach . . . or counting the same grain again and again and again. Though this swarm was running different com codes and partially disconnected from the Clade entire, it did receive telemetry updates. He understood from this that it delighted in chaos and order equally. In the Graveyard, a swarm of eight hundred units was fomenting war between two factions of humans aboard a large space station. Meanwhile, a few light years away from there, three hundred of them were building a structure out of molybdenite crystals that had been free-floating in vacuum. It had no use—it was just neat. The proposition the Wheel had presented to the Clade entire had fascinated it, and so it assigned a large portion of itself to that end. Trike could only suppose that the Wheel had penetrated this particular swarm of the Clade as he had, else it would not have carried through the Wheel's plans to their conclusion.

"You are nothing," he said.

It became aware of him and formed a virtuality in which to communicate, where trees floated upside down in a pink sky wrapped in a ring of rock. He allowed himself to be drawn in. The Clade presented itself as a pink axolotl by his feet. He put his foot on it and crushed it. Giggling, the virtuality retreated. He realized then that madness was its choice and that it could also decide to be sane. And it sometimes did, if the democracy of its mind allowed it. The reflections in himself were painful. He recognized that he had made his choice too, but was unsure if he had the mental integrity to carry it through.

"The Clade here is no more," he said to Blade. "The rest of it you will find at these locations." He showed Blade the places: the crystals, the fomenting war, the moon wrapped in weird, convoluted factories that manufactured Clade units in its core. The other places, the stray lone units, the ones that thought they were men, or Golem, or thought not at all. Then he sent the signal that turned hundreds of AI crystal spheres to dust. Focusing on what was in front of him, he saw the unit he held issue a puff of dust from the rear of its skull and slump. He dropped it into the current.

18

One could believe that, unlike the past, the prador war would not fade from human memory. Humans have lifespans that are now mostly a matter of choice rather than biology. So many who fought and lost friends are still around. However, humans bury old memories under new, and the weight of the passing centuries makes the war vague to them. Also, memory is a matter of choice now too, and many of those whose experiences were traumatic have had the worst of it edited from their minds. The AIs, by contrast, never forget or choose to forget. Our AI rulers always "learn the lessons of history" and can in fact recall them in eidetic detail. They also understand that the prador were not an enemy once under the influence of some toxic ideology. It is their biological nature to be aggressive and xenophobic, and that is not something that can pass away in a generation. Their medical technology and gerontology is not at the level of the Polity, because that requires a degree of cooperation and submission to physical examination by their fellows which they find abhorrent. However, they are still long-lived, and many of those who fought are still alive. Therefore the AIs perpetually monitor the Prador Kingdom. Weapons developed there will always have a counter in the Polity. The stock of Polity warships is always high. And, it is certain, interventions are often made. This is just plain good sense. Because even if the prador do not become warlike again, we may yet encounter another race like them.

—from *Quince Guide,* compiled by humans

ORLIK

Orlik had apparently accepted the necessity for the complete destruction of the remaining eighty ships. But Diana knew there would always be a big question mark over what had happened here. And she knew that King Oberon would be thinking very deeply on the matter.

"They will come to the conclusion that Clade units penetrated those ships," said Hogue out loud.

"It's only logical," agreed Seckurg, adding, "First."

"Perhaps I should have said that to them," said Diana, "rather than suggesting a Jain-tech infection aboard."

"Nah, better to let them work it out and feel clever," said Jabro. "They'll then assume that the Clade got aboard those ships before they came here."

"That may well be the case," said Seckurg. "Yes, the Clade is quite capable of discovering the loophole in the bounce gates, but your assumption that it used them to break on board may not be correct. The Clade would have needed to use a runcible gate of some kind to access those gates. Therefore the units had to be already aboard one of their ships or . . . maybe one of ours."

"You are correct," said Hogue abruptly.

"About what?" asked Seckurg.

"Confirmation has just been made," said the AI. "Data have become available to me. When the legate Angel visited his base of operations before departing to the Cyberat world, a reaver was present, which departed before Angel. It seems likely Clade units were aboard and that this reaver joined Orlik's fleet before it came here."

Nobody said anything and Diana felt herself first grow cold and then angry. This was something she should have known about and it was certainly something Earth Central *had* been aware of. The ECS agent, Captain Cog, had transmitted telemetry and reports whenever he could. The only time he had gone silent was under the USER disruption around Cyberat. So what was the game here? She realized it must still be the old one. When the fleets had been sent here it was because Orlandine had been, ostensibly, murdered. No one knew anything of U-space blisters and hidden ships.

"A police action," said Jabro slowly. "Another sharp reminder."

He was thinking along the same lines as her.

Earth Central had probably decided that the objective of the Wheel, Angel and the Clade had been to put the Kingdom and the Polity at each other's throats. It would have surmised the purpose of the reaver in that.

Perhaps even that Clade units were aboard and aimed to seize control of more prador ships and have them fire on Polity ships. It had not prevented this nor warned Diana. She could only assume that the intention, just as Jabro said, had been to allow a limited military action to go ahead. It had been certain at that point that her fleet would have won. The arrival of the *Kinghammer* had screwed those calculations. She winced. It was like the war. Though it would have been a pyrrhic victory thereafter, still the prador would have received a bloodied nose and again been reminded of Polity military supremacy. Also production supremacy. The king would have lost a substantial portion of his forces, while the Polity only a small percentage of its many warships.

"Like training an animal not to shit on the floor," Jabro added.

Exactly.

Diana tried to dismiss all this from her thinking. She had to deal with the now, not the past. First she viewed telemetry from the Polity fleet, noting that the prador ships were moving out of formation. It seemed the alliance had ended and she gave a tight, bitter smile at that. She then turned her attention to casualties and damage.

The ships were scattered over a wide swathe of vacuum. Wreckage tumbled between but also spread in a cloud away from the fleets. Those ships that had been hit by the disruptor beams had completely fragmented, with nothing left larger than the occasional structural beam or hull plate. Collision lasers flashed all across, vaporizing fast-moving chunks that might cause damage, and it seemed as if all the ships were in the midst of a thunderstorm. Occasional detonations occurred from free-floating and ruined munitions. Damage was still occurring out there, and loss of life.

"A salutary reminder of the results of warfare," said a voice.

She had been aware of a presence moving in close to her, as close as Hogue. The comlink to Earth Central had always been open to transmit telemetry and other fleet data, but that AI had remained remote for some time. Now it seemed to be breathing in her ear.

"You knew about the Clade," she said.

"If one has the capacity, one must focus both on detail and upon the big picture. This is something Orlandine has been receiving some painful lessons in, and which, I was sure, you had learned long ago."

"Oh, I learned," replied Diana. "But that does not mean I am comfortable with the knowledge."

"Neither am I, but my discomfort is ameliorated by my perfect recall of what happened during the war, as well as my predictions, whose accuracy can of course be questioned, of what will happen if such a war occurs again."

"Interesting justification," Diana said flatly.

"Look out there and multiply it by many orders of magnitude. Include worlds denuded of life and the deaths of many billions of humans and prador," said EC.

Larger wrecks were visible where ships had not been wholly destroyed by the U-space weapon the Species ship had deployed. She watched a Polity dreadnought turning end over end as it fell away from the fleet, hollowed by fire and still burning inside. Checking other views, she saw hold doors open on her own ship, the *Cable Hogue*, and extra-vehicular activity units shooting out. The things were like giant crabs and resembled the armoured prador out there in vacuum—some either dead or without the motive power of their suits. Others headed under chemical drives to the prador ships that would take them in. Her EVA units were on their way to collect up survivors: AIs, Golem, drones and humans who had managed to eject from their ships or were blown clear. The artificial intelligences were secondary to the suited humans, because their survival time was measured in centuries, whereas the humans, depending on the nature of their suits, had a more limited life span. She watched one EVA unit in pursuit of a heavily armoured human soldier who was dropping back towards the accretion disc. The front of his suit was open and his ruptured intestines spread like tentacles.

"Understand that the king of the prador will only go to war with us if he has some chance of victory," EC continued. "It is my job to ensure he is aware he has no chance, and to perpetually remind him."

"I understand this. I don't like it but I understand." She felt calm and cold now. Of course she understood—she wouldn't have been allowed to captain such a massive engine of destruction as the *Cable Hogue* if she did not. It was all as surgical as warfare, and the prevention of warfare, could be. The prador inclination towards battle was an abscess that periodically had to be drained. The prador, just as Jabro had said, needed to be trained not to shit on the floor. She also wondered, sometimes, if the present king of the prador was complicit in all this. He and his mutated family seemed more concerned about the advancement of the Kingdom and were fighting their own battles against the xenophobia and self-destructive impulses of the bulk of *normal* prador kind.

"So what now?" she asked.

"Orlandine is alive and reaffirming her grip on the reins of power here," said EC. "You will remain while the prador fleet remains too, and will only leave when she requests that you *both* leave."

"That I assumed . . . but there's something else, isn't there?"

"There is the Client and there are anomalies. I assume you are aware of these?"

"I am." Diana grimaced. "If the sole aim of the Wheel was to have us destroy that Species ship, why did it hold those two hundred Clade-controlled prador dreadnoughts in reserve? I must suppose that those ships had another purpose and were only used when the bombardment by the platforms failed. The only other purpose I can presently think of is to put prador and Polity at each other's throats. If so, why?"

"That is my conjecture too," EC replied.

"And the Client?"

"Very powerful."

"It would take all our firepower," Diana stated.

"So is not at present feasible."

"Why?"

"Because you would need to move your fleet to the Jaskoran system, which is inadvisable at this time." EC paused for a moment, as if waiting for something, then growing impatient, said, "I will withdraw—you are there because I wanted someone on the scene whom I trust to make the correct decisions. You now need to take a close look at the accretion disc." Earth Central blinked out of her consciousness with a sound like a glass stem snapping.

Diana looked through ship's sensors at the accretion disc. What had once been the disc's sun was still shrinking and still displaying the surface patterns it had exhibited prior to the Species ship departing it. But something new had begun to occur.

The matter of the disc still fell into the black hole. In fact, even as she watched, a small planet began breaking up to spread into a ring of debris around the thing, burning and heating up to emit heavy EMR. U-space disruption remained high. But the disruption from the mines which the Clade-controlled prador ships had deployed had faded within the noise of that central event. A line of division had appeared, lying twenty light minutes out, as if a barrier there prevented the material of the disc outside it from falling into the hole. Also, outside the division, swirls had appeared, and remaining planetary bodies, moons and asteroids were breaking up smoothly, like soluble pills dissolving in water.

"So what the hell is happening there?" Diana asked generally, even though she was reviewing the data on these events from Hogue. After a pause, she relayed the data to Orlik and left com open to him. She ensured the others knew this, so there would be no further discussion of the Clade or bounce gates. Orlik needed to be fully aware of the phenomena—perhaps then he would reconsider withdrawing his ships. She felt, in her gut, that separating the two fleets, and having them nose to nose again, might not be a bright idea.

"Combined gravity and U-space phenomena," said Jabro. "The substance of the cloud is moving very fast." He shook his head. "Unbelievably fast. There's also organization in there at levels I can just detect but cannot properly identify."

"Information too," said Seckurg.

They turned to look at him.

He explained. "Jain signatures are proliferating and changing. In EMR I'm detecting the kind of back-spill you get from an induction warfare beam, but on a massive scale."

"Orlik?" she enquired, focusing on the disposition of the two fleets.

"Sprag is running through accretion disc data, but hasn't found any instance of this happening before," replied the prador. "But then no one dropped a black hole in it before either."

"Perhaps we are just seeing something that will add formulae to current theories of the universe," said Diana wryly.

Orlik, who didn't understand her tone, said, "I think that highly unlikely."

Diana noted that the prador ships were no longer moving out of formation. Orlik had obviously ordered them to hold station.

"I think I should talk to Orlandine—if there is an explanation for this she will have it," said Diana.

"If she cares to share it." Jabro's comment had its elements of anger.

Still changes were occurring in the outer part of the accretion disc. It was becoming increasingly difficult to penetrate. In the human visual spectrum, it turned milky yellow, like a polluted fog. Other EMR began bouncing and scattering, and sometimes the central black hole ceased to be detectible to usual forms of scanning. The fog thickened and then finally it was only possible to locate the black hole on a gravity and U-space map of the system.

"When my scanners become obscured," said Orlik, "I tend to think someone doesn't want me to see something."

"The prador have always been a little paranoid," Diana replied.

Demonstrating that he did understand human badinage, Orlik came back with, "And of course that's an evolutionary trait you humans sidestepped?"

THE CLIENT

The Client gazed upon the core of the Species ship in confusion. Her attempts at communication had ranged across the spectrum, in every information format she could think of, including the language of the Jain. She had garnered responses, but nothing whose source was sentient. She had received ancient telemetry which, after analysis, she realized must have been from the far past, when this ship fought the Jain. There was stuff from what seemed to be a damaged translation device—a sub-AI language computer that gave responses as if attempting to learn how to communicate, but never quite managing it. Random information too, utterly out of context.

Finally, frustrated by the lack of any progress and utterly aware of the precarious position she was in, she consigned attempts at communication to a subprogram. Meanwhile, she began to assess damage to her platform and attack pods.

It had been a difficult jump through U-space. Disruption had been high, and she had needed to encompass a massive object in her U-field, within a complex web of combined drives. Having to jump without setting a destination, she had just allowed the nearest gravity well to drag her back up into the real. She could have ended up in the sun or in one of the planets of the Jaskoran system. Or found herself, as seemed usual for her, sitting in a wreck fighting for survival. She had been lucky, but still the situation was not good. Every single U-space drive had been damaged. The drives of her attack pods were a mess. Three of them only had cavities where their drives had been, while another four pods were completely missing. They had sustained minimal physical damage beyond that, and still possessed most of their weapons and defensive capabilities, which was something.

The U-space drive of the platform was also out of commission. The thing itself had twisted, but not beyond the recovery parameters of the memory metals and hydraulic adjustment of its structure. Also, the platform's weapons and its hardfield were good. This was odd. She realized she must be missing something and began to study the interconnection between the U-space drive and grav-engines, enclosing hardfields and weapons. She started to incorporate the math, buried by sheer quantity of data in her mind, that was integral to the shriek of the Librarian, whose mind was now part of her own. Gradually the shape of it became clearer to her.

The hardfields fed the energy generated by the impact of weapons into the underlying U-twist—a kind of energy storage spring, from which she could also draw energy for all other purposes. But hardfields were also, in themselves, a U-space effect. They put a dividing surface into the real... Investigating further, she saw, in the memories of Pragus, that some Polity ships had deployed hardfields to fend off the effects of disrupted U-space on conventional matter... The math and the theory pulled together into a perfect whole. A U-space drive was, in effect, a perfectly enclosing hardfield—a bubble that scooted its contents through that continuum. And further hardfields merely enforced the U-field. But what about the energy? Surely it would ramp up to infinity? No. Because dropping into U-space inverted the effect and the twist sat *outside* the hardfield. But that meant...

She switched her attention, via her sensor arrays, to the core of the Species ship. It had bounced out of the U-space blister and, when attacked, had thrown up incomplete hardfields. This made no sense. It should have had the technology to deploy a complete, enclosing hardfield, just like she could, no matter if its U-engines were knocked out of kilter. This, combined with the lack of any sensible communication, meant that something was seriously wrong. And perhaps it had been wrong before the Species ship even left the U-space blister.

Were her people dead? Had the ship simply responded to the attempts to destroy it on automatic?

She brought her attack pods in nearer to the object to get a better view, and to scan the thing closely. The plug of matter, like a thick coin, lay fifty miles across. Its outer rim was pocked with ports, closed off with tri-section doors half a mile in. Around the interior of the ports lay tangled masses of wrecked technology—almost certainly connections to the rest of the destroyed ship. Its upper and lower surfaces were mostly flat planes of armour—an exotic metal and ceramo-carbon composite, with superconducting and bearing layers. These could resist massive stresses and distribute point heat of hundreds of thousands of degrees. It was much more resistant than the armour had been on the rest of the ship. Hit this with a particle beam and it would take whole minutes to make an impression. The composite also reflected much of active scan, which meant that the Client struggled to look inside.

But she could partially see.

Slowly, scanning through the ports because they weren't so reflective, she began to build up shadowy images of the interior. Tunnels speared in from the ports and then took all sorts of twists and turns. The whole looked like a massive fruit whose flesh was made up of closely packed technology, wormed through with maggot holes. Near the centre, these all converged on a chamber ten miles across. Scanning also revealed temperature and pressure. The outer tunnels were cool and airy, in her terms, while the central chamber was just right for her: a little over a hundred degrees Celsius at two Earth atmospheres. She realized she had found the living quarters of her kind.

So what now?

First she had to repair those U-space engines. Around the world of Jaskor sat two potentially hostile fleets that could move against her at any moment. She immediately ordered the recall of her attack pods, because she could rebuild their drives more quickly using the facilities of the platform. Next turning her attention to the platform's drive, she set in motion its repair. Thankfully this time she would not need to build new, super-dense components, as had been the case before. Also, the Jain-tech integrated system throughout the platform meant many other components could be repaired in situ, rather than having to be replaced or hauled off to factory units. As the first attack pod arrived to be drawn into a repair bay, and as robots and Jain tentacles began to disassemble or penetrate the platform drive, she comprehended some idea of the time scale. It would be two hundred solstan hours before she could go anywhere.

Now, my people, she thought.

She only had one option. Scanning from outside would not provide her with the answers she required, so she must go inside to find them. But, of course, she would not send the entirety of herself. She quickly decided on an amalgam of the remotes she had used before. She wanted something with the ruggedness of the one she had deployed to penetrate the library, but with the ability to access and glean information, like the ones she had used to fight the Librarian and Dragon. In the last link in the chain of her being, she altered and adjusted the genome of a single cell. Then she injected the nutrients to set the process going. The remote would be on hand long before she was ready to leave this system. Should she send it across at once or wait until she was somewhere she could be free from interference?

No, it would be better to know if her people were alive before trying to U-jump that ship's core again. To take the platform, pods and that structure far enough away would be as dangerous as the last jump she had made. Yes, she had been prepared to take that risk to rescue her people from destruction. But taking the same chance again to transport what might only be an oversized coffin?

The Client also felt she needed to explore other options. Did her previous resentment towards the prador and the humans any longer apply? Was she being too hasty in excluding them from her calculations? She must never forget that, with what was coming next, she might not be able to run away far enough . . .

BLADE

Blade began pulling out its units from the tunnels, peevish, annoyed. Yes, it was good that the Clade threat here had been eliminated but it couldn't help thinking, *My job*. Trike had done well. He'd penetrated the Clade and got precisely what Blade had been after, finding out the locations of other Clade infestations. Then he had done more than well by breaching the coding the Clade used to sacrifice units should they be infiltrated, sequestered or captured. Now they were all lying in Jaskor's tunnels—inert lumps of complex technology.

Blade hesitated for just a second, then redirected its swarm. Rather than withdrawing, it hunted down the fallen Clade units and started collecting them up. Yes, the things were mindless lumps of hardware, but very sophisticated hardware and they could be given minds—subminds of Blade. This opened up all sorts of interesting possibilities for Clade penetration. The swarm AI, who had once been a black-ops attack ship, now had to think beyond Jaskor to the continuing fight. It was time to dismiss resentment and get on with it.

As it gathered up the Clade, it directed its attention towards Trike. The man showed no inclination to head for the surface. After standing for a while fighting some internal battle, he had set out, taking a route Blade projected led to where the drainage system connected to the underground cave network. Why? It had some idea. It had listened in on the exchange between Trike and Cog. Keying back into the ECS data sphere, it saw that the man's wife, Ruth, was on the point of resurrection. Perhaps he needed to think about that. Perhaps he needed to flee it. Blade could see how the whole situation posed a bit of a problem. There had been a human relationship and now Trike had ceased to be human. But it wasn't Blade's problem—the AI was a soldier, not a relationship counsellor.

"How are you doing?" Blade asked another down in the tunnels.

"I am making repairs, but they go slowly," replied Angel.

The android had crawled into a hole in the side of the tunnel where part of the wall had collapsed. He was lying on his back. Splits in his body revealed internal glittering movement.

"I thought you were tougher than that," said Blade.

"I don't think it was deliberate. Trike used weapons he did not know were at his disposal when he hit me."

"Meaning?"

"Besides the blow having the force of a hypersonic projectile, he gave me an induction warfare pulse. This killed my ability to absorb, distribute or otherwise disperse the shock. It also generated malware throughout my body that interferes with repairs and continues to attack me even now."

"Doesn't sound deliberate at all," said Blade.

Angel didn't respond to that.

Blade contemplated that there might be another reason Trike had retreated deep into the tunnels. The man had come close to destroying Angel and was sitting on a big psychopathic impulse. He had also recently taken on some nasty and, almost certainly Jain, military programming. The combination of the two was quite likely toxic. Perhaps Trike was removing himself to a place he would not be a danger to others. Yes, let that be the reason.

"Do you need assistance?" Blade offered, reluctantly.

"All I require is time, and you have other matters to attend to."

"Good luck," said Blade, relieved.

The first of its units heaved open a drain grating and rose into the air. Immediately, it became the target for three particle beams, induction warfare and a tripod-mounted micro-bead railgun so powerful its recoil dampers were larger than the gun itself. Blade dropped its unit straight back into the drains but fared better than another unit whose point of egress sat below an airfire drone. A particle beam strike, directly on top of a railgun hit, had obliterated the thing.

"Are you fucking paying attention?" Blade yelled into the data sphere.

"My apologies," replied Commander Gemmell. "You are clear now."

"What the hell happened?"

"Orders," Gemmell replied. "On their own cognizance they fired on the Clade."

Blade grudgingly accepted that. Other units had risen to the surface unscathed, but those two had been carrying defunct Clade units close to their bodies.

"Okay," it said.

More units began surfacing. Meanwhile, the soldiers set to guard the drainage system started packing up their gear and withdrawing, while the airfire drones moved to their locations. With nothing left to fight on the surface of the planet, would both go back into storage? Blade thought not. The situation had by no means been settled by the destruction of the Clade here or out at the accretion disc. Though the role of the swarm AI had been major, it had not been the prime one. However, it was the main actor in Blade's drama, beside Blade itself. And the time had come for the two stories to diverge.

Blade rose and swarmed above the city, swirling around the core of its original self, which hung in the sky like a bone stripped of meat. Next, those carrying the mindless Clade units began sweeping in where tentacular, gecko-stick grabs snared the silvery snakes and dragged them inside, packing them into armoured storage. Soon after all the units were neatly packed away, it was time to reconstitute.

Blade's components spiralled in around the central core of the erstwhile attack ship. Beginning at the stern, they began attaching like leaves to a branch, working their way forwards to the nose. Some were missing, of course. But Blade had a small factory inside that could produce more. Hanging in the sky like a long, open pine cone, but a black and immense one, it took stock. The Client was out there with the core of the Species ship. Weapons platforms were ready to jump to the accretion disc. Prador and Polity war fleets were poised to respond to all of this, and quite possibly to each other, but . . .

Not my business.

On grav-engines, Blade rose into the sky, its component units folding down flat to return it to sleek lethality. The landmass below dropped away, became framed by sea and then by the circle of the world. The black of space encroached, leavened by stars, by warships and the paraphernalia of Orlandine's *project*. And it was she who acknowledged Blade's departure.

"Thank you, *Obsidian Blade*," she said. "And good luck."

"Luck?" Blade enquired. It saw her down below, sliding through the sky from the mountains—a coiled dense mass of technology with something once human at its core.

"Don't be pedantic—go kick ass."

"Catch you later," said Blade. It faced out beyond Jaskor, ducked into U-space and was gone.

19

The accretion disc, whose nearest neighbour is the Jaskoran independent state, contains a large infestation of active Jain tech. This is continuously generating Jain nodes which are the seeds of that virulent and dangerous sequestering technology. Many experts have proposed that the disc is the source of all Jain nodes that have ever been discovered—that it was the site of an experiment which went wrong. However, others claim this is disproven by a find hundreds of light years away and dated at what is cited as the time of Jain extinction five million years ago. The previous experts then argue that, since there is no way to date accretion disc infestation, those Jain nodes discovered later could still have come from the disc. Also, the margin of error for dating both that find and the Jain's extinction is hundreds of thousands of years wide. The argument continues and is the source of many lengthy dissertations and studies. Such is the way with experts. However, one thing is clear: in much older finds that have been attributed to the Jain, no nodes have been found. They did, at one time, have a complex and highly advanced technology that was without the tendency to eat your face off. Some experts have recently proposed that this validates the earlier thesis that the more recent, dangerous technology was what did for them. Other experts, even now, are preparing their refutations of this.

—from *How It Is* by Gordon

ORLANDINE

Hovering over the city, Orlandine studied the situation here. Where the runcible facility had been located was now a crater half a mile across. Around that lay a ring of rubble, and scattered beyond were buildings that had just about survived the blast, but would have to be demolished. The rubble crawled with robots. Some with shearfields, laser cutters and heavy grabs burrowed in here and there, while others no larger than ants were deep inside. They extended scans where materials blocked them and diligently searched every crevice. These she keyed into and gazed from a million multifaceted eyes.

She focused on a military autodoc, which was in a space created deep beneath the remains of a foamstone wall. A woman lay there, still breathing but unconscious, as the doc severed her trapped and mangled legs. Meanwhile, only a short distance away, another doc laboured on a corpse so badly burned it could not be identified as either male or female. The thing had trepanned the skull and was now extracting a ruby memplant. Both these humans were, in essence, survivors. Others were not. Or, rather, whether they got to live again was debatable. At the crater sat a big zero-freezer—an object like a chunk of honeycomb in a framework to revolve it. The most damaged corpses were put in there to be vitrified and frozen. Those less damaged, across the rubble pile and elsewhere, were going into stasis or stop coffins. And all were flowing in towards the medship, beside which Cog's ship lay at rest—

"Orlandine!"

She decided to stop ignoring the comlink as, in her Jain mechanism, she descended towards the roof of her old apartment block.

"Yes, I have seen it," she replied, looking at the face of Diana Windermere.

She had noted the changes in the accretion disc right from the start. They were highly anomalous and she simply had no immediate explanation for them. So she had set the resources she had out there—remaining attack pods and some working debris from wrecked weapons platforms—just to gather data.

"So what, in your *expert* opinion, do you think is going on?" Windermere asked.

Orlandine looked through the failing sensors of one attack pod actually within the cloud. Here she saw a small, heavily cratered moon, grey and silver in the dim light except in one area. A bite out of that moon emitted blue-white light. Matter poured into the crater and flowed towards the centre, as if a singularity had been fixed there. However, from that central point, it fountained out into vacuum. This fountain was dust at first, then coagulated as it rose into lumps that were blurred to scan but showed organization. It could be some crystallization effect, but she very much doubted it. Energies were involved here and she could not locate a source. Nor would she be able to before the attack pod finally failed.

"The Jain tech has been stimulated in some way," Orlandine replied. "It was activated once before when Dragon injected power into and interrogated the Jain AIs in U-space. I suspect something similar here."

"Those AIs are causing this?"

"Possibly . . . or it could be a programmed reaction—like an ants' nest being disturbed with a stick. In this case the stick is a black hole."

"I'm going to need more than that," Windermere spat.

Orlandine felt a surge of irritation. In her mind, she had a wide mosaic of explanations for events out there. Most of them had their validity, and all of them were quite a large jump away from being provable. But this was beyond the mind of the woman she was speaking to. Instead she requested another comlink to the mind of Windermere's ship—to Hogue itself—and transmitted that mosaic of reasoning.

"The black hole. The blister in U-space," said Windermere.

That gave Orlandine pause. The woman had just upgraded her thinking, meshing with her ship's AI. Interesting how she could so easily connect and disconnect. Perhaps Morgaine could learn something from her? Orlandine felt she herself had nothing to learn since she no longer possessed a separate human element to connect or disconnect.

"It is the largest imponderable in any calculation or prognosis. The next being the Jain tech itself," she replied. "We at least know something about Jain tech, but we know very little about a U-space blister opened by a black hole."

"Suggestions?" Windermere asked.

"I will investigate this phenomenon when my platforms have returned there," Orlandine replied. "But beyond that I can help you no more than I have."

She considered adding something more about certain fleets departing but decided against it. She was still dealing with a lot of unknowns and, though this was her realm, she thought it worth keeping the extra

Polity and prador firepower around for a while. Besides that, she was reluctant to push. If she told both the fleets to leave, that might compel either the king or Earth Central to . . . react. With the Client here and odd things still occurring in the disc, either might decide their agreements concerning the disc had become a hindrance to the best interests of their realms. She wanted her defences and her weapons platforms at their optimum in such an event.

"Well, thank you for that, at least," said Windermere, now back fully human and just a little resentful.

Orlandine cut the link, then abruptly changed course. Instead of settling on top of her old apartment building as she had intended, she tilted in mid-air, opened the bands of armour on the back of her mechanism and fired up the fusion drives. She shot straight upwards, the city receding and shrinking behind her, then the continent. Off one edge, fifty miles out in the ocean, she noted the red eye of the Sambre volcano at the base of a plume casting a shadow across the waters. Within just a minute, she punched through a cloud layer and saw the plain of rumpled white spread out below her. Then the sky darkened and stars began to blink into existence. As the air grew thin and faded away entirely, she noted the rhythmic rise and fall of her chest and cancelled it. This facsimile of her human body had no need of air, nor did the remaining elements of her original body, since they were stored inert throughout her *whole* structure.

Out in vacuum, she swung into a curving course taking her a quarter of the way around the planet. Meanwhile, she noted the departure of another ten evacuation platforms, and saw the remainder were rapidly filling. Soon she had a direct line of sight into the inner system and where the Client sat in orbit of Adranas, the hot giant planet in close orbit of the Jaskoran sun. It was time to talk.

She could, if she had wished, have opened communication with the Client while down on the surface—through her systems scattered up here, or even via machines she had mining heavy metals from the crust of Adranas itself. But she was wary. If she used com with too many relays involved, she opened windows for informational attack. Also the tech wrapped around her was some way in advance of those elements of her older self. She now viewed Weapons Platform Mu via numerous orbital arrays, noting activity out there. Weapons pods were returning to the platform and others were departing. Doubtless the Client was calling them in for repairs. However, those pods and the platform were markedly undamaged from their short jump through disruption, and not having had a set destination.

"We need to talk," she said.

She had tightened the U-com and used a completely different coding format from what she operated to link her dispersed parts. Bandwidth, if it could be so described in U-space, stayed narrow. At present, all it could carry was only a binary coding of her words in text.

"You may need to talk," replied the Client.

The alien had replied at least, so it was prepared to talk. She ignored its snippiness and continued, "Have you communicated with the survivors of that ship yet?"

"I have not."

"They are not responding to you," Orlandine guessed.

After a long pause the Client replied, "No, they are not."

"Perhaps they are in stasis—cryogenic storage?"

Again a long pause then, "Perhaps so."

"What are your intentions now?"

"To leave."

"That being your intention, it would be no loss to you to provide me with information."

"And no gain."

"Perhaps you should not leave," Orlandine suggested, then wondered what impulse made her say that. Brief analysis of her own thought processes provided the answer and it disconcerted her. In complex situations, it was always best to keep as many pieces in play, so as to have as many options open as possible. Simplification could lead to impasses and dead ends and was the resort of simpler minds. She realized Dragon thought like this.

"There are prador and Polity forces here that might move against me," said the Client.

"But you are in neither prador nor Polity territory," Orlandine noted.

"The realm of Orlandine."

"Quite." Orlandine left that for a moment then continued, "I calculate that an attack by the ships here would be unable to breach your defences. Let me propose a deal."

"I am listening."

"I will bring you under my aegis as an adviser and order all Polity and prador forces to take no action against you."

"And they will listen?"

"Six hundred weapons platform will be a great aid to hearing."

"You mean five hundred platforms."

Orlandine acknowledged that with a grimace. "Quite."

"And in return you want . . . what?"

"Your advice, of course. You provided a brief history of what happened here millions of years ago to Diana Windermere in an attempt to stop her firing on the Species ship. I would guess . . . no, I am certain, that the data you provided was limited to that end. You know a lot more about events here and I need that knowledge. You understand the technology much better too—this is materially evident in what you have done to Weapons Platform Mu. I want data, Client."

Another pause ensued, a much longer one this time. Before the Client could reply, Orlandine continued, "It is a big universe and you can run far away. But do not underestimate the assistance I may be able to provide. Nor should you dismiss how useful it is to have friends."

"Very well, I accept," said the Client.

That was very quick and worryingly so. It made her think that the Client had already been thinking along these lines, which indicated the alien might well *need* assistance and friends.

"Morgaine," said Orlandine, her attention now directed towards one of the dreadnoughts sitting out from Jaskor. The four-mile-long slab of technology wasn't state-of-the-art but could still turn moons to rubble.

"I'm listening," replied its interfaced captain.

"The Client is now an adviser in the Jaskoran independent state and as such comes under my protection. Kindly relay this information to Diana Windermere."

"I will," replied Morgaine, "but I would be interested to know why you did not tell her yourself."

"It's quite simple. She is at the accretion disc and if any orders come from Earth Central concerning the Client it will be you who responds to them."

"And if I receive such orders to engage?"

"That would be unfortunate." Orlandine transferred her gaze to the weapons platforms hanging in vacuum out beyond Jaskor. The *Morgaine* might well be able to turn a moon to rubble, but just one of those platforms could do the same to a planet. She sent an image of the platforms as an addendum to their exchange.

"Understood," said Morgaine. "Anything else?"

"That's all for now."

The link closed and Orlandine noted the same resentment in Morgaine as she had found in Windermere. Inevitably, being in charge of such massive engines of destruction caused a degree of arrogance in the two captains that did not respond well to her. Once a Polity citizen and now an outsider, she did not accede to their will.

"Good enough?" she asked.

"Yes," said the Client, "but understand that if you betray my trust I will destroy you."

"Fair enough."

"Now ask your questions."

"First: what the hell is happening with the accretion disc now?"

"Chaff," the Client replied. "Something doesn't want to be seen. Yet."

COG

Ruth lay comfortably on the bed, breathing evenly, seemingly asleep. Cog sat on his director's chair to one side, while on the other Mobius Clean hovered, shimmering. The new occupant of the room had joined them only a few minutes earlier.

"Don't you both have work to do?" Cog asked.

The forensic AI waved a dismissive, feathery tendril. "I copied across subminds to control the medical machines here. The work is prosaic and uninteresting."

"Really?"

"Routine interventions and restorations," Clean replied. "The damage the Clade caused was merely brutish and physical—no viruses or nano-machines, no genetic or mental disruption, just wounds and burns and death."

"So you are here . . . ?"

"You know why."

"Trike."

The crinoid forensic AI shrugged.

"And you?" Cog focused on Gemmell, the commander who had come in too. The man was big, rugged and tough-looking, with cropped black hair and black stubble on an angular and slightly cruel face. Muscle packed his ECS uniform and it certainly wasn't cosmetic. He had an air about him, a body confidence and strength Cog recognized. This guy would be no pushover, even for an Old Captain.

Gemmell smiled calmly. "I can give orders wherever I am, and my presence is not required unless something untoward happens." He gestured to Clean. "As with him, it's all pretty routine now."

Cog watched as the man returned his attention to Ruth. There was something going on there. He had come here perhaps out of curiosity, but his reaction on seeing Ruth's face had been . . . notable. Now the man turned away and headed to a fabricator inset in one wall and began inputting instructions. Cog shook himself and turned back to the AI.

"So Trike," he said.

"There are two items that I wish to inspect. Trike is one of them. The android Angel is the other."

"You're done with me then?" Cog eyed the blue square of scar tissue on his arm. He had agreed to give a sample and the AI had taken it before he could reconsider. It had moved fast and excised a chunk of his arm before he had a chance to draw breath.

"Your DNA is interesting in how it relates to your brother Jay Hoop. I can see certain structures that could result in malformations in the brain. In your case, this did not occur. Perhaps Jay was more genetically predisposed towards these but, as we have noted, there is an element of choice in this. It goes back to the old debates about nature and nurture."

"Choice," Cog repeated woodenly.

"Ten per cent of humans born without genetic assay and correction can be so disposed. Only eight per cent of those experience . . . problems. Those are due to environmental and social factors. Nurture, in essence." Clean paused for a moment, but Cog had found himself able to read the thing and knew that it wanted to say more. It continued, "I would like a memcording of your mind so as to study this relationship."

"That's not going to happen," said Cog.

"I understand the difficulties related to the Spatterjay virus—"

"As do I," Cog interrupted. "Memcording the mind of a hooper is difficult because of the viral fibres, but doubtless could be achieved by a forensic AI. You're not getting one because what goes on between my ears belongs to me. Now let's talk about Trike."

His response obviously agitated Clean, but it finally relented, "Okay. I can reduce his viral load and return him to human form without killing him."

"But?"

"The Jain technology also occupying his body is beyond my present scope. Therefore a *cure* for Trike would be a lengthy process of experimentation, investigation and constant intervention."

"Do you think it can be achieved?"

"It is not impossible, but then very little is." Clean touched a tendril to Ruth's head for a moment, then pulled it away. "However, I would need his complete cooperation. I am a forensic AI with many powerful tools at my disposal, but I would not countenance any intervention even on you without your agreement. Old Captains are ridiculously strong and rugged and notoriously difficult to render unconscious. Trike is much more than that. Without his cooperation I could end up dead."

"So I need to bring him back and he has to be willing," Cog stated, but distractedly. Gemmell had reached out to brush back a lock of Ruth's hair which Clean had dislodged, and his hand was lingering overlong on her face.

"Do you know her?" Cog abruptly asked.

Gemmell withdrew his hand. "She reminds me of someone I knew." He glanced up towards the ceiling. "How she once was."

"But she's not that woman," Cog stated.

"When she was human?" asked Clean.

"Yes, then," said Gemmell.

Obviously Clean knew about this woman too. Cog got back to the point. "Trike has to be willing . . ."

"Exactly." Clean shrugged again. "I have been in communication with the android Angel, who has been allowed access to the ECS data sphere here. He has gone after Trike, who has gone deep into the cave systems below us. But I am not sure that Angel can reason with him."

"And that's why," said a hoarse voice, "you let me hear all this."

Cog peered down at Ruth. Her eyes were open now and she was looking across at Gemmell. She sat up, the sheet dropping away from her naked body. Cog couldn't help but stare. There wasn't a single blemish on a torso he had seen open and eviscerated just a few hours ago. Gemmell, meanwhile, held out a jacket for her. He'd got clothing from the fabricator—Cog should have thought of doing that himself. She pulled the garment on, with his unrequired help, and muttered her thanks. Cog turned away and tried to stop his mind slipping into cynicism. When he turned back she had fixed her gaze on him.

"We must bring my husband back," she stated.

Cog nodded, aware that her eyes were glassy with incipient tears and that something had changed.

ORLIK

The great fog was coagulating, shifting, reshaping. Orlik keyed into the feed from the probes the *Cable Hogue* had U-jumped out and above the accretion disc. The outer part of the disc seemed to be bunching up in one place and lying directly between the black hole and the fleets. The inner part, still falling in towards the black hole, had also turned opaque.

"It's very fast," Windermere commented.

"Sprag?" Orlik enquired.

"Pretty damned anomalous," Sprag replied. "There are things in there moving at close to light speed, otherwise it could not reshape so fast. We are, after all, looking at something that is nominally eight light hours across."

Orlik was glad to be reminded. As ever in space, one could lose a sense of scale. So, something was shifting the Jain cloud out there, altering it and making it opaque to scan, somehow skating elements of it across vacuum without dropping them into U-space. This meant utterly appalling amounts of energy were being used, in ways he, and quite probably Windermere, did not understand. Did the AIs?

"Do you understand how this is being done?" he asked. Sprag had, after all, become a high and mighty ship AI.

"I haven't a clue," Sprag answered.

"I presume that is your ship AI that I hear speaking," said Windermere.

Orlik bubbled irritation. He hadn't remembered to cut her out of his exchanges with Sprag. "Yes, that's my ship AI."

Windermere looked mildly puzzled. "You speak to it in Anglic."

"Evidently."

She shrugged. "I hadn't expected it to sound like that."

Privately to Sprag, he said, "You could have prevented her from hearing."

"I could have," Sprag said, "but the cat is out of the box since I communicated with Hogue and the other Polity AIs. They are aware that there's something unexpected about me for a prador design."

Orlik could not help feeling a little suspicious about that.

"The cloud is more opaque between us and the black hole," said Windermere, "but I suspect that opacity would be the same for us wherever we moved and it's not due to the material shift." She paused contemplatively. "We don't even know—"

"Now that's a material shift," Sprag broke in.

Orlik had seen it the moment Sprag interrupted and doubtless all the faster minds in the combined fleets had seen it too. Objects were now sliding out of the Jain cloud and heading towards them. Tens of thousands of them. Orlik immediately focused his sensor array on one of them. It looked like a conglomerate of the internal organs of a prador and was coated with bluish metal. Pulling back, he saw that most of the swarm consisted of these, though other objects were evident too. Deeper scanning revealed tangled technology and a super-dense power supply. The things were travelling fast—a high portion of light speed. Even as he watched, they all fired up high-powered ion drives to ramp up their acceleration. But what could such small items, which would take a long time to reach the fleets, do?

A series of particle beams lanced out from the *Cable Hogue*—probing shots. Orlik saw them strike fifteen of the objects. As the beams winked out they revealed tumbling cinders.

"Take them out," said Orlik.

The *Kinghammer* opened fire—a fusillade of railgun slugs hurtling across vacuum. The order, relayed by Sprag, had the rest of the prador ships firing railgun slugs too.

"Why have you stopped firing?" Orlik asked Windermere.

"Because they are ineffective," she replied.

"What?"

Her face was back in his vision. "They don't have U-space drives. We can move out of the way any time we like." She shook her head and Orlik surprised himself by recognizing something unpleasant in her expression. "And, in reality, they are not our problem but Orlandine's."

The prador ships opened up with particle beams—lines of royal blue slicing across vacuum. Railgun slugs and the beams struck simultaneously. Plasma explosions lit vacuum, the approaching objects blackened dots in silhouette. The beams drilled into these, splashing sun-hot particulate. Then targeting began to get sketchy, as it became difficult to find targets in the steadily increasing EMR. U-com was unaffected, however.

"And there we have it," said Windermere dryly. "Destroy enough of them and you cannot see the rest. Some will get to us."

"U-space," said Orlik, pedantically.

"Take a look," she replied.

Sprag relayed U-space imagery and a gravity map through his interface. Certainly, Jain signatures were detectible, but they were dispersed, shifting. That, combined with the intense EMR, made it impossible to nail down the positions of the ones that had not been hit.

"We need to relocate," he said.

The new coordinates arrived even as he spoke the words. Sprag transmitted them to the prador ships as he felt the falling twist of the *Kinghammer* entering that continuum. A second later, his ship was out again. It now sat slightly above the plane of the accretion disc. Other faster ships were arriving too—slower old-style prador or Polity dreadnoughts trailed behind. The formation was in disarray. The disruption from the black hole, the proximity of other ships making it impossible for each to jump accurately, and the timings, all contributed. But Orlik was pleased to see how quickly his ships regained their positions relative to each other, and to the Polity ships. He wasn't pleased for long.

"More of the fuckers," said Sprag.

Other things came too this time: bacilliform objects a hundred feet long, hollow down the centre. These heated up internally so that their ends looked like the throats of furnaces. A moment later, they spewed out intensely orange ion beams. These reached out across vacuum and splashed on hardfields. Again the prador ships replied, and Sprag coordinated fire on the bacilliforms, since they seemed to represent the greatest danger. These could take more than one beam hit, but a railgun slug caused a satisfactory explosion. However, the explosions ramped up EMR again. And still, Orlik noted, the Polity ships were inactive.

"You're still not firing," he said tetchily.

"I am not firing because these things will just deplete our armouries," Windermere replied. "Cease firing."

It was about the first direct order he had received from her and he didn't like it. He ground his long mandibles together in irritation. He finally acceded, "Tell them to cut it, Sprag."

All the prador ships ceased firing at once, though tardy railgun slugs continued to impact. The bacilliforms carried on firing. None of their shots was getting through but obviously they were eating into the fleet's energy reserves.

"Tactics," he said.

"Something stinks," Windermere replied. "This seems too organized to be just another Jain-tech outbreak. If we stay here we will eventually have to open fire. We can back off or keep shifting position . . . I don't like either. We're being driven."

"By what?"

Windermere had no answer for him. He contemplated this for a moment then said, "Orlandine . . ."

"She is aware but saying nothing as yet."

This got a response.

"My weapons platforms are still rearming and developing weapons and defences," said Orlandine. "I will not move them in until they are ready."

"But what we are seeing here is precisely what your platforms were designed to stop," Windermere argued.

"As you have noted, these objects are . . . thus far, incapable of jumping through U-space. Their spread is a concern, but they can easily be tracked and dealt with at a later time."

Orlik grudgingly conceded that she was talking sense. "Tactics," he repeated. "We're bleeding power like this."

"Calculating for all ships," replied Sprag.

"Perhaps we should go in," Orlik suggested, broadcasting an image of the accretion disc with a square frame over the inner separation point.

"Too close," said Windermere tersely. "We'll have those fuckers coming at us from every direction and they'll be more concentrated. And still this is not our problem."

Orlik was annoyed at himself. Trying to think outside the box, he had not recognized that the inner cloud around the black hole would probably contain the same hostiles.

"So what now?"

"I don't know," replied Windermere acidly. "I'm swiftly coming to the conclusion that Orlandine would like us to do her work for her and that it is perhaps time to leave." During the ensuing pregnant pause there was no response from Orlandine. Orlik assumed she was either no longer listening, or simply did not care to refute Windermere, who continued, "Either that, or by not bringing her platforms in, she is pushing me to make that decision."

Your decision, thought Orlik, *for your ships.*

Windermere continued, "But I've had nothing from Earth Central so I think it best we watch and wait until we're sure what the situation is . . . whether it requires us."

"It's pretty damned obvious, really," said Sprag abruptly. "We jump out, leaving attack ships on watch."

"In microcosm, Orlandine's tactics," commented Windermere, with something of disgust in her voice, Orlik thought. And still no response from Orlandine. "But I agree for the interim . . . I need to talk to Earth Central."

Via his interface, Orlik noted the new tactical plan. The fleets would jump out two light hours. Fifty-three stealthed attack ships and hundreds of watch probes would be left to spread about the disc, themselves jumping and shifting to avoid confrontation. They would form a sensory sphere that would enable greater penetration of the cloud, through to the black hole. Also one Polity dreadnought, with immense hold space, would stay to pick up remaining survivors scattered about space from the previous encounter with the Species ship. Even as the *Kinghammer* dropped into U-space, Orlik wondered how long this tactic would remain viable. What if that cloud just kept pumping out Jain-tech objects for months? What if nothing else happened? He really needed to talk to his king.

Hiatus . . .

Orlik stared at a slightly more distant view of the accretion disc. Meanwhile, a second image, sent by U-com from the attack ships and probes, gradually cleared. This closer view of the disc lost enough of its opacity to reveal the black hole, a beady eye sunk deep inside. Abruptly it became sharper still—the haze dispersing. Now he could see planets, planetoids and asteroids issuing great fountains of matter into vacuum, flickering twists in U-space and massive ionic energy surges. There were plasma vortexes, flashes and streaks of raw power, as of a storm within. And scattered throughout in their millions: coagulating Jain-tech objects. Those things that had already attacked swarmed there like some massive infection.

"We should have scanned like this before," he commented.

"We're not seeing clearly because of our scanning," said Sprag. "Seems something has decided it doesn't matter what we see now."

"Look at the black hole," said Windermere.

It was even smaller, the pattern of conjoined hexagons over its surface bright and clear. A line then cut around its equator and a powerful U-signature crashed through that continuum. It even affected the cloud, causing it to flinch, almost like an amoeba touched with a hot wire.

"Oh hell," said Windermere. "Whatever's in there, we've just done precisely what it wants."

"We go back in," said Orlik, but he knew he was too late.

The even pattern over the surface of the black hole dissolved, spread, the orb briefly flashing to the brightness of a sun and emitting an intense pulse of EMR. Then the thing darkened and shrank, losing its artificial expansion. U-com dropped out as it collapsed, from the size of a G-type star to a minuscule point a mere eight miles across. It was as if the rubberized sheet of U-space had been smacked with an immense club.

And an object had come out.

ANGEL

The storm drains were emptying—their flow of water little more than streams running down their centres. Angel finally hauled himself upright. With mud sucking against his feet, he clumped off in the direction Trike had gone earlier.

I am Golem, he thought.

He understood that Trike had initially intended to knock him out of the way, but then the Jain technology had responded to other levels of his mind. This was why the blow had been so hard, and why it had hit him with induction warfare and destructive viruses. Trike might be consciously trying to accept Angel as one of the good guys, but unconsciously he still wanted to kill him.

The diminished flow of water had left all sorts of detritus in the layer of mud: clumps of waterweed like bleached lettuces leaking blood, oozing transparent nematodes the length of his forearm. Occasional mudfish backed against the wall and barked like asthmatic dogs as he passed. And there were pieces of the Clade. In one area where he found these, he looked up and saw the damage to the tunnel ceiling. He realized this was where Trike had finished off the swarm AI—finally killing it with its own destruct program. Angel moved on, scanning ahead, trying to find some trace of the man. Trike had to be blocking to be so invisible, so did not want to be found. However, he had neglected his traces in the physical world, and soon Angel followed big claw-toed footprints in the mud.

The trail took him into a series of interlinked side tunnels and finally to a shaft plummeting into darkness. Scanning down, he realized that here the flood water poured into natural caves deep below, to underground rivers that flowed to the sea. The sides of the shaft bore the markings of a tunnel borer, just like those underneath the Ghost Drive Facility. Angel eyed the chipped and broken stone where Trike had climbed down by the simple expedient of driving his fingers and toes into the rock. He followed, using the handholds provided.

The bottom of the shaft opened out in the ceiling of a cavern, small stalactites growing around its rim. Angel released his hold and dropped fifty feet, landing heavily in a squat, with stone shattering under his feet. Alerts rippled through his body, since his internal repair systems were not yet up to speed. He rose carefully and searched his surroundings. He could find no footprints here and Trike had a wide choice of caves into which he could have ducked. A river ran down the side of this cavern, flowing into distant darkness towards the sea and Angel followed it. Basic psychology informed his choice. When he passed a series of newly snapped-off stalagmites, he guessed he had made the right decision. Later, a footprint in a sandy deposit beside the river confirmed this.

"Captain Trike!" he bellowed, his voice echoing eerily.

Briefly a flash of EMR far ahead, quickly concealed. He broke into a run, heading for that location, but on reaching it found no one there. But his sensorium, still reinstating from the damage he had received, started giving him more. In infrared he began picking up heat traces on the cavern floor. A few miles further on, and these became clear footprints like those in the mud above. He considered calling again but decided against it—Trike might try to conceal himself further.

The cavern became steadily narrower, the river occupying more of its floor. In a little while Angel walked along a ledge beside it and knew that soon he would have to go into the water. Then he felt the attempts at communication. It wasn't U-com since he had lost that earlier, along with his connection to the ECS data sphere, but tight beam terahertz com. Too much rock lay between himself and the sender, though, and he failed to lock it down. He responded with his own signal in the direction of the beam. Whoever was there would at least know his location.

Finally, he dropped into the water. The packed density of his body took him straight down to the bottom but then some tinkering with his internal grav brought him back to the surface and he let the flow carry him. He wondered if Trike could do the same now, and what the man's limitations were. Trike had become terrifyingly strong and fast, his body as densely tech-packed as Angel's own. But his capabilities were greater. Angel knew that even when he had been linked to his wormship, he could not have done what Trike had done to the Clade. Nor would he have been capable of going one-on-one with a war drone like that lethal creature called Cutter.

Daylight began to penetrate and soon Angel saw a crack above showing sky. This grew steadily, until the cave widened out into a canyon. Com established—this time simple radio—and Angel once again opened into the ECS data sphere. Data flow had slowed because U-com was down, apparently due to a wave of disruption spreading from the accretion disc black hole. He received a query and the identifier for the forensic AI Mobius Clean, but hesitated to open communication. Angel was just the kind of item Earth Central would want taken apart and studied by a forensic AI. But in the end he relented.

"What do you want?"

"You, and Trike."

"I have no intention of surrendering myself to ECS."

"And ECS does not have the power here to take you."

A data package arrived and, after scanning it internally, Angel finally opened it. Apparently Orlandine had given him citizenship of her realm and he now came under her protection.

"All I want from you is the data you will allow," said Clean. "All I want with Trike is to help him, if he, also a citizen here now, will allow it."

Ahead, the canyon walls fell away and Angel could see the river opening out into the sea, mounded shingle on either side. He thought about why he had decided to follow Trike and the resolution he sought.

"I cannot make decisions for Trike," he said. "As for me, right now, I give you my permission to study me. Let us hope you will have something to study." Before Clean could question that, Angel ended the communication.

Where the river cut through the shingle beach, Angel scanned the banks and saw where they had been disturbed. He swam over and climbed out, following deep footprints. Again he questioned his present actions and again he came up with the same answers. Despite what he had done in the tunnels, he still felt he owed Trike something. He also felt he needed absolution from the man, some forgiveness. He had to face Trike, alone, and they must resolve what lay between them before either of them could move on. And there he was.

A boulder field lay ahead and Trike sat atop one of them, gazing out to sea at the distant plume of the Sambre volcano. Angel felt a shudder run through him at the utter certainty of the danger he faced here, but resolutely strode forwards. After a moment, Trike slumped, dipping his head, then abruptly swivelled on the boulder and dropped off the side.

"You should not have come," he said.

"We need to make things right," Angel replied.

But Trike was already on the move, accelerating, his clawed feet kicking up shingle. Angel stared. He had anticipated something else. He had expected there to be reason but he saw none in the thing hurtling towards him. He turned to run but could not build up the acceleration on the shingle. A clawed hand clamped on his shoulder, nails driving into his metallic skin. Trike hauled him off the ground and threw him hard. Angel slammed headfirst into one of the boulders, the impact smashing his head down against his chest, compacting metallic bones, systems breaking inside him. Induction warfare hit him in a wave, generating hostile viruses, surges blowing out nanowires. He looked up, neck straightening with a crunching, tinny sound of metal components straightening.

"You should not have come," Trike repeated woodenly, reaching down for him.

20

Somewhere, in U-space, there is a great mass of Jain AIs. Our own AIs assure us of this but, apparently, the only place where it is possible to communicate with these products of the Jain is near the central sun of an accretion disc. This disc is also packed with supposedly dangerous Jain tech, and to engage with the AIs, one must inject energy in the process to enable them to think. We can't go there—any ships even approaching the area are summarily destroyed. What are we to make of this? I think we must take a long, hard look at our own AIs and speculate on what the future might bring. The prevailing idea is that those Jain AIs voluntarily ensconced themselves in that continuum to escape whatever it was that wiped out their creators... But, of course, we cannot ask them about this. So let me make a new suggestion: their creators imprisoned them there and went on to live out their material existence free from AI interference. The Jain created a massive civilization whose technology we know to be utterly beyond our own. Most certainly, they were peace-loving creatures who made the utopia all races can achieve without soulless AIs holding them back and dragging them into unnecessary conflicts. This civilization existed for millennia, if not millions of years, and achieved the unalloyed heights of racial purity before it moved on. That our AIs, and those quislings in thrall to them, sneer at this analysis, I think proves that the movement of a civilization to a higher plane of existence is valid. I feel the religious zeitgeist of the past just reflected this truth, and that our ruling AIs deliberately quashed it. Are we truly to believe that some rogue technology, created by the Jain, wiped out the later, highly technical alien civilizations of the Atheter and the Csorians? No! They moved on to that higher plane of existence too—one that is denied to us by AI oppression!

—from *The Separatist Handbook*

ORLANDINE

The wave of U-space disruption slammed out. Orlandine read its intensity on a map of that continuum, until even the instruments for detecting it ceased to function. However, she got enough data to place the accretion disc black hole as its source. No vessels would be travelling through that continuum for some time. Even U-com, the transference of data by electromagnetic means through U-space, crashed.

To Orlandine, it felt as if all her perceptions had slowed, as her project and her mind, distributed throughout the Jaskoran system, began switching over to the slow drag of laser com. She fielded queries from platform AIs, from prador and Polity ships, from sub-AI systems, until she raised a subpersona to deal with them all. This provided the various iterations of one answer: "I don't know." She then directed a tight, blue-beam BIC com laser into the inner system and asked, "Something does not want to be seen?" She did not have to wait a whole eleven minutes for the circuit of question and response, because a com laser locked on her just a moment later with the continuation of their exchange.

"My species is a branch of the Jain family tree that they tried to wipe out. You saw part of that attempted extermination in the data I sent to Diana Windermere." The Client paused, then continued, "Must we continue to communicate in this ineffective manner, with such delays?"

Orlandine opted to trust, and opened up bandwidth via the laser. Now they could communicate with more than just text, and pack the exchanges with data. She then decided she really needed to speed this up, so created a subpersona to transmit to the Client—one that could ask questions and respond immediately. The Client was equally as fast, and Orlandine recognized the AI format of the data coming in as its subpersona. She routed it to secure storage, but opened bandwidth from it for complex com, and watched it grow within her. At once, it showed her a fleet of alien ships, all of which bore a resemblance to seashells. She identified the Species ship amidst them as they fell into a solar system, closely past a gas giant.

"Four of the Jain allied themselves to attack one of their kind," the Client persona intoned. "One must understand the Jain to know that it was not the attack that was unusual but the alliance. The progress of Jain society was achieved through constant conflict and theft of knowledge and materials from each other."

It gave her a graphical representation and she understood at once. Their behaviour was rooted in their biology. Sex is a mingling of genetic data, whose purpose is overall evolution to optimum survival, in given environmental circumstances. From the start, for the Jain, sex was genetic rape, a fight—the winner taking the genetic material of its victim, or mate, and making an eclectic selection for the best offspring. But, through evolution and their own alteration of their biology, it extended beyond that. They became potentially immortal and individually followed varying developmental paths. They mated and stole genetic material from each other, sometimes for offspring, more often in order to incorporate the best in themselves. They also pilfered information from each other's minds, and technology and material resources from one another. They mixed genetically and technologically to advance. Sex and warfare were the same thing to them.

"This was how they lived and how they wanted to live," it continued. "This was why they never spread out widely, because they wanted to stay proximal to potential mates and victims. The Librarian was an outlier, insane in their terms, who wanted to create a form of their kind more like the social insects of Earth. This was anathema to them, hence the alliance against that one."

"The Librarian," Orlandine repeated.

The Client had prepared well, because its persona immediately gave her compacted detail of the Client's encounters with that entity, though she felt sure it had redacted information from the final encounter, when the Librarian died. Something to investigate another time—she just accepted that the Client had garnered a great deal of knowledge and history from the creature.

"The Librarian created its Species, whereupon four Jain allied to hunt it down and destroy it. Over many centuries, the Species and the Librarian defeated three of them. The last of them, in possession of a new lethal technology, a technology then spreading in the Jain realm, ambushed them in the solar system you saw. And then this happened . . ."

She again saw the final battle that wrecked a solar system and resulted in a disc of debris that looked like an accretion disc. In this disc spread the remnants of the new lethal technology the Jain had deployed. As she watched the appalling destruction, Orlandine realized, "Their technology killed them."

"The new Jain technology was essentially one of them. It finally incorporated them all. Yes, it killed them as individuals. Yet the Jain lives on in its way. Like the Atheter in some respects: brute survival of a kind at the cost of conscious intelligence."

"I understand—the Jain tech in the disc is the detritus of war. I thank you for all of this, but your explanation is incomplete."

"There were two ships," the Client persona replied.

She saw the Species ships fleeing: the one that stayed to face the remaining Jain, then both of them falling into a U-space blister in the system's sun, putting it out.

"A Jain ship is coming," she stated, remembering the king of the prador's fear of this. How had he managed to extrapolate that, on so little data?

"Correct," said the Client persona didactically. "The Wheel's aim was to release the Jain ship from the U-space blister, but it must have known that the first ship to exit it would be the enemy. My people. It therefore set things up so that ship would be fired on."

"Okay . . ."

"My people's ship was damaged when it took the Jain ship into the U-space blister."

"Why did the Wheel set that up? Wouldn't the Jain ship, if undamaged, have been able to deal with the Species ship?"

"Data required," said the persona.

Orlandine waited impatiently for the Client to update the thing. However, in that time she set things in motion, based on what she had received already. She first contacted Gemmell and others down on the planet: no more selectivity with the refugees to the evacuation platforms. Send as many people as possible, as quickly as possible. She then contacted those remaining platforms in orbit: take on more supplies and life support for the refugees and rig for conventional space travel until the disruption has passed. She followed that up by making the necessary alterations to the supply chains. It took only minutes. Eleven minutes later, a large block of data arrived in the persona and it spoke again.

"It was inevitable that driving you to use the black hole would focus the attention of Earth Central and the king of the prador—that those fleets would be sent anyway."

"But the attempt to have me killed ensured it . . ."

"Yes," said the persona, obviously ready for this. "But when about to face an enemy, isn't it a good idea to see them in combat first, preferably with another of your enemies?"

And that's how the Jain think, thought Orlandine.

"What else may have occurred in that blister, I do not know. There is the temporal issue . . ." The Client persona paused to let that sink in, then continued, "For the Jain to have sent the Wheel means that time was not in stasis within the blister."

Orlandine realized she had to reassess. Okay, it seemed two warring ships had gone into that blister. And now the "temporal issue." When that Species ship appeared, they had been thinking in terms of it being locked in a U-space blister—locked in time like an insect in amber. But now the Client had told her the Wheel had been sent from the Jain ship to manipulate exterior events. This meant there had to be a time flow in the blister. She was appalled. Had those two ships, and whatever crews they contained, survived a whole five million or more years in the blister?

"The prador ships that fired . . ." she said. It suddenly seemed so obvious now: the Clade had penetrated them. The swarm AI's primary purpose had been to get everyone firing on each other, after the platforms destroyed the Species ship. Thus the Jain ship would have safer passage, or perhaps see further action to assess. Was that right? Of course it was. She realized the Clade-controlled ships would have fired on her weapons platforms, had she not recalled them, and that the platforms would have responded.

"Such destruction," she said, reviewing the mayhem and potential mayhem in her mind.

"It is what they are," the Client replied, eleven minutes later.

"Yes, I see that," she said tightly, and contemplated all she had learned.

Here was a newly encountered, intelligent race, and the response should be overtures of peace, until whatever reaction they made clarified matters. Was she too obsessed with her mission to prevent Jain technology escaping the disc, and in turn destroying the Polity and the Kingdom? Yes and no. This wasn't just about the Jain tech. It was about the nature of that technology, which she knew intimately. Its nature was hostile and destructive. Now she had the Client's data and extrapolated from that. This showed a race whose warlike tendencies rooted in them before they even developed intelligence. They destroyed and pillaged each other and could not countenance a branch from their evolutionary tree, let alone some other alien race. Of course, the Client could have massaged the data, but it fitted. Orlandine was utterly certain the Jain were xenophobes, more extreme even than the prador. For such creatures, *not* attacking the Polity and the Kingdom would never even be an option.

They must stop that ship.

Orlandine relayed her thinking to the weapons platform AIs who, now devoid of directives, were freethinking and changing fast. She expected some argument on the matter but they were all in immediate agreement with her. They must face the Jain, and deal with it.

Eleven minutes later, another message came through directly from the Client: "It will destroy the fleets out there, and then it will come here. The ship of my kind was severely damaged and . . . there is something wrong with the crew, yet you saw what it did. The Jain ship, undamaged and controlling that technology . . ."

A little while after that came another brief comment, "I don't know if there is anything, either in the Polity or the Kingdom, that can stop it."

TRIKE

Trike hauled Angel up by his fractured neck and scanned down the android's body. He could see points of attack, areas he needed to destroy. He mapped the networks of power and data, the nodal reactors, electromuscle and ceramal skeleton, and drew back his hand for an eviscerating blow. Then he hesitated. What was he doing?

He could feel the Jain tech and the essence of the soldiers responding to the whole of him—both in his conscious and subconscious mind. But its response to the stronger, knotted blackness of his twisted-up anger and hate was greatest, and it fed that into his consciousness, driving him. He had to stop now. Yet even as he tried to pull back, Angel's fingers screamed with an intense vibration and his hand stabbed up. The spiked fingers hesitated for a second, then started boring into Trike's forearm. Pain and damage fed back into the system and Trike flung him, his impact cutting a groove through the shingle and sending a wave of stones. Angel rolled out of this and came upright, then accelerated towards Trike. Almost with a kind of relief, Trike faced him.

And with hunger.

Angel slammed into him hard, driving him back a pace and raining blow after blow against his torso. His fists also issued intense disruptive ultrasound pulses, scrambling things inside. Trike backhanded him, snapping his head over on the already damaged neck. It straightened with a crunch and Angel's eyes reddened. His laser informational warfare beam flashed and blinded Trike, viral propagation in his human mind, ripping in. Humanly blind, Trike could still see so much more with other sensors throughout his body. He spun and drove his foot into Angel's torso, lifting the android off the ground. Angel reached down, horribly fast, and caught his ankle, spun back in and drove his own foot straight into Trike's mouth. Teeth broke, even as Trike swept a claw down and drove it into Angel's back, closing his fingers about artificial ribs.

The hunger grew and emotions and intents blurred. He wanted to break Angel apart and destroy him. But he also wanted to take everything from the android and make it his own. This all made no sense, but still he let it drive him.

The face of a boulder now. Trike slammed Angel into it again and again, bending and fracturing the android's internal skeleton, seeing inside as components shorted and winked out. He grabbed an arm and heaved, tearing it from its socket and tossing it aside. Angel's other hand came round at an impossible angle, driving spiked fingers into Trike's eyes and partway into his skull, spewing attacking nano-machines. Down on the shingle and knee in the back. Trike caught the wrist in his free hand and tore off the other arm. No thought now, no doubts. From the hand gripping Angel's ribs, he issued tendrils, extending them through the android's body, penetrating and connecting. Memories were there, knowledge, systems—the whole technical peak of what Angel was—and he began to tear them out. Angel's head turned to face him on its broken neck.

"It is resolved," he said.

Nano-machines spreading from the tendrils created material weaknesses, debonded layers and opened cracks. Trike reached down to grab one shoulder, and folded Angel up, snapping his spine. Finally, he withdrew the tendrils and released the ribs in order to take the rest apart, hardly noticing the red glow fading from those eyes.

GEMMELL

The grey slug of a military grav-transport slid through the sky just inside the canyon. Gemmell studied the walls on either side. They were sheer basalt cut through with inclusions of smoky quartz. Here and there clung scrubby bushes loaded with sparse green needles and violet fruit like chillies. Earlier, accessing his gridlink, he had discovered that they were chillies adapted to this world, as was so much of the flora here. A world it seemed Orlandine was now anxious to evacuate as quickly as possible . . .

"How long till we get there?" said Cog.

"What?"

"How long till—"

"Ten minutes," Gemmell replied tersely, after checking coordinates and airspeed in his link. He returned to overview the changes to the evacuation for a moment. Something critical had happened, something big, and it related to the present disruption of U-com.

"Is my husband still there?" Ruth asked behind.

Gemmell flinched a little at that and dismissed the evacuation stats from his gridlink. Ruth and Trike had twinned U-mitters in their skulls that told each the location of the other. She had provided the coordinates to which they were heading. He did not like to examine too closely why that irritated him. Or why it pleased him now that, since U-com had gone down, she had lost her connection.

"Yes, he is there," said a silky, whispering voice. "Angel is not."

"I thought you said Angel had reached him?" said Cog.

"I did," said Clean. "And now I see him clearly from the ECS satellite."

"And Angel?"

"Is not there."

Gemmell made no comment on that, though he felt sure Clean was concealing something. He made his own search in the ECS data sphere and found the satellite Clean was probably using, since all its sensors focused on one point on the coast ahead. Clarity was good. The cams on that satellite could image objects smaller than a human fingernail. He saw then that Clean was both correct and wrong. Angel was not there, and he was.

The canyon wound through a rocky landscape, its walls gradually falling away. The river grew wider and then opened out in a shingle beach. Gemmell brought the military transport to a steady hover. He took a tight breath. This was probably going to be ugly. He turned to inspect his passengers. The crinoid forensic AI, Mobius Clean, rested behind the other two, now a balled-up mass of metal strips and white cords. Cog's wounds had healed and he had lost the bluish tint from earlier. Gemmell's gaze came to rest on Ruth, sitting beside the man. She met his look and he felt sure, more than ever, that his attraction to her was reciprocated.

He shook his head and returned his attention to flying. He knew the time had come for him to cut himself away from Morgaine. She would never be what he wanted, and there would never be a return to the relationship they had had before. So was he already feeling the loss and trying to replace it? Was he suffering from transference? The moment he had met Ruth, he had seen a young version of Morgaine, and it had tweaked something inside him. He now realized the similarities were only vague.

Easing the joystick down, he brought the craft in over the spit of shingle and landed. Looking over towards the boulders, he could see Trike perched on one of them like a large blue and grotesque gargoyle. He hit the door control, unstrapped and stood up. Cog reached the door as it began hinging down into a ramp, and Clean started unfolding and rising too, issuing static discharges. As Gemmell moved forwards, Ruth stepped in beside him. It seemed quite natural to place a hand on the small of her back as the ramp finally crumped on the shingle, and she didn't object. But at the head of the ramp she froze.

"Trike," she said, leadenly.

Only now did Gemmell realize that though she had seen recorded imagery and was up to date on all that had occurred since she ended up in a cold coffin, this was the first time she had seen him in the flesh since his transformation. She walked on down the ramp and he thought it a testament to Clean's repairs of her body and mind that her reaction was so muted.

They all moved out across the shingle, Clean rolling ahead like a stray beach ball with Cog hurrying to catch up. Ruth did not hurry, her pace remained reluctant and slow. Trike meanwhile swung his nightmare head towards them for a moment, then back to look out to sea. He continued doing what he had been doing, which was to skim flat stones out across the swell. Gemmell followed the course of one as it hit the water with a sonic crack and continued for an improbable distance. Finally, he and Ruth came up behind the others.

"What the hell have you done?" Cog growled.

He'd seen, and now they could all see. At the foot of the rock lay the remains of Angel. Trike had torn the android apart. He had strewn the limbs here and there and folded the torso in half. A short distance away from this, the head lay on the shingle, eyes gazing sightlessly up into the tumbling sky.

"I'm sorry," said Trike, turning to peer down at him like some prehistoric raptor considering its next meal. "It was unavoidable."

"How the fuck was that unavoidable, boy?" Cog demanded.

Trike stared at him. "I am not a boy."

That seemed enough to silence Cog as Trike now focused on Ruth. Gemmell felt her lock rigid beside him. "You're alive," he said in a dead voice.

She squeezed Gemmell's arm, then abruptly moved forwards. "Trike and I need to talk," she said. "Alone."

Gemmell felt his hand drop to his sidearm and saw Trike's head twitch towards him. He slid his hand away. Stupid to be so defensive of a woman he had just met, and really, what could he do? This Trike, who had once been a man, had, so he understood, gone head-to-head with the war drone Cutter and snapped one of its limbs. Shots from a gas-system pulse gun were hardly likely to have any effect.

"Do you think that's safe?" asked Cog.

"You won't hurt me, will you, my husband?" Ruth asked Trike.

He bowed his head. "Angel and I had something to resolve. It is now resolved. There will no longer be any unnecessary violence."

"So this was necessary?" Cog asked, obviously still livid.

Ruth put a hand on his arm. "He won't harm me."

Gemmell watched this interplay, then turned around and walked away. Sitting on the shingle, he himself started looking for flat rocks. A moment later, Clean and Cog joined him, while Ruth climbed up onto the rock to sit beside Trike.

"What do you think they're saying?" asked Cog, slumping down on the shingle.

"No idea," said Gemmell.

"Clean?" asked Cog.

"Human stuff," said the AI. "Prosaic."

"What do we do if he decides not to go back to the medship with us?" asked Gemmell, utterly sure that was the decision he wanted Trike to make.

"That is not really viable," said Clean. The AI moved down to the edge where waves slopped in strands of pink weed like sodden Christmas decorations.

Gemmell skimmed a stone out across the waves beside the AI. It bounced once and sank. The AI picked up a stone in one tendril and skimmed it. This stone shot out with a sonic crack like the one Trike had thrown. It somehow seemed an omen of what might occur. "Not viable" meant Trike would be coming back with them whether he wanted to or not. Gemmell looked across at the remains of Angel. Ugly, very ugly. He dipped his head and started sorting further stones.

"She's done," Cog noted.

Ruth climbed down from the boulder to march back across the shingle. Gemmell reached her first and saw her wiping her eyes. She halted and gazed at them all.

"He's not coming back," she stated. "He says he needs some time . . ." She abruptly stepped round Gemmell and headed back to the transport.

"We'll see about that," said Cog. With Clean rolling behind, he headed towards Trike. Gemmell was torn for a moment. He wanted to go back to the transport, then cursed himself. He had been out of human company for too long and was responding like an emotional adolescent. Hand on his sidearm, he followed the other two.

"So you're not coming back with us," said Cog. "Decided to sulk for a while because your excuses for anger and violence have gone and it's time to return to your life?"

Trike swung his head round and gazed at Cog for a long moment, then pushed himself up and dropped down off the boulder. His landing scattered stones all around and he sank to his ankles. This showed just how heavy he must be, but he moved smooth and fast.

"There is no returning to my life," he said. He gestured with one claw, first towards the remains of Angel, then towards the transport. "That's gone now." He pointed to himself. "And what I once was has gone too."

"But it can be returned to you," said Cog, indicating Clean.

"You are assuming I want it back," said Trike.

Trike spoke with perfect rationality, Gemmell thought, but still he had felt the need to take a step back when the monstrous man came down off the rock. He looked like a monster because of the changes the Spatterjay virus had wrought in him, but Gemmell couldn't dismiss the idea that the look reflected the inner reality. All he needed to remind himself was a glance down at Angel's severed head.

Trike swung round to stare at Mobius Clean. "For my own good?" he enquired.

Clean crackled with energy and shot forwards, the feathery tendrils reaching out like the tentacles of a hunting squid. It struck Trike and engulfed him. A flash of power ensued and flung Gemmell flat on his back. He felt as if he had been hit in the chest with a shovel. After another concussion, chunks of smoking rock rained down. A moment later, Cog stooped over him, reaching down with one hand. Gemmell grasped it and Cog hauled him up.

"What the hell happened?" he asked.

"Seems Clean underestimated him," Cog replied, gesturing.

Gemmell studied the balled-up form of the forensic AI. Its tendrils were shifting weakly, smoke issuing from between them. He transferred his attention to Trike. The man-monster seemed undamaged but for a couple of pink whip marks across his chest. The boulder behind him lay in steaming chunks.

"Orlandine thought it best for me," said Trike, "and made an agreement with this AI that I should be taken back."

He was peering out to sea, towards the plume of smoke from the Sambre volcano.

"But I choose what is best for me now," he added, turning to look at them.

"You've changed, boy," said Cog.

Trike made a coughing sound that might have been laughter. He shrugged and abruptly strode down towards the sea. He waded out into the waves and just kept going, finally submerging and then gone.

DIANA

It took ten seconds for laser com to establish across the fleet.

"Seems Orlandine won't be coming," said Orlik.

"Seems like," added the voice of the prador's distinctly odd AI.

Diana made an instant decision: "We go in—steady and wary."

"No more wait and see?" enquired Orlik.

"What would your king say?"

"Yeah, okay," the prador admitted.

Fusion drives ignited throughout the fleet. With U-space disrupted, it would take some time before they could even see what was occurring at the accretion disc. In fact, conventional sensor arrays still showed the two fleets there and would do so for two hours. They would have no new scan data on the cloud until then. It would also take them a lot longer to get there. As their acceleration increased, Diana felt something creeping up her spine. What exactly had happened?

"What have we got?" she asked. "What data before the disruption hit?"

Seckurg replied, "Before it collapsed, something came out of the U-space blister. Through Hogue I'm collating scan data from all our ships—from the prador ships too."

"Another Species ship?" she asked.

Seckurg shrugged. "Who knows?" He then added, "I have something now."

An image came through from collated scan data. It tracked the skating U-jump of the object that had left the black hole to materialize in the outer ring of cloud. That cloud reacted to it at once, as to a stone dropped into immiscible fluids. Swirls generated all around and the whole mass seemed to be shifting. Seckurg tried to focus in on this object, but the closer he got the more blurred and insubstantial it became. There just wasn't enough data for a clear image. Diana grimaced and turned her attention to the fleet.

The ships had arrayed themselves in a neat, close formation—with even spacing between them all. She counted them in her mind—how many were already gone. If what they found in the cloud was another Species ship, then fine—they would just let it go. But this manipulation of the cloud, of the Jain tech there, made her think otherwise.

"We have to do better this time," said Orlik. "If battle is necessary."

"I concur," Diana replied, studying his ship. Already a girder structure was stretched across the great hole in it, and armoured prador and robots were there making repairs.

"Suggestions?" Orlik asked.

"We need to loosen our formation, but in groups of ships to cover for that disruptor," she stated. Only that layered hardfield and imploder defence worked against this weapon. She sketched out a tactical map in her mind and Hogue at once firmed it up.

"This is supposing what comes next possesses such a weapon." He added, "And uses it."

"I would say that only the second case applies, and we must be ready."

"Your tactical map needs some adjustment."

Diana reviewed it and could not see what he meant. "Why?"

After a long pause Orlik reluctantly admitted, "Only reavers carry imploders, and not very many."

"Then it is time for you to properly tie your telemetry with ours," Diana suggested tightly. Obviously the telemetry they had been receiving had been . . . edited. Trust was still apparently an issue.

"Very well," said Orlik.

As Hogue began to receive the corrected data, it changed the tactical map: groups of three or four ships now, with every group containing at least one Polity vessel loaded with imploders.

"Seckurg?" she enquired.

He did not need her to ask any more to know what she wanted. "I've analysed the induction warfare the two hundred C— . . . the two hundred prador ships were using. Transmitting to all our vessels now, and the *Kinghammer*."

"You mustn't call them crabs. Not while Orlik is listening," said Diana.

Seckurg rolled his eyes and cracked the palm of his hand against the side of his head. He hadn't been about to say "crabs" but "Clade." It was a quite glaring error for a Golem to make.

"Anything else?" Diana asked, also putting the more detailed query through Hogue and thus across the fleet. Hundreds of analyses flooded in and Hogue incorporated them in battle plans. They all related to the Species ship, which was everything they had to go on—the places to hit and the weapons that would cause the most damage. How that central portion that the Client had snatched away should be the main target. A crucial analysis Diana noted was about the disruptor beam. It showed this might contain a heavy data component related to the atomic forces of varying materials. And in turn that an induction warfare strike might be able to counter it.

Diana watched as the ships began shifting position into the new formation. She kept checking telemetry as their systems linked for the disruptor defence. An hour went by, and then another. When the time disparity passed and she saw, through *Cable Hogue*'s EMR arrays, the fleets departing the cloud two hours in the past, she focused on it again. For a moment, nothing new revealed itself. Then a surge hit every sensor, every receiver across the emitted spectrum, and even came over U-com, despite the disruption. This shriek, this data scream reverberated in the ship all around Diana, in the air, in her, in her bones and blood. It felt utterly primal and seemed a challenge, a demand, and a question all in one.

"What the fuck is that?" she asked.

"Communication," Seckurg replied. He was Golem but wincing like a human, his hand claw-like on the console before him.

"Warfare," Jabro slurred. Deep into the ship's systems, and taking the full brunt of that shriek in his mind, his eyes were glazed and his mouth hanging open. Diana quickly cut him out and he jerked, as if waking from nightmare, and shot her a grateful look.

"It is an intellectual challenge," stated Hogue.

Diana put up mental defences and delved into the periphery of the thing where Hogue began interpreting it. The data were highly compressed and unravelling them took up masses of processing space, but she could see some of what Hogue indicated.

It consisted of a series of problems and questions: open-ended U-space formulae, unsolved mathematical equations where pi was a perfect number, questions about particle physics that devolved into Mandelbrot complexity. It required solutions for quantum impossibilities, probability theory paradoxes and chemical equations. And all of it was posed in a language that itself needed to be cracked: speech from something that used light, sound and huge biological molecules for communication.

"From the Jain tech?" she asked.

"I don't think so," said Seckurg.

"And it's not just fucking information," Jabro added.

Diana had to agree: she knew it was more than that. She could separate herself from the sensory input via her interface, yet the shriek would not go away.

"It's the thing in that cloud," said Seckurg. "Getting transmissions from our attack ships and sensors on site now."

Imagery came through clearly. Around the object that had appeared in the cloud, the swirling spread and then began to tighten inwards. A whole mass of the cloud, millions of miles across, started to detach from the rest. Next, from within it, came high-intensity EMR flashes, and the sensor probes they had left behind began to malfunction. A view from the sensors of an attack ship gave her a view of one of those probes. The round-ended cylinder, five feet long, flamed along its length and boiled away, quickly turning into a smear of hot vapour.

"Gamma-ray lasers," noted Jabro.

Next, a stealthed Polity attack ship, invisible until a beam found it, glowed like hot iron. It hurtled across vacuum emitting streams of plasma as it tried to cool. A disruptor beam speared out from the cloud and nailed it. The thing shattered into black, glassy debris interlaced with spreading guts of molten metal. She tracked across sensor feeds as another attack ship went, then another. In both cases, the gamma-ray laser found them initially, then the disruptor beam took them out. After that, it seemed their attacker had found a way to find them through their chameleonware without lasering them first, because disruptor beams flowered from the cloud and turned the rest to expanding vapours of scrap.

"The dreadnought," said Jabro leadenly.

That ship lay further out than the attack ships, and around it crowded surviving prador in armour, three ejected prador sanctums and excursion robots toting AI mind cases. A disruptor beam hit it on the nose and tracked down its length, like the point of a knife stripping fish scales. The ship began to break up. But it seemed that was not enough. An object hurtled out of the cloud at sub-light speed and struck it dead centre. The strange detonation seemed without explosive force. Fire flared at the point of impact, blue-white, electrical. It began eating up matter, extending around the ship to consume more and more. It then flicked out tendrils like lightning strikes, touched armoured prador and incinerated them, burned through the captain's sanctums, hit the excursion robots and mind cases. Finally it went out, leaving a tumbling mass that looked like fractured charcoal.

Diana nodded slowly to herself. These were not the actions of something intent on escape. It had destroyed the watchers with methodical precision and left the easy target until last, as if it wanted to take its time, play with its weapons and relish their effect. Focusing her attention on that great mass of cloud, she could see it was now very definitely on the move around the object, or vessel, at its centre. The cloud began flowering, stretching out tendrils that scanning from the *Hogue*'s arrays showed consisted wholly of Jain-tech objects. It reached like some titanic, clawed hand, out and out, towards her, towards her fleet. At the centre, it began to clear, revealing at last what lay there.

"So, not a Species ship," Jabro commented.

The thing was a leviathan—on the same scale as the Species ship—but of an utterly different construction. Its bulk, measuring over a thousand miles long, resembled an immense leaf-like and grotesque mantid, fashioned out of smoky quartz. It appeared to have limbs folded against its body, but they were melded there and immobile. Perhaps they were just decoration or, more alarmingly, the trace remains of the *growth* of this thing. From its head end, sprouting from a thin neck, jutted great black pincers capable of grasping small moons. It also seemed it had possessed an outer tegument that had decayed and split, shrinking back to reveal the underlying crystal structure. Massive clumps of organic technology clung to its underside, like copepod parasites that had fed too well, or perhaps they were its children. These alone were bigger than most of the ships of the combined fleet.

Like the shriek now dying away, this thing elicited in Diana a repulsion, a fear—something primal. None of them had said it, but it had been implicit right from when the cloud started to move and when they realized something was directing it.

"My king was right," said Orlik.

"Really?" said Diana, next taking a steadying breath—trying to think coldly and logically about weapons and tactics in the face of this thing.

"Seems the Jain have arrived," Orlik finished.

NEAL ASHER is a science fiction writer whose work has been nominated for both the Philip K. Dick and the British Fantasy Society awards. He has published more than fifteen novels, many set within his Polity universe, including *Gridlinked*, *The Skinner*, and *Prador Moon*. He divides his time between Essex and a home in Crete.